oc*CULT*

THEY DIDN'T THINK IT COULD HAPPEN IN THEIR CHURCH

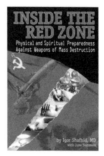

oc*CULT*

THEY DIDN'T THINK IT COULD HAPPEN IN THEIR CHURCH

~ A Novel ~

June Summers

Global Strategic Resources

OC *CULT*

Published by:
Global Strategic Resources
1725 S. Rainbow Blvd., Ste. 2, Box 171
Las Vegas, NV 89146

First Printing 2005
Printed in the United States of America

Cover Design by Robert Aulicino
Editing by Val Dumond

Library of Congress Number: 2005921643
ISBN 978-0-9754214-8-2 (0-9754214-8-4)

I dedicate this book to my dearest and longtime friend, Stacey Wright, who, in her darkest hour, showed true grit for the Gospel truth, refusing to allow mortal men the right to possess her mind and plunder her conscience.

ENDORSEMENTS

"June Summers has written a compelling book that relates to an increasingly frequent theme in American life—which is the heartbreaking consequences of destructive cult involvement. Her fiction mirrors the facts of and answers many puzzling questions. How do people fall prey to cults, why do they stay, and is there hope for those who leave?"

Rick Ross, *Veteran Cult Watcher, Rick Ross Institute*

"In working with clients who have been victims of indoctrination, I find Ms. Summer's account of situations and experiences to be factual. Although this is a work of fiction, I believe it will help victims heal and others to understand and be wary of the signs and manipulations of the perpetrators."

Joan Elvidge *M.S., M.F.T./Psychotherapy, Masters of Science in Counseling, Psychology, Licensed Marriage and Family Therapist*

AUTHOR'S NOTE AND ACKNOWLEDGMENTS

Due to the cult and the occult subject matter, this book is intended for adult reading only.

This book, though a work of fiction, is inspired on true events, all which were documented in newspapers, television news reports, talk shows, and by the testimonies of those members who had been involved.

All of the characters in this book are fiction and any characterizations that might resemble anyone living today are purely coincidental.

There are between seven and ten million Americans involved in cults or cult-like groups, with three to five thousand groups active in the U.S. These groups will recruit about 180,000 new members each year. There are different types of cults, non-religious groups, political extremist groups, and religious groups, with some dabbling in the occult. They all engage in some form of mind control, exploiting their members financially, physically, and psychologically.

It is not always easy to admit that a church, a place that is supposed to offer hope and peace, might be a breeding ground for destructive cultic or occult behavior. But it is an occurrence that happens all too often, as confirmed by the statistics. This is why believers hold a serious responsibility, as the Apostle Paul admonishes, "to guard their salvation with fear and trembling," searching the scripture daily to make sure that what they hear is from God.

Despite ministers who twist and pollute scripture and lead many astray by doing so, the pure Word of God stands a true and unshakable witness of righteousness, salvation, and hope to all who call upon the name of the Lord Jesus Christ.

I would like to thank my wonderful husband, Igor, and daughter, Star, for patiently allowing me the many hours to complete this manuscript—and their constant encouragement to do so.

I also want to extend a deep gratitude to my editor and friend, Val Dumond, for her unwavering support.

To my friends, Stacey Wright, Randy Bukowski, and Arlene Hurlburt, who read the manuscript and provided me with helpful critiques and fair evaluations, I am very grateful!

For God hath not given us the spirit of fear; but of power, and of love, and of a *sound mind*.

—II Timothy 1: 7

And no marvel; for Satan himself is transformed into an angel of light.
Therefore it is no great thing if his ministers also be transformed as the ministers of righteousness; whose end shall be according to their works.

—II Corinthians 11: 14, 15

~~~~~~

Know, likewise, that in witches, those are most bewitched, who, with often looking direct the edge of their sight to the edge of the sight of those who bewitch or fascinate them; whence arose the saying of "Evil eyes." For when their eyes are reciprocally bent one upon the other, and are joined beams to beams, and lights to lights, the spirit of the one is joined to the spirit of the other, and then are strong ligations made; and most violent love is stirred up, only with a sudden looking on, as it were, with the darting look, or piercing into the very inmost of the heart, whence the spirit and amorous blood, being thus wounded, are carried forth upon the lover, and enchanter.

—*Natural Magic*

~~~~~~

PROLOGUE

I am dancing in church, spinning and twirling; arms raised in adoration to Jesus. I feel holy before God. The skirt on my dress swirls high in the air with each spin, flashing slender thighs and silky underwear. I am oblivious to the male eyes watching me. I dance all over the sanctuary, up and around the pastor, weaving in and out of the elders. The congregation begins to dance too. My attention is on God, on God, on God...

One by one the men in the church dance up and form a tight circle around me. The pastor sashays forward and pulls me against his body, resting his hand upon my breasts. The male members gyrate, possessed, faster to the music, their lusting eyes open wide while shouting praises to God. The other females in the church are dancing and shouting to God in unison with the men, but their eyes are closed, not seeing anything...

Penny woke with a start. Like a tiny light poking its way into a black chasm and illuminating its once bleak surroundings into something tangible, Penny suddenly saw what she had not quite got before. Waves of shame hit her...

"Oh God, oh God! Satan is out to destroy our marriages! I need my husband. I need you, Rick. Oh Rick, what have I done?" She leaned over, holding her stomach, crying out to God until she could weep no more.

OC*CULT*

CHAPTER ONE

Five years earlier...

His lisp was like a magnet. The people of Grace church loved him.

"Pwaise God! Pwaise God!" Pastor Mark shouted from the wooden pulpit. "Give God a hand!"

The congregation clapped and shouted *amen* and *hallelujah*.

"You are God's chosen people. Hallelujah! Can you feel His Spiwit? He's here today, moving like a wind to heal your hearts and touch your bwoken bodies! Have faith in Jesus!" Pastor Mark held out his arms. "Let Him inside you. Do you want to be healed? Stop whining and start believing! Do you want pwospewity? Quit complaining and start giving! You can't receive if you don't believe!" His cobalt blue eyes challenged his loyal recipients. "Are you ready for God today, church? Let's pwaise Him! Music ministwy, come on up here and let's sing pwaises to God!"

The pastor's excitement rose along with the jubilant response of his church. He flashed a charming smile before leaving the platform and joining his wife Donna in the front pew. The choir filed into rows on the raised platform and began to sing. As Mark settled in the pew, he noticed a new face in the choir. The attractive woman bounced as she sang. His eyes followed the rhythm of her bosom while his church members closed their eyes, worshipping and crooning with delight as a billowing energy moved over them in time with the lively beat of the music.

As the *spirit* touched the assembly, some people were knocked backwards under its power, babbling in strange tongues; others wept, the majority raised hands high, singing, swaying, laughing, and shouting praises to God.

While his church was enjoying the supernatural visitation, Mark's mind flitted back in time forty years to the old white farmhouse he grew up in. *Thank you, God. I've accomplished all this, just like I told Pop.*

"Son, come wash up, dinner's about ready. Remember church service starts early tonight."

His father had been a serious fellow, the pastor of a small Baptist Church, a dedicated man who oversaw his family with an iron pan of rules, seldom seasoning those rules with any type of affection.

"Coming, Pop!" thirteen-year-old Mark hollered back at his father from upstairs. He had lost track of time reading the girlie magazine he had found in the trash outside the old gas station not too far from their church. The pictures of peach-skinned beauties dressed in nothing but underwear awakened his young body, and he had to stall. He quickly shoved the magazine back under the loose floorboard in his bedroom and slowly walked downstairs, trying to think of something that would cool his loins. He entered the kitchen and zoomed into his chair next to his brother William, and grabbed a warm biscuit, pressing it into his mouth.

"Mark, wait for prayers," his mother scolded as she placed a platter of fried chicken on the table and sat down.

William made a face at his younger brother and shook his head. "You are certainly the prodigal son, Mark. I won't be surprised if you end up sleeping with the pigs."

"Now boys, no fighting at dinner," their father ordered. "Let's pray and give God thanks for this food." Mr. Garrett bowed his head to pray. "Father, bless this food to our bodies and make us strong in You. Minister to the souls that attend service tonight. May they find comfort and joy in You. Amen."

"Pop," Mark stole the next word, "think I can give the altar call tonight?"

"Sure, son."

"So, dad, what's the sermon tonight?" William asked as he poured gravy over his biscuits. He was sixteen and a head taller than Mark.

"It's called, *Doing God's Will*," Pastor Garrett said.

"Pop," Mark asked, "Don't you ever want to be pweaching to a bigger church?" His speech impediment seemed to add to Mark's charm, and he liked to exaggerate it when he wanted something. At school he had no problem flirting with the girls this way. They all seemed flattered at the way he talked. "Someday I want to pweach to thousands and own a big house and dwive those fancy cars like the pweacher in Evansville. I want a successful ministwy like that Revewend Bill. He has style."

William rolled his eyes as Mrs. Garrett sighed out a reply, "Honey, Reverend Bill might love God, but he's a bit overboard when it comes to his view on material possessions."

"Mom, why do all pweachers have to be poor? So Revewend Bill has money, so did Abwaham and King Solomon. They were successful, why can't I be? Hey Mom, can I have some jam and milk?"

Mrs. Garrett sighed again, put aside her napkin, and rose to the bidding.

"I believe you will be successful," Pastor Garrett admonished his youngest son. "But make sure what you seek is the will of God. Remember, self gain leads to no good. Keep your eyes fixed on God's word, and He'll reward you with riches that nothing here on earth can compare to."

Mark ignored his father and said, "Hey mom, you haven't touched your food. Sit down and eat!"

The sudden silence from the choir was a distraction that brought Mark back to the present. He rose from the pew and bounded up the steps with his Bible in hand, smiling wide.

The Boeing 727 roared its engines as the flight attendants made their final safety check before takeoff. Penny Adams, biting at her lower lip, gazed out the tiny window wondering what her future would hold. She had no idea how jittery she was until she tasted blood. Relieved that the man next to her preferred to read than talk, she got out a tissue from her handbag and dabbed at her mouth, all the while allowing her racing thoughts to go as fast as the speed of the takeoff.

Leaving Chicago and her family was momentous. Where she got the courage to do this still seemed amazing. She sighed and closed her eyes for a moment. Though nervous, the excitement at the adventure awaiting her buoyed her up higher than the plane. Aunt Joann's invitation to live with her in Portland, Oregon, was the offer of her lifetime. She couldn't refuse. At twenty-one, she was ready for this. That constant nag of emptiness that filled her soul wouldn't let her back out, even though part of her wanted to. She was leaving behind her boyfriend, lots of friends, and a good steady job. But leaving behind the sticky Illinois summers and cruel winters was something she would not miss. That small rural city she grew up in had nothing much to excite the soul. Cornfields and nagging mosquitoes seemed to be all there were in her world, probably because her parent's standoffish love never seemed to open her heart to much more than that.

Chicago shrunk to a dot on the horizon as the plane soared higher. Penny's eyes were as intense as the blue painted sky. Four hours in the air. It was too long a wait.

"There's no life here," she had complained to her mother two months earlier. "I need mountains and oceans, blue skies and sea gulls. I need something...just something." What she needed, she didn't quite know herself. But, whatever it was, she wasn't finding it in the Midwest, or from her family.

Her mother nodded without emotion. Penny longed to be closer with her, with Dad; but displays of affection were rare; and hugs only came at funerals. Her two older sisters were just as aloof. Though they lived ten minutes away from Mom and Dad, one would hardly know it from the few times they came back to visit. Of course, Dad's demanding and insensitive ways were no lure for anyone. As to be expected, none of her family had seen her off. It was Rick who drove her to the airport and kissed her goodbye, with a wishful *you'll be back soon* look hovering over his sad blue eyes.

I'm not coming back.

She loved Rick, and could feel the stab of pain at their separation. He had promised to come out and visit after his golf competition in Chicago. She smiled at the memory of their relationship. He was a romantic. She remembered the time he first told her he loved her—smack dab on a big billboard in the center of town. It must have cost him a small fortune to rent that for one day. She was proud of his achievements. At his age, he was already moving in the fast lane with the top golfers in the country. She loved going to his games and supporting him from the sidelines with his other fans. But finding herself and searching for her own niche in the world were more powerful drives than her feelings for him. Something was missing in her life, and she had to find it. The constant void inside her heart had set her on a quest for fulfillment for as long as she could remember. Would she ever feel complete? She hoped so.

The plane's descent into Portland displayed green, statuesque mountains in the distance. October looked good out in the Northwest, real good.

The 727 rolled to a silent halt in front of gate B-1. Penny felt numb with excitement. She was starting over, a new beginning. She wondered what the next few years would hold for her. She gathered her backpack from the overhead bin and trailed off the aircraft. Aunt Joann was waving as she exited the jetway.

"Penny, you made it!" Joann squealed, hugging her niece tightly.

Penny was surprised that her mother's sister showed emotion. It made her feel braver, and she squeezed her back.

"How many bags did you check?" Joann asked.

"Two…big ones." Penny chuckled. "I can't believe I'm here, Aunt Joann. It's a beautiful city." The hustle bustle of the crowd around her added to Penny's excitement and she talked fast, trying to keep her tongue in sync with her traveling thoughts.

At baggage claim they retrieved the luggage from the moving belt. "I'm double parked, so let's fly!" Joann said.

As they scrambled outside through the sliding doors, the crisp breeze tangled Penny's long, blonde hair into her face and around her neck. "It smells fresh here, and clean," she said, fighting her windblown mane so she could see.

"That's ocean air you smell. You'll love it here, Penny."

After hoisting the luggage in the rear bed of the small pickup, niece and aunt climbed into the cluttered cab. Joann pulled a small package from her purse and tossed it on Penny's lap.

"What's this?" Penny asked.

"A welcome gift."

Penny unwrapped the tissue. *Welcome to Portland*, framed in delicate red and gold embroidery made her smile. "Did you make this?"

"No, sorry, just an airport trinket."

They grinned at each other as Joann steered the truck towards the freeway.

"First thing I need to do is find a good job," Penny quipped as she watched rolling, lush green hills and full, swaying trees pass by the window. The blue-gray skies, dotted with puffs of white clouds here and there, reminded her of the oil paintings hanging in the Chicago Art Museum.

"I have an extra car you can use, as long as you need it. And there's a huge mall not far from my house...our house." Joann's toffee eyes danced. She continued, "Let's see, oh yes, you have your own room and your own bathroom. We can split groceries, once you start working." She reached over and patted Penny's knee as she turned onto Eighth Avenue.

"Hey, what's that?" Penny pointed to a monstrous-size brick complex spread out across a massive parking lot. The biggest building, with a unique looking half-round, half-rectangular shape, was completely enclosed except for a few windows peeking out from the second floor. A sign in bold black letters read, *Grace Church*. "Oh, it's a church."

"Yeah, that went up about two years ago. A woman I work with goes there. It's all she talks about. There is a Lutheran church by our home. That's where I go. The pastor is sweet. It's a small congregation; that's why I like it."

"Aunt Joann, you forget, Mom switched to Catholicism because Dad refused to let her raise us Lutheran."

"Oh, that's right. I don't know how your mom puts up with that overbearing father of yours." Joann shook her head, adjusting the overhead mirror as she talked.

"Even when mom became a Catholic he refused to let us pray before dinner. Mom would have us say our prayers at night because he never came into our bedrooms to say goodnight."

"Well, now you're free to do whatever you want."

"Yippeee!" Penny shouted, and threw her head back.

Each day, all week long, joyful members at Grace Church came and went, busily attending church services, prayer meetings, college classes, the library, or the bookstore. It was always a busy place, and took a lot of governing by the pastor and his appointed eldership to maintain the 500-student Bible College, large Christian school, and 2500-membership church.

The pastor's office, the elders' offices, and the ministry and counseling centers were all located on the college campus, not too far from the sanctuary and Christian school. Elders' meetings were held twice a week inside a conference room near the small college campus chapel.

Monday morning Pastor Mark stood at the front of the room with his arms crossed. "Good morning, gentlemen," he said as his twelve elders settled in their seats. His blue suit complemented his striking eyes. "I'll twy and keep this week's meeting bwief as possible." He flashed a smile to put the men at ease. "Donna can't make it today. My wife has an urgent counseling appointment, so we will go ahead and start."

The only furnishings in the small conference room were a long metal table and thirteen fold-up chairs. Three dismal paintings of Portland's rainy piers graced the walls. There were no windows. The table was bare.

Ted Hunter, the thirty-nine-year old senior elder and head counselor, sat lazily on the pastor's right, drumming his fingers lightly on the table. As he leaned forward, his starched white shirt stretched tautly against his lengthy back.

Ted's impressive business degree, and leadership qualities had caught Pastor Mark's attention years earlier when Grace Church was just forming. Mark had taken the remarkable young man under his wing as apprentice, using him as his personal secretary and business advisor. A few short years later he was promoted to head counselor—under Donna's supervision. Ted did not have a counseling degree—none of the elders did—but Mark insisted that their demanding eldership status warranted them instant degrees in psychology. Ted's wife Betty was an asset as well, and Mark placed her in charge of overseeing college schedules and elders' meetings. She had become quite a pillar in the church and a great example of the perfect wife for the females in the assembly.

Avery Baniston, Mark's son-in-law, sat beside Ted with his chin resting on his fist. His olive green eyes looked bored. At twenty-seven-years of age, he was overly confident. He had accomplished a lot in a short time. He had flown in from South Dakota in the early days shortly after the first chapel and Bible College were built. His dad knew Pastor Mark's old college buddy, who insisted Avery meet Mark and check out Grace Church. After Avery graduated from Grace's Bible College, he did not waste any time in proposing to Gayle, the pastor's daughter. That move boosted him into a solid position as Bible college teacher and elder.

Joe Fellows, closer to the pastor's age, was the head financial advisor, and was seated on the pastor's other side. His pencil-like lips stretched into a serious grimace as he leafed through his notebook. Joe had been with the church from the beginning. He and his wife Christina, married twenty-five years, were committed Christians, and had been years before they met Mark and Donna Garrett.

The remaining elders, all Bible college teachers in their mid-thirties, sat rigid and attentive as the pastor spoke.

"Gentlemen, I'm concerned about our finances." Mark sat down. " Joe tells me there has been a dwop in giving the last two months. Nothing sewious, but it could be if it continues."

"What do you suggest?" Ted asked.

"I'll talk to the congwegation. But I want you college teachers to plant some seeds, firm seeds, into your lectures. Use wisdom of course, but get the point acwoss." Mark scratched at his thick brow then placed his hands flat in front of him on the table.

"We depend on tithes to keep this body and our satellite churches running smoothly. Our Fwance church is supported solely by us; we can't afford to take losses."

The elders murmured in agreement.

"Let's remind the people that the more they give, the gweater their blessings. Our assembly must be obedient to God. Can I count on you gentlemen to encouwage our flock?"

"Absolutely, Pastor," the elders answered.

"Good, good. I count on your support." Mark's glare was intimidating. "Joe, keep me informed on the incwease."

Joe didn't answer, but kept scribbling in his notebook with one hand and poking at his ear with the other.

"You will keep me informed, *Joe?*" Mark asked again, annoyed.

Joe closed his notebook. "Yes, Mark," he said, this time making eye contact with the pastor.

"Good. Vewy good. Avewy, do you have anything to add on this issue?" Mark turned his attention to his son-in-law.

"No, Pastor. I'll work it into my lectures today." Avery leaned back from the table and crossed his skinny legs. His cell phone went off, and he quickly silenced it.

"Good. Vewy good." Mark glanced around the table. "Any other areas of concern today, gentlemen, before we hit on the Dexter case?"

"Um...uh...pastor, there is another problem that has come up," Joe stammered uneasily. He fiddled some more with his ear, than clasped his hands over his notebook and took a deep breath. "Laurina Addison telephoned me last night. She...uh...claims you...uh...made inappropriate...she claims you might have touched her inappropriately." Joe shifted uncomfortably in his chair under Mark's glare. "I tried to calm her down," he continued, "and get to the bottom of what would cause her to say such a thing, but she was not too agreeable. I am almost positive her accusations against you are influenced by Jolene Dexter. They are good friends."

The pastor took on the expression of a wounded puppy. "Joe, thank you for bwinging this to our attention. I have nothing to hide. You gentlemen know this accusation is not twue. Poor Lauwina," he said, shaking his head, "She has such pwoblems with male authowity. She's an imaginative young lady from a difficult childhood. Since her mother died, she has thwived on getting attention any way she can. I feared this vulnerability in her might make her weak against the wicked ploys of people like the Dexters. They know how I care about Lauwina, and that I promised her father I would watch over her. This is why they have twied so hard to plot against me.

They know she is like a daughter to me." Mark threw his senior elder a scrutinizing look. "Ted understands this weakness about Lauwina, as he has counseled her often. Right, Ted?"

"Yes, this is correct." Ted cleared his throat and sat straight. It was payback time and he knew it. Though it was already four years since he had ended his affair with Laurina, it seemed liked days. She was sixteen-years-old when she had waltzed through the doors of his office the first time. Exceedingly beautiful, he could not help but get weak-kneed at her presence. A year later he was cheating on his wife with Laurina every Tuesday and Friday afternoon in his office. Laurina was vulnerable and insecure, and he was there to comfort her. Five months later a guilty Laurina confessed their affair to Donna Garrett. Betty found out, and his marriage would have ended if Mark and Donna had not persuaded Betty and Laurina to forgive and forget, and keep their mouths shut. None of the elders ever found out. Mark had covered him well, burying the ordeal before it caused an awful scandal.

Ted moved his thoughts back to the meeting and said with confidence, "Laurina is dealing with the death of her mother, along with feeling abandoned by her father. Jolene is trying to pollute Laurina's mind with these false accusations against Mark. The devil is fighting mad now. Laurina is using Mark as a target to get even with her father, along with wanting to support her friend Jolene. Laurina needs extensive counseling." Ted boldly returned each man's look. "Pastor Mark has been like a father to her. I have counseled her personally about all of this. Laurina likes to tell tall tales. I believe we need to deal with this without overreacting. She needs love and strong guidance. We can give her that. Now that she is married, her husband is willing to support this church government and help his wife through her difficulties. Cody is very aware of her problems. It's vital we support our pastor in this situation."

"He's right," Avery interposed. "Gayle has spent time talking with Laurina and she also suggests she be counseled on a regular basis."

The pastor took back the conversation. "You men know I would never do anything to jeopardize the position God has placed me in." He rolled his pudgy hands together on his lap. "Ted, set up a meeting this week with Lauwina. Keep it small. I don't want her to feel uncomfortable. Ted, I want you and Avewy there, and I will join you. We need Lauwina's husband to side with us on this, so ask Cody to come. We will talk to him first, but I don't want him in the room duwing the meeting. He has always submitted fully to this church government, and I believe he will be supportive. I twust we can put this matter to rest."

"What do you propose we do to stop the Dexter scandal?" Avery asked.

"You men know I did not touch Jolene either. She has twied to get me to pwomote her husband as elder for years. I do not agwee with his teachings, and I can't subject this church to compwomise." His jaw muscle twitched. "Jolene has found a way to retaliate. Gentlemen, I will not be coerced into ordaining someone if it is not in God's will. It is sad that Jolene would stoop so low. And I'm disappointed that her husband would go along with her folly. They have given themselves over to the devil. We have to stop their gossip before it destwoys this church. I will hold a special service on Sunday to discuss this matter with the assembly. We need to stay joined and fight against the powers of darkness. God will pwevail!" Mark stood to signify the end of the meeting. "Can I count on your support, gentlemen? I can't run this church alone."

The eldership nodded. "Yes, Pastor. We're behind you."

Penny's new hostess job at the mall's Green Café gave her the opportunity to start helping her aunt with groceries and rent, and to meet new friends. Friday was her first day.

"Hello, I'm Callie Dusten." A waitress, around her age, greeted her with a big smile and a handshake. "You look like you could use a friend."

"How did you know?" Penny reciprocated the hearty handshake. "I just moved here from the Chicago area. I don't know a soul except my aunt."

"Well, I know this town inside and out. I grew up here. I can show you the sights sometime when we both have a night off."

"That would be nice. I would enjoy that very much. Thank you."

Callie looked over her shoulder. "Oops, my order's up. I will talk to you during break."

At break time Penny and Callie talked about their lives and goals. They had a lot in common, except that Callie loved horses, something Penny didn't know much about.

"So, do you own horses?" Penny asked.

"No, it is my dream though. My parents could not afford to buy me a horse, so when I was a kid I would dress up my two large dogs with makeshift saddles and prance them around the living room."

Penny noticed how her new friend's large green eyes lit up like a Christmas tree when she smiled. Even though she wore no makeup and did little to enhance her mousy brown hair, laughter on Callie was a complete makeover in itself. Still,

Penny thought, a little makeup would turn Callie into quite a pretty girl. She, herself, never left the house without eye shadow, mascara, and lipstick.

"Callie, is that an engagement ring?" Penny motioned to Callie's hand.

"Yes! My fiancé's name is Petey Graves. I met him last year. I thought he was so clumsy when I first met him. But he somehow charmed me silly."

"Is he still clumsy?" Penny joked.

"Only when he is embarrassed. I love it though. He *can* be outspoken, but he is *sweet potato pie*."

"I look forward to meeting him."

"Do you go to church?" Callie asked nonchalantly.

"Not since I moved here. My Aunt Joann, that's whom I live with, she is Lutheran. But I'm Catholic."

"I was born a Catholic too. But since I gave my life to Jesus, I don't go to a Catholic church anymore."

"What do you mean?" Penny asked curiously.

"I am a born-again Christian now. I accepted Jesus into my heart last year. As a Catholic I didn't know much about God. They were so steeped in traditions that I never understood who God really was. I had no idea that I was a sinner, or what to do to inherit eternal life. Jesus is my whole life now."

Now Penny understood more why the girl lit up like a Christmas tree—something inside her glowed. What was it? She felt drawn to the woman, and Penny wanted to know more about why Callie talked about Jesus as though He were *a real person*.

Callie smiled and touched Penny's knee. "Hey, our break is up. If you are interested in going to church, you can join me tonight at my church service."

"Church on Friday night?"

"Yes, we have Friday night, Sunday morning, and Sunday evening services."

Something inside longed to go. "Oh. Sure. I guess so."

"I'll pick you up tonight about seven. I'll get your address later." Callie grinned and headed for the kitchen.

Laurina Addison entered Ted's office at exactly two. She wore a simple white blouse and navy cotton skirt. Her silky hair was swept up to one side with a silver comb. She stiffened at the sight of Ted seated behind his desk. He made sure his eyes didn't trail her figure as she walked into the room. He signaled her to sit on the couch near the wall and pretended to work on his computer.

"The pastor will be here shortly, "he said. "Would you like some coffee?"

"No."

"Is Cody here?"

"Yes, he's right outside the door." She fidgeted with her hands.

"Laurina..." Her pouty face made him want to run his fingers down her cheek and whisper in her ear that everything would be all right. What was it about her that made men do crazy things?

"What?" she asked defiantly, tipping her nose up.

Ted backed down. "Nothing...I...everything will be fine." He quickly quashed his feelings and looked away.

"You men are all alike," Laurina spat.

Ted did not reply.

"You know me, Ted. I don't lie."

"Do I know you, Laurina? I thought I did at one time." He busied himself with papers on his desk.

She grunted and shook her head in disgust. A muffled noise outside the office door made Laurina turn her head. The door opened and Pastor Mark and Avery walked into the room. Laurina could hear her husband's drawl beyond the open door before it was shut again. The men greeted her with weak smiles.

Pastor Mark nodded at Ted and sat down on the opposite end of the couch, away from Laurina. Ted rose from his desk and joined the group, seating himself in the leather chair near Laurina. Avery pulled up a chair close to Mark and crossed his skinny legs.

"Honey, I'm glad you came today," Pastor Mark purred, almost fatherly. He leaned forward, offering a wan smile. "This is difficult for me, too. I'm sort of confused at this whole mess. I hope we can stwaighten things out today."

Laurina did not answer.

"Cody is waiting outside the door. If you need him at any time, let us know." He opened his suit coat. "Now Lauwina, I understand you believe I might have made some inappwopwiate advances to your person. Is this twue?"

Laurina glared at him grimly. "Yes." Dread began to replace the anger she had, and she felt her reserve start to crack. Her hands rocketed like yo-yos up and down her arms.

"I've called this meeting, Lauwina, to clear up any misunderstandings that might have twanspired between us. I'm gweatly twoubled by your implications. A charge like this can damage this church and Bible College. Is this what you want, Lauwina?" He pronounced his lisp slowly, using it for his advantage, knowing the calming effect it had on women. His expression turned into one of benevolence.

"No." She wiggled uncomfortably.

"Lauwina, I was raised in a secure family enviwonment. I tend to forget sometimes that not evewyone had the fweedom I had gwowing up. I'm like my Dad. He was a hugger. If you misunderstood my touches…"

"How can touching my…chest be hugging?" Laurina glared at him until his piercing blues made her back down. She dropped her eyes into her lap.

Ted cleared his throat and Avery's brows shot up.

"Honey, if my hands slipped against you, that was an accident. Now, think back, did I say anything sexual to you?" Mark spoke softly.

Laurina rubbed her arms faster. "Well…no."

"Did I hurt you?" He almost whispered.

"No."

"Were we alone at the time?"

"No, but…"

"See, Lauwina, you're implying something that would not have happened. I would never touch you, especially in a public place. And fwom what Joe says, you're saying it happened in the libwary?"

"Yes. But no one saw you."

"That's exactly my point, Lauwina. No one saw me. Maybe this is not about me, maybe it's about your loyalty to your fwiend Jolene."

Laurina started to weep.

Ted got up and retrieved a box of Kleenex from his desk. He kept a good supply of tissues on hand to meet the demand of the many ladies who wept during his counseling sessions.

Laurina wiped her eyes with the tissue and Ted took his seat again.

"Laurina," Avery said, taking the floor, "I understand you feel misunderstood. We're not here to judge you, or attack you. We love you and want what's best for you. Your husband understands this too. That's why he's here, too. He trusts us with your heart. Will *you* trust us?"

Laurina blew her nose and glanced at him.

"Laurina," Ted added tenderly, "Your life has not been easy. But you can't blame every man for your loss. Your father didn't send you here to abandon you. He sent you here because he loves you and felt we could give you better guidance than he could. Your pastor loves you and has looked out for your welfare. You know this, don't you?" He looked over at Mark who was wearing a pleased look on his face.

"Yes...I know. I want to trust Mark." She looked over at him and cried some more. "I don't want to leave this church." Her shoulders shook with her sobs.

"Of course you don't," Avery said. "Your friends are here, your support. Laurina, I know you love your friend, Jolene, but if you follow her, you will find yourself walking out of God's will. You can lose your salvation. Is this what you want? To leave the covering God has placed over you?"

"No."

"Honey," the pastor scooted towards her, "I'm on your side. Please forgive me if I've hurt you in any way. I pwomise to be careful with your heart." He kept his hands in his lap. "I believe Satan has twied to influence your mind against me by using Jolene. I did not touch Jolene. She has pwoblems you are not aware of. She is being used by the devil now to destwoy this church. Is this what you want? To see all these people thwown to the wolves?"

"No, Mark." Laurina sighed with a shiver. "Maybe I'm just confused by their words. I...I..."

"Laurina," Avery interrupted, "Can you say for sure that your Pastor sexually abused you?"

Laurina shook her head no and started crying again. She felt foolish.

The pastor nodded at Ted to go get Cody. "We can forget this whole matter ever happened," he said. "God will reward you for standing against the enemy's lies." Mark bent forward with a sappy expression. "Will you forgive me for being insensitive?"

Laurina nodded and gave a weak smile.

Cody came into the room and lowered himself beside his wife. He stretched his arm around her shoulders and drew her close. His eyes, like turquoise tropical pools, were a refuge for her. "You okay, Laurina?" he asked. His sallow face softened at her brokenness.

"I'm fine. I...I think I got confused about Pastor Mark." She rubbed at her eyes.

"Sweetie, everything will be alright."

"I don't want to hurt this church," she said sobbing.

"You won't, Babe. We all make mistakes. It's part of growing as a Christian." Cody gave Ted a gracious look. The two men had come to a silent understanding about Ted's affair with Laurina. What happened in the past was past, buried and over, and Cody felt no inward concerns about it.

"She's coming along fine," Ted crooned. "She's been through a lot, and patience is needed here."

Mark smiled. He was relieved and it showed. "Good, good, Lauwina. Do I have your support fwom here on out?"

"Yes, Mark." She kept her face hidden in Cody's shoulder.

"Lauwina, I want you to know that your submission today to this church government is, in a sense, establishing your heart of submission towards your husband as well. I am pwoud of you. And I know Cody is too." Mark spoke gently. "God called Cody to Gwace Church. You know this, Lauwina. God saved him from a life of dwugs and is now using him here to encouwage the youth. You don't want to go against God's calling for his life and ruin his chances for the ministwy, do you?"

"No, of course not." Laurina looked up at Cody. He shrugged and smiled passively.

"Good. You're a good girl. A vewy good girl."

oc *CULT*

CHAPTER TWO

Ted Hunter had to mention the meeting to Betty. It was the pact he and his wife had made—no more secrets. He handed the mashed potatoes to his perky thirteen-year-old daughter, Connie, then reached for the bread. He cleared his throat. "I had a meeting with Laurina Addison today." He quickly added, "Mark and Avery were there as well."

Betty stiffened.

"She concocted some false accusations against Mark." Ted could sense his wife's insecurity, but he kept talking. "Jolene Dexter and Laurina were friends, so, put two and two together."

Betty didn't comment.

Ted took another bite of steak. He hated Betty's jealousy. She had changed so much since he first laid eyes on her during his college days. He had eaten breakfast and lunch at the corner café every day just so she would wait on him. It took awhile to get her to go out with him, but once she did, Betty was zesty and willing, and he took full advantage of her willingness. When Connie was born nine months later they tied the knot. During their first years together she was a wildcat. Why she lost that zeal, he didn't know. She had gained some weight, but not enough to matter to him.

"What accusations?" Betty asked. She brushed at her short bangs and looked over at Connie. "Sweetie, take your plate and finish in your bedroom."

"Okay, Mom," Connie replied and left the room.

Ted kept eating. "Laurina says that Mark touched her breasts. Of course, it wasn't true. She claimed he did it in the college library. Common sense alone tells you Mark wouldn't do something so foolish in front of college students and jeopardize his pastoral position."

Betty shook her head. "Poor, Mark. He's a good man. Why are these women lying like this? He's got a heart of gold." She resumed eating for a while then asked, "So, what did you say to her?" It still bothered her to say Laurina's name. "Do you think it was wise for you to be the one counseling her?" Her voice took on an edge.

"I'm senior elder and head counselor." He was irritated. "Mark requested my presence. Don't turn this into a fight. It's not about me and Laurina, it's about Mark and Laurina." Why couldn't Betty let the past go? He loved the Lord and worked hard to keep his marriage together. It was *his* commitment to Christ that saved their marriage. He didn't leave her for Laurina. It was Betty who had filed for divorce when she found out about the affair. It took a lot of work on his part to stop her from going through with it. Why couldn't she let it all go?

Betty stiffened and pushed her plate away. "That woman's trouble. She seems to thrive on destroying relationships." She stood and picked up her plate, throwing Ted a cool look before leaving the room.

Connie walked back into the room. "Is Mom mad at you, Dad?" she asked.

"She'll get over it." Ted helped himself to more potatoes. "After you finish your homework, we can play Scrabble. Loser does the dishes tomorrow."

"Oh, Dad!" Connie giggled and blew him a kiss. "You've got a deal. You'll lose."

"Never. There's something you need to know about your dad; I never lose."

That night before service Laurina Addison snuggled with Cody on the sofa for reassurance and support. He soothed his new bride with soft strokes until she stopped crying.

"Are you sure you want do this?" he asked, his face creased with worry.

"Yes, Cody. I'll support Mark publicly. I need to do it if I want to stay in the church. And for you." She looked at him lovingly.

Laurina was tired of having to endure everyone else's problems and feeling guilty about them. She remembered her struggles in Iowa when she was thirteen years old. She spent two years nursing her dying mother, watching the cancer spread slowly through her body, while her father escaped the horror by working long hours every day. Even her older brothers found excuses to leave Laurina with the brunt of the responsibilities, doing all the chores, cooking, and cleaning her mother's messes. The funeral brought relief instead of grief, along with a never-ending guilt for feeling that relief. As she grew older, she got plain tired of the whistles and cat-calls from men. She hated being treated like a sex object, especially when she had proved herself stronger then even the men in her family. At first it angered her when her father sent her to Portland to live with his Christian friends, Joe and Christina Fellows. He insisted she would be safer in a good family environment. Once she settled, she liked the atmosphere of love and support she received at Grace Church. She met many new friends and felt accepted for the first time in her life. She didn't want to leave the church.

Cody pulled Laurina close. "We don't want misunderstandings to destroy what God's doing in this church. I think it wise to give Pastor Mark the benefit of the doubt."

Laurina trusted her husband's judgment. He was the first man who treated her with respect. God had changed him so wonderfully, saving him from a world of drugs and a prison sentence, igniting his heart with fire from the Holy Ghost. Cody, too, grew up in the Midwest, in a small town in Southern Kentucky. A series of life-changing events transpired after he gave his life to Jesus. Cody found his direction after meeting Grace Church's Kentucky satellite pastor, Gary Evans. Soon afterwards he moved to Portland to attend Grace Church Bible College full time. Though he was only six years older than Laurina, his life with drugs had aged his twenty-six years, leaving his skin blotchy and tough. But Laurina had seen his heart. His generous eyes held depth and compassion. She had to hang in there for him. God brought him to Grace Church. Mark was right about this. Cody was next in line for youth pastor. She had to support her husband, even if it meant some sacrifices.

That night Penny readied herself for church by donning a pair of blue dress slacks and an ivory blouse. She had painted her nails ruby red to match her lipstick, and pinned her long hair up in a French roll.

The doorbell chimed. Penny finished dusting her face and set the powder brush down. "I got it!" she yelled to her aunt and rushed for the door.

Callie stood there smiling. The *too* frilly pink dress she had on seemed out of place with her plain face. Penny complimented her anyway and invited her in.

Joann walked into the room and Penny made introductions. "Aunt Joann, this is Callie."

"Hello, Callie, glad to meet you," Joann smiled.

"You too," Callie replied joyfully.

Joann returned to the kitchen and Callie frowned, "Penny, maybe you should put on a dress. Pastor Mark doesn't want women to wear pants at church."

"Oh? Well, okay. Why's that?"

"He wants the congregation to maintain a high standard for God."

Penny accepted the explanation and dashed to her room. She returned five minutes later wearing an ankle length black skirt and flat pumps.

"That looks nice," Callie said, grinning again.

Callie's old Ford chugged a bit and than started right up. She backed out of the driveway and headed south. To Penny's astonishment, Callie pulled into the same spacious lot that housed the huge oblong church she had noticed the first day of her arrival into Oregon. The sign still said, *Grace Church*.

"So, what kind of church is this?" Penny asked, suddenly nervous.

"It's a non-denominational fellowship. We are not Catholics or Lutherans or Methodists. We are just Bible believing folks who love the Lord."

Penny changed the subject. "Will your boyfriend be here tonight?" she asked.

"No, he works tonight. He's looking forward to meeting you though." Callie's face warmed. "Petey's the only man I love. And I'm glad he loves Grace Church. I wouldn't date anyone that didn't go to Grace Church."

"Oh, how come?"

"Mark encourages us to stay within our own."

"What do you mean?"

"He wants us to date fellow *churchites*. So our marriages are equally yoked and we stay one with Grace Church's vision."

"*Churchites?*" Penny asked, puzzled.

"Oh, that's a term we give ourselves. You know, church members that attend Grace Church."

Callie found a spot close to the church and parked the car. Together the two girls entered the vast church through a pair of wooden doors.

"Wow, this place is huge!" Penny exclaimed, gaping at the spacious size of the foyer. Coat racks lined both sidewalls of the red-carpeted forum. A long bookshelf separated the doors that led into the sanctuary. Stairs on both sides of the foyer led up to a second floor.

Callie followed Penny's gaze and said proudly, "Upstairs is the Christian school. And we have a full Bible college. It's the large campus next door. I'm going to college there!"

Through the next set of doors the sanctuary area itself, full of people, was a vast sea of red carpet that seemed to go on forever. Too many pews to count, wide aisles, and the choir's platform were all red as blood. Thick red curtains covered the entire long length of the back wall. The side walls were plain brick. Unlike most churches, the walls and pulpit areas were plain with no crosses or religious artifacts gracing them. The place was abuzz with friendly chatter.

"Our church is big too," Callie exclaimed, "We have over two thousand members."

Penny could not help but gawk at the differences in Grace Church compared to the Catholic Church she attended back in Illinois. One would think that the ornate human-sized statues of the various saints and the costly icons displayed on every pillar and wall in that church would make Grace Church pale in comparison. But, not so. This massive space, with the many glitzy-dressed people roaming its regal red runways, seemed to outshine any palace. The over friendliness of the people gave the otherwise stark warehouse-size sanctuary surprising warmth.

Callie guided Penny into a pew near the front on the left side of the sanctuary. She kept glancing around. The women were dressed to the hilt and the men were spiffy looking, all clean-shaven, sporting dress suits and ties. Not only did the churchgoers look great, they smelled it too. It was hard for her nose to ignore their tangy mixture of perfumes and cologne.

Callie stayed close to Penny's side, talking softly. "Grace Church has satellite churches all over the United States, and ones in Italy, Germany, and France. We also have our own music and publications studio. All the Christian tapes sold in our bookstore are from our own choir and singers. Pastor Mark has authored many of the books we sell, too." Callie turned and pointed to the back of the auditorium. A man stood inside a small-enclosed glass area overseeing a panel of buttons and knobs. "That's the sound system," she said. "Every service is taped, so if we miss church, we can make it up."

The lights flashed off and on, signaling the start of service. The room quieted as the choir filed in rows onto the raised stage behind the podium. As the music started, Penny noticed most of the people in the congregation closed their eyes and raised their hands high above their heads, some swinging, others waving, some still. Some stood; some sat; a few kneeled in their pew and prayed. She felt out of place, nervous, but oddly drawn to the lovelorn looks on everyone's faces.

As the heavenly music played, its melody settled upon her like sweet oil. Perspiration dotted her brows as she fought the strange feeling warming her insides.

What's happening to me?

She fought to retain composure, but her body ignored the fight in her mind and followed the response of her heart. Tears flowed as she felt this newfound love permeate her insides, filling her up with joy. Her eye mascara smeared and she knew her cheeks probably resembled tomatoes. This embarrassed her even more.

Callie gave a sheepish grin as she removed two tissues from her purse and handed them to her crying guest. Penny kept her head down, trying hard not to cry. But the more the choir sang, the worse she blubbered.

"You're feeling God's Holy Spirit, Penny," Callie whispered. "He loves you."

Penny nodded, hoping no one was watching her lose her cool. She was relieved when the singers stopped and returned to their seats.

The Pastor took his cue and scurried up the platform and stood behind the wooden podium. Though small in stature, he presence was as big as the room. He was impeccably dressed in an expensive gray suit and paisley tie. His full head of chestnut "Elvis" hair was obviously dyed, for at his age the gray usually had surfaced.

Cindy leaned over to Penny and said quietly, "That's Pastor Mark. Pastor Mark Garrett."

"Good evening," Pastor Mark smiled, flashing his even white teeth. "Glad you made it tonight. Pwaise God for Gwace Church. There's no other church that compares with the teachings and the moving of God's Spiwit like this church! We are a chosen people, set apart for His calling in these last days!"

His cocksure mannerisms and lullaby lisp captured Penny's attention.

The pastor continued, "Stay rooted in this church, my *sheepies*. Stay joined with this church government, for they care for your soul. Submit to autho*w*ity and God will reward you with great outpou*w*ings of His Spi*w*it. Are you joined with me, believers? Are you willing to be part of His t*w*ue church?"

"*Yes Pastor!* and *Amen!*" bounced back at him from the congregation.

"Tonight I will p*w*each on the life of the Apostle Paul. But first, I want to p*w*epare you for a special service Sunday morning. I want all of you to be here, because it's very important. I can't discuss it now, but it's a se*w*ious matter and we need to pull together against the attacks of Satan. I don't want to instill fear in your little hearts, so p*w*ay, and come supporting your pastor. God will have the victo*w*y!" He pumped his audience's curiosity with dramatic arm gestures and a stern tone.

They responded with supportive calls.

"Also, we are getting a lot of new members, and so before I get into tonight's message, I want to give a b*w*ief reminder of our church's rules. I ask that women attending this church d*w*ess modestly. Avoid heavy makeup. Red lipstick and nail polish has always been related to harlots, and I prefer our women to be examples of holiness and walk in their natural beauty. Men, no beards or moustaches. If you're making G*w*ace Church your church home, please shave. Men, let's be clean soldiers for God!"

Penny squirmed in the pew at his words. Though Callie did not wear makeup, most of the other women did, but she was the only one wearing red lipstick. She licked at her lips and hid her red-nailed hands in her lap.

The pastor pushed his arms straight in front of him and kept talking. "Men, tweat the ladies with respect. No fwont hugging is allowed between singles, especially the Bible college students. Side hugging is appwopwiate."

As the pastor underscored church policies, the assembly listened attentively, nodding their heads in agreement to his words, leaving their pews only for the bathroom or to remove a crying child.

"I forbid any rock-n-roll beat in our music, so this is the reason our bookstore sells only our own choir's music. When you purchase music or teaching tapes here you are supporting your church, and making sure you are getting fed with twuth. Should you need more information on why we don't listen to rock music, you can check out the tape called, "The Dangers of Rock Music." With the full range of gifted individuals in this body of believers, there is no need to go anywhere else to buy books or music. *Churchites*, are you listening? Let's sepawate from the compwomise of the world and be partakers of His holiness."

A cell phone went off in the sanctuary. The pastor turned toward the annoying sound and scolded, "I forbid cell phones during service. I want them shut off. I pwefer you leave them at home. This is God's time. I want respect in the house of God."

More *Amens* flew at him.

Forty-five minutes later the pastor closed his sermon. Before he left the podium he added, "If you know someone who did not make it tonight, please make sure they get a copy of tonight's service. We must all be our bwother's keeper. I don't want anyone left behind."

A male and female duet took his place, ending the service with a song. Again, the Holy Spirit tugged at Penny's heart and tears flowed.

Callie reached over and took Penny's hand. "Penny, would you like to give your life to Jesus?"

"How do I do that?" Penny murmured self-consciously, keeping her chin tucked down. The convicting presence was nudging her gently and she knew it was God.

"Pray the sinner's prayer with me."

Penny agreed, and repeated the prayer with her new friend. "Jesus, I'm a sinner. Forgive my sins and enter my heart, and be my friend, my Lord, my God. Be Lord over all my life."

That feeling of love, so pure, like a gentle caressing wind, enveloped her, and she felt as though she would burst from the sheer delight of what was happening to her. She was giving her heart to Jesus, and for the first time in her life, she knew she found what she had been searching for all her life.

After service Callie sat in the pew and took Penny through scripture. It was then that Penny understood John chapter 3, verse 16: *For God so loved the world, that He gave His only begotten Son, that whosoever believeth in Him should not perish, but have everlasting life.*

"Aunt Joann, last night changed my life!" Penny exclaimed the next morning at the breakfast table. "For the first time in my life I know what I want to do."

"What's going on?" Joann cracked some eggs into the frying pan.

"I gave my heart to Jesus last night at Grace Church. Remember the big church we passed when you picked me up from the airport? That's were I was! I never knew God could be so real. Aunt Joann, I want to spend my life serving Him."

Joann turned the heat down on the burner. "Penny, you sound nuts. Don't get caught up in fly-by-night emotions."

"This is real, Aunt Joann. I can't explain how I feel. But I'm different inside. I'm born again. I never understood what that meant, until now. I was a sinner, and I didn't realize how much of a sinner I was until last night when God's Holy Spirit shined His light on my heart." Penny put a hand on her heart and sighed, her eyes teary. "That emptiness inside me is gone. Jesus forgave me and He loves me! He has my life now. This is why I've decided to sign up and join their Bible College next week."

"Your friend Callie goes there?" Joann asked, raising a wary brow.

"Yes. She is a great girl."

Joann carried the skillet to the table and sat down. "Penny, don't be jumping into anything drastic. Look into this church and find out more about it. Is their college accredited?"

"I'm not sure. But it doesn't matter; I want to learn about God for myself. A degree isn't my goal. Aunt Joann, I've been lost for a long time. That's why I moved out here with you. I thought being with you would take care of the inner aches that weigh me down. But, I was wrong. Only God could do that. And He did."

"Pen, the woman I work with that goes there is always talking about the place like it is the only church that exists. She talks funny too, almost phony. Be careful. I've heard the pastor runs the place like a heavy-handed sergeant does his battalion. Please do some research on their beliefs."

"Don't worry, Aunt Joann. How could a church that size be wrong when so many people love Jesus?" Penny leaned over and hugged her aunt happily.

Joann threw her niece a wary look. She finished breakfast and walked to the sink, flipping on the radio near the window. An old song from the Beatles came on and Penny jumped up from the table and turned the station.

Anxious Christians, Bibles tucked under their arms, filed past Penny and Callie Sunday morning as they entered the church foyer. Expectation in the crowd was thick.

Penny was excited. Friday night had changed the course of her life, made her a new person, and today the anticipation to hear more about God pushed her emotions into high gear. She felt as though she were seeing through a pair of new eyes. Praying was a whole new experience. She found herself not wanting to stop. And the words in the Bible that once seemed confusing now made sense. Her relationship with Jesus was indeed intimate and personal. Life suddenly made sense to her. She had wanted her parents' love to fill the void inside her, but even if they did love her like she wanted, only God could bring her dead spirit to life.

"Do you like college?" Penny asked Callie as they settled in the pew.

"Yeah, a lot. I'm getting to know Jesus more and more by learning His Word. Are you planning on enrolling? I hope so, you'll treasure the knowledge you receive."

"I plan to sign up for the winter quarter! I am so excited about this, Callie. I cannot even explain what the Lord has done inside me. I feel like a new person."

"You are!" Callie beamed.

A hand flew into Penny's face. "Hello, you must be Penny." A tall fellow with wavy black hair all slicked back with grease behind his ears, was leaning over the pew grinning widely.

Once he winked at Callie, Penny knew who he was. "Why, hello, you must be Petey," she said, shaking his hand heartily.

On Petey's nose was balanced a pair of black thick-rimmed glasses. Two brows almost caressed each other above his coal eyes. His attire was conventional—black pants and a crisp white shirt with blue tie. He moved into the pew and plumped down between her and his fiancé.

"Callie told me wonderful things about you," Petey said loudly. "One, that you love Jesus. Praise God! Hallelujah!"

Penny liked him instantly.

Strange animal-like noises began echoing around her. "What's that?" she asked.

Petey quickly said, "There are two levels of prayer space behind the front wall." He pointed to the small entranceways, one on each side of the stage. "Christians are praying *in the spirit.*"

Penny wondered what *in the spirit* meant, but didn't ask.

A nice looking couple moved into the pew in front of the them and turned around with broad smiles. "Hi Callie, Petey," they both said.

"Hello back," Callie sang. "This is Penny."

"Hi, I'm Marcy Nason." The woman extended a slim hand to Penny. She was in her late twenties with strawberry-blonde hair and smoke-gray eyes. A single diamond twinkled from her finger. Her fluffy hair graced her shoulders, and the light blue suit she wore slimmed her five-foot-five-inch frame.

"I'm Owen, her better half." The man with dancing light brown eyes tipped his thinning blonde head to one side, grinned, and stuck out his hand too. He looked exceptional in a tan suit and green tie.

Penny smiled, crossed her arms, and shook both their hands at the same time.

"You must be new," Marcy said sweetly. "Are you from Portland?"

"No, I'm from Illinois."

"You single?" Marcy's inquisitive eyes dropped to Penny's hand. "Lots of single gents around here," she added with a mischievous glint in her eye.

"Actually, I do have a boyfriend—I think. I left him to move out here. He wanted to get married, but I wanted a change in my life. But now that Jesus has given me the change I needed, maybe I might say yes to his proposal. Rick is supposed to come out next week to see me."

"Introduce us when he arrives," Marcy said.

"Does Rick know about your new commitment to Jesus?" Petey blurted, pushing his glasses close to his nose with two fingers.

"He comes from a Catholic background too. I hope he can accept this church. It's different than what he's used to. He's a professional golfer, travels a lot, so I don't know if he'll want to live here. We're discussing it."

"Impressive," Petey announced. "I'm looking forward to meeting him and talking to him about the Lord. I will walk him through scripture. Let us know as soon as he arrives."

Callie patted Petey's arm with an embarrassed smile and said, "Petey does get a bit anxious about getting people saved."

"Once he walks through these doors, your boyfriend will be hooked," Owen Nason added with a wink.

Penny hoped so. When she had called him yesterday, Rick didn't seem as happy as she about her newfound relationship with Christ.

The lights flashed and the choir gathered on the platform.

Penny whispered to Owen and Marcy, "Nice meeting you both. I hope to see you again soon."

"You will," Marcy replied, still grinning. Instead of sitting down, Marcy scooted out of the pew and joined the singers on stage. Someone handed her a guitar and she led the group in song.

The congregation stood and sang along, worshipping with raised hands. God's Spirit brushed Penny again and tears came freely as God's sweet presence poured over her. The music lifted her into a peaceful place where nothing in life mattered at the moment but being with God.

After fifteen minutes, Pastor Mark signaled the end of the song service and everyone sat down. A buxom woman with a small waist walked up to the pulpit, almost swaying as she went. An expectant hush fell over the crowd as she began speaking into the microphone in a language that was not English. She looked to be in her early fifties, though she dressed much younger. A long, bouncy yellow wig overpowered the attractive face.

"Who is that?" Penny asked Petey. The woman wore a lot of make-up, something the pastor didn't like, and Penny found this odd.

"That's Donna, the Pastor's wife," Petey replied. "She's so in tune with God and the most spiritual person in this place."

"What's she doing?"

Callie bent forward and put her finger to her mouth and whispered, "I will tell you later. She's being *anointed* by God. She will translate what she is saying in English."

Donna finished the powerful words in the English language, speaking with God's authority to stay close to His Word.

Amens and *Thank you, Lords* resonated throughout the sanctuary.

Pastor Mark moved up to the platform, behind the pulpit. "Praise God," he cooed. Everyone got quiet again.

"Now, listen up, people. I want all of you to come to service tonight. I have decided to postpone that important matter I told you about Fwiday night until tonight. I feel it is important that you all stay after service and pway about this. I want God's will to be pwesent in how I tackle this difficult subject. I need your support! Can I count on you?"

The audience's supportive response was loud.

Mark leaned over the podium with authority and opened his Bible. "Now, let's pway before I get into today's message."

After service ended, Petey opened his Bible and showed Penny a verse in the Book of Acts, chapter two. "Penny," he explained, "Donna is blessed in the gift of prophesy and tongue and interpretations. When you heard her speaking at the beginning of service, she was speaking in an *unknown tongue*. Afterward she interpreted that language in English. It was a message from God."

Penny looked confused.

Petey continued. "In the days of Pentecost, God sent His Holy Spirit to comfort, guide, and teach us all things. While the disciples and their friends were praying, God's Spirit came upon them like a rushing wind and scripture says they began to speak in new tongues. The gift of tongues was a sign for both the believers and the unbelievers, to prove God's promises, but most importantly to keep His children in close communion with Him." He looked up at Penny. "Sometimes

English words aren't enough to empty a burdened heart; praying in tongues, or *in the Spirit*, can release our burdens to Christ. I know it looks and sounds bizarre, but God's Word tells us all about this."

"Is that what it means to be *anointed*?"

"Anyone so used by God is anointed when His Spirit comes upon them," Callie added.

"Is that the noise I heard in the prayer rooms?"

"They were praying in tongues. You can ask Jesus for it any time you want. It might seem very strange at first, getting this new language, but after a while you will use it more in prayer then not."

Penny opened her Bible to the same place in Acts and started reading. "But, this part here in verse six says that the people hearing were of different nationalities and understood their own language being spoken. Was the pastor's wife speaking in Chinese or something?"

"No," Petey chimed in, "You are reading it wrong. They were speaking in an unknown language."

"Oh? The Bible's wrong?" Penny replied, a bit confused.

"No, its translated wrong, or misinterpreted incorrectly."

Penny accepted the explanation. Besides, if it was from God, she wanted it too.

"Pastor asked us to pray," Callie said. "We must *stay joined* so that Satan cannot attack our pastor and this church. Do you want to go down front and pray with me for a while?"

"Sure."

Petey patted Penny's shoulder and got up. "Penny, it was nice meeting you. I will see you tonight."

"Okay, Petey. Bye bye." Penny returned his smile.

Petey squeezed Callie's hand and told her he would see her later. He headed for the prayer area.

"Callie, what does *stay joined* mean?" Penny asked, as they walked to the altar down front underneath the stage. Some members lingered in the aisles between the pews chatting, others remained in their pews to pray, but the majority headed for the altar and back prayer areas.

"It means submitting ourselves under our pastor and obeying that authority God has put over us."

"Oh." Penny thought Grace Church had a language of its own, even without the unknown tongues.

They knelt on the floor, and Callie bowed her head and prayed, but Penny, still getting used to her surroundings, kept glancing around. She spotted Pastor Mark in a pew, laughing with a blonde woman. The attractive woman's mouth was stretched wide back at him.

Penny put her head back down to pray, but could not help but be curiously attracted to the pastor. It was not a physical attraction, for he was older and not good looking in the sense of what she thought was handsome, but there was a certain magnetism about him. She continued to sneak peeks at him until Callie finished praying.

The musician returned to the piano and began playing. Everyone around them began to respond to the music. Some stood and swayed, some wept. As the two women stood, Penny noticed a small group standing around a man, their hands all over him, praying. Suddenly the man fell backwards, unconscious, onto the floor. Some of the prayers caught him going down, but he still hit the floor hard.

"Is he okay?" Penny asked, worried.

"Yes," Callie said, taking Penny's arm. "The power of God put him under. That is what we call being *slain in the spirit*."

"Oh, where is that found in the Bible? I would like to read about that."

"It's not in the Bible…because it's a response to God's Spirit moving on us."

"Oh."

They walked back to the pew to retrieve their Bibles, and when Penny turned and stepped into the aisle, she bumped smack into Pastor Mark. He caught her elbow and flashed her an electric smile. She froze and her stomach flip-flopped. She lowered her head self-consciously. But he kept going.

"Penny, you're red as a beet," Callie cajoled. "Don't feel bad. I have been going here a year and I'm still nervous around the pastor."

"You are?"

"Yeah. I don't know why. But I better get over it because I'm supposed to start praying for him next week," Callie said. "God has been using me in intercessory prayer, and two of his intercessors have invited me to join his prayer meeting."

Callie saw the blank look on Penny's face and explained further, "An intercessor is someone that stands in the stead for someone else in prayer, someone anointed by God to pray a request or problem to victory. It involves spiritual warfare against demons. It's an important ministry."

"Can anyone pray for the pastor?"

"No. That's why I'm so nervous. Some members have tried for years to get into his prayer group. But God has opened these doors and I must be obedient to go where He leads me."

Callie and Penny found Petey, and together they headed for the exit doors in the foyer.

"Those guys policemen?" Penny asked, as two men in blue uniforms with black guns hanging from their holsters opened the doors for them.

"Security guards," Petey said. "They're church members hired to patrol and protect our church."

That evening Penny took special care to dress modestly. She slipped a blue knit dress down over her head and examined herself in the mirror.

I wonder if this is too tight for church?

She was anxious to get to church and hear what the pastor had to say. It sounded awfully important.

Her cell phone rang…once, twice…she answered it in the kitchen. "Hello?"

"Penny, it's me."

"Hi, Rick."

"I thought I'd catch you before you head for church tonight. How's that going anyway?"

"I have so much to tell you, Rick, about this church!"

"Penny, are you sure about this God stuff?"

"Absolutely! Oh, Rick, I can't explain it, you just have to get here and see for yourself."

"I'll be there next week. I love you." His voice lacked confidence.

"I love you too!" Penny hung up, grabbed her purse and Bible, and shoved the cell into her purse. Remembering the pastor's rebuke about cell phones, she hastily removed it, set it on the kitchen counter, and rushed to the door. Church started in thirty minutes and she didn't want to be late.

"Hey, don't I get a good-bye?" Joann came up behind her.

"Sorry, Aunt Joann." She hugged her. "I'll be home around ten."

"You look nice."

"Thanks, Aunt! I feel wonderful!" Penny waved and scurried outside.

The fall evening held a chill, so Penny turned on the heater before slowly backing the Datsun out of the driveway. As she looked in the rear view mirror, the shadow of a man caused her to slam on the brakes. Quickly looking over her shoulder, Penny spied an old gray-haired man standing behind her car, looking confused. He turned this way and that, as if he was lost.

Penny rolled down the window and yelled out, "Sir, do you need some help?"

The man approached her. Even in the dark Penny could see his trench coat was soiled. She guessed he might be homeless. Dark sunglasses kept her from reading his intentions. A wooden cane, looking more like a crooked staff, steadied him.

"Hello," he said in an upbeat voice.

"Hello," Penny said.

"I was wondering if you could be so kind as to direct an old blind man to Fifth Street. I seem to have lost my way." A quick smile gave the stubbly face character.

Penny caught sight of the Bible wedged under the man's arm. She lit up. "Are you a Christian, sir?"

"Of course!" He got excited and bounced a little.

"I'm a new Christian. I just got saved at Grace Church, the big church down the street on Eighth Avenue."

"Ah…"

"Sir, excuse me, I don't mean to be rude, but how are you able to find your way?"

"My child, Psalms 146, verse 8 says, 'The Lord openeth the eyes of the blind and the Lord raiseth them that are bowed down. The Lord loveth the righteous.' Sight comes by hearing the Word of God! Don't ever forget this, my child."

Penny stuttered, "C..c..can I give you a ride, sir?"

"No, no. I can use the exercise, dear."

"Fifth Street is down two blocks on your left."

He thanked her and moved slowly down the sidewalk. Penny watched him walk away. She backed out of the driveway and decided she was going to pull over and make him get in the car. As she straightened out the front of her vehicle, she turned her head back around, but the man was gone.

CHAPTER THREE

Penny drove into the packed church grounds as parking attendants, waving bright orange neon flashlights, were directing people to the overflow area. She parked near the college campus and hiked the long walk to the sanctuary. Maple trees, leafed in red and gold, positioned over the grounds like soldiers in a row, looked festive with yellow and orange marigolds dancing around their bases.

"Penny, hello, nice to see you again." Marcy Nason, the guitar singer she had met that morning with her husband Owen, came up and hooked Penny's arm. "You alone?" The glaring overhead lights rimming the front entrance made her hair, which lay in fuzzy curls around her face, look copper red.

"Hello, Marcy!" Penny offered a hearty grin.

"Why don't you sit with Owen and I? Owen's parking the car, and will be in soon."

"I'd like that. Callie and Petey will be here soon too."

"They will find us."

Penny followed Marcy into the crowded sanctuary. The anticipation for what Pastor Mark had to say was evident. A group of people rushed to their pews, their energy bubbling over like an exploded soda can.

Marcy led Penny past the busy aisles towards the back of the church. "Service is about to start," she said. "Come on, let's sit down."

The women moved into the padded pew and sat down.

"Penny, are you going to make this your church home?" Marcy asked as she removed her jacket.

"Yes. I mean, I think so. I'm not sure what Rick will want to do when he arrives."

"Penny, if you know God has brought you here, don't let anything stop that. Pray and ask the Lord to direct Rick's path so that you both can serve God together. I don't know of any church that has the freedom in God like this one. If you leave Grace Church, you will find this out. Your relationship with Jesus is the most important thing in the world and you don't want to lose it. It's important you stay in a *spirit filled* church so you can be ready for Christ's return."

Owen arrived and sat beside Marcy. He leaned over and saluted Penny. Again he was impeccably dressed. Penny looked behind her, searching for Callie and Petey. She spotted them standing at the back of the aisle looking around. Standing up, Penny waved them over. They hurriedly marched toward her and moved in beside Owen.

"Good evening, my flock." Pastor Mark purred into the microphone before the lights were able to give their usual "on and off" signal. He looked dandy in a navy blue suit and red tie, his hair styled up high in a wave. His piercing eyes met the crowd with confidence. "I'm glad you came today to hear this special service," he said, "and to support your pastor who loves you ve*w*y much."

The crowd hushed.

"This morning I've asked music minist*w*y to remain seated. I want to get right on with what needs to be add*w*essed. This service will be taped the same as eve*w*y service. Please tell those not attending today to make sure and get a copy. Let's p*w*ay."

The assembly backed the Pastor's prayer with hearty *Amens*.

Donna was seated in the same place as before, below the platform in the designated pastoral pew. The pews behind her were reserved for close friends and special visitors. Across the main aisle, to the right of that section, the middle eight rows were set aside for the eldership and their wives.

Donna flew out of her pew and rushed up behind her husband. She put her hand on his shoulder, and he stepped back and closed his eyes as she *prophesied* into the mike in her unknown tongue.

"Thus saith your God," she said aggressively, swaying side to side. Her arms moved with her body as though they were speaking in a language all their own. "It is no coincidence that you are here. I have called you to this place, to this church. I have called you to be a beam of strength for your pastor against the evil designs the devil has plotted against him and this church. Trust me and look to my Word and I will deliver you from the hands of the evil one."

She stopped and dipped her head humbly before returning to her seat.

Mark paused, giving the congregation time to swallow her words. Then he lifted his voice and started talking. "Certain people in this assembly are twying to destwoy this church. I've spent days pwaying and cwying unto the Lord over this. I don't want to lose one sheep. I'm your good shepherd who cares for your soul; but when one or two sheep purposely undermine me and what God is doing here, then I have no other choice but to put those rebellious ones out of the pasture."

A crying baby broke into the stillness. The mother slipped out of the pew with the babe and sped down the aisle.

The pastor continued, "Bob and Jolene Dexter, are no longer part of this fellowship. They have undermined this church and would not repent. They have been *disfellowshipped*."

The audience gasped. The couple, regular members from the beginning, had been close friends of Mark and Donna Garrett. They had been stable fixtures in the pew behind them for years.

"I want you to twust me as your pastor and to twust my reasons concerning this situation. Just as the Apostle Paul in the New Testament had to disfellowship rebellious sinners in his church, I must also follow scwipture and remove the rebellion out of our assembly. If I don't, their sin will cowwupt some of you and cause a dissension within our body."

Penny hung onto every word, not sure what to think of it all. The pastor spoke with such humility and sincerity that she felt moved with him.

"They are spweading vicious gossip, and I see no reason to repeat it. The last thing I want to do is give the devil glowy. I am asking you to twust me in this church's decision. It pains me gweatly to expel them, but we have exhausted all gwace." Mark rubbed his forehead and shook his head sadly. "I have pwayed and pwayed about this. It has been a huge twial for me. But I refuse to let the devil have the upper hand. I've been your pastor and you know that I have thought good for you, *my flock*, to teach you God's Word and to help you gwow in Chwist. Satan wants to destwoy me so that he can destwoy you. And I won't have it!" As his voice rose in pitch, he slammed his fist against the podium. "I simply won't have it!"

Amen! and *Preach it, Brother!* shot up from the assembly.

The Pastor turned his attention to Laurina Addison seated in the elder's section next to his daughter, Gayle, and his son-in-law Avery.

"Lauwina," Mark wooed from the pulpit, "Honey, would you come up here and share with us what's on your heart?"

Avery nudged the young woman and she spirited out of her seat.

The pastor's hands roamed down his lapels as sweat moistened his forehead. He traced her delicate steps up the platform.

Laurina smiled nervously as he placed a reassuring hand on her shoulder and guided her close to the microphone. The tan dress she wore displayed a curvaceous figure, and her auburn hair looked like spun silk as it fell across her shoulders. Her mouth quivered as she eyed the inquiring faces. Inhaling, she leaned toward the mike and spoke. The melody in her speech brought an even bigger silence.

"As you know, Pastor Mark is our shepherd, and he cares about us," she said softly. "He's like a father to me, and has been for five years now, since I was sixteen, after my mother died of cancer. Some people have misunderstood Pastor Mark because he truly has a father's love for us. And, well…" her lush voice lowered, "the pastor is a very affectionate man, like a father to his children. And this is what he has been to me. Jolene Dexter was my friend, but I cannot call her that anymore. She has tried to convince me to lie about my pastor, to accuse him of inappropriate actions. But I can't, before God, go along with her lies. I stand here today to tell you all that we need to believe in our pastor and trust him."

The audience stayed mum.

"The Dexters are angry at pastor because he would not compromise his stand for holiness. They are spreading falsehoods now to get people to leave our church. Pray for them, but don't talk to them! They almost had me convinced, and I am so thankful God protected me from their web of deceit. I want to set straight any gossip that might hurt our pastor. God bless you."

Laurina walked down from the platform. As she passed the front pew, Donna averted her eyes.

The congregation watched with fascination as the service progressed, and Penny wondered what the whole mess was about. Elder after elder, member after member stood up, dedicating their loyalty to Pastor Mark. Some cried; others repented for not doing enough for their pastor. Through each affirmation, Penny's mind wandered back to Laurina's strange words. What exactly did it all mean? She hoped to meet the beautiful woman someday and find out more.

A woman in her forties moved up to the pulpit. Her sleek hairdo and slit-long eyes contrasted with the girlish dress she wore. With great emotion she stated, "I had a vision last night during my prayer time." The woman exuberated the same swaying mannerisms as the pastor's wife. She continued, "Satan, in the form of a large black octopus, was trying to attach itself to each one of your hearts with its tentacles. These tentacles represented deception, to blind you from the truth to God's word. Be warned, the devil wants to destroy this church. We need to support our pastor, our eldership, one another." She finished and pitter-pattered down the steps.

Pastor Mark took over the pulpit again.

"I'm asking you to leave here today encouwaged, yet cautious. Guard yourselves against gossip! Let's put this matter to rest. The Dexters are never to be mentioned again. As your good shepherd who cares for you, I must forbid you to associate with them. This is a pwotection for you, my flock. Don't give Satan room to destwoy this church. Stay under this church's covewing." Mark slowed his words. "I am His repwesentative, His mouthpiece, so if you disobey my words, you are disobeying God Himself. He has bwought you here and put me over you for your safety. Stay joined. Stay in the boat.

God bless you and thank you for coming and supporting me today."

The service had lasted three hours. At the end, Penny remained as confused as she had in the beginning. By Mark's orders, no one would ever know the whole reason for the banishment of the couple. Even the church bulletin read only: *Bob and Jolene Dexter have been disfellowshipped. They are now considered dissidents to this church body. Please do not have any association with them.*

The choir took the platform and began to sing soft songs. The music became a gentle vehicle back to God's sweet presence, a safe place for Penny to bask in His love. She didn't understand everything, but God had brought her here, and she would submit to the church and trust her pastor. The love she felt from Jesus was too beautiful to deny and she wondered why anyone would try to destroy something so wonderful.

As the throng exited the building, Pastor Mark, Donna, and Laurina Addison disappeared into a side room off the foyer. Donna and Mark sat on a chair and Laurina just stood in the center of the room.

"Well, I did what you asked," she said.

"Yes. Thank you, Lau*w*ina. I am p*w*oud of you. God is p*w*oud of you. Let's put this behind us now and move forward."

Laurina nodded. Donna said nothing.

"Honey, by submitting to this church government, you are allowing God to p*w*epare your husband for the minist*w*y. You know I have allowed Cody special p*w*ivileges from the pulpit; and I've decided to p*w*omote him as youth leader. You want him to *gwow*, don't you?"

"Yes," Laurina said.

Donna patted at her big hair, saying nothing as she watched the young woman walk out. She felt irritated and slightly humiliated by Mark's request to meet Laurina after service. Mark sensed her mood.

"What?" he asked.

"Couldn't we have let this go? I think she feels awkward enough."

"She is still ang*w*y at me."

"This little encounter didn't help any."

Mark smiled at his wife with resignation. "Maybe you're right. I'm over cautious. I was thinking of you. I don't want you to think bad of me, or be persuaded by the rumors."

"Is that why you asked me not to attend the last elder's meeting?"

Mark feigned a 'you caught me' look. "Is that what's bothering you, Donna?"

She didn't answer. A lot more than that irked her, but she held her tongue.

"Honey, this has been unbea*w*ably hard on me. Emba*ww*assing..."

"I understand."

Mark took her hand and drew her onto her feet. "T*w*ust me. I'm t*w*ying to do the right thing in all this." He hugged her.

She squelched her feelings and returned the hug. "The service went well, Mark," she said, letting him have his way. "God's grace is big, and...so is mine. We do have a big responsibility for this flock. They are our first priority."

She hoped Mark would open up to her and talk about the Jolene mishap and Laurina's accusations, but he simply pulled away and said, "Let's go eat."

Rick Duncan's plane landed at the airport on the first Thursday in November. The flight from Chicago gave him time to think about the changes in Penny. He loved her, and wanted to marry her, but her newfound religion made him nervous. He remembered when he had first met her, at his buddy's birthday party; it was like walking into a sauna and finding frost instead of steam. She gave him that kind of kick. Her long legs, rosy cheeks, and great smile made him do a turn-about. Getting her to go out with him was not an easy task, especially when she found out he was married. She was the excuse that pushed him to go ahead with a divorce. His marriage had long since been dead, and hanging on was something he did for no good reason. But meeting Penny gave him the reason to move ahead and do what he knew he should have done before. God, he wanted her so bad. She was a carefree spirit—would her recent *conversion* change this? He worried it might. She already told him she quit drinking, which was okay, but telling him she would not sleep with him before their wedding day took the cake. How was he supposed to respond to that bit of news? With a gallant bow?

To top it all off, his parents were not behind his decision to get the divorce, and they did not like Penny. If only he had the guts to be more direct with them about his feelings. He gave them no clues about his sour marriage for years, so the split surprised them—for the worse, for him. If he had found the courage to tell them his marriage was a pitiful mistake, then maybe they would not be so distant to Penny. It was as though they blamed her for what had transpired. Penny's folks weren't the most caring people and he hated to have his own parents reject her too. He hoped what she was going through was just a passing phase, and that she would return to Illinois and marry him. In time, maybe his parents could learn to love her. Penny had to understand his golfing career was at stake, and living in Portland was not a consideration. He had worked too hard to give up his lifelong dream. Not only did it take most of his parent's money to get where he was as a pro golfer, but his own hard work in winning national tournaments molded his life. Golf was who he was.

Rick sauntered off the plane wearing jeans and a leather jacket. He spotted Penny right away, dropped his bag, and grabbed for her. She moved into his arms. "Penny, hey." He kissed her hard, pulled back and swooned into her face. "Boy, I've missed you!"

"I missed you too, Rick." His rugged smell excited her. She couldn't wait to marry him.

They broke apart and scurried down the busy escalator to baggage claim. Rick retrieved his two suitcases off the conveyor belt.

"Aunt Joann is out of town for a few weeks," Penny said. "She couldn't pass on a free ticket to England. She told me to tell you hi."

"So, we have the whole house to ourselves?" Rick asked mischievously, his eyes turning a dirty brown.

"Yes, silly. But, don't get any ideas. Remember I talked with you about my new commitment. We will be married soon, so waiting a little while won't kill us."

She smiled but he didn't. They walked outside and headed for the parking area.

"What's wrong, Rick? You do still want to get married?"

He didn't answer.

"Rick?"

"Yes, of course I *want* to marry you. Let's get the luggage to the car, then we can talk."

"Okay."

"You driving *this?*" he asked, when Penny stopped at the beat-up Datsun. "Does this thing run?"

Penny jabbed his ribs and got into the car. Once they were settled, she started it up and skidded out of the parking lot into the traffic.

"Portland's a beautiful city. The mountain range is spectacular. I can see why you love it here." Rick rolled the window down a few inches and breathed in the cool air, then looked over at Penny. "You look different. What's different about you?"

Penny shrugged.

"Ah, the dress you're wearing. Pretty. Sort of frilly."

"I'm trying to look more like a lady."

Rick slid his hand over her knee. "I like it."

"You came on a good day. November is usually the rainy season. You'll love it here though; the people are friendly and the food is great."

Rick nodded, than sputtered out what was on his mind. "Penny, I love you, plain and simple. I want to marry you. But I am concerned about moving here. You know my golfing career has really taken off now. I can't live out here. I have to stay close to my contacts. Why don't you come back home and we get married there. My parents will help us with the wedding…"

"Your parents hate me!" Penny shot back. "I can't believe you expect me to move back there. You know I've signed up for Bible College. I have to stay here. It's important to me."

"And my career isn't?"

"No! I didn't say that. But I have to do what Jesus wants me to do!" Penny's face turned crimson. She shifted into fourth gear and pulled onto the freeway. The clean outline of downtown Portland loomed behind them.

Rick threw up his arms and shouted, "Jesus, Jesus, Jesus!"
Penny started to cry.

"Penny, I'm sorry. I didn't mean that. You are throwing a lot on me now, you know. Let's not fight. I love you." His voice softened and he rubbed her shoulder.

"I love you too." Penny surrendered a sheepish grin. "We can talk about it later. Okay?"

The car sputtered to a stop in front of Joann's rambler. Rick unloaded the suitcases as Penny unlocked the front door.

"It's messy, but comfy. Aunt Joann has collected a lot of stuff from all her overseas travels. Working for a travel agency has been rewarding for her. Anyway, she won't let me organize the messy rooms. Drives me nuts."

Boxes full of old newspapers and magazines were stacked against part of the living room wall and scattered mail and other papers completely covered the dining table. Rick set his luggage down in the hallway and spun around and pulled Penny into his arms.

"I want you now," he said huskily and tugged at her sweater.

Penny wiggled out of his arms. "Rick, stop, come on, I'm serious; we have to wait."

"We've done it for two years," he whined, exasperated.

"Pastor Mark says it's a sin. I want to obey God. I need to. Please understand." She traced her finger around his dimpled chin. "Please? For me?" She pecked his nose and mouth with kisses.

"Stop that if you want me to abstain," he retorted. "You go from one extreme to the other. It's just another crutch for you." He tromped off into the kitchen.

"Rick, that's not true." She followed after him. "Jesus is not a crutch. Coming to know Him has given me a reason not to drink or want to do anything that goes against His will."

"Shouldn't teasing be a sin?" He leaned against the sink, sulking.

"I can't believe you're acting this way. Is that all you want me for is sex?"

"Penny, I haven't seen you in two months. Of course I want you."

"Let's not fight. Come on, we can still smooch and cuddle." She put her arms around his waist, but his pride would not give in.

"You're so different; I don't know, I have to get used to your new ways."

"Rick, I'm still me, come on, I love you."

He stayed angry.

"Why did you come here Rick? For sex or for me?" She kicked the kitchen cabinet with her foot and stormed out of the room.

Rick stayed put. What was her problem? What made her so holy all of a sudden?

It would be one long, lonely night.

Rick woke with a slight headache. He hadn't gotten much sleep knowing Penny was lying in the room next to him. He felt like a heel for ruining their first night together. Waiting for sex was not that bad. In fact, the wait would add more excitement for the big day. He grinned and jumped out of bed, remembering their fight and amused that Penny hadn't lost her feisty spirit after all. If he could convince her to fly home with him, they could be married within two weeks.

Relieved at Rick's improved behavior, Penny cooked him a fantastic pancake breakfast and afterwards gave him the tour of the downtown area. They hit the public market place and scoured the long rows of handmade crafts, paintings, and baked goods. In the afternoon they shopped at the pier and ate fried fish and clam chowder. Lazy seagulls watched them from atop the ships docked nearby. At dinnertime Rick and Penny feasted on hamburgers at a small diner near their home.

"I've had a great day, Penny," Rick said as they left the restaurant.

"Rick, do you want to understand why I have changed?" Penny asked.

"Sure, you know I do."

"Well, Grace Church has a service every Friday night, and I was hoping you'd want to go tonight."

Rick surprised Penny with his reply. "You're right, I need to understand. Let's go."

They entered the sanctuary at six forty-five. The place was aglow with smiling people.

"Penny, hello," Callie said, walking up to them with Petey in tow. "You must be Rick." She extended her hand. "I'm Callie. This is my fiancé, Petey."

"Yes, hello." Rick reciprocated the handshake.

Petey shoved his Bible under one arm and extended his free hand to Rick. He was taller than Rick by a head. "Hello," he said with a floppy grin, "nice to meet you."

Rick feigned a smile and shook back. "Nice to meet you both." He was out of his element and did not like the feeling.

Penny hoped Petey would not pressure Rick with the Gospel at the moment. Everything was too new for Rick and she didn't want to scare him off.

"We hope to see more of you Rick," Callie added, sensitive to Rick's discomfort. "Maybe the four of us can have dinner sometime."

"That would be nice," Penny said.

"It's nice meeting you, Rick," Petey said, putting an arm around Rick's shoulder. "Enjoy the service and if you have any questions…"

"*Come on*, Petey. Let's let these lovebirds be. Bye, guys." Callie pulled her fiancé away.

Penny breathed easier and led Rick into the sanctuary. They sat near the back, and the service started. The choir lifted their hands and voices in praise. Members swung their arms back and forth with the beat of the music.

Rick looked around nervously. He kept glancing at his watch and at Penny. She wore the same odd, blissful look as everyone else.

The music ended and Donna tiptoed to the microphone in ruffles.

"Who's that?" Rick asked, pointing.

"The pastor's wife." Penny pushed his finger down. "She is a wonderful lady; very knowledgeable of the things of God."

Donna's husky voice boomed out across the spacious room. She related a dream about Jesus and His love for the church.

Rick edged forward in the pew, wringing his hands in front of him. "That guy talks funny," he said smartly as Pastor Mark began preaching his message.

Penny scowled at him.

Rick looked at his watch every five minutes until the service ended. It did, two hours later, much to his dismay.

"Well, what do you think?" Penny asked him in the car.

No answer.

"Rick, say something."
"What?"
"Anything."
Still silence.
"Rick, say something, please. You hated it, right?"
"Drop it Penny. Just drop it."

"Callie, come on in," Pastor Mark greeted sweetly, opening the parsonage door. "Thwee on the nose, you're right on time. I'm glad to meet you. Welcome, welcome." He shook her hand. "You're the first one here. The other ladies should be here soon. I know we normally don't pway on Saturdays, so thank you for coming."

Callie stammered something indecipherable and would not look at him. Immediately Mark got aroused, which surprised him because he didn't find her beautiful. What was it that made him react so? He scanned her figure. Slim hips. He studied her face. No makeup, but nice large green eyes. She blushed under his glare and suddenly he knew what it was— she was bashful and afraid of him! This is what excited him. He grasped her hand and led her down the mirrored hallway into his living room. He liked the feel of her hands stiffen under his. This encounter reminded him of the first time he met his wife. Donna had once been extremely shy. Though she had not been as pretty as most of the women he dated, he liked the challenge of helping such a *timid bud* blossom into a vibrant rose. He got her to do things that none of the other women would.

The doorbell rang and Mark went for the door. The women's voices and warm greetings gave Callie courage, and she relaxed.

Pastor Mark watched the women chat. He remembered his high school days when he discovered his *dreaded* lisp was suddenly a huge wonderful asset with which to woo the girls. When his notoriety with the ladies was established; he gained the respect of the male classmates as well. He never had trouble getting the girl.

"Mark, are you ready?" one of the women asked.

"Yes." He smiled and looked at Callie. Her lids fluttered down.

Mark sat down and sprawled backwards on the carpeted floor, resting his head on a soft pillow. The intercessors surrounded him on their knees and laid their hands on his torso.

"Callie, honey, sit here," Mark said, patting the floor near his right hip.

She obeyed and moved closer. "That's a good girl. I won't bite." He flashed her his best smile and watched her adjust her gray skirt over her knees. He reached up and took her hand and placed it over his heart, then covered it with his own. As his women began to pray, Mark closed his eyes.

"P*w*aise God," he said, "P*w*aise God."

CHAPTER FOUR

The rain continued to fall all weekend into Monday, giving the city the appearance of a giant mud puddle. But still the rash of college students arrived at campus, stomping their muddy shoes and shaking out wet umbrellas.

As the halls were abuzz, Pastor Mark secluded himself inside his quiet office. His office, though near the other ministry offices on campus, was privately set off from the rest. Water paintings in various shades of blues and gold brought the windowless room to life. His desk, a large cherry wood piece, was immaculate. Only his Bible, a phone, his laptop, a cup of pens, and a cup of coffee touched the surface.

A double rap on his door broke his concentration of Bible study. He picked up his steamy cup of coffee and said, "Come in."

His senior elder walked in.

"We've got another problem. Just came up," Ted Hunter said, sitting down in front of Mark with a blank expression.

"What this time?" Pastor Mark continued thumbing through his Bible, not looking up.

"Frank Serris molested his step-daughter last night. I just got the news."

Mark raised his head and threw Ted a disgusted look. "Not again. Ring his wife. Tell her we want to see them right away. Did they report it to the police?"

"No."

"Good. Tell them to let us handle this. Make the appointment at four."

"Do you want us to relieve him of his duties in the bookstore?" Ted's back took on the length of a surfboard as he leaned forward.

"No, no, we don't want this to get out." Mark exhaled slowly. "Let's see if we can smooth this over. Maybe his wife will be willing to move to California and attend the satellite church out there. Keep Fwank here. I want to sepawate them. Hopefully this will dewail the pwoblem."

"Okay."

After Ted left, Mark grabbed the phone and called home.

Donna answered.

"It's me. Listen. Ted just left. He said that Fwank molested his step-daughter again."

"Oh, not again!" Donna moaned.

"Yes, again. Ted is setting up a four o'clock meeting with the Sewwis's and so I need you to be here for that. We need to nip this in the bud so that it doesn't hurt our church. This means convincing Fwank's wife and daughter to move to California. If we keep Fwank here, away fwom them, this might settle the affair for now."

"Mark, do you think it is wise keeping this from the authorities? This is the second time he's done this."

"We can't allow another scandal so soon after what happened with the Dexters. Let's just get this fixed. See you soon." He hung up and leaned back in his leather chair.

"The county closed his church down."

"Why Pop?" fifteen-year-old Mark asked. "Pastor Tim reported it to the police. He did the right thing."

"I don't know, son. But God does, and we need to trust Him to restore Brother Tim's church."

"But if the church member touched that kid and not Pastor Tim, why did they close the church? He didn't do anything wrong."

"I don't agree with it. You try to do the right thing and sometimes it seems to backfire. Pastor Tim is a good man...it's in God's hands now..."

The intercom buzzed.

Mark brushed aside his thoughts and hit the button. "Yes?" he asked.

"Pastor," his secretary said, "Callie Dusten is here to see you."

"Good, good. Send her in. And no disturbances while she's here." Mark removed his suit coat and straightened his tie. He walked to the front of the desk and sat on the corner's edge, plucking at a brow in anticipation.

Callie knocked, opened the door, and peeked in.

"Come on in dear," Pastor Mark said. He watched her hesitation. "Sit down, over on the couch."

She obeyed him with a dippy smile. Mark noticed she had curled her hair, but it did little to improve her appearance. She looked visibly tense, so he put on his best grin.

"Thank you for coming in today. I know you're pwobably wondewing why I asked you here."

"Sort of," she said.

"Last week during our pwayer gwoup, I received so much fwom your spiwit. I felt a renewed connection to God as you interceded for me. I received a healing I did not know I needed."

"Really?" Callie perked up and crossed her legs. "I know He's called me to a ministry of prayer. Thank you for the confirmation."

"He's calling you to more than that. God has laid it on my heart to find a pwayer partner, someone I can completely twust my heart with; someone that can pway me thwough to victowy during the demonic battles. I'm in a position of leadership and it's important that I find the right person. Satan is a powerful foe and I cannot afford to let my guard down. This church needs me." Mark moved away from his desk and took a seat beside Callie. "You are the person God wants to use. You have the right gifts from God to fight the principalities and powers of darkness that might come against me."

Callie didn't know what to say.

Mark took her hand. "Will you join yourself with me and accept this ministwy? Will you say yes to God and pway for your pastor? Donna is aware of my decision and my secwetawy will be right outside the door the entire hour, each week you come here."

"A..are you sure?" she stuttered. "I d..don't know if I can..."

"Honey, God sent you to me. You're the one he's chosen." He put his hand on her knee. "Will you join me in this?"

She gave him a weak smile. "Yes, Pastor, I will minister to you."

"Good. Good. Is this time good for you each week?" He ran his hand up and down her arm.

"Yes."

"And Callie, I want you to be able to share your heart with me as well. I'm here for you too. This goes both ways."

She squeaked out a meek, "Okay."

Later Pastor Mark phoned Ted's office.

"Ted, is that position still open in the ministwie's office?"

"Yes, pastor. I'm interviewing for that job now."

"I have someone in mind. A good fellow, I hear."

"Oh?"

"His name is Petey Gwaves. His fiancé is Callie Dusten. She is one of my intercessors. I think he'll make an ideal candidate for the position. Call him today, Ted, for an interview. "

"It's a done deal. Anything else?"

"Yes. Call an informal meeting today with the elders at three. I want you to fill them in about F*w*ank Se*ww*is."

"Will do."

Five minutes after three Ted strutted into the conference room. The elders were already seated. "Thank you for all coming on the spur of the moment," he said. "Sorry I didn't know this information during our morning meeting. The reason I've called this unscheduled meeting is to update you on Pastor Mark's recent decision regarding Frank Serris. Frank's wife will take her daughter to our satellite church in California and Frank will remain here, doing what he's doing. Because each of you is aware of what happened before, and because of the latest dealings with the Dexters, Pastor Mark wants this incident buried immediately. He doesn't want to cause our body of believers to be hurt through another scandal."

"Did Frank touch the girl again?" Avery asked, leaning back in his chair, fingering his forehead.

"Yes, and he's willing to get repeated counsel. We're to support him in prayer, forgive him, and trust God for Frank's deliverance against that demon of molestation."

"Do the police know?" Joe Fellows asked.

"No, the family wants it quiet. They want to trust God in all this. Is everyone clear on this?"

Everyone agreed.

Ted finished with a prayer and the elders dispersed.

Frank arrived for the meeting on time. Everyone else was already there. Donna and Ted sat near Mark's desk. Mark stood near Frank's family, who were seated on the sofa.

Frank's bumblebee eyes flew from his wife to Mark. The bald spot on his head, peeking through his combed over strands of hair, was sweaty. So was his upper lip.

"Hello, Fwank, be seated." Mark pointed to the chair near the sofa. He despised Frank for allowing this to happen during such a critical time in their church. He wanted to bury the man, but he couldn't. Frank had a silent partnership with a booming retail business in Ohio and received large sums of money every month from the successful business. He generously tithed to Grace Church. After what he was doing for Frank today, Mark hoped he would be even more generous.

Frank sat down and rubbed his clammy hands over his thighs. Mark walked behind the teenager and placed his hand on her shoulder. She looked older than her fifteen years.

"Fwank, your wife and step-daughter have agweed to live apart from you in California. We feel this is the best answer regarding this pwoblem. We don't want to get the authowities involved, and so this is the only solution to do that. Gwace Church will pay to relocate them. They will fellowship at the satellite church out there."

Frank refused to look at his wife. "I understand," he said.

"You have repented," Pastor Mark sighed, "So let's end this uncomfortable session with pwayer. I want this young lady to know that we love her and that we are doing this for her safety and future."

The scared minor leaned against her mother. She was having a hard time facing her stepfather.

"Let's pway," Mark said. He raised his voice. "Dear God, Your love is gweater than our understanding. Fwank accepts your forgiveness, and his family forgives him, not with their own stwength, but with Your stwength. Cover them with your love. Restore their twust in Your time, in Your way. In Jesus name, amen."

Donna tiptoed behind mother and daughter and put her slender hands upon both their heads. She swayed as she prophesied, "Thus saith your Lord, I have seen your pain, and your hearts are not far from me. I will separate you for a season for growth and restoration. I am your healer and your deliverer; turn to me and let me guide your steps and mend your broken hearts. Submit to the authority I have placed over you in this church. I will use them to keep you safe and under my great care."

The daughter broke down and sobbed on Donna's shoulder and Pastor Mark embraced Frank's distraught wife. He looked over at Ted and nodded. Ted rushed Frank out the door.

"Whew, Donna, I hope nothing backfires," Mark announced after mother and daughter left. "Fwank needs to be more discweet."

"Like you?" She plumped down on the sofa.

"Now Donna, don't talk like that. Jolene came on to me. I told you this."

Donna couldn't hide her feelings any more. She needed answers. "You didn't tell me much." She tilted her head up bravely. "She insists you made a pass at her."

"Why are you bwinging this up now? We discussed this weeks ago. It's over. You need to twust me and let go of your suspicions." Mark sat down beside his wife and took her hand. "Honey, you know I love the Lord. Yes, I haven't been perfect in all the years we've been ma*ww*ied, but I've always been faithful to you."

Donna looked him square in the eyes. "Then tell me what really happened with Jolene. Stop leaving me in the dark. Don't you think you owe it to me to let me know the details? Keeping that from me only makes me suspicious. I need to hear what happened from you, not Ted or Avery."

Mark stood. "You're right, Donna. We need to be open about this. The last thing I want is to have Satan come at our ma*ww*iage. I can see it is bothe*w*ing you g*w*eatly. I t*w*ied to shield you from all this, but I was w*w*ong in doing so." He circled the room as he talked. "That Tuesday night when Jolene came over to p*w*ay with me...when the other two intercessors didn't show up...she lifted her blouse."

"And?"

"To be honest, I was tempted. I mean, she is att*w*active, but I didn't touch her. I told her to leave. She and Bob have been our f*w*iends for years. I was so shocked by her actions."

"You didn't touch her?"

"No, why would I jeopardize my pasto*w*al position, and our ma*ww*iage? Donna, she t*w*ied to seduce me; yes, I will admit it a*w*oused me, but I am human. I feel guilty about that eve*w*y day! Please t*w*ust me, I did not touch her!"

"Why would she do such a thing?"

"I asked why she wanted to jeopardize our f*w*iendship. She said she was att*w*acted to me for a long time." Mark went to Donna. "I need your support, Donna." He sat beside her and ran his thick thumb over her rouged cheek. "Forgive me for being involved in such a te*ww*ible indignity. I didn't realize it hurt you so bad."

Donna placed her head against his shoulder. "And Laurina?" she asked.

"Lauwina's a baby, like a daughter. But I made a big mistake being too fatherly towards her. I learned a hard lesson with her."

"Well, I do know Jesus is in this church, Mark. And for this reason I support you. This body of believers is important to God's heart. We need to move forward and put all this to rest now."

Donna knew she had no choice but to let this go. She could not allow their church to fall apart. She and Mark had spent their life working together to obtain this kind of ministry. No matter what mistakes they made, they would overcome them. She knew Mark liked to flirt, but that was what attracted her to him in the first place. If women were drawn to him, what was that to her? Mark did love God, and the church was growing because of his dedication. When she first met Mark at Christ Centered Bible College in San Diego, her parents disapproved of the overbearing suitor, but she knew that drive in him would bring him great success. As an only child growing up in South Dakota, she had been showered with love and taught a solid foundation of God's Word. But her folks forbid her the worldly pleasures of attending town dances or viewing the shows at the movie house. Marrying Mark gave her liberty without losing God. He was everything she was forbidden to be. His *freedoms* enticed her, downright tempted her silly. He introduced her to fast cars and the Dancing Elks Club. Her mother found out about the dancing and screamed, "Child, that man is leading you astray. Dancing is of the devil and will lead to destruction." But Donna's blood was already injected with his germ. Despite the fact he was a ladies' man, with flirtatious mannerisms and a brash attitude, she didn't care; she wanted him. Though her parents swore one day his over-confidence would hurt his ministry, Mark's love for the

Bible finally put peace in their hearts. They need have not worried because her commitment to God never wavered, even when her parents died in that awful train derailment shortly after her marriage. She missed them every day still. She soon found that Mark was unable to fill the void her parent's death had left. It was Jesus that did that for her, and she could never let Him go.

She had a church to think of now, a flock of God-hungry people that needed truth. She would do whatever it took to keep them safe. Mark was their lifeline, and so was she. They had to pull together and not allow mistakes to destroy what they had achieved. As far as Laurina, she was a weak young woman with too many problems. Mark would not touch her again.

CHAPTER FIVE

"**R**ick, will you please talk with one of the church elders?" Penny begged him over breakfast Tuesday morning. "It might help you to understand my decision to go to Bible College." He had been unusually quiet since visiting Grace Church, and she was worried.

Rick felt caged. He loved Penny, but he also loved his career.

"Penny, you've already made it clear that you want to stay here. You know I can't live in Portland. So, it sounds to me like there will be no wedding." He chomped into his toast. He felt confused and distraught over the entire mess.

"Rick, Jesus is my life now. Can you understand this a little?" She reached over to touch his arm. "I love you with all my heart. But I can't turn away from what I've found. I've searched all my life for this. Now that I have it, I can't walk away. Jesus has given me the reason to hope. Loving Him has opened my heart to loving you more, Rick." She pleaded with her eyes and then confessed, "If you must know, before I got saved, I was not sure I was going to marry you. This change showed me how much I really needed you. So, you might think it a bad change, but I happen to see it as a good change."

Rick stared at her. How could he argue that? It seemed he lost her either way. He took a swallow of juice and stood up. "Okay, you win. I'll talk to your church person. But...well...maybe you need to explain to me more about how you feel; what made you change? I'm in the dark now and before I agree to meet with him, I want to understand your heart as much as I can."

Penny scrambled into his arms. "Rick, thank you! I love you so much!"

"Penny, more than anything I want to marry you. I mean, golf is my life...but without you I have no life. I realized this while we were separated. I was miserable."

"Babe, we *both* need Jesus." She brushed at his brow tenderly. "Golf will never satisfy you if you don't fill your heart with God. I'm not enough to fulfill you Rick. Only Jesus can fill that void. Life is too short. We have to consider our eternal welfare and we must plan for that future as well as our future here on earth."

Rick tipped her face toward his. He smiled. "Okay, I can't fight the almighty God. What do I do to be...what is it...*saved*?"

"Oh Rick!" Penny squeezed him hard around the waist. "Your name will be written in God's book of life."

The next afternoon Rick could not keep anything down; he had a bad case of diarrhea. Meeting with the church elder made him more nervous than the beginning of a golf tournament. This God thing was new to him and plenty different from his church upbringing. He thought about that. Since his church never talked about being born again, he had never dwelled much on the afterlife. But in Grace Church that seemed all they talked about.

At the college campus, Rick and Penny managed to plow through the hustle and bustle of scrambling students and find the counseling office on time. Rick felt like his tie was strangling him, and he tugged at his collar. He was nervous and he knew it showed.

"You okay, Rick?" Penny asked as they sat in the reception area.

"I'm a big boy." His muscles tensed as the office door opened and a tall, lanky man stepped out from behind the door. The brown eyes which met his reminded him of bullets, aimed straight at his heart.

"Hello, you must be Rick. I'm Ted Hunter."

"Yes. Hello." Rick stood and grabbed Ted's hand. "This is my fiancé, Penny."

"Nice to meet you, Penny." Ted nodded at her.

He put his hand on Rick's back. "Would you like to come into my office?"

"Sure." Right about then Rick wanted to run, but Penny's hopeful expression kept him from doing so.

"Penny, you don't mind waiting out here while I chat with Rick?" Ted asked.

"No, not at all; he's all yours."

Ted led Rick into his office and shut the door. He took a seat behind the desk. Rick glanced around the room. Sailboat paintings hung on the walls and three shiny bowling trophies sat on top of the tall bookshelf. Ted's name was engraved on all three trophies. The other shelves were lined with Bible commentaries and Bible dictionaries. One row was nothing but paperbacks. Rick noticed the titles, *Godly Marriages*, *Saving Your Marriage*, and *Biblical Perspectives on Marriage*. A few of them he couldn't read; they were placed upside down as though hurriedly put back.

"Sit down, Rick. Make yourself comfortable."

"You bowl?" Rick asked, taking the chair nearest the desk.

"Yes, in my spare time. It's relaxing." Ted swung his chair to the right and looked up at his trophies. "I got those years back in college. I don't compete anymore. I just bowl for fun now." He swiveled his chair back to Rick. "I hear you are a pro golfer. That's quite an accomplishment."

"I love the game."

"I bet your parents are proud of you. Is your father a golfing fan?"

"Oh, yes. But Dad likes baseball more. He never missed one of my brother's games. I wish I could get him to as many of my games." Rick laughed, suddenly uncomfortable as to why he was telling a total stranger something so personal. He rushed to change the subject. "I love my career...and I love Penny. I guess the reason I'm here is to understand why I'm here."

"Rick, you're not alone in how you feel now. I know you have a lot of questions you want answered. In time you will understand God's calling on your life and why you are here today." Ted propped his elbows on the desk and scratched his temple thoughtfully. "Penny says you've accepted Christ as your personal Lord and Savior."

"Yesterday. I didn't feel much. But I want to learn more about the decision I made."

"That decision is the best decision you will ever make in your life, Rick. You have gained eternal life. Do you understand the importance of this?"

"I think so. Well, Penny explained how the Bible says we must be born again to get to heaven. I thought being good was enough, but she said no, we had to accept Him as our Lord, ask of Him forgiveness, and live our life for Him. It's hard for me to understand how to do this on a daily basis."

"Rick, in time you will fully realize what a colossal and important decision you made yesterday. You have secured an *insurance policy*, as I call it, which guarantees you a place beside the Lord when you die. Most people are busy buying up death policies for their loved ones for when they pass on, but they don't even consider the afterlife. That is why God gave us His Word, and why we study the Bible, so we can grow as we go and be prepared for Christ's coming. I'm still growing and learning about God and I've been a Christian for ten years. But I have great peace because I know if something were to happen to me today, I would be with Jesus."

"I see."

"That's why Bible College is such a wise choice. Many of our students are not attending solely to get degrees to become ministers; many are taking the courses to establish a closer relationship with Jesus. The more they learn about Him, the more they fall in love with Him and understand their path in life."

Rick listened, thinking that Ted had a way of making it sound plausible.

"Rick, playing sports is fun and exciting to our flesh. It's a great outlet for stress. And of course, because God created us as competitive beings, we enjoy the game. The important factor is that your love for the game doesn't overshadow your commitment to Jesus and His will for your life. Working towards a trophy is good," Ted swiveled his chair again and pointed to his bowling trophies, "but they cannot give you eternal life. When I die, those trophies are worthless. What can they give me then? What will I have accomplished if I forsake Christ, die, and lose a future in heaven? A short lifetime of self-seeking glory and dust-collecting trophies will not satisfy my soul in death. Rick, make sure your path leads towards *His* will for your life. If you gain the world and lose Christ, what have you?"

"I understand." The drawn shades were starting to make Rick feel shut in.

"You must choose the most important thing for your life. Penny has." Ted leaned back. "Rick, the Bible says 'wide is the gate to destruction, but narrow is the path to eternal life.' Think about this. The choice is yours."

"So, you're suggesting I give up my golfing career?" Rick's heart hammered.

"Rick, Penny's desire to attend Bible College may not seem important to you, but I can assure you she is doing something more valuable than any profession the sports world could offer her. She is preparing her life to serve the Lord, now and for eternity. If you force her to forsake this path, she is in grave danger of losing her soul. Do you want to be responsible for this? Once you know God and His intimate love, turning away is not an option. The Bible says it is better if you had never known Him. If you marry Penny and put Christ at the head of your relationship, you will have a solid foundation and a full life."

Rick shrugged his shoulders. "Wow, I'm outnumbered."

"Rick, Jesus loves you. Have you contemplated the reason you might be sitting here today is because God directed it so?"

Rick didn't know what else to do but nod, though his mind teetered with doubts.

"Let me pray with you, Rick," Ted said.

Rick bowed his head. His stomach began to feel like one of Ted's bowling balls dropped inside. Giving up pro golf was like asking him to cut off his legs, or worse. He felt disheartened when he left the room and even more so when Penny gave him an enthusiastic hug and said, "Jesus has your life in His hands, Rick."

Over the next few days Penny found Rick's mood distant and sour. He wouldn't look her in the eyes and he refused to talk about his discussion with Ted. She didn't know what to do.

"Penny, we have to talk." She was relieved but nervous when Rick came up behind her at the sink and touched her shoulders.

She dried her hands and nodded. He led her into the living room and sat on the couch. He pulled her down beside him. "Pen, I cannot give up my career. It will tear me up to do so. I love you. I don't want to lose you either. I feel so torn to have to make this choice. It just doesn't seem fair to me that I have to. I feel angry toward you and I feel angry toward God. I feel miserable."

Penny took his hand and put it to her lips. "Sweetie, I would give up everything for you. Do you not love me enough?"

"Would you, Penny, give up everything for me? It is me that is the one giving up my life for you, not the other way around." He hung his head and took back his hand.

"I gave my life to Jesus. It wasn't a light decision, Rick."

"Why can't you serve Jesus in Illinois?"

Penny averted her eyes.

"Huh, Penny? How come I am the one giving up every thing. You have what you want. Can't we compromise?"

"I hate Illinois. I can't go back there." Penny started crying. "I am different. I can't go back to my old life." She cried harder.

"I want to fly back home and do some thinking. I have to think some more. Clear my head. It's a tough decision I'm facing."

"Rick, please don't go. If you leave, I'll lose you. Let's get married next week! Please? Please? I can't live without you. Maybe you can travel from here to some of your tournaments." She sobbed into his shoulder and he cried with her.

A week later Rick and Penny married in the smaller chapel on campus. Aunt Joann still vacationed in England and, since Penny and Rick were new at church, there were no crowds to share their joy. Callie and Petey stood beside them as maid of honor and best man. Penny wore a tea-length white gown made of chiffon and Rick matched her in a white tux trimmed in gray. Marcy sang a love song for them with her guitar, and her husband Owen took pictures. The church donated fresh flowers and a small cake.

Penny beamed from ear to ear as Rick slipped the ring on her finger. He smiled back at Penny, feeling numb, trying not to think of the awful phone conversation he had yesterday with his manager. Right now his life felt hazy and unclear, seemingly spinning away from him, and he didn't know how to get it back. He wanted to scream out and stop the whole speeding train, but something stopped him. Was it God? Or Guilt?

Ted held the open Bible in his hand with a plastic smile. "Do you, Rick, take Penny to be your lawful wedded wife? To cherish, and honor…"

Rick's thoughts tangled with Ted's words. Still, he squeaked out a yes.

When Ted announced, "I now pronounce you man and wife," a sick feeling shot through Rick and he got a weird sensation that he was attending his funeral instead of his wedding.

The December chill on Monday morning made Owen jump out of bed and turn up the heat. Marcy watched him, hoping he would return, but he didn't. Instead, he dashed for the shower.

Her husband seldom wanted to be intimate. Today he responded dutifully because of her peak time. He seemed to do it only for the motivation of having a baby, nothing more. He did not find her desirable; this was as clear as the water now running over his body.

She sank down under the covers and closed her eyes, trying to blot out depression with thoughts of a baby. Getting pregnant might bring their marriage together. She hoped so.

Owen returned from the bathroom dressed to kill. He mumbled a sentence that sounded like, "I'll see you later."

"Owen, why are you leaving so early? You don't start work for another two hours."

"Got lots to do at the office. Two clients want to close on their properties early." He pecked her cheek and sped out of the room.

At times Marcy wished her parents were still alive so she had someone to confide in. She was nineteen the night they died. The memory haunted her. It had been a rainy night and she was supposed to have been with her parents at the annual leukemia fundraiser, but an argument erupted when she told her father she did not want to go to medical school. Her father, a respected surgeon, got angry and called her a lazy bum. He did not let up, so she spit back, "I hate you," and refused to go with them to the fund-raiser. They drove away while she glowered at their departure. The truck killed them instantly just a block away, and the pain of their loss and the guilt never left her.

Visiting Grace Church four months later saved her life. Pastor Mark and Donna Garrett walked her through those dark hours. She laid the guilt of her parents' deaths at Christ's feet and enrolled in Bible College. Soon after, she discovered her niche; she could sing. She took guitar lessons and loved it. Donna encouraged her to join the music team, and within a short time she was singing alone before the assembly. She loved watching the happy faces praise Jesus as she sang. It lightened her burdens.

Numerous men at college had asked her out, but she was drawn to the shy blonde man, her age, who sat alone in the back pew each service. He worked for a prominent title company downtown and always had enough money to dress nice and tithe well. His pooch brown eyes, giving heart, and reserved manner attracted her, and she befriended him. He was different from the other men. He didn't flirt with her and send her flowers. Instead he treated her like his best buddy. He loved to cook and would spend lots of time in the kitchen with her, teaching her how to make gourmet meals. He liked the arts and took her to different art shows and museums. By sharing his aspirations during those times together, he made her feel secure and special.

Owen never right out told her he loved her. That bothered her, but Pastor Mark assured her he just wasn't that kind of guy, and to accept him as he was. He encouraged her to marry Owen because he was a great catch. Alas, she did, but their honeymoon turned out to be a disaster. Her husband threw up all night, and they did not consummate the marriage until the following week.

Marcy turned over and cried into the pillow.

That same blustery morning Penny drove north towards the parsonage. She had volunteered for the cleaning position at the pastor's home, and did so with a bit of trepidation. Pastor Mark made her skittish, but she was banking on this job to cure her of that, especially since her friend Callie was way past her jitters with him. That girl was now praying for him twice every week!

Penny, bundled in a wool jacket, with a matching hat, knocked at the door. What would she do if the pastor answered?

A young black woman wearing a simple blue skirt and sweater opened the door. "Hi," she said. "You must be Penny. I'm Marilyn Elston. I'm in charge of this ministry."

Penny followed Marilyn inside, watching her own slender figure walk through the all-mirrored house. White colonial sofas and matching wingback chairs encircled an elegant black marble fireplace. The black and white theme continued into the open-spaced kitchen. Black and white tiled counter tops and white cabinets complemented a unique black dining table.

"As you can see, it takes some work cleaning these mirrors," Marilyn stated. She led Penny out of the living room and down a hallway. She pointed to a closed door. "That's the pastor's study. It's off limits at all times."

"What a beautiful house," Penny commented as she entered the master bedroom and saw the large king-size bed surrounded by ornately carved bedposts and matching white highboy dressers. Four slim black glass vases filled with clear, crystal flowers reached from floor to dresser top. The bed's shimmery floral spread was a blend of black and white silk. "Does the pastor own this house?" she asked

"Sort of. The church pays him extra for his home and car," Marilyn replied. Her beautiful brown skin and attractive eyes needed no makeup. "He also gets a great salary and five paid vacations a year. Great huh? I hope my husband becomes a pastor." Her chestnut eyes twinkled and she tossed her head sideways and thrust out her left hip. "But, hey, not for the money!" she teased.

Penny liked her immediately.

"We had better get to work." Marilyn led Penny into the bathroom. It too was completely mirrored. "This is where you will work. Today all you need to do is clean up the sink area and wipe down the mirrors. The bucket of cleansers is in the closet. I'll check in on you later. Okay?" She left Penny to work and shut the bedroom door behind her.

Penny got curious. She walked back out into the bedroom and plopped down on the gallant bed. She bounced slightly and lay back, spreading her hands over the silky fabric. The sound of the vacuum cleaner whirring in the next room made her sit back up and scurry back to the bathroom. She scoured the sink and polished mirror after mirror. The room glistened. Once the task was finished she took advantage of the mirrors and bent close, dabbing at her eye makeup. The violet shade on her lids made her eyes look bluer. She stepped back and turned sideways, patting at her tummy. It still looked flat despite the fact she had gained five pounds.

"Hello." The pastor's amused reflection looked back at her.

Startled, mouth dropping, Penny spun around.

"You look perfect," he mused. "What is your name, Honey?"

"I'm Pe...Penny Duncan." She extended her hand as Pastor Mark stepped close to her side. Instead of shaking it, he gripped it and drew her near and encircled her waist with his free arm, allowing it to run slowly down and around her hips. Hypnotic blues focused on her stricken face. He didn't say a word. Then, without warning, he dropped his arms, let her go, and walked out of the room, leaving the strength of his cologne behind to remind her of his invading presence. Penny felt strange. But she was too embarrassed that he had caught her gawking at herself in the mirror to dwell on his unusual actions.

Why didn't I say something?

Too flustered to leave the room, Penny remained in the bathroom and scoured the sink a second time.

"Hey girl, you done?" Marilyn poked her head through the door.

Penny jumped and laughed nervously. "Oh, yes." She put the bucket away. "I'm such a dingbat. The pastor came in earlier and caught me primping in the mirror."

Marilyn laughed. "Don't worry about it. He's a kind man. I was surprised when he showed up. He usually isn't here at this time."

"Well, I'm glad I met him anyway. I've been too shy to approach him at church. Boy, his eyes are so blue."

"I think his hair is too poofie," Marilyn joked.

"What?" Penny laughed and got on the bandwagon. "Marilyn, I didn't realize Donna had so many wigs. The bathroom looks like a zoo."

"Yeah, I wonder what her hair really looks like. I do know she used to be flat as a pancake."

"Marilyn! Shhhhh, he might come back." Penny roared with laughter. "Should you be saying this in the parsonage?"

"Why not? The rooms aren't bugged. At least I hope not."

The women bonded right then and there.

"Marilyn, you are so funny! Listen, how about going to get some lunch with me?" Penny wiped at her eyes, trying to keep from laughing.

"Sounds good. How about *The Grill*? Lots of churchites hang out there."

They left the parsonage in separate cars and parked at *The Grill* ten minutes later. Penny recognized other church members as they entered the establishment. They slid into a booth near the back.

"Marilyn, what is your husband's name?" Penny asked as the waitress set down two glasses of water and menus.

"Jason. We met in Las Vegas at a Christian conference. He's a great guy. He grew up in New Hampshire, in an overly religious family of Presbyterian pastors. Jason was expected to follow suit, but he wanted to be a lawyer. So he rebelled and instead got accepted in law school."

"He's an attorney?"

"Yep. He often does legal work for the church. Anyway, while we were at that conference in Vegas I got saved. I had been going to college there and a friend invited me to go with her. I am so glad she did! Guess who I sat down next to? Jason."

"Small world."

"Jason and I met a student that day who was going to Bible College here. The rest is history. Jason attends Bible College part-time and works at a law firm not too far from here."

"Is his dad glad he's going to Bible College?"

"When he found out this was a charismatic church, his dad threatened to disown him."

Penny liked Marilyn's strong character. "Why is that?"

"He says we prioritize experiences over the Word of God, and trust in feelings instead of scripture. He just doesn't understand the working of God's Spirit!" She continued. "I thank God He led us here. Grace Church is a wonderful place. The Spirit of God is changing lives. We've met wonderful friends, and Pastor Mark, despite his poofie-do, is a dedicated man."

They laughed again.

"What does your husband do, Penny?"

"Rick was a pro golfer, but he gave that up not too long ago to live here in Portland and attend Bible College. We are both from the Chicago area. Now he works as a roofer."

"Oh. Jason likes golf."

"Rick misses the game." Penny looked over her shoulder. "Oh look, Callie and Petey just walked in. Do you know them?"

"Yeah. Jason and I love them guys. Callie, Petey, over here," Marilyn hollered.

"Hey, you guys know each other!" Callie exclaimed as she and Petey scooted into the booth, removing their coats.

"We met today while cleaning the pastor's house," Penny said, handing a menu to Callie. "It's wall to wall mirrors."

"I know," Callie said.

"Sounds kinky," Petey joked, with one hand to his mouth.

"Petey, hush!" Callie slapped his arm. "I can't believe you said that."

"Just making sure you holy rollers are on your toes."

"Pastor's house is mostly black inside," Marilyn said as she flipped through the menu. "I guess his tastes aren't too bad."

They all hooted at that.

"Are you guys ready for your big day on Saturday?" Penny asked her friends.

Callie exclaimed, "I'm marrying the finest man. Of course, he's getting the finest woman." She looked up at him with a sneaky grin.

Petey tweaked her nose. "You're the best."

"Ah, marriage, what a wonderful thing between two people," Marilyn jeered. "What God has put together, let no man tear asunder. Not even because of dirty dishes or smelly laundry!"

"Oh, look, there's Marcy and Owen," Callie exclaimed. She waved them over.

"Aren't they are the perfect couple!"

Petey and Callie's wedding day was delightful, despite the slippery snow that surprised everyone and stuck to the ground. Callie had added some mascara and a little blush with Penny's prodding, and she looked exquisite in the flowing, white satin gown. Petey stood at her side beaming with pride. Ted pronounced them husband and wife and the couple kissed long and hard.

"She's lovely," Marilyn whispered as the wedding progressed. She and Jason sat next to Penny, Rick and Owen. Marcy was maid of honor.

"If it wasn't for Callie, I wouldn't know Jesus today," Penny replied quietly. Unlike Penny's wedding, the chapel was crowded

"I wish I had seen your wedding," Marilyn said.

"Me too," Penny smiled and patted her friend's knee. "We were new here and didn't know many people. But now God is bringing us wonderful friends."

Rick pulled Penny close as Callie and Petey marched down the aisle as husband and wife.

The reception was held in a large room adjacent to the college chapel. Pink and white streamers with floating balloons decorated the ceiling. The wedding cake sat between two silver platters of finger sandwiches and a frothy purple punch. Callie, grinning with delight, moved behind the cake while the photographer snapped pictures. Afterwards they went back to the chapel to snap more pictures. The guests continued eating and having a good time.

Since Rick and Jason were engrossed in a golfing discussion, and Marilyn and Marcy had headed for the bathroom, Penny sauntered to the table for some punch. She reached out to grab the ladle when another hand smacked her wrist.

"Oh, excuse me," a lush voice rushed out. "I am so clumsy today!"

That voice! It was her; the young woman who had supported Pastor Mark from the pulpit months ago.

Laurina stood there looking apologetic.

"No damage done." Penny smiled. "I'm Penny Duncan."

"Hello. I'm Laurina Addison."

"Yes, I know, uh, I mean I know who you are. Glad to meet you."

Laurina filled a cup with the fruit drink and handed it to Penny, then poured another for herself. "Are you a new member?" she asked.

Penny was taken aback at Laurina's extreme good looks.

"Yes, we... my husband Rick and I've been attending Grace Church for almost four months now. We love it here."

"I have never seen you."

"I remember you from that special service back in October. You gave a testimony, and well, it was one of my first visits, so it stood out in my mind."

"Oh. What a bad day for your first time. I am surprised you stayed." She put on a quick smile. "Where are you from?"

"Rick and I are from a small town close to Chicago. That's him over there." Penny pointed to the far table. "The blonde guy."

"I'm from Iowa, and my husband Cody is from Kentucky!"

"Oh, I didn't know you were married."

"Yes. My husband is the one that exhorted the congregation last Sunday night, before Mark got up. He's the youth pastor now. Pastor Mark recently promoted him. He's good with teenagers. He came out of a life of drugs and can really relate to the kids." Laurina sipped at her punch, then wiggled her left foot. "My shoes are killing me," she complained.

"Mine too. What size do you wear? Maybe we can switch." Penny looked down at Laurina's feet. "Nope, I have gorilla feet next to yours."

Both women laughed.

"Is your husband here?" Penny asked.

"No, he's at home studying. He's taking a semester of college. Actually, I don't know the bride or groom. I was next door renting the tape from last week's sermon and got thirsty. Chapel weddings are open to any member, so here I am."

"Well, I'm glad you're here. Hey, would you and Cody like to come over for dinner next Saturday night? I'll make my famous lasagna and chocolate cheesecake."

"Really? Sure, we're open, no plans that I know of. Thank you."

They exchanged phone numbers.

As Laurina walked away, Rick strolled up.

"She's so pretty," Penny said.

"Who?"

"Laurina, the girl I was talking with. Did you see her?"

"Yeah. Who is she?"

"Laurina Addison. She's from the Midwest too. I invited her and her husband for dinner Saturday."

"What's her husband do?"

"He's the youth pastor now. Laurina said he spoke right before Pastor last Sunday evening."

"Oh, yes, I remember him. In fact, I met him already. He was on my basketball team last week. He's a good player."

Penny was relieved to know Rick had an outlet for playing sports. It kept him from being too down over the loss of his golfing career.

"Let's go hassle the newlyweds," Rick said.

Laurina telephoned Penny twice before the weekend. They chatted for hours, and by the time Saturday rolled around, Penny knew she had found a soul mate. The two couples became instant friends over lasagna dinner.

"The food is great, Penny," Cody chimed.

"I married a great cook," Rick said.

"Flattery will get you both some cheesecake," Penny responded.

"God is so good," Cody said, as he passed the bread. "Six years ago I was a strung-out drug addict. Now I am a youth pastor. Only God can do that with a person." Cody's words flowed easily. Though not a handsome man, his confidence and love for God was an attraction in itself.

"I know what you mean," Penny interjected as she helped herself to more salad. "Christ filled up that empty space inside my soul. Who needs booze and drugs when you have Jesus."

Laurina nodded in agreement.

Rick remained quiet. Penny was glad the conversation stayed on God because Rick did not share the same passion to talk about Jesus as she did.

"So, Rick, are you going to continue in college?" Laurina asked.

"No, not next semester. We are tight on finances, so Penny and I are going to take turns."

"Rick, God will provide your tuition if you really feel led to be there. It's important to learn everything there is about God. Trust Him to make it happen."

"Thanks, Cody, I'll pray about that."

After dinner the men chatted in the living room, while Penny and Laurina got lost in conversation over a sink full of dirty dishes.

"Laurina, I'm glad you and Cody came tonight. I feel so comfortable around you guys." She dried her hands on a towel and tossed her long hair over her shoulders.

"Me too, I needed a good friend."

"My whole life is so changed now, Laurina. For the first time in my life I feel accepted, like I have found a true family."

Laurina grinned. "That's what keeps our church strong," she said as she continued scrubbing the dirty plates. "Love and forgiveness between one another. Despite Pastor Mark's mistakes, God cares about us and is moving in our lives."

"Mistakes?"

Laurina raced to undo what she had said. "Oh, I mean we all make mistakes. The Bible says we have all sinned and come short of the glory of God. God is forgiving and merciful to forgive any of us when we screw up."

"Oh."

Laurina finished the dishes and put them away. "Can you keep a secret?" She moved near Penny and lowered her voice.

"Sure."

"Before I married Cody last year, I had an affair with one of the elders. I can't say his name, but we both repented. You are the first person I ever told this to. I feel so one with you; I hope you don't mind me opening up to you about this."

Penny was stunned, but honored that her new friend would trust her. "No, I'm glad you told me. How did it happen?" she asked, with wide eyes.

"It just did. He understood me more than anyone else—and he made me laugh. I was going through some difficult times and he was there for me. One thing led to another and…you know."

"How long did you guys see each other? Did his wife find out?"

"Yes, she found out because I confessed to it. The affair lasted five months. But since that time, God's completely restored our relationship and his relationship with his wife."

"What did the pastor do?"

"Pastor Mark kept him on staff because he understood mistakes happen."

Penny frowned. "Wow!"

"It's *under the blood*, now. Please do not repeat this to anyone; Rick too. I don't want this to get past you. Okay? I needed a good friend to share my heart with. Cody knows about it."

"My lips are sealed. I guess being a Christian does not mean we are exempt from temptation. I needed to hear this today, to see how easy Satan can work."

The phone's ring interrupted them.

Penny answered.

A woman on the other end cried, "Hello, this is the emergency prayer chain. Becky Thomas died an hour ago. She committed suicide. Pray for the family, her husband and two children."

"Oh no! I'll pass on the request." Penny hung up the phone and told Laurina the news as she swiftly dialed another number.

"Not Becky!" Laurina wept.

"Who is she?" Rick asked, appearing from the living room with Cody.

"She's in the choir, married with three kids," Laurina blubbered. "She's battled depression for years. You've probably seen her husband. He's the head usher. Frank Serris is her brother. You might have seen him at the bookstore. He works there."

"Let's pray," Cody said, taking charge.

They stood in a circle and held hands. Cody led in prayer.

"We rebuke you Satan, you will not touch that family with fears and doubts," Laurina shouted, moved by her emotion. "We pray the blood of Jesus over the entire situation. In Jesus' name, amen."

Rick, skittish at the loud prayer response, kept quiet.

The phone rang again. Relieved for the interruption, Rick picked up.

"Rick, this is Callie. Did you guys hear about Becky Thomas?"

"Yeah, we were just praying about it. Hold on." He handed the receiver to his wife.

"Penny, Petey and I knew her. We are so upset. Do you mind if we come over?"

"Sure. Laurina and Cody Addison are here too. Come on by, we'd love to see you."

"Oh, I didn't know you had company. We can make it another night."

"No, no, come on by; you can meet Laurina and Cody. Come, come, come!"

"Okay, we'll be there in ten minutes."

Callie and Petey arrived a short time later.

"Hey, you newlyweds, come on in," Penny said, opening the door. "This is Laurina and Cody."

They all greeted one another.

Laurina wiped at her eyes. "Oh, I look terrible. I'm sorry, I knew Becky and this is such a shock. I didn't think she'd do this."

"I can't believe it either," Callie replied. "She seemed so happy."

"We just finished praying for the family," Laurina said.

"Well, not much we can do now." Petey shook his head and changed the subject. "You from the south, Cody?" he asked. "Your drawl gives you away."

"Yep, from Southern Kentucky."

"Get comfortable, guys, I'll dish out the cheesecake." Penny clamored towards the kitchen.

"Callie, how do you like married life?" Laurina asked.

"I love it!" Callie sat down on the sofa and nestled into Petey.

"How did you come to Grace Church?" Laurina asked.

Callie pulled her legs up under her and squeezed her husband's arm. "Through Petey. We worked together and he constantly told me about Jesus. My family has a hard time with our Christian commitment, though. My sister thinks we're off the deep end, and my mom can't understand why we got rid of our television."

"Why did you get rid of your TV?" Rick asked, suddenly embarrassed at his own big TV propped against the wall.

"Pastor Mark encourages us not to watch TV because there is too much compromise on the shows."

"As new Christians we want to be careful what we feed our minds," Petey said.

"Well," Rick mused, "Pretend you don't see our television over there."

"Rick," Laurina asked, "What did you think when you first came to Grace Church?"

"The poor boy thought he entered a circus arena," Penny cut in, returning from the kitchen with a platter of sliced cakes.

"Yeah," Rick said, "I thought the people acted strange. I mean, the lady next to me is crying, the man in front of me is swaying and chanting in some weird language, then the pastor's wife is bellowing out some dream she had. It scared me. I thought, 'What is Penny into?' I was ready to skip town, but Penny talked me into going back again."

"When did you get saved, Rick?" Laurina asked.

"After a night of wild sex I told Penny I wanted to accept Christ," Rick snickered.

"Rick!" Penny exclaimed. "That's not true. We never did *it* until later."

"True, you wouldn't let me," he chortled. "We'd been having sex for two years then she gets religion and decides to get holy on me. About drove me nuts. I flew here desperately wanting her and she says *no!*"

"Rick, you gossip!" Penny blurted. "Yeah, it killed you to wait a few weeks."

"Well, I'm human." Rick shoved a forkful of cake in his mouth.

"We almost waited until marriage," Laurina admitted, smiling at her husband.

"Hush, woman." Cody turned red. "She seduced me." He pinched his wife's cheek playfully.

"What do you mean you *almost* waited?" Penny kidded, sitting down beside Rick.

Laurina moved her finger over her lips, "Don't tell anyone, but we did it the night before our wedding day."

"Doesn't count, you know," Petey joked. He pushed his glasses to his nose. "Thank God for the blood of Jesus to cover all our sins."

When the laughter died, Callie spoke up. "I wonder how Pastor Mark is dealing with the news about Becky? She was his favorite singer."

"She's singing with Jesus now," Laurina added.

Mark paced the floor in his study. He tightened the belt on his robe. The clock said eleven. He telephoned Ted.

Ted answered with a grunt.

"Ted," Mark said without apologizing for the lateness of the hour, "a suicide in the assembly isn't good. I have decided to go ahead and bwing this up tomowwow morning."

"All right, Mark."

"Telephone the elders tonight and schedule an informal meeting tomowwow morning at eight. We'll meet at the office at the sanctuawy. Contact Fwank Sewwis too. I'm sure he'll need some support."

"She wasn't a strong woman, Pastor."

"I know. We need to soften the blow to our congwegation. God bless, Ted." He replaced the mouthpiece. His stomach burned. Dealing with the pressures exhausted him, but his conquest to maintain power did not. He had built the godly empire from scratch, and he would face every obstacle thrown his way. Mark took a deep breath and shoved three Tums into his mouth.

As everyone was mourning over Becky, Marcy, unaware of what had happened, was tailing Owen down the seedy back streets in Portland's downtown area. The night's clouds, pasted along the mountain ranges like wet cotton balls, were illuminated by the full moon.

She had concealed her hair under a dark scarf, and kept a good enough distance so that her husband would not suspect she was following him. He had told her he had a late work meeting, but she suspected he might be seeing another woman. She steered her Honda past teetering bums and topless bars, onward towards First Avenue. Owens' car veered sharply into a wide dead-end alley and stopped. Marcy inched a half block past the alley and parked her car, then strained her head back to see where her husband was going. A single neon light flickered inside the window of a worn building next to the alley. It said: *Bar*. She breathed hard.

How could he pretend everything's rosy? He acts like a saint...he's a jerk!

She noticed a few men going into the bar. How could he cheat on her? Especially when she might be pregnant. She didn't know how long she sat there. She didn't seem to have the courage to get out of the car and go inside and confront him. But she didn't have to. Owen appeared back in the parking lot. This time he was with another man. For a second Marcy felt relieved, but the way his arm was linked around the other man's waist brought on a sickening feel. She rolled down the car window. The brisk air hit her face as she stuck her head out. The men disappeared behind the cars. Without thinking she shoved the door's handle downward. The door swung and remained open as she scuttled towards the dark alley. She moved behind Owen's Buick. The sight of her husband wrapped in the arms of the young man caused her to wail, "Nooooo, Owen, noooooo..."

He pulled out of the embrace and looked around with a horror-filled expression as his wife doubled over, retching.

CHAPTER SIX

Sunday morning the weather was cold and windy. A slight breeze blew leftover leaves from trees, fluttering them to flight in crisp silent spins to the ground.

"Good morning," the pastor said bleakly to the elders as he entered the room near the sanctuary. "Glad you could make it on such short notice." Donna, who came in on her husband's arm, took a seat beside Ted.

Mark, dressed in a black three-piece suit, stood before the group and said, "As you know, Becky Thomas committed suicide yesterday. This is a sad moment for the family and for our church. She was a sweet and gifted woman. Her stwuggle with depwession has come to an end, fweeing her into the arms of Chwist. She died loving the Lord and we *must* emphasize this to the church."

"What can we do?" Joe Fellows asked.

"Today I must addwess this twagedy to the congwegation. My flock must hear it from their shepherd first, not some newspaper. It will be a shock, so I'm asking each one of you to help me put out this fire."

"When's the funeral?" Avery asked.

Ted answered. "Tuesday, in the college chapel. I'll perform the service."

"Make sure each of you contact the family," Mark insisted.

The elders agreed.

Service began. The choir sang soothing tunes and Mark allowed the music to go on longer than usual. He moved up behind the pulpit, closed his eyes, and started singing too. The pianist lightened his fingers on the keys and the singers quieted to let the pastor be heard. His baby-like voice crackled with emotion into the microphone.

"We love you Lord, We love you Lord, King and Savior. You are able to heal eve*w*y b*w*oken heart; catch eve*w*y fallen tear."

The congregation became subdued at the tenor of the service, knowing it was leading up to something. The pastor ended the lyrics and kept humming, preparing the crowd for what he had to bring.

He stopped, clapped his hands together against his nose, and sighed long and mournfully. The music quit and he kept moaning, his eyes closed.

The audience responded to his somber mood and began praying in tongues. His moans, mingled with the people's haunting gibberish, set the tone perfectly. Mark raised his hands to silence the crowd. They obeyed, and he began to pray.

"Yes, Jesus, we believe you, in your power to t*w*ample even death. You are the Lord of heaven and earth and our lives are in Your hands. We t*w*ust you in eve*w*y situation, and in eve*w*y circumstance. Even when we don't understand those t*w*agedies in our life, we know You are working eve*w*ything out for good, in Your time."

Mark cleared his throat and stretched his arms forward before resting them on both sides of the rostrum.

"Now my flock, today I have some bad news. This is not easy for me to share, but it's important that you all know so that p*w*ayers can be released to heaven." He paused for greater impact, than continued. "Last night Becky Thomas went home to be with the Lord. She committed suicide."

As gasps rolled throughout the sanctuary, Marcy doubled over, panting. Owen put a hand on her shoulder, but she jerked from him and dashed out from her pew. Owen put his head down and stayed seated.

Penny saw Marcy flee and said to Rick. "Marcy must have known her. I'll go after her." Rick nodded and Penny left the pew.

"The pwayer chain got word of her death last night and has been interceding for the family. Becky was a delightful woman, beautiful singer, and a gweat mother; but she battled depwession for years. Life was too much on her fwail mind. She is with Jesus now, fweed from her personal turmoil. Her family is going thwough a difficult time now, and we need to be sensitive to their gwief. I don't want this church dwelling on how she died, I want this church dwelling on her life and all the good she gave." The pastor turned as he spoke. "I will not be giving a sermon this morning. I am going to let the choir have the floor the rest of the service. I will announce the funeral details tonight. Meanwhile, let's turn our tears into pwaise!"

Marcy's heart ached. She drooped across the sofa watching the rain and the wind, sounding like screeching owls, plummet the bay window. How could she face her prayer meeting tonight? It had been over a week since she caught Owen at that bar making out with another man. The memory haunted her. His response that night almost killed her. He did not reach out in comfort, but instead grabbed his partner's arm and pulled him into his car, speeding off and leaving her alone to vomit in his trail of exhaust fumes. Without Donna's support, she would have faced an insurmountable mountain. She had no idea dear Becky had died that night. Yet Donna, even in the midst of dealing with that tragedy, did not hesitate to come to her aid.

"You're a leader," Donna had admonished, putting her arms around Marcy, "a pillar in this church. Be strong for Grace Church, for the people. God has called you to be an example for the women in this assembly. They look up to you. Don't let Owen's mistakes ruin your life and everything you have accomplished. Owen has this weakness. Mark and I have known about it for a couple months now. He confided in us because he wants to be free of it. The important thing is that he still loves you!"

Finding out that others knew of his problem made Marcy angrier.

"Owen called me a few minutes before I came here. He was crying. He was too ashamed to face you, Marcy. Will you talk to him?"

Marcy bawled on Donna's shoulder, but finally gave in.

"You need to forgive Owen, and continue to submit under his authority, Marcy. He is still your husband. I will call him now."

The sound of the doorbell lifted Marcy's head. She ran a hand through her hair and hoped none of the women could see her sorrow. She went to the door and, with a pasted smile, opened it wide.

February came with more freezing rain. Penny had been kneeling on the big round rug in her living room, wrapped in a sweater, with her Bible next to her, talking to the Lord, when the doorbell rang. Though she loved her prayer meetings at church, her favorite times were at home, just communicating quietly with God on her own time. It was during these times that she was able to truly release her burdens and share her heart to her Heavenly Father. She spent many an hour each week on the rug or kneeling beside her bed. Even Rick had no idea how often she prayed. Having a relationship with Jesus Christ had changed her life so wonderfully and she owed Him everything. It was nice to wait on Him alone and allow His Spirit to talk to her through His Word.

Penny wasn't expecting anyone, so she rushed to open the door. Her mouth dropped at the sight of Callie.

"Callie?" she asked, taken back at her friend's appearance.

"What do you think, Pen?" Callie swung her head side to side. A thick, curly blonde wig cascaded down her shoulders. A heavy made-up face glittered like a neon sign.

Penny raised her voice to an excited screech. "What did you do?" She pulled her friend into the house. "What is all this? False eyelashes too?"

Callie strutted around in a circle. "Pastor Mark talked me into it. He says I have great eyes." She flitted her lids. "He's been such a blessing to me, Pen. I mean, God is moving in our prayer times together. Not only am I ministering to him, but he has also been ministering to me. My new look is because of him!"

Penny kept staring at her friend. She hated the wig.

"I love my new look. Mark...I mean Pastor Mark, thinks I look fantastic. He said that after Donna started wearing her wig and adding more makeup, her self-esteem shot up. And Donna looks great! I was so insecure about my looks, and well...Mark is helping me to overcome my shyness." Callie pranced around the room. "I feel grand. Do you like the blonde color?"

"Yes, but instead of the wig, why don't you just color your own hair?"

"Mark says I needed some fullness."

Penny noticed Callie's fake nails. "Well, you look more mature. And...not so innocent anymore." She smiled wanly. "I'll have to get used to your new look. Does Petey like the wig and all?"

"Petey says he likes me the way I was before. He does not see the potential inside of me like the pastor does. Pastor Mark says I'm a budding rose ready to bloom."

"Oh." Penny didn't quite know what else to say. "Can you stay for lunch? Come on, I made some chicken salad earlier."

Callie followed Penny into the kitchen. "Look at these." She twiddled her fingers in a showy manner.

"Fake nails. I noticed them. Be careful you don't scratch Petey's eyes out tonight."

"Pastor Mark is the kindest man. I know God is preparing him for a mighty ministry in the future. God has given me so much love for him. We have become one in heart. We're so blessed to be under his teaching, Penny. Sometimes I feel like I want to crawl inside him when I'm praying for him. That's how strong a love I have for him."

"I can see you have more confidence now, Callie."

"All because of Mark...I mean Pastor Mark."

"I'm glad God is doing good work in you. I'm happy for you."

Callie felt alive and beautiful. She had noticed the two men staring at her at the grocery store. What a feeling of power that gave her. By changing her appearance she could change the way people viewed her. She loved the attention. And it was all because of Mark.

"Penny, sometimes when the pastor talks to me, I feel like Jesus himself is talking to me. I would die for that man."

Monday morning Callie wiggled into the Pastor's office smiling and wearing a plum sweater and floral dress. Springtime had finally come, and Callie liked that she didn't have to hide her new figure under a heavy coat.

"Callie, how's my girl today?" Mark lit up when she charged up beside him.

"What do you think?" She straightened her shoulders. Her chest size had doubled.

"You did it! You look wonderful!" Mark clasped her waist and gawked at her large bosom. "I am amazed!"

"Mark, thank you for encouraging me to do this. I feel so alive now. You're right, I feel more feminine and confident." Callie spun around, still displaying her new mounds. "The two thousand dollar bonus you gave Petey paid for it all!"

"Well, he's been doing a good job on staff." Mark could not stop staring. She had blossomed just as he expected she would. The wig, the makeup...she looked perfect. His body responded

Patience...patience...

"Shall we pway?" He stretched down on the sofa.

Callie knelt beside him on the floor. His eyes followed her full breasts, until she looked up at him. Then he shut his eyes. Her long fingernails raked his chest as she positioned her hands on him for prayer. The feel of her hands and the scent of her perfume seduced him to sleep.

An hour later Callie left her pastor sleeping on the couch. She tiptoed out of the room, giving his secretary the hush sign.

The secretary nodded and smiled back.

"Is Petey busy?" Callie asked the receptionist in the ministry's office next door.

"No, go right in. He'll be glad to see you."

Callie brushed past the copy machine and two file cabinets, waved at her husband's co-workers behind the glass partition, and entered his office. Petey looked up. He was on the phone. His dark eyes softened and he motioned her to sit. She plopped down in the overstuffed leather chair across from his desk. His office was small, but richly furnished. His oak desk filled one fourth of the room.

"Great, yeah, okay," Petey chimed into the phone. "I'll announce the marriage retreat in this Sunday's bulletin." He replaced the receiver and pushed his chair away from the desk. "Hey, Sweetie, what's up? You pray for the pastor?"

"He fell asleep." She shook her head with amusement. "He's such a wonderful man."

Petey walked behind his wife, bent down, and kissed the side of her mouth. "You look nice today."

"You think so?"

"Yes, just wish you'd let me see these more." He pushed her shoulders back, leaned forward, and growled in her ear.

"Petey, stop it, someone might come in."

"You've always got an excuse." He dropped his hands, suddenly irritated.

"Petey, come on, let's not argue. I love you. I've been tired, that's all."

Petey walked back to his desk and sat down. "Yeah, I know. It's just that I spent two thousand dollars for that operation and I would like to see more of what I paid for." He relinquished a smile. "I mean, we're still newlyweds, aren't we?"

"Oh, Petey, don't be so selfish. You have me every night." She brushed him off with her hand.

"Callie, I miss the old you sometimes." Petey chided her. "Remember our tumbles in the hay?"

"Petey!" Callie laughed. "Yeah, if my grandparents ever knew what we did in their barn."

"Let's go out there tonight!" Petey's eyes widened.

"What? No."

"Why not?"

"I have a prayer meeting tonight."

"Can't you cancel it?"

"No. I don't want to."

"Come on, we can bring a couple flashlights..." His grin froze at the scowl on her face.

"Petey, no. Listen, I have to go." She stood to avoid the hurt in his eyes.

"Will you be home late?"

"No."

"Okay."

Callie left him alone to sulk. Petey just didn't understand her anymore. Not like Pastor Mark did. She passed the large office window and caught her reflection. She had to admit, she looked great, really great.

She straightened her shoulders and pranced out the door.

Thursday evening all the women showed up on time for Marcy's prayer meeting. Penny arrived in comfortable blue dress slacks, Laurina wore a beige wrap-around skirt and pink sweater, and Marilyn had on a yellow flowered sweater and jeans. Marcy wore a purple dress that made her gray eyes look blue. She had swept her hair up in a roll and applied extra makeup around her eyes to hide the tired creases.

"Is Callie coming tonight?" Penny asked, lounging on the couch near another intercessor, Suzie Hatley. Suzie's black hairstyle softened her broad chin, but her tight suit made her hips look big.

"No," Marcy replied, finding a seat. "She's not coming anymore. She's busy ministering to Pastor Mark. She's also been praying for the elders' wives as well. She's praying for Betty Hunter tonight. The Lord is really using her in the area of prayer. Her schedule is pretty full these days."

"I'll miss her," Penny said.

"Me too," Marilyn added.

"Let's start," Marcy said. "Any prayer requests?"

"Yes, I have one," Suzie raised her hand. "It is serious. My husband wants to leave Grace Church and go to New York and minister to teenagers."

"Is the ministry connected to our church?" Marcy asked.

"No, its not. That's why I am so worried. I told him I didn't want to go because he is making a big mistake leaving Grace Church. Donna has tried to talk some sense into him, but he refuses to listen. He says he has to follow God and not man. The devil has convinced my husband that God is calling him to New York."

"So you aren't going with him?" Laurina asked, looking concerned.

"No," Suzie declared, "He says I'm wrong. But I know God called me here. I can't follow him and disobey God!"

Marilyn cleared her throat. "Excuse me, Suzie, but have you considered the fact that maybe God *is* calling your husband to New York?" Her question was met with perplexed looks.

"How could that be? God is not the author of confusion. He would have put it on my heart too." Suzie crossed her arms and looked agitated. "He brought us both here, now why would he move my husband to a different church? Satan doesn't want him to be here!"

"There's always a time and season for everything." Marilyn treaded carefully with her reply. "Are you sure it's the devil moving him? I don't see why the devil would lead him to another ministry. It sounds more like something the Lord would do."

"Marilyn," Suzie griped, "Satan hates what God's doing in this church. He knows if we leave this place we'll miss out on being part of God's bride. Satan wants to keep my husband from Grace Church because this is the only church that has an intimate moving of God's Spirit. Besides, Donna said I don't have to submit to him if it goes against my moral conscience and jeopardizes my salvation."

"But the Bible says we are to submit to our husbands. Even the pastor says that..."

Marcy interrupted the conversation. "Let's take it to prayer now. I have to agree with Suzie. Satan doesn't want any of us here. There is no other church that has the teachings and freedom in the spirit like Grace Church. God is preparing us for something wonderful; we can't afford to miss it. Let's ask God to deliver Suzie's husband from deception."

Marilyn glanced at Penny with a dubious expression, but Penny simply shrugged. Marilyn felt odd. She knew Suzie's husband, and he was not a frivolous man. In fact, he was a strong Christian man who served God without compromise. She wondered why the group could not understand that possibly...maybe...God wanted him in New York. Pastor Mark preached that wives were to submit to their husbands, and she was stunned that Donna was telling Suzie the complete opposite.

The women moved from their seats to the floor. Together they began speaking in tongues. Soon the room became a roaring chorus of shouts at the devil.

"I rebuke you, Satan!" Marcy shouted, putting her hands on Suzie. "You will leave Suzie's husband now, in Jesus' name!"

The group screamed along, and as the energy danced among them, some began prophesying, others were laughing, some were chanting loudly. By the end of the hour, two women had gotten visions that confirmed to Suzie that she had to stay under Grace Church's covering no matter what.

The knock came at three, between Sunday services. Mark, sporting a pair of casual slacks and a blue pullover shirt, opened the door to Callie. He had summoned her after morning service to come to his house and minister to his weary soul, while Donna stayed behind at church to counsel Suzie Hatley and Marcy Nason.

"Hello, Mark, how are you?" Callie said, sashaying into the living room, watching herself in the mirrors as she walked. Her tailored blouse flattered her new figure.

Mark followed. "Callie, honey, thank you for coming. I'm under so much stwess now twying to keep things running smooth at the church. I needed some extwa filling up today from God."

"I'm here for you, Pastor."

"Want some tea, Honey?" he asked.

"Sure, sounds good." She followed him into the kitchen and perched on top of a stool.

"Callie, do you mind if we talk instead of pway? I feel God wants to minister to me this way today." He filled a kettle with tap water and placed it on the stove.

"Sure, Mark." She smiled and leaned over the counter, resting her decorated face in her hands.

Mark opened a cupboard and retrieved a box of donuts. He pushed the box her way.

"Oh, no, Mark, I'm watching my weight. Thanks anyway."

"What? You have a beautiful shape now." Mark scanned her chest and smiled. "Callie, you're a special lady and your spiwit is gentle. I hope you don't mind if I'm a bit forward with you. You know, without your sacwificial heart, I wouldn't be able to pweach the sermons I pweach. Your pwayers have allowed the Holy Spiwit to move thwough me in wonderful ways. For this I am thankful." He reached across the counter and stroked her cheek. "Do you know your eyes are like emewalds?" he charmed.

Callie batted her eyes at the compliment.

Mark removed the whistling kettle from the burner and filled two cups, than came around next to Callie. He set the cups down and leaned sideways against the counter, facing her.

"You're my gift from God, and I need to expewience more of God thwough you, even in aweas that might not seem spiwitual."

"What do you mean?" Callie looked puzzled.

"God is in evewything. What might not seem spiwitual to us is to God. For instance, sex. It's cweated by God to be something holy and beautiful, though duwing sex we might not be thinking on the things of God—but it is a gweat spiwitual experience between two people."

Callie blushed. "Oh, yes, I know what you mean." She poured a little cream into her cup.

"Callie, I need to share my heart with you today. I feel God wants me to empty my soul for spiwitual cleansing. Can I twust you, Hon, with a difficult subject?" He wore a boyish face.

"Of course, Pastor. I'm here for you." N o

"This is difficult to talk about, and that is why I wanted you here. You are the only person I can completely open my spiwit too."

Callie put her hand on Mark's shoulder for support. "Say whatever you need to say, Mark," she reassured him.

"Okay. I will just say it. I have been having a hard time desiwing my wife. I have been having this pwoblem for a while now." Mark took a deep breath. "I need to be fwee from this. I want to please my wife."

"Pastor, I totally understand. I have been going through similar problems with Petey."

"You have?"

"Yes. I have been praying about it too. I am glad you confided in me. It is good we pray about this together."

"No, no, Callie, let's not pway. I feel talking about this with you is what I need now. I feel comfortable with you, and of course, since I know your husband, I feel safe sharing such personal matters with you." He picked us his cup and took a sip.

"Pastor Mark, you're a virile, good-looking man. Don't let this problem crack your self-esteem. Just as you encouraged me during my low times, I want to be an encouragement for you." She tossed her synthetic curls behind her shoulder and leaned her face close to his. "I'm with you, Mark. I'll help you get over this small hurdle. And by helping you, I know God will help me too."

"Yes, I agwee. I think maybe I'm stwessed from the ministwy. You know my schedule is demanding." He reached a finger out and traced her lips. In a father-like tone he said, "Such a pwetty mouth you have, Honey."

Callie kissed his aging fingers innocently in response to his compliment. As she reached for her tea, Mark grasped her arm and drew it back to him, massaging her fingers.

"I think maybe if we twy a test of some sort, I can loosen up. I know that whatever I say or do, you will not judge me."

"What kind of test?"

"Since we're so far apart in age and you're like my own daughter, I thought, well…" He dipped his head, pretending embarrassment.

"Pastor, finish."

"Instead of interceding on Donna's behalf spiwitually in pwayer, would you stand in her stead *physically*, as if you were her—my wife?"

"I don't understand."

He exaggerated his lisp. "If you could wub my back to welease my tension, maybe speak some special words to build my ego—as my wife, of course—then I can close my eyes and project myself with Donna. If you speak faith, God can set me fwee. Oh, my, does this sound too forward? Oh, I don't want to make you uncomfortable. Maybe I am asking too much fwom you!"

"No, no, I'm fine. I mean you encouraged my breast operation, you knew…"

"Twue. I wanted to help you build your self-esteem. And at first you were nervous, but afterwards you became comfortable with the idea. I guess I'm nervous now." Mark motioned to her chest. "These are my rewards in a way. Seeing you at ease and confident makes me feel better about sharing my own pwoblem."

"Let's do it, Pastor."

Later that night, after the evening service, Mark stayed busy in the kitchen making sandwiches. "Hope you're hung*wy*," he said to Donna as he smeared mayonnaise on rye bread.

"Starving," she said looking over his shoulder.

"Have you heard from our daughter?" He piled pastrami high on sliced cheddar cheese, then bit into a pickle before adding it to the sandwich.

"Gayle called this morning after church. She's bringing the boys over to join us for dinner tomorrow. Avery has a basketball game." She filled her glass with Coke. "I think she and Avery are having some problems."

Donna loved their daughter, Gayle. She had turned out to be an intelligent woman—though she wished Gayle took more care of her appearance. That could be why Avery wasn't as attentive. Gayle had inherited Mark's short stout frame, his chubby nose, and his plump cheeks. She did not have any of his charming wit, but instead inherited her own quiet nature. She had studied hard to get her degree as a teacher, and Donna was proud of her daughter's ability to connect with children. She was a great mom to her two little boys. She herself had never acquired this gift, and wished she had, for Gayle's sake. But Gayle grew up a good girl anyway.

"What? Why? He's a g*w*eat guy, a good father, a good teacher. Gayle needs to be careful." Mark washed his sandwich down with a glass of milk.

"Well, I don't know for sure; she doesn't say much, but I suspect it. Just from the little things she says." Donna set her plate down and unclipped her belt and set it on the stool.

Mark cleaned the counter and replaced the condiments in the refrigerator. He grabbed an orange from the bottom shelf. "Well, she takes after you."

Donna ignored his remark. "I'm going to bed. I have to get up early for a counseling session with a young couple. The girl is pregnant…"

"Is she in Bible college?" he interrupted.

"Yes, they both are."

"I don't want any more gossip to fly in our assembly! What will people think of our church? With discwetion, counsel her to abort the baby."

"Mark, are you sure about this? You've condoned abortion from the pulpit only if a rape has occurred. How can we tell this young lady to murder her child?"

"Donna, we're twying to run a delicate ministwy; we have to make some sacwifices and twust God will back up our decisions. We have to think of the whole church."

"There's also a problem with one of our Christian school teachers."

"Another pwoblem?"

"Suzie Hatley's husband wants to leave the church to join another ministry in New York. Suzie refuses to go with him. He's upset that she's not supporting his decision."

"Counsel her to stay put. Her husband has always been too independent. He never fit in here. She needs to put God first. Her salvation is more important than her mawwiage. Gwace Church is her covewing. If he refuses to submit to this church government, he will be on his own."

Donna nodded. "I told her this." She shuffled past him towards the bedroom.

Mark shut out the kitchen lights. He washed up in the bathroom, and than crept into the bedroom and climbed into bed. He rolled opposite Donna and fell asleep.

Aunt Joann rang Penny's doorbell. There was no answer. She knocked on the door. She knew Penny was home because her car was parked out front. She was about to walk away when Penny answered, head wrapped in a towel.

"Aunt Joann. Why didn't you call? I was in the shower. I didn't hear you." Penny shooed her inside.

"When I call, you're always too busy to talk. So I thought I'd come by and see if I could nail you down in person for a few minutes."

"You look like you're expecting a blizzard. Gloves and a hat?"

"Hey, it's cold out here. I wouldn't be surprised if it snowed."

"Snow in March would be fun."

As Joann removed her outerwear she noticed the pile of dirty dishes in the sink. "Dirty dishes? Since when did you become the messy one?" She sat down at the kitchen table.

"Rick and I've been attending a three day marriage seminar. I haven't had time to clean. The seminars lasted all day."

"How are you both doing?"

"Great. Sorry we don't visit much. We're so busy with college and..."

"Yeah, yeah...blah...blah...blah...excuses, excuses."

"Well, we are." Penny brushed her off with her hand and laughed.

"Does Rick like your church?"

Penny dried her wet head with the towel. "Of course. He loves Jesus."

"Well, so do I, Penny."

"I know. I meant that Rick's happy." Penny grabbed two cans of Coke from the refrigerator and handed one to her aunt. "But Grace Church is the best church, Aunt Joann. You should visit."

"I like my church."

"But it's important to attend a spirit-filled church…"

"A what?"

"A spirit-filled church. Does your church speak in tongues?" Penny sat down beside Joann.

"What!?"

"If your church doesn't speak in tongues, then your church doesn't have the Holy Spirit."

"Says who?"

"Pastor Mark."

"Is that what the Bible says?"

"If Pastor Mark says so, then it's what God says."

"Penny, not every church has the same views as yours."

"God is moving in our church, Aunt Joann. You would see this if you came."

"Penny, stop trying to convert me. I'm happy where I am."

"But the Bible says you must be born again…"

"And go to Grace Church?" Joann mocked.

"Well…maybe." Penny smiled and patted her aunt's hand. "I'm sorry to pressure you. It's just that I love you and want you to go to heaven. Since we've joined with Pastor Mark our lives have changed. We are so free now. Being in the spirit is like finding a piece of heaven on earth."

"My dear niece, you talk funny. Anyway, I don't know about this tongue thing you're talking about. A lady at work told me her sister is a white witch. I don't exactly know what the difference is between white and black witches, but she said she went to one of their meetings just for the heck of it, and they were all chanting in some weird language."

Penny shrugged. "It's not the same."

"I can see why your mom's worried about you."

"My mom worried? I doubt it. She never even calls."

"Penny, your mom loves you."

"I have a real family now. They love me. They would die for me. Would my mom? I doubt it."

Joann shook her head. "Penny, I doubt these new friends would either. I guarantee you, if you left that church, you'd be history to them."

Penny smiled. "You're wrong. Besides, I would never leave Grace Church."

Months flew by and the unusual July heat surprised everyone. But despite the sticky weather, the Friday night service was packed. Hundreds of fans fluttered back and forth like myriads of flapping butterflies to cool down the expectant spectators. Mark stood at the pulpit wearing only a shirt and tie.

"Before I intwoduce a special guest we have tonight, I want to let all of you know how much God has been changing me inside! As most of you know, Callie Gwaves has been ordained by God to pway for me on a regular basis. Her sacwificial ministwy has enabled God to move in my life in ways I never thought possible. I am so thankful for her *pwayers*. I ask each one of you to pway for her as well as me. It is important that I am fwee to teach and guide this flock in the ways of God. Satan has been twying to hinder me, and it is your pwayers that will give me the total victowy."

Callie blushed, sitting in the front pew section.

Mark smiled at her, than changed the subject. "We have a visitor from Nashville, Tennessee. He is a longtime fwiend of my son-in-law's father. Avery asked if I would give him a few minutes to intwoduce himself. Please welcome Bob Owenings. Come on up, Bob."

The congregation was curious and surprised. Mark never allowed anyone outside the sphere of Grace Church to take the pulpit.

A gray-haired man scurried up the platform. He was older, with a round face, jovial eyes, and a posh belly. Mark shook his hand and left the platform.

"Good evening ya' all. It is nice to be here." The man's heavy drawl was boisterous. "Jesus is here an' He wants to meet your needs. This mornin' I feel nudged by His Spirit to minister to ya' in the area of healin.' I have seen legs grow, tumors disappear, the lame walk, an' the deaf hear. Do ya' believe, Ladies and Gentlemen, that Jesus heals today jist as He did thousands of years ago?"

The congregation answered in excited shouts.

Bob prayed, and the room charged up like an electrical storm.

"There's someone here with stomach pain. Ya' battled this pain for years an' no doctor 'as been able to diagnose its cause. If this is you, stand up, God wants to heal ya'!"

Bob paced the floor under the *anointing,* waving his arms and shouting, "Praise God! Stand up an' let God heal ya'!"

A young woman with long, straight hair jumped to her feet.

"Be healed in Jesus name!" Bob cried.

Tears flowed down her face. She stood, shaking.

"You're healed! Praise God!"

The woman sat down, crying with joy.

"Whoever 'as that pain in yar' neck, God is healin' ya' now. Stand up."

An elderly man rose up out of the pew. His bony hand waved through the air.

"Arthritis, remove yar'self from this man of God, now, in Jesus name," the evangelist bellowed.

Mark squirmed in the pew. He didn't like the minister's style, or the way he was taking over the pulpit. It wasn't what he was asked to do. He tugged at his shirt collar, annoyed.

I can't lose control of this flock...

As Bob bounced around the stage, Mark sizzled. No amount if fanning could cool him down. He bounded up the stairs, trying not to let his insecurities show, and removed the microphone from Bob's hand. "Thank you, Bob," he said, without looking at the man, "God wants to use *me* now in the area of healing. Let's thank Bob for p*w*epa*w*ing the Spi*w*it of God to come forth."

The evangelist stood there dumbfounded. When Mark ignored him, he walked back down to his pew.

Donna's face paled as Bob passed.

"P*w*ay with me, church! God wants to continue healing this body of believers."

But Mark couldn't conjure up the power working through Bob. The congregation was disappointed.

"I feel Satan is h-hi-h-hinder*w*ing me," Mark stammered. He squeezed his eyes shut and ordered prayer. The church prayed. But nothing happened. Without ado, he spent the next ten minutes blaming Satan for the sudden "dry" spell. He cooed the spectators back to his side, and as they relaxed he released the pulpit for testimonies and songs.

Camp Bachter, a secluded, woodsy area with log cabins surrounding a picturesque lake, was the perfect place for the marriage retreat. Mountains lined the backdrop of the serene campground, and long pathways led to colorful patches of secluded woods and fish-filled streams. There were paddleboats and rowboats moored against the dock near a good-size lake, and two tennis courts nearby. But the church couples spent little time playing. They came for prayer, to find God, to seek miracles, to be changed.

The meetings were held in the main cabin hall, a spacious cozy atmosphere. A large stone fireplace, wooden tables, overstuffed sofas, and woven rugs thrown over hardwood floors gave the place a homey country feel. Twenty couples sat around the spacious room singing praises to Jesus, while three musicians accompanied them on guitars.

Penny snuggled with Rick on the floor against the fat couch and closed her eyes as she sang to Jesus. Callie and Petey, seated on the couch beside them, raised hands high and prayed softly in tongues.

Marilyn and Jason, the only black couple attending the retreat, stood in a circle with some other couples, praying.

Cody Addison left Laurina's side and walked to the middle of the room. He clapped his hands loudly to get everyone's attention. The room quieted. "I hate to interrupt you all, but I sense there is a hindrance here today. We need to *feel* God's Spirit, and I'm not feeling it! Are you?" he shouted.

"No!" everyone yelled back.

"Let's pray the Holy Ghost into this place!" Cody lifted his hands toward heaven. "Lord," he prayed, "we're expectant for Your spirit to touch our lives in wonderful ways. Change our lives, Lord; make us more like You. Restore our marriages! Heal our hearts! Give us a renewed vision for You. Pour Your Spirit on us today like rain!"

Amens backed up his prayer. Soon Cody was praying with his *other* language. Everyone joined him, and as they united into one noise, and the spiritual energy filled the room, some members rocked on their knees with tears streaming down their faces. Others paced the floor with hands raised or hands clapping. The believers expected God to break the powers of darkness and meet them.

Callie got up and strolled over behind Marcy and Owen, who were seated near the fireplace. Marcy, now eight months pregnant, smiled up at her friend. Callie laid her hands on Marcy's head and slowly began to sway back and forth, murmuring in whispered tongues. As her garbled words became louder, her hands started shaking. Moved by the power, Callie began vibrating. She shouted against the principalities of darkness she could not see. Petey came up behind Callie and placed his hand on her back, supporting his wife's intercession. Two other female intercessors belonging to Mark's prayer group joined Callie and Petey in the spiritual battle. Marcy rested her head on Owen's shoulder and cried. He put his hand on her knee and continued praying softly, eyes closed.

Callie started praying in English and turned her attention to Marcy. "You demon of unsubmission, you rebellious spirit, get out of Marcy, in Jesus name. Get out you foul spirit, leave this child of God, in the name of Jesus!" The heat from her wig dampened her forehead and neck as the pitch in her voice rose to a shriek.

Marcy trembled and shouted her response. "Get out of me unsubmissive demon in Jesus name! Teach me, Lord, to be a better wife and a faithful woman of God."

A supernatural zing shot through Callie's hands into Marcy. Marcy groaned as the glorious feelings swept inside her. The praying group no longer were shouting and fighting; now they were laughing.

Couples in other parts of the room responded in similar fashion. Laurina, Cody, Marilyn, Jason, and Rick were laying hands on Penny's shoulders and praying as she knelt on the floor. Penny's tears could not adequately express the glorious reception she received from Her Savior. Inside she felt like ministering waves were knocking against her heart.

"Oh, Jesus, yes, you cleanse her heart, restore her broken heart," Marilyn prayed quietly, "Yes, Jesus, heal the wounds inflicted from her father. Help her to forgive him."

Marilyn got silent before the Lord, waiting to see if God's Spirit would reveal anything else.

Laurina spoke up. "Oh, oh, I received a vision, Penny, of you being rocked in Christ's arms. On the ground was broken glass everywhere. You had some cuts in your feet, but Jesus had reached down and saved you from enduring any further painful steps." She than began to sing to Penny, "*My daughter, my cherished lamb, You know my life was slain, to keep you near my heart, free from all hurts and pain. My eyes see every scar you bear; stay close to me, and do not fear, for I am your healer. I am always, always near. I am the Lamb that was slain; I am the Lamb that was slain.*"

The retreat lasted three days, with constant prayer sessions. On the last night the God-seeking group found themselves drenched in a whirlwind of mystical love. Standing couples were slammed to the ground by the force, and others wept from the sheer joy of the supernatural permeating presence. Not one person could stand because the "spirit" had them so *drunk*.

Then, out of the blue, the entire group started singing the same melody in tongues. No one had ever heard the tune before, but as one female started singing, another joined, and another, and instantaneously the place became one unified "tongue." They were all *singing in the spirit*. It was something new, something glorious, and the couples rushed to their feet in one accord and raised their hands toward heaven and sang the evocative melody over and over and over—despite the fact not one person understood what they were singing.

CHAPTER SEVEN

Another year passed and Penny was busy keeping up with the fast-paced social life, numerous *intercessory* prayer meetings, help ministries, and college classes. August had arrived, and with it came the annual camp meetings—Penny's favorite time of the year. The meetings lasted four days, with three services held each day—mornings, afternoons, and evenings. Satellite pastors and elders flew in from all over the country to attend the special services.

Rick was active, but not as involved as Penny. He too enjoyed the anticipation of each service and the yearly camp meetings. It was like living inside a daytime soap opera, being part of a lifestyle that never allowed for a dull moment. He still missed the professional aspect of golf, but he had acclimated well to Grace Church's stimulating world. Though he was disappointed that he could not land a better job, he played lots of basketball and golf whenever he could. Roofing paid well and gave him a flexible schedule, but it didn't replace professional golf career. Yet, he kept centered on his goal, and that was to graduate from Bible College.

Penny had left early that Friday morning to meet Laurina and Marilyn at the sanctuary before the first camp meeting service, so Rick agreed to meet Cody and Petey at *The Grill* for breakfast. Other well-dressed *churchites* were seated at the restaurant and Rick greeted most of them before taking the back booth beside his friends. The server took their order.

"Rick, you been golfing lately?" Petey asked.

"Yeah, quite a bit. Cody's been playing with me. Want to join us after this weekend?"

Petey took off his glasses and polished them with a napkin. "Sure. Callie is gone so much anyway."

"Praying for Mark?" Rick asked.

"Praying for everyone!"

"I hear you. Penny is gone a lot too. I have to make an appointment just to see her."

When the food arrived, Cody buttered his toast and said, "Rick, did you get that last job you bid on?"

"Yeah. I start Monday. But I can take off early. My clubs our aching to be used."

Two tall beautiful women, a blonde and a brunette, squeezed through the crowd and took the empty booth beside them.

The three husbands stared.

"Who are they?" Rick asked.

"Janice Certs and Ellen Barker. Both are church members. I don't think either one is married," Cody said.

"I thought I saw them before," Rick said, ogling Janice, the blonde. She looked over at him and smiled. He turned red.

"Hey, buddy, battle that flesh, put it under," Petey teased.

Rick brushed Petey off with his hand. "Ah, just looking. She's gorgeous though."

"Yeah," Cody said, his twang going up an octave. "She is high class. Look at the way she dresses. Like a fashion model."

Petey laughed. "Ellen is prettier," he said, "But I know you like blondes, Rick."

"I like my wife. Period. Though sometimes I feel like we are in more of a competition than a marriage these days."

"What do you mean?" Cody asked.

"Penny feels God's presence so much. I can't relate to that. Pastor Mark tells us men to be the spiritual heads in the family, but I ask you, how can I compete with her abundant spirituality?"

"Relax, Rick," Cody admonished. "God deals with everyone differently. Women seem to be more in tune with spiritual things because of their emotional makeup. They're intuitive creatures. That's why God placed them under us, because we got it together."

The men chuckled.

"I never feel anything. Guess I am as dry spiritually as this spoon." Rick lifted his spoon.

"Keep plugging in," Cody persisted. "God will meet you. One day you will have an experience that will blow your mind. Keep in prayer."

"Yeah." Rick finished his breakfast and continued to steal glances at the blonde in the booth.

Members had arrived at the church early to save pews, pray, and worship. The prayer rooms were chock-full of noisy people, and hundreds of other churchgoers stood below the platform in the altar area, *singing in the spirit* in one perfect harmony. The unified garble became catchy and those sitting in the pews began singing along, until the entire auditorium had joined in. Mark let the singing go on for ten minutes before breaking in.

"Pwaise God, Pwaise God," he bellowed into the microphone as the crowd took their seats.

"My sheepies, your shepherd loves you. Pwaise God!" the pastor baby-talked into the microphone as pleasant compliments came back at him from the audience. "Let's have Marcy Nason sing a song before we begin."

Marcy climbed the platform with her guitar, smiling.

Penny looked behind her and saw Owen sitting in the soundproof nursery holding little William. Their delightful baby boy was already a year old.

"I feel God's about to do something different today." Laurina nudged Penny.

"Me too," Penny said and glanced back over her shoulder. She spotted Rick, Jason, and Owen standing near the back wall. They were ushering to help seat the overflow of people. They waved at her. "Remember the last camp meeting when everyone laughed in the spirit for two days?" she asked, turning back around as Marcy was tightening her guitar strings.

"I couldn't even eat," Laurina said.

"His love was like waves inside me."

"God is moving in this church! We're so fortunate to be here," Laurina exclaimed.

Marcy started singing, and the room worshipped God. People stood and worshipped, weeping, and singing, as the heartfelt melody drew them into its world. The place sparked with electric emotion, and different members began falling backward to the ground, crying and whooping as they went down under the *power* seducing their bodies.

"God's meeting us!" Laurina exclaimed as the church reacted to the flow of the tempo. "I was so dry this morning when I prayed, but God's here now. He's drenching us in His love!"

"Praise God!" Penny replied, swaying back and forth in the pew, hands raised up high, singing loudly.

Marcy sang the song fifteen more minutes to allow the people to relish in the supernatural experiences they were receiving. Finally, at the finish of the song, the pastor took the pulpit, looking giddy and happy at the way the service was going.

"Yes, my flock," he bellowed, "God has chosen this church to be His spiwitual bwide. We must seek to expewience Him. Those of you who are dwy in the spiwit must bweak thwough and get into the holy of holies, into God's intimate presence. We must obtain the higher things of God. Don't stop pwaying until God dumps His glowy on you!"

Mark paused long enough to get his breath. He lowered his voice. "The Bible says Chwist is the head of the church, and we, the church, are His bwide. The only way to be His bwide is to *feel* Him! This type should not be bwoken, and for this reason is why I pweach stwongly that wives submit to their husbands. Ladies, God has placed the male as authowity over you for your safety. Stay obedient to God and He will reward you."

Penny's face took on a defeated look as Mark exhorted. His constant speeches for the husbands to "take their positions" as spiritual heads only succeeded in leading her and Rick into heated arguments. She badgered Rick to be more spiritual so she could submit, and he pestered her to be more docile so he could feel more spiritual. Neither one could attain these roles without feeling pressured. They seemed to fight more and more these days.

Donna Garrett dropped to her knees and faced the pew, covering her face in her hands, praying softly.

The crowd tensed, expecting something.

She rose and rushed up the platform. She was crying as she staggered under *the anointing*. Her slender hands waved through the air like a symphony conductor, her long pink nails a bewitchment to all three thousand eyes. She swayed on high black heels, her flounced skirt licking at her thighs as she moved.

"Tender flock, last night in prayer God gave me a warning for this assembly." She moaned, displaying an agonizing expression. "The devil wants to bring a deception into this body, an evil lie that will beguile and deceive God's people if we are not careful." She bent over and clutched her chest. "I have never had God speak to me in such a way as this. All I could do was weep. We must all make new commitments today to stand for God and His Word. Let us pray."

A solemn hush came over the assembly and members slid to their knees as Donna prayed.

There was no sermon that morning. Donna closed the service with exhortation to draw nearer to God. People were responding and repenting as the Spirit of God moved gently across the sanctuary. The elders from both Grace Church and the satellite churches supported the repenting crowd with the *laying on of hands* as the Christians filed down front to pray.

The prayers subsided, and the pianist played quiet melodies until members began dispersing for lunch.

Visitors and satellite pastors rushed up to greet Pastor Mark, but he hurried over to Laurina's pew, shaking more hands as he went.

"Hello, Lau*w*ina, my dear," he said as he reached her pew. "How are you today?"

"Fine, Pastor."

"Why, hello. Haven't we met before?" Mark asked politely, turning his attention to Penny.

Penny blushed. "Yes, in your bathroom, when I cleaned your house. It was a long time ago; you might not remember. I'm Penny Duncan." Her words ran together.

The pastor chuckled. "I do remember! Good to see you again, Penny."

Mark turned his attention back to Laurina. He allowed his eyes to roam over her form long enough to notice the blue skirt that hugged her hips.

"Lauwina, are you busy now? Would you like to join me in pwayer with a few of the satellite pastors?"

Laurina wouldn't look at him. "No Mark," she said. "I can't. Penny and I are on our way to lunch. Sorry, maybe another time."

"I understand," the pastor said. "You have a good camp meeting, my dear. God bless you." He squeezed her shoulder, smiled at Penny, and left the pew.

"Duh?" Penny said, gaping at Laurina with surprise.

"Penny, Mark's too insecure; I can't meet his needs." Laurina turned away from Penny and gathered her things from under the pew. She was sorry she had blurted that out.

"What do you mean?"

"Penny, there are some things I can't share. Forget I even said anything. It wasn't right."

"What things?"

"Penny, I have known the pastor a long time and so I just know some of his faults."

Penny looked bothered, so Laurina tried to make light of it. "Really, I love Pastor Mark. None of us is perfect is what I am trying to say. Anyway, I promised lunch with you. Remember?"

After lunch Cody, Laurina and Penny returned to their saved seats. Rick squeezed into a back pew with Marilyn, Jason, Owen, and Marcy. Men and women, all dressed in their best attire, scurried down the aisles. Callie and Petey, part of the oozing crowd, passed by Penny's pew.

"Hey, Callie, hello," Penny called out after Callie. She felt bad that she seldom saw her anymore.

Callie looked over her shoulder and waved. Penny's now *famous* intercessor friend and husband scooted in behind Pastor Mark and Donna in the reserved section. Penny was resigned to the fact that Callie was not the same anymore. She and Petey were definitely inside the pastor's *elite* circle. Petey seemed more mature since he began his job at the church office, and Penny was glad to see him do so well. Rick still got together with him often, and she was glad about that.

Petey turned in the pew and caught her staring. He cocked his dark head and threw her a clumsy grin with a quick salute. She saluted back. Petey hadn't changed at all; he was still the same funny guy.

Penny scanned the elder's pews one aisle over. Ted and Betty Hunter sat together, ignoring each other. Ted's younger brother, Kurt, a single fellow who taught a class at the Bible College, sat beside his brother. Penny thought he was very good looking and not like Ted at all. All the girls loved his class. Huddled beside them and cooling herself with a frilly pink fan was their daughter, Connie, now a pretty fifteen-year-old. The pastor's daughter, Gayle, and her husband, Avery, sat beside them. Penny noticed that Gayle seemed uncomfortable. She was fanning herself pretty hard and looked awfully hot in the dress she wore. She had never met Gayle, but had heard she was a great teacher and mother. The church was so huge, and although not everyone had met each other personally, everyone still *knew* everything about everyone. That's how it was. Being in Grace Church was like being a character in a book.

Penny flung open her fan, whipped it at her face, and snooped some more. She watched Avery lean over and chat with Connie, who obviously admired him. He was too thin for Penny's taste, but his youthful features did give him a likeable appeal.

Behind Gayle and Avery were Joe and Christina Fellows and their three children. Joe had a pleasant face—a too thin nose and a pair of string bean lips that sort of made room for his benevolent eyes. His short wife was always smiling.

"Ohhh, God, pwaise Your holy name, ohhh, Lord, come to us today, we are open to Your Spiwit…" Mark invaded Penny's wandering eyes and grabbed the room's attention. He kept praying in his child-like tone while the congregation prayed along with him softly.

"Go to hell!"

The rough intrusion stunned the crowd. They strained around in their seats to see who would dare to speak in such a manner.

A hoarse voice bellowed out from the back of the sanctuary. "This is nonsense and garbage. To hell with you all! Go to hell!" A further stream of profanity ripped through the auditorium, rendering the Christians speechless.

Mark halted, then yelled into the microphone, "Secuwity, remove that man." But before the man could be restrained, he flew up the aisle and stood beneath the pulpit, his arms flaying erratically at Mark.

"I am Jesus. Worship me," the man cried, his eyes like black glass. His deep voice seemed out of place with his thin body.

Three security guards stormed up the aisle and wrestled the middle-aged man to the floor. The congregation moved to the edge of their seats, gaping in horror at the puny little man hurling the guards away from him like the Bible character Samson did with the Philistines. The possessed man sneered at Mark, hissing, than cackling at him.

"What's the matter, man of God? Can't you tame me?" He flung himself to the ground in a wolf position and howled.

Two more guards joined the charade, and the five men subdued the loathsome man.

Mark, afraid he might lose face, spoke into the microphone loudly. "Church, pway and intercede for this man. This man seems to be demon possessed."

Murmurs rose up across the auditorium.

Gary Evans, the satellite pastor from Kentucky, bounded up the steps. He stood no taller then Mark as he conversed into his ear in rapid whispers. Mark nodded, then shouted into the microphone.

"I want this assembly to back Gawy and me up in pwayer. I'll explain later. Gawy believes God wants to deliver this man. This man is a Chwistian."

Gasps shot through the church like gunfire.

Pastor Gary shouted, "Pray, church, deliverance is here. God is victorious!" He ran down from the platform and cautiously approached the bound man. Mark followed him, for the first time caring less that another pastor was taking the lead.

"Hold him down tight," Gary ordered the guards. The wild man was still spitting out cuss words when Gary placed his hands on the man's head and commanded, "In Jesus name, I command you, evil spirit, to come out of this man."

The enraged man recoiled under the touch of the pastor.

Mark approached the other side of the man and placed his hand on the man's shoulder. Dark eyes darted from Gary to Mark and the deep voice growled, "You like me, man of *God*."

"Who are you?" Gary commanded. "In the name of Jesus, I command you to answer me."

The demon spoke. "I am of the witch lineage. His generation fondled my wisdom."

"Why are you in this man?" Gary asked.

The man's body, contorted by the strength of the demon, relaxed, and the guards loosened their grips. The voice snarled quietly, "He let me in."

"How?" Gary asked, leaning closer to the man's leering face.

"He played with me."

"I am asking you again, why are you in this man?"

"He likes Ouija boards and tarot cards. He likes séances." The evil smile faded. "Leave me alone. I don't want to leave." The voice in the man cried out, sounding like a wounded puppy, cowering himself away from Gary's touch. "Leave me alone! Don't touch me!"

"Come out of him, in Jesus name, now!" Gary ordered.

Gary and Mark kept praying and insisting the demon leave in the name of Jesus, and as they did so, the power of the demon weakened.

As the battle between good and evil raged on, Penny watched in fascination, glancing away long enough to meet Rick's astounded gaze. The elders, Donna, and Callie sat poised, ready to move if necessary. Petey shrunk into the pew and Laurina grabbed Cody's hand for support. Jason squirmed at the manifestation, and Marilyn, perched on the edge of her seat, prayed in tongues. Marcy and Owen, mesmerized at the outburst, flew to their knees in the pew to intercede.

For two hours no one left the grand room; everyone waited and watched the pastors rebuking the unclean spirit.

Pastor Mark grew more confident and began to overshadow Gary's prayers with scripture. Gary backed off and let Mark take over the commanding. "You must obey God!" Mark shouted.

"You should talk..." the demon quipped out at Mark before finally giving up and fleeing the skinny man, who at the same time fell limp in the arms of his captives. The dark eyes brightened to a light brown as the man sighed and looked around him, embarrassed.

"What happened?" he whispered.

Pastor Mark jumped up and left the man with Gary. He jostled back up to the pulpit and spoke into the mic. "My sheepies, my flock, the hour is late. God allowed what you have witnessed here today. Despite the fact that God is exposing demons, we know the victowy is His. This man was set fwee by the blood of Jesus Chwist. I will discuss all this at the evening service. Go eat dinner and rest up. We will resume service a half hour later tonight since this has been an exhausting episode for all of us. Thank you for your pwayers. God bless you."

The man who was freed from the demon spirit was led to the pastor's pew. Gary and Donna counseled him concerning the matter.

Mark closed the service and found Ted, still seated in the elders' section of seats.

"Ted," he said, "I've never expewienced an encounter like this before. I have to admit, I'm shaken." Mark cleared his throat. "I want you to awwange a meeting with our eldership before the next service. I want Gawy there too."

"It is hard to believe this can happen to a Christian," Ted said. He looked concerned.

"Yes, stwange indeed. Awwange the meeting for five-thirty, in the conference room at the college."

"Done."

"Can you believe what happened?" Penny asked her friends as they all devoured two pepperoni pizzas at the Pizza Hut not too far from the church.

"Man, it was eerie," Rick said, rubbing his dimpled chin, and shaking his head.

"Yeah," Cody agreed. He was troubled. "I never thought demons could possess a Christian. I've met that man in Kentucky. He's not a violent person. He attends Pastor Evan's church. As far as I knew, he didn't have any major problems in his life."

"I know him too," Owen said, wiping at his nose with his handkerchief. "He didn't have an angry bone in his body."

"The Bible mentions in numerous places about demon possession," Laurina said. "What about the verses in Matthew chapter 12, verses 43 - 45? *When an unclean spirit goes out of a man, he goes through dry places, seeking rest, and finds none. Then he says, 'I will return to my house from which I came.' And when he comes, he finds it empty, swept, and put in order. Then he goes and takes with him seven other spirits more wicked than himself, and they enter and dwell there; and the last state of that man is worse than the first. So shall it also be with this wicked generation.*"

"Isn't God admonishing Christians here?" she asked, "Maybe this scripture implies we need deliverances as Christians."

Jason filled his cup with coffee. He didn't raise the cup to his mouth, but instead played with its rim. His perplexed eyes were as dark as the coffee. "I have a problem with this.

Christians should not have demons. I need to hear what the pastor says about all this."

"Yeah," Petey replied, scratching his nose under his glasses. "Me too."

"I thought I was in the 'Twilight Zone,'" Rick added, "Are you sure this guy wasn't a paid actor? He was good."

The group laughed.

"I don't know," Petey said, flexing his back. "Callie can out-scream that demon during her prayer times."

"Now, Petey, Callie is not here to defend herself!" Laurina said jokingly. She pulled another slab of pizza onto her plate.

"Where is Callie?" Penny asked.

"On the moon," Petey said flatly.

Penny ignored what he said. "You know, people are going to think we're crazy," she said.

"I can't imagine what your folks would say," Marilyn said to Jason.

"Well, I should call my dad and talk to him about it. He is a pastor and should know about these things," Jason replied.

"He'll disown us, Jason!" Marilyn cried.

"Owen's parents already do," Marcy said, leaning back in the booth, rocking her little boy in her lap. He had the same berry-red hair color as his mother. "They think our lifestyle is too holy. They hate the fact we won't drink a glass of champagne, watch television, or put up a pagan Christmas tree. They stay away from us because they think we're brainwashed."

"My family never calls me; they could care less. And Rick's family would freak out." Penny reached for a napkin, "My Aunt Joann who lives here thinks I'm running from reality. So do my parents. They are so blind from the truth. I pray someday they can see Grace Church is the only way. We can't settle for less, especially when Jesus wants our best. Anyway, all of you are my family now."

Her friends smiled.

"Well, I refuse to let demons take control of me!" Marilyn declared.

"Yeah, really, who do they think they are anyway?" Penny retorted.

That evening Mark approached the podium and signaled the choir to remain seated. Fans whipped at the hot air, babies cried in the background, shoes shuffled under pews, and numerous anxious members ruffled through Bible pages. Ushers led the last minute cluster of people to their seats.

"Pwaise God," Mark said. "Church, I'm glad you made it back for the evening service, especially after the last service." He flashed a captivating grin. "Today an extwaordinawy event happened, but God prwevailed, pwoving Himself in contwol, prwoving His Word, and showing us that we have victowy in the name of Jesus." His speech impediment became more pronounced in his excitement.

The church shouted agreement.

"Gawy told me this afternoon that his church in Kentucky had a similar expewience. During a pwayer meeting a young woman manifested in similar fashion. After much pwayer God set her fwee. We have been seeing God bwing in fwesh, *new waves of His Spiwit* in this church. The last one, *singing in the spiwit*, has unified this body. Thwough that new experience, God is now opening us up for further revelation. We are going deeper into the things of God! No other church has the dedication and commitments Gwace Church stwives for. Your pwayers have moved mountains and the demons are twembling. They are manifesting because your pwayers are diswupting their plans."

Mark paced, something he seldom did.

"According to scwipture, we know Mary Magdelene was delivered from seven demons. We know Jesus delivered many followers from demons. Can Chwistians have demons? Can we be possessed?" He added more oomph to his speech and paced some more.

"I believe because of our own past sins, or genewational sins that have come down through the family lineage, we have allowed demons on our backs, so to speak. The man today that was set fwee told my wife that he had spent much of his time in the occult before he was saved. Somehow that demon still had a hold on him. Today God exposed it and set him fwee. If this is what God is doing in our midst, we must be open to it and stwive for delivewance in our own lives."

At the pastoral pew, Donna slid to her knees, causing an anxious expectancy to hover over the congregation.

Mark kept talking. "What I want to do is give God a chance to move today. Pastor Gawy has agweed to pway for individuals who feel they need delivewance. Gawy, come on up here. I want the eldership and all Bible College teachers up here for backup, but only the men. I don't know what might happen and I don't want any females hurt. Let's keep this in order."

Ted, Avery, Joe and the other elders and teachers filed down to the altar.

"Now, I want only those of you who have dealt with witchcraft in your past to get up fwom your pews and file down fwont and form four lines. I am not sure what will happen, but whatever does, I want this church to stay seated and pway quietly."

Donna came up behind her husband and prophesied. "My church, my tender flock, keep your eyes on Me. I am your great deliverer. Do not fear and do not tremble, for the only one trembling today is your adversary, the devil. My Word has prevailed and I shall set you free, my beloved children. Keep your eyes centered entirely on My Word, do not sway from My truth, and you shall remain victorious, saith your God."

Donna returned to her pew, where she knelt down and started to pray. Callie and the other intercessors from Mark's "inner circle" followed suit and knelt at their pews as well.

"As we pway for delivewance, I want the pianist to play "All Things are Possible" very softly," Mark said.

As the music played, a dozen or so members walked down front. An overweight woman was first in line. As Gary stepped towards her, the woman suddenly shrieked and fell down.

"She's mine," a scary voice screeched from her.

The assembly again ended up at the edge of their pews.

"Hold her," Gary shouted.

Ted and Avery pinned her arms while Gary placed his hand upon her forehead. "Get out, demon, in Jesus name," he prayed with authority.

"No," the demons growled. "We want to stay."

"Why are you in this woman?" Gary commanded.

"She let us in. Hssssss, and we love having her... Heeeeeeeee! She likes praying to us."

"How many of there are you?"

The woman's body twisted like a rubber band. "Three of us. We came in a long time ago. She loves our power!"

"The blood of Jesus defeats you," Gary said confidently. "This woman is a believer and covered by the blood of Jesus.

Get out of her now. She is cleansed by the Blood of Christ. Remove yourselves in Jesus name."

The demons wailed as they battered the woman's large frame. Her tongue hung out while her eyes rolled back in her head.

Mark came up and joined the battle.

"Eeeeeehhhhhheeeee..." A shriek from the audience made everyone jump. A young black woman was thrashing in a back pew uncontrollably.

Donna ran down the aisle and charged to the young woman's side. Callie bounced up from her kneeling position to join her. So did four other women. Petey stayed behind, ashen-faced.

As the service went on, demons started exposing themselves all over the church. With eerie screams and wild movements, people were being taken over by an evil power they could not stop—and only until the Word of God was spoken and Jesus' name mentioned, were they forced into silence.

CHAPTER EIGHT

The months sped by for the *churchites*. The new *deliverance move* had pushed everyone's already busy life into full speed. The pace was demanding, both physically and spiritually.

"Rick, I can't believe all the prayer meetings I'm involved with," Penny said enthusiastically on a Monday morning as she got ready for her meeting with Laurina. "God is so good. His Spirit is moving and we are part of this!"

"That's nice, Hon." Rick searched his drawers, then slammed the bottom one.

"Penny, where are my socks?" he asked, irritated.

"Did you look in the dryer?"

He strode out of the room and returned—angry. "They are in the dirty laundry," he griped.

Penny ignored his remark.

"Penny, with all these prayer meetings you're involved in, nothing gets done around here. You seem to forget you have a husband."

"Rick, I can't do everything."

"Well, if you can't keep up with the housework, then you'll have to cut back on your prayer meetings."

"Why are you so grumpy?"

"We have no groceries, the clothes are still dirty, the bills are unpaid, the sink still full of dishes…what do you want me to do, smile?"

"Rick, you have two legs. I'm tired of your jealousy towards my walk with God. If you would pray more instead of complaining, maybe you wouldn't be harping at me!"

"I gave up golf for you; don't make me small!"

"That's it, then, isn't it? You gave up golf for me. I thought you did it for God! How sad for you!"

Rick winced at her words. No matter how much he tried to forget, he couldn't. No amount of prayer lessened the loss. He knew his reply would cause an argument, but he didn't care. "It's always what you want, Penny. What I want doesn't matter. I've given up my life for you, so the least you can do is buy me some groceries!"

"You need to get delivered, Rick, from a *golf* demon!" Penny spat.

He glared at her. He was so angry he wanted to smack her.

She saw his mood and grabbed her purse and jacket and stormed out the front door.

Rick grabbed a glass out of the sink and flung it against the wall. He sank down at the kitchen table and stared at the broken pieces shattered all over the floor. He felt just like that glass. No amount of deliverance against demons could put his torn self back together. He had prayed for hours and hours, and had friends pray for him for hours and hours, but nothing ever happened. Though he knew Bible college was not wasted time, it was evident his lack of spiritual experiences kept him from moving in the *fast lane* with everyone else. Why wouldn't God give him the breakthrough he needed to take his position as spiritual head in his marriage? He did everything the pastor told him. He joined prayer meetings, got prayer, read the Bible, but nothing changed. It was humiliating to see his wife *soaring in the spirit* while he sat on the sidelines, dry as tumbleweed.

Penny and Laurina met at *The Grill* for bagels and cream cheese before heading for their intercessor's prayer meeting at the college campus. Male heads turned as they strode in and took their seats.

"Laurina," Penny asked, "What do you think of the deliverances?" Penny's blonde hair was swept up in a French Roll and she looked chic.

"What do you mean?" Laurina pulled at the turquoise scarf around her neck. Its color made her hazel eyes look very green.

"Sometimes I think Satan loves the manifestations. I don't know, but it seems like we give the demons too much room to talk. We ask them who they are, and then two hours later we realize we've just been led on a wild goose chase." Penny spread jam on her bagel. "I miss the old prayer meetings when we praised God; now it seems like all we do is battle. I'm exhausted."

"I know." Laurina's eyes widened as she cocked her pretty head in thought. "Hearing demons talk has become normal for us now. We forget people on the street would freak out if they heard them."

"And another thing, Laurina, whenever I get upset or tired, Rick antagonizes me and asks, 'What demon is that talking?' I feel like I am starting to wonder who I am. I mean one guy gave a testimony of being delivered of a spirit of flatulence. Please! Even gas is now demonic!"

Laurina laughed. "Cody needs deliverance from that demon. It manifests way too much. I think face masks are the best way to deliver him."

Penny burst out laughing. She liked how Laurina knew how to bring her back to herself.

"How are you and Cody doing?"

"We have argued a little over our busy schedules."

"Me too! Rick and I just fought this morning. He says I don't care about him anymore. I have even caught him looking at other women."

"Penny, you are so pretty. Don't be insecure about that. Rick loves you."

Penny grunted.

"So Rick still misses golf?" Laurina asked. "Do you think that is why he is mad at you?"

"Yeah. He hasn't fully surrendered it over to God yet, so he blames me for his quitting. He seemed to be fine about it for a long time, but now it is really bothering him."

A plump server refilled their water glasses and removed the empty plates.

"Let's pray for him at Marcy's this week," Laurina said.

"Okay. Oh, look, Ted and Betty Hunter just came in."

Laurina uncrossed her legs and swung around to see the elder and his wife. They saw her and she put up her hand.

Ted waved, but Betty pretended not to notice.

Suddenly Penny understood. "You had that affair with Ted, didn't you?" Penny asked in a hushed tone.

"Shhh. You are too smart, Penny. That was years ago. Penny, please keep this confidential. Promise me."

"His wife doesn't like you."

"I know. It's between them now. Besides, we talked it all out and, like I told you, we forgave and forgot."

"I don't think she forgot," Penny said as Ted kept glancing their way.

Jason's dark hands sped nervously down the sides of his blue suit before he took his seat in front of the elder's desk.

"Well, Jason, what can I do for you?" Avery asked, smiling, looking relaxed in the leather chair.

Jason licked his lips and leaned forward with a frown. "Avery, I graduated from Bible College a year ago, and I'm feeling anxious to use my degree. I don't see any doors opening for me. I see a lot of graduates sitting in the pews and, well, I don't want to be a pew warmer. Pastor Mark exhorts us to minister, but every time I try to do this, I am told *no*, to wait. I love Jesus and I want to use my God-given talents."

Avery scratched his temple and crossed his skinny legs. "Jason," he said, "I'm glad you have a desire to minister. There are thousands of needs in this church. Witnessing teams, deliverance prayer…"

"I know this, Avery. I've been doing all those things. But I want to *use* my degree."

Jason felt smothered. How could he tell this to Avery? The only ones allowed to preach were satellite pastors, elders, or college teachers. He hated seeing the graduates collect dust in the pews, especially when there was a whole world of hurting and lost souls. He wished the church would give them more freedom to go out on their own and exercise their potentials.

"Jason, be patient. God will raise you up in His time. It's important that you place yourself under this church government and wait for God's leading in your life. Your place is here. Aren't you happy as an attorney?"

"Yes, of course. I worked hard to get my degree and become a lawyer. But the difference is that I am utilizing this degree and not utilizing the degree I also worked hard to get, here at Grace Church Bible College. Being an attorney is not enough for me. I have a calling of God in my life."

Avery picked up a pencil and played with it. "God is using you to help this church with legal matters. This is a ministry in itself. The pastor is extremely happy that you do this." He scratched at his nose with the eraser. "I remember being in your shoes. Someday you'll find yourself in the position God has ordained for you. Be patient. Meanwhile, be a good lawyer."

"Thank you for your time, Avery. I'll keep praying." Jason straightened his tie, stood, and bent forward to shake the minister's hand.

"Good, Jason. Thanks for stopping by."

Jason walked out with the same nagging doubts he had brought in with him.

Marilyn had been waiting in the reception area for him. She caught his disheartened look as he came out of the office.

"Sweetie, you okay? What happened?" she asked. Her dark eyes were worried.

"Nothing, Mar, absolutely nothing."

Marilyn grasped her husband's hand. "What did Avery say?"

He wrapped his arm around her waist and pulled her close. "He told me to be patient, Marilyn. I feel trapped. Why do I feel this way?"

"Because God has called you, Babe. You have His heart and you don't want to sit still. That's a good sign. Don't be hard on yourself. Keep praying. Give God time to open doors for you."

"Yeah, I need to trust Him. But why do I feel so empty inside? You know, Babe, I am a lawyer with a good clientele. Mark uses my services; I am bright enough to keep his church out of legal entanglements, yet I don't seem to be good enough to head up a satellite church or lead a ministry. I don't quite understand it."

Pastor Mark flipped through the pages of his notebook, than looked up at the somber couple facing his desk.

"Owen and Marcy, I am glad you came by today. How's little William?"

"He's fine," Marcy replied with a forced smile.

"He's as cute as a button, that boy," Mark stated, trying to relax the tension in the room.

"Yes, he is," Marcy smiled.

"Okay, let's face this pwoblem between you," Mark said.

"It's not my problem, Pastor," Marcy asserted.

Mark ignored her remark. "Now, Owen, I hear you're still having some stwuggles?"

"Yes," Owen said softly. He stared blankly at his lap.

"Owen, Marcy, I know things seems overwhelming now, but God is a God of restowation and delivewance. Do you agwee?"

"Yes," Owen murmured. He pulled his handkerchief from his shirt pocket and blew his nose.

"Owen has gotten prayer after prayer by the best deliverance teams. Yet there is no change. He is still gay. What am I supposed to do as a woman? Never have sex with my husband?"

Mark shifted in his seat and sighed. "Honey, you have to submit this to the Lord and accept your husband as your spiwitual head, even if he does not meet up to your standards. In God's eyes, you are his wife, and your place is under him. You have no choices here. I cannot allow you to divorce Owen. I cannot allow Owen to divorce you."

Marcy began to cry. "How can I go on pretending my life is fine? I have fooled all my friends. I feel like I am in a prison!"

"Owen, you must continue to seek delivewance against this spiwit of homosexuality."

Owen nodded.

"I can't take any more of this, Pastor," Marcy pushed on, "I'm living a double life. He lives this sick lifestyle and I'm forced to cover for him and put up with his love affairs with other men."

Owen sniffled.

Mark opened the Bible and read a scripture about wives submitting to their husbands. Marcy sobbed harder.

"Marcy, I do try to stop," Owen insisted. "I still love you and William. Be patient with me."

"We have no sex life, Owen. I can't live like this."

Mark handed her a tissue and cleared his throat. He wanted to end the session as soon as possible. Times like this he was thankful his weakness was for pretty women and not other men.

"Marcy, Owen is twying to overcome his pwoblem thwough counsel. That's why he's here. He's willing. I can't let you divorce him. Otherwise you show unwillingness and I will be forced to put you out of this church. I cannot allow a bad example within this body of believers."

Marcy dabbed at her puffy face with a tissue. "No wonder Becky Thomas killed herself," she blurted.

"Marcy, I want you to meet with Donna twice a week now instead of only once a week. She will help you get through this. Can you do this?"

Marcy blew her nose and nodded.

"I've got another appointment now. Let's cover one another, Marcy." He got up and moved beside her. He put a finger under her chin and said, "You're going to make it, Honey. Stay in the boat."

He led the emotionally spent couple to the door and wished them well.

With a sigh of relief, Mark returned to his tidy desk.

A knock, then Callie's face appeared around the door.

"Hello, Pastor, are you ready for me?"

"Hello Honey," Mark purred. He rose and gave her a small hug. He quickly locked the door and said, "No one intewwupts us today!"

Callie shrugged and smiled.

"This week has been fewocious. I need some filling up fwom your spiwit."

Callie came up behind him and scratched his back. "How are things with you and Donna?"

"You've helped me so much in my mawwiage." He took her hand and led her to his desk chair. He sat down and pulled her close.

"Want me to pray or minister in Donna's stead for you today?" she asked, standing there with her hands on his shoulders.

Mark sighed and rested his head on her bosom. "Ah...ummm...Honey, you're a gem. Go ahead and stand in the stead for Donna. Lets see if we can complete my healing."

With ease Callie ran her hands up his neck. "You have a strong mind," she said, massaging his temples and acting out the same duties she had been doing often at their meetings over the last year.

He moaned, "Yes, Jesus, thank you Lord."

"Your mind is like a bull," she said, caressing his ego, "sound and sure, and your body responds with great strength."

He pulled her onto his lap, surprising her. "You don't mind, my sweet daughter, if we do something diffewent today?"

"No, sure, Pastor."

"Would you go over there and turn on the tape player. Let's get some music in here to worship the Lord with."

Callie, eager to be off his lap, went to the cassette player. She hit the button. The choir's music filled the room.

"Turn up the volume, Callie."

She obeyed and returned to Mark. Again he pulled her back onto his lap.

"Relax, Callie."

The music was hypnotic and she gave in to its haunting melody.

"Close your eyes and feel the spiwit."

He pulled her close. The strong tang of his aftershave mingled with the minty smell of his breath.

"I want you and I to expewience God's intimate love. Release yourself to God and let me become Chwist to you. If we can bypass the flesh and allow God to move thwough us, I can be fwee to love my wife."

He held her hips down with his hands. "Jesus loves you and I love you. Do you believe this?"

"Yes."

Mark's charm moved with the music's tempo. As soon as he felt her relax, he moved his hand up under her cotton blouse. Callie stiffened and stopped him. He cooed into her ear. "Don't fight God's pwesence. It is not you I am touching; this is Donna. Twust me."

Callie released his hand and he continued fondling her. "Ohhh, Donna, I need your love. Ohhh, Jesus, I need your love. I want to be one with you! I am open for your love, Jesus!"

Callie did not want to break Mark's place in the spirit, so she did not flinch when he slid his other hand up her back and unhooked her bra. His breathing intensified as he rocked his hips underneath her and grabbed at her breasts.

She tried to think of Jesus and ignore his intrusive pinching. She knew she had to relax and not hinder his spiritual journey, so she envisioned it was Petey rubbing her. Her skirt bunched up around her from his gyratory movements.

He groaned with delight. "Pwaise God, pwaise God," he murmured, grasping her tightly until he reeled back down to earth.

He opened his eyes and pushed her off his lap.

Callie fumbled to redo her bra and straighten her skirt. She felt odd, ashamed.

"Thank you Callie. Oh my, I was with Jesus! I was with Jesus." He feigned tears and lowered his head. "Oh, I was with Jesus! You have no idea what you did for me today! Tonight Donna will reap the rewards of your ministwy. She and I will meet Jesus together!"

Penny and Laurina ran into Callie scurrying down the campus hallway.

"Callie, hey where you going?" Laurina asked, catching her by the arm.

"Oh, I'm late for a d-d-doctor's appointment," Callie stammered. She blushed and fumbled with her purse strap.

"Are you okay, Callie?" Penny asked. She had never seen her friend so nervous.

"Yes, yes, I'm just running late." She put on a smile and tried to look normal.

"Callie, Pastor Mark asked me to come to his prayer meeting this week," Laurina said. "Will you be there?"

"Yes. I will."

"I don't really want to go…"

"Why?" Callie asked.

"Mark and I sometimes clash."

"Give him a chance. We all make mistakes." Callie dropped her eyes at that.

"You're right," Laurina said. "I will be there. It might be a good time for the pastor and I to connect."

"See you then. Talk to you later, Penny." Callie patted Penny's arm. "Call me, maybe we can get together this week." She hastened away.

"She seemed a little uptight," Laurina said.

"Ah, she's like that now. She's changed a lot since she's been praying for Pastor Mark. I hardly see her anymore."

Laurina wondered how close Callie and Mark had become. She threw the thought out. Callie really admired him and Mark would be foolish to spoil that.

Penny tugged at Laurina's elbow and her eyes widened. "Hey, I didn't know you're invited to be in the pastor's prayer group."

"I forgot about it. No big deal. Listen, Penny, you're coming with me to his prayer meeting."

"Me? I don't think so, Laurina."

"Yes, you. Or I am not going! I'll have Cody telephone Mark tonight. If he wants me there—which I know he does—he'll invite you too. Besides, you're an intercessor."

Late Wednesday afternoon, Penny and Laurina arrived at the parsonage wearing comfortable dresses and flat shoes. Pastor Mark answered the door looking casual in brown slacks and a blue cotton shirt.

"Lauwina, I'm so glad you could come, and Penny. Come on in, we're about to start."

Laurina smiled, but not as sheepishly as Penny did.

Mark's gaze skimmed Penny's slender figure before moving it back to Laurina's voluptuous one.

Ten female intercessors, including Callie, greeted them in the living room.

Mark grasped his hands together happily and said, "Ladies, thank you for coming. I've asked Lauwina and Penny to join us today."

He sat down on a big pillow on the floor and the ladies settled around him. "Lauwina," he said hopefully, "I hope you don't mind if we have the ladies pway for you and I? We have had some hurts between us, and I think this is a good time to ask the Lord to heal and mend us both."

Laurina nodded.

"Come closer, Lauwina, sit here by me," the pastor said.

Laurina scooted over. Callie came up behind Laurina and placed her hands on her back. Penny followed suit, while the rest of the ladies put their hands on the pastor's shoulder.

The group started taking turns praying for God's *anointing* to come into the room. Suddenly, like an attacking tsunami, Callie shouted, "Get out of Laurina, you demon of rebellion, in Jesus name!"

A growl escaped Laurina and she flung backward. Mark opened his eyes and reached for her arm. She shot forward with a vicious yell.

The evil spirit hurled Laurina back and forth as soft hands held her down.

Mark took command. "Get out, you dirty demon. Let her be."

"No, you just want her for yourself," the demon snickered.

"Shut up," Mark ordered, "In Jesus name, depart now."

The battle raged for twenty minutes before Laurina fell limp against Mark's chest.

"It's gone," she said awkwardly and started weeping. "My, I didn't know that thing was so strong. I feel so foolish," she cried. "I have been harboring ill feelings toward you, Pastor. I am so sorry! Satan has tried to convince me that your kindness toward me was impure! He is a liar!"

Callie lifted her hands off Laurina and put them in her lap. She looked down and remained quiet the rest of the meeting.

"Lauwina, Honey," Mark urged, "I would never hurt you or do anything to make you mistwust me. I have always loved you as my own daughter. It has hurt me to know you have seen me any other way."

Laurina cried some more. "I am so sorry, Pastor."

He hugged her and said, "It is okay. God is here and He is healing us both."

The prayers shifted to Mark, and he slid back onto the floor, stretching his stocky frame across the white carpet, snuggling his head into the pillow. The women kneeled over his relaxed form and covered his chest with their perfectly polished hands, petitioning God in song to touch their pastor.

Mark relaxed. They would pray and sing, but not rebuke demons from him. He made sure of this by telling them God used only his wife to pray for him in the area of deliverance. He refused to give in to the ugly manifestations. Besides, his knowledge of scripture kept him free. He may have weaknesses, but not demons. No siree. He was the pastor. A man of his position could not have demons.

Mark woke an hour later and sat up sighing, "Ah, how glowious. Thank you, Jesus, thank you, Jesus!" He smiled and spoke to the group. "Jesus gave me a vision."

The women clapped their hands with excitement. "Thank you, Lord!" they cried out together.

"I am overwhelmed at what He did!" The pastor shook his head in amazement. "He placed a medal of honor on my shoulder. He told me I was going to hold a gweat pwophetic ministwy, one that will be known acwoss the world."

"Oh, God has a mighty plan for you!" one of the women shouted. She closed her eyes and moved her hands in a circular motion in front of Mark's face. "As we were praying, I saw Jesus walk you to the front of the earth. You stood before kings and presidents. Than Jesus disappeared inside of you and everyone worshipped God!"

"Oh, praise you, Lord, for Grace Church, for Your truths, for our loving pastor," another woman said. "I saw our church turn into a building made of glass, and we were transparent, and the world was watching Jesus' reflection from our windows."

Everyone rejoiced until Mark abruptly stopped the session. "Excuse me, ladies, time has run out. I have another appointment." He peered at Callie. She took his cue and walked to the bathroom.

Mark led the women to the front door. "Ladies, thank you for coming." He put his hand on Laurina's arm. "Thank you so much for this, Lauwina. I appweciate your willingness to pway with me."

"God bless, Mark." She hugged him.

"Will you be here next week, Lauwina?" He patted her back. "Bwing Penny of course."

"Sure." She and Penny left with the group and Mark shut the door.

He turned around. Callie was leaning against the wall, facing him. How he wished that it was Laurina looking back at him.

"Donna won't be home for dinner," Mark said coyly. "Want to spend some time ministewing to your pastor?"

She was tired and wary of what he wanted—and still confused about what happened in his office. "Petey is expecting me home early tonight."

Mark caught her reluctance and walked up to her. Lifting her chin lightly with one finger he said, "Callie, I hope you had the same expewience I had duwing our last meeting. I told Donna about it, and that night we had the closest, most intimate sexual encounter we have ever had. It was so holy."

"You did? Donna knows?"

"Yes." He dropped his hand. "Oh Callie, I wowwied that you might have misunderstood what happened between us. I was completely caught away in the spiwit, and you had become my wife, you see, and so I hoped that what or how I responded did not offend you."

Callie sighed. "Oh, I am so glad. I was a bit nervous about it all. But, now that Donna is really part of this, I feel good about how God is freeing you and her."

"Can you stay, Callie?"

"I guess."

"Are you hungwy?" he asked.

"No. Not at all."

"Let's go talk in my study."

Callie sat on the leather couch across from Mark's huge desk. He joined her and took both her hands in his.

"Would you feel better if we told Petey about all this?"

"Oh, oh...uh...maybe not yet. I am not sure my husband would understand this depth of God's spirit."

"Maybe you're right, Callie. He is not really in the same spiwitual place as you are. We will pway about that. Okay?"

"Okay."

The corners of Mark's mouth tipped up. "Should we see what God will do today? Do you want to go deeper in Him?"

She jiggled her head, a little nervously.

"I might touch you again. Will this be okay?"

Callie didn't say anything. Instead she reached back and unhooked her bra.

Mark smiled and went over to his desk and flipped on the cassette player. The music filled the small room with a soothing melody.

Callie started praying and Mark came up beside her and started *singing in the spirit*. He didn't touch her for a few minutes, allowing the music to do its magic. Than he moved closer and began praising Jesus out loud and rubbing her arms, up and down. Callie felt strange again, but this time she blocked it out and let herself respond to the music and Mark's touches.

"You're a tweasure fwom God."

His hands groveled underneath her blouse as he lowered her down, panting.

"No, Mark, no, I am not sure…" She gasped and tried to get up.

"Yes, yes. Look to Jesus. Don't stop the spiwit, Honey." He pinned her with his arms.

She is running with Jesus through flowery fields of yellow and white daisies, His hand is in hers and they are laughing. They lie down on the flowers and sing.

The cool air starts to feel warm…warmer…hot…hotter. The blue sky is closing in on her. Closer, and closer, penetrating blue, probing, piercing into her face…

"Oh, baby, baby…gweat stuff."

oc*CULT*

CHAPTER NINE

"**W**hy did your prayer meeting last so long?" Petey prodded his wife as she sat at her makeup dresser that evening. He still didn't like the blonde wig cascading down Callie's back, but he couldn't help but admire her for going after changes that made her feel good about herself. He plomped down on the bed and watched her clean her eyes. She wouldn't look at him.

"God was moving." Callie replied. She eased the hairpiece off her head and placed it on the dummy. Her own bland brown hair was locked up in bobby pins.

"I don't like the fact you're spending so much time away from home. I'm missing you."

"Petey, stop being selfish."

"Okay," he said. He rose off the bed, put his arms around her shoulders and kissed her cheek.

"I'm tired."

Petey dropped his hands. "You're always too tired for me, Callie." He hated being jealous, but it seemed like the pastor spent more time with his wife than he did. "I feel like the only reason the pastor gave me this job at the church is to pacify me somehow."

He went into the bathroom to brush his teeth and returned to find Callie in bed. He felt like a heel. Why was he overreacting? Pastor Mark did need lots of prayer; he had a tremendous responsibility, and Callie was used in the area of prayer. He had to learn to release her to God and not be so angry. Grace Church was his home and he loved what God was doing in their lives.

He crawled in beside her. "Hey, Cal, I'm sorry. You're right. I'm too jealous. Forgive me?"

"Of course, silly." She didn't turn over.

He tried to snuggle with her but she was like stone.

Two weeks later, on a Saturday evening, Donna swung the door open wide with a delightful whoop as her two grandsons threw their arms around her. "Hello, boys." She gave her daughter a kiss and patted Avery on the back. "Come on in. Dinner is almost ready."

Gayle and Avery followed their kids into the living room and Donna, wearing slippers, pitter-pattered into the kitchen to prepare the meal.

"What's for dinner, Mom?" Gayle yelled as she removed the boys' jackets.

"Roast, dear," Donna called back.

"Hey bunnies, hug your gwandpa," Mark shouted as he entered the room.

Both boys giggled and ran to Mark. He squeezed them and gave them both some candy.

"Go play, boys," Gayle said. She wished her father would take more interest in his grandchildren, but he never was one to spend much time with youngsters. Her children sensed this, the same as she had growing up. As a child she could seldom get her father to leave his study and play with her. He was always reading in the Bible or doing things at the church or gone off on some ministry. But, boy, when he met Avery, it was as though *he* was marrying him. He wouldn't stop talking about his old college buddy's fantastic son, and pushed and pushed her to meet him. She finally did, only because of his insistence. At first she didn't like that Avery was so skinny or that he piled so much goop on his hair. It was his cocky self-assurance that did finally grab her attention, and he was a likable sort around people. Oh, she loved Avery, but sometimes she wondered if she married him more to please her father than herself. Soon after the wedding Mark ordained his son-in-law as minister and full-time Bible college teacher.

"You guys going to Hawaii next week?" Avery asked Mark. He watched his reflection sit down on the sofa.

"Yes, for ten days. We need a bweak. Avewy, I would like you to lead the services while we're gone. Can you do this?"

"Will do."

"How's the classroom this year, son?" Mark asked.

It was a rare moment when Mark called him son.

"Going well. This group seems really motivated."

Gayle joined her husband on the couch while Donna watched her family from the kitchen. She carefully arranged silk flowers into a thin vase and placed the arrangement on the dining table.

"Come eat," she called.

The display of roast beef, baby potatoes and glazed carrots looked and smelled appetizing. As usual, Donna put out a beautiful spread.

"This looks great, Mom," Gayle said.

She had learned a long time ago to stay out of the kitchen when her mother was cooking. Mother never wanted to share the glory for her fabulous cooking or its presentation to the guests. She had to have things perfect, and simply did not carry the patience for interfering hands. Besides, her mother's tastes all around were quite exotic compared to her own. Like the way she dressed. Donna had a beautiful figure—thanks to the breast implants—and she dressed to the hilt to show it off. It was almost as if her dress was a purposeful attack to wrestle against her shyness; but that contrite demeanor of hers was too much a part of her. Besides, that was why everyone adored her.

The family sat down to eat. Gayle wished her mother would not use the expensive plates; the boys, expected to act like angels, could shatter one. If they did, they would never hear the end of it.

"You outdid yourself, Donna," Mark said heartily.

She smiled and passed the bread.

"Callie Gᴡaves called me last night. Seems the intercessor's retᴡeat expeᴡienced a rather exciting visitation from God." Mark took the bread and passed the plate to Avery.

"What happened?" Gayle asked, digging the spoon into the carrots.

"I believe God is directing us into another new *move* of His Spirit," Donna chimed with excitement. She patted at her artificial tresses and then folded the silk napkin across her lap.

"What happened?" Gayle asked again.

"As they were *singing in the spirit*, God's power fell and everyone began to dance. Callie told Mark the group danced for hours."

"Wow, this I got to see," Avery remarked as he ate.

"Are they going to share it tomorrow morning, Dad?" Gayle had put a small portion of food on her plate and hoped her dad wouldn't notice.

"Yes, if God diᴡects it so." Mark reached for the bread and handed it to Gayle. "You're not eating enough. Have some bᴡead."

The next morning members walked into the service stunned to see the intercessory group dancing below the platform, spinning and twirling to the joyful music being played by the pianist. The new expression of worship was a pleasant sight, a grand relief from the exhausting battles with demonic spirits. When the lights flashed on and off, the choir took to the platform and the dancers remained, flapping their arms and skipping everywhere like a group of first-time dancers stealing the floor inside a Fred Astaire dance studio.

Rick, Penny, Laurina and Cody sat together, fascinated by the fun.

"I hope they don't expect me to get down there and do that," Rick said, pulling Penny close.

Penny thought it was a welcome sight after the exhausting *move* of demonic deliverances. "I think this is beautiful," she said, leaning against her husband.

"Me too," Laurina added, taking Cody's hand. "Jesus is so good. What a special way to adore Him. You know, King David danced before the Lord in the Old Testament and so did Moses' sister Miriam after they crossed the Red Sea."

Penny wished she were down there dancing too, but she doubted she would ever have the nerve to do so. Though she loved to dance in her *old* life, it was only because alcohol had given her that boldness. Only Jesus could give her that freedom now.

"Hey, look!" Laurina exclaimed. "Petey and Callie are dancing. I forgot they went to the retreat."

Callie, her cheeks flushed from the exercise, had one hand in Petey's and another waving in the air above her head. Her expression was pure joy. Petey looked clumsy, but his face was like a Cheshire cat.

Mark reached the pulpit and raised his arms to quiet the music. The dancers and singers reluctantly returned to their pews.

"Pwaise God." Mark's enthusiasm tumbled off his tongue. "Another *fwesh new wave* of God's Spiwit is being poured out on this church. We have been faithful and Jesus is blessing us. We are going deeper, Church. Enter into His love. Taste His glowy!"

Christmas was a festive time for the churchites, despite the fact Pastor Mark did not decorate the sanctuary. He encouraged the holiday as a time for members to share the good news of the Gospel.

"Getting them saved is not enough," the pastor would exhort to the adoring multitude. "Getting them twained as soldiers is vital. Gwace Church has twuths no other church possesses. Invite those new converts to your church so that they can gwow and expewience the Spiwit of God."

The dancing had brought a new freedom into the assembly, and slowly people gave in to the physical display of worship. *Dancing in the spirit* overshadowed the demonic deliverances, and in time people decided to dance instead of fight demons. It had taken only a few days for Penny, Laurina, Marcy, and Owen to join Callie in the dance. Marilyn, Jason, Rick, and Cody held out for one month, and then jumped in with all the rest. The contagious new *move of God* broke down barriers, unifying the entire body. Everyone, both male and female, now arrived at church service carrying dancing slippers as well as Bibles. People were more open and giving, and the joy spread out into the community. The counseling office lost business as troubled marriages and other problems seemed to disappear. Rick and Penny stopped fighting, Marcy and Owen seemed to unite; and Callie was having so much fun she buried the guilt she often felt after she left Mark's office.

Dancing was her escape and she lost ten pounds in the process. On top of that, she and Petey were getting along superbly.

So many people were dancing, almost the whole church, that Mark ordered a new sound system installed so that live or taped music could be pumped into the main sanctuary, the foyer, or upstairs into the classrooms to accommodate the overflow of people. After services, dancers continued to dance for hours longer if they desired to.

Two days before Christmas the pastor's wife took the pulpit and bounced up and down in her glittery slippers. She wore a shiny green taffeta dress with wide ruffles. A large matching bow ornamented her blonde wig. "Oh, praise His name," she wailed joyfully into the microphone. "Praise Him for everything!"

The assembly responded with enthusiastic Amens.

"I must tell you," she huffed back at them, tuckered out from the dancing, "what Jesus does always surprises me. He is not a God of format. He loves to reveal Himself in new ways!" She began hopping up and down with small jumps. Her full breasts were dancing as well. "Oh, yes...oh, yes...thank You, Jesus! Praise You, Jesus." She raised her arms high above her head and closed her eyes as she acknowledged God. "Hallelujah!" she shouted over and over.

The excited congregation joined her. "Hallelujah! We love You, Jesus." A sea of arms waved at her.

Donna shouted, "I want you to know the counseling office is empty. People are getting free. We don't have to counsel when the mighty counselor Himself is doing it for us. The dancing is setting people free! Enter in with your whole heart and allow God to set you free! Surrender your entire being to Him. Will you do this, church?"

"Yes, we will, we will," they chanted back at her.

"What do you think of the dancing?" Marcy asked Penny a few months later in early March over lunch.

Marcy's festive kitchen had an all-year-round spring feeling with its floral wallpaper, brightly colored stenciled cabinets, and flowery pots that filled the bay window.

"I love it! It's ushered me closer to God than I ever thought possible." Penny took a forkful of chicken fettuccini and glanced out the bay window. The wet rain-blown bushes rattling against the glass couldn't steal the sunny feeling inside.

Marcy's two-year-old son, seated in a highchair beside them, started throwing Cheerios. Marcy grabbed his hand.

"I can't believe how big Willy is getting. He looks like you, Marcy."

Marcy reached for the garlic rolls and gave one to her son. She passed the basket to Penny. "Penny," she asked, taking on a serious frown, "would you pray for me this week? Get some others together? I could use some deliverances."

Marcy longed to confide everything about Owen and how miserable she was. It was hard faking her life. Though the dancing had brought her and Owen to an even plateau for a couple months, Owen went right back to his old tricks. She had found him at that same bar on Second Avenue again. His reply was another outbreak of false tears. She dreaded the day their son would find out about his father's *real* life. But even worse, she worried that her son would become like him. The Bible talked about generational curses handed down through the family line, and she had ulcers worrying about that possibility. She wanted to talk to Owen's mom, but she couldn't. His Mom was not a Christian and she would be devastated. She was so angry with Owen lately, especially because she believed his sole reason for marrying her had been to cover his own gay hide. He had not even considered what it would do to her.

"How about during our prayer meeting?" Penny asked.

"No, I'd rather just a couple of women pray."

"Okay, I'll call Laurina and Marilyn." Penny tickled Willy. "You know, Marcy, I'm thankful you invited me to join your prayer meeting. The last couple years have been wonderful. The Spirit of the Lord meets our group in such sweet ways. You know, I tried for years to join two other intercessory prayer groups, but the leaders kept saying no. You said yes. And now look, I'm praying for the pastor."

Marcy tapped Penny's hand. "God knows where you belong."

"Thanks for having me over. The lunch was great. You're such a beautiful example for me, Marcy. You're a wonderful wife, loving mother, and you always think of others before yourself. You have been a wonderful friend to me."

The front door slammed and Owen rushed into the kitchen with an apologetic smile on his face.

"Sorry to disturb you ladies. I forgot my client's paperwork in the den." He bent down and planted a kiss on Marcy's head. "Hi, Willy!" He kissed his son's messy cheek before running into the other room. In a moment he returned and said, "I'm in a hurry. I'll see you tonight, Marcy. Bye, Pen." He rushed back out the front door.

"What a great guy Owen is," Penny said.

"Yeah, the best," Marcy said, being careful not to let the pain travel from her heart into her eyes.

The phone rang in Petey's office.

"Petey speaking."

"Hello, Petey. This is Mark. Do you have a minute to spare?"

"Yes, of course."

"Can you come by my office now?"

"Sure, Pastor, I'll be there in five minutes."

Petey arrived and stood before Mark, a tad apprehensive.

"Petey, sit down." Mark directed him to sit in the chair beside his desk.

Petey sat down, stretching his long legs out in front of him. When he realized he might look too indolent, he drew his legs back up to the chair.

"Callie tells me you're stwuggling with the time she spends ministewing to me. Is this twue?" Mark picked up his pen to occupy his bored hands. His staunch blue eyes didn't back down.

"Well...yeah. I seldom see her. She spends a lot of time away from home."

"Petey, God has called Callie into a special ministwy of intercession for me. I can put a handle on this, but I feel I'll be stifling the work God is doing in me thwough her. She is your wife and I want to honor that position. It would be hard to replace her. And I don't know what kind of effect this will have on Callie. She twuly has the heart of God for me."

"No, Pastor, my heart is not to stop Callie from ministering to you or anyone." Petey felt foolish. How could he put his needs before his own pastor? "I'll work on my insecurities. Don't worry about me." Petey stood, pushed at his glasses, and leaned over Mark's desk with an outstretched hand. "I am behind this church, Pastor, and you have my support."

Mark returned the shake. "God bless you, bwother. God will reward you.

CHAPTER TEN

The Friday evening service began with dancers twirling in and around each other; some danced in groups; the majority danced alone with arms up-stretched in praises to God. Mark spied Laurina dancing among a small group near the front of the church. He joined them and, to his satisfaction, she responded, laughing and praising God, spinning her pretty form in delicate circles around him and the others. Merriment filled the group as they swirled in one circle praising their Lord.

Twenty minutes later, Mark forced himself to stop. He hurried to his pastoral pew and retrieved his suit coat, than climbed the platform and signaled the singers to take their seats.

"My flock, good evening," Pastor Mark chirped. He moved his arms around before resting them back down on the podium. "What a gweat way to get in shape," he chuckled.

The assembly laughed too.

"I've been noticing how many of you are gifted in the dance; it's a beautiful sight to watch you soar like swans before our Lord. I want this church to maintain a pure level of holiness and I want worship to be a pleasant sight for visitors."

Mark strutted, puffing out his chest, and said, "What I want to do is form thwee categowies for dancers. I will call these Gwoup A, gwoup B, and gwoup C. Over the next two weeks, my wife and I are going to pick out the best dancers and categowize them into one of these thwee gwoups. Gwoup A will be the most gifted dancers, and so on down the line. We'll contact the members we choose. Not evewyone will be part of these thwee gwoups. Evewyone is welcome to dance down fwont of course, unless I request, by micwophone, for gwoup A, B, or C to be down here. Then only those designated dancers will have the fwont. The rest will have to move to the aisles, the foyer, or take their seats."

A couple babies in the audience wailed.

"Mothers, please use the sound-pwoof nursewy room; that is what it's there for," Mark ordered.

He continued, "I want to talk about tithing for a minute. Giving has been down this month, and I am going to start making the non-tithers sit in the back pews if they don't start giving pwoperly. I will publicly make it known who you are so that the people who do give are not over-burdened by you slothful ones."

Amens arose from the pews. Some lowered their heads.

Mark finished and handed the pulpit over to church members.

Joe Fellows walked up. His thin lips tensed as he spoke yet his big eyes wore compassion. "Jesus loves us and wants the best for our lives," the elder said, "but we must remember Him. Last night in prayer I had a vision, and in this vision I saw our church dancing and spinning. Jesus stood in the center of the dancers, but no one noticed Him. We were too busy with the dance and we forgot why we were dancing. Jesus just stood there, ignored, weeping. Please, church, let's not forget the reason we dance. Let's keep our eyes fastened on Jesus. I've noticed prayer has decreased greatly since the dancing. We must not forget how important prayer is."

Donna rushed upto the platform next. "Last night I also had a vision. I saw our church split. Half of you filed out the side door while the other half remained." Tears streamed down her face. "Church, Satan wants to destroy us. Joe is right, we must maintain unity in prayer and continue to submit to this church government. Let's not allow the devil to break in two the beautiful unity we have here as a body!"

The service ended with Christians filing down the aisles towards the altar to pray.

The three-day elders' retreat took place at Camp Finland, a large private camp nestled in the wooded mountains west of Portland.

On the first day during breakfast, Laurina asked, "Penny, who are you praying for this morning?"

The large log-cabin cafeteria was filled with numerous wooden picnic-style tables where elders and invited intercessors mingled together, eating pancakes and scrambled eggs.

"Avery and Gayle. How about you?" Penny replied.

"Pastor Mark, of course; he's requested me."

Penny nodded and buttered her pancakes.

"I don't know how this retreat could be more wonderful than the last one!" Laurina exclaimed.

Across the room Callie sat on a bench between Petey and Pastor Mark. Donna, perched on Mark's opposite side, smiled as sweet as sugar as she offered a basket of muffins to Avery and Gayle, who were across from her.

Penny noticed that Donna seldom talked to Callie, even though Callie was always around their clique. She bent close to Laurina. "Laurina, do you think it bothers Donna that Callie and Mark are so close now?"

"Yes."

"Really? Callie wouldn't do anything to undermine Donna."

"Penny, Donna is the most submissive woman I have ever known. She trusts her husband and stands behind him. But, she is human, just like you and me. Wouldn't it bother you a little bit?"

"Yeah. Rick says that it's bothering Petey a lot. I guess the pastor talked to him about it. But Petey is still jealous."

"God will work it all out. We all need to keep praying for Mark. We all have to make sacrifices for him." Laurina looked down and changed the subject.

After a few more minutes of conversation, Penny noticed that Ted, seated beside Betty, kept stealing glances their way.

"Maybe you and Betty ought to get prayer," Penny stated.

Laurina shot her the look of a dagger.

After breakfast the intercessors and elders filed into the main hall. Lights were lowered and a crackling fire glowed in the stone fireplace. Over the mantle an old stuffed moose head with drooping antlers kept watch over the room.

Penny and two female intercessors prayed for Avery and Gayle, on a couch near the wall, while Laurina and Callie prayed for Mark, on the floor near the fireplace.

Mark, his hands folded over his abdomen, was cozily stretched out over a thick layer of blankets. He admired Laurina's natural beauty as she leaned over him; she needed no wigs or implants. He smiled. She was the first woman he would not want to change. He closed his eyes and switched his thoughts back to spiritual matters.

After lunch the afternoon meeting resumed with dancing and *singing in the spirit*. Feet frolicked gaily unto the Lord as the women's skirts and hair flew through the air in sync to the music. The atmosphere became doused with the supernatural presence of joy. The men followed the women around the room, and soon it became one big circle, with everyone weaving and swaying, shouting praises to God.

Mark leaped over to Laurina's swaying form. She opened her eyes and smiled at him, and kept spinning as Mark pranced around her.

As the jolly circle began to split, Callie looked up and saw Ted dancing around her. He looked awkward, but happy. As she swirled with him, a warm feeling moved up inside her and she moved closer. The elder's eyes flew open, triggering a lightening bolt like energy between their eyes. The ethereal power surge seemed to fuse their spirits as the invisible beam ricocheted back and forth between them. They couldn't look away, nor stop the power. Neither did they want to. They were so smitten by the experience that they had no idea that they had moved in closer and were gawking at each other like two love-struck teenagers.

Callie was overcome by the spiritual journey, and when Ted took her hand, she was met with waves of glorious bliss. The potent love-spell ousted her from reality and into a spiritual sphere she had never known. Ted got it too. It ministered up and down his body and he felt like he was flying. Callie, a woman he did not find attractive, became the most beautiful woman he had ever seen. He wanted to burst from the sheer joy of it all. They were enslaved by the love bond— spirit-merged. The passion soaring through their members scared them—but they did not stop.

Ted's wife ran up to Donna and grabbed her arm. "Donna, what's going on? Why is Ted doing that with Callie?"

"Betty, calm down." The pastor's wife looked over and winced at the romantic exhibition going on in the corner. "They seem to be in a spiritual trance of some sort."

Other members were noticing and stopped to watch the progression of what was quite obviously *taboo* for Grace Church.

"Stay here and let me deal with this," Donna said, hushing Betty with a jerk to her forearm.

Donna moved between the couple and grasped their shoulders with her hands. "Excuse me," she ordered in a whisper, "Ted, Callie! Time out...now!"

The "connected" pair did not want to stop.

"Let's stop this!" Donna demanded. She pushed at the two dancers. Callie obeyed Donna, but it took every ounce of emotional and physical strength to fight the *spell* still binding her heart captive to Ted.

Donna jiggled Ted's arm and clutched Callie's hesitant hand, then pulled them off the floor and led them into the small room near the fireplace.

"What's happening between you?" Donna asked the dazed *lovers*.

Callie fell back against the wall, clutching her stomach with laughter. "I don't know, Donna. God is all over me. I have never felt this kind of love!"

Ted looked dazed.

"Ted, talk to me. I realize something's happening here; help me to understand." Donna tapped at his cheeks.

"Yes, yes, Donna." He could not stop laughing either. His brown eyes moved like lazy slugs. "I feel light, deliriously happy. God's glory is all over me and I feel so much love for Callie. It's beautiful, more beautiful than any earthly love I have ever experienced. This is God!" His eyes flew to Callie. "I see...I see Jesus in her."

Donna could not deny the captivating "zing" hovering between the couple, yet she knew she had to stop it.

"Ted, your wife needs you now. No matter what you're experiencing with Callie, you must put your wife first. Do you understand?" Donna shook his shoulders. "Go get some water. Callie, go the opposite way and get some fresh air. This experience is too new. Let's give God a chance to reveal Himself a bit more regarding what just happened. Okay?"

Callie and Ted reluctantly agreed.

During the strange encounter, Pastor Mark had been lost in dance with a small group on the other side of the room and missed what had transpired between his senior elder and sidekick intercessor. At lunch he was confused at Callie's lack of attention. She seemed to be acting awfully giddy and woozy, and completely uninterested in him. He did notice that she could not keep her eyes off Ted. And oddly enough, Ted was acting just as strangely. Something must have happened.

"Donna," he leaned over to his wife, "Betty looks upset. What is going on? And why is Ted ogling Callie that way?"

"Let's go to the cabin. We need to talk."

Mark wiped his mouth and excused himself from the table. He took his wife by the elbow, and together they left the cafeteria and headed for their lodging.

"Mark, something strange is happening," Donna said. The breezy day whooshed tree branches together as they tracked through the woods.

"What are you talking about?"

"Today, during worship in the dance, Ted and Callie experienced a strange *connection* through the eyes. They were dancing slow and gazing into each other's eyes...very intimately."

They reached the cabin and went in.

"What do you mean?" Mark asked angrily. "Callie and Ted did what?"

Donna sat on the bed and removed her shoes and massaged her feet.

"They seem to be experiencing God's love through their eyes. At least that is what they told me. Now you know Ted and Callie are complete opposites, so something like this has to be supernatural."

The pastor sat beside her. "Donna, we can't allow this to happen again. Callie and Ted are ma*ww*ied to other people. How do you justify something like this? I don't want my church going off the deep end into something that will cause us to be the talk of the town."

"Mark, I felt the energy. The spiritual charisma bouncing between them was like a thunderstorm."

"Keep Callie and Ted apart. Period."

"Half the members saw it."

"I will address it only if I have to."

"Callie, what happened this afternoon?" Petey asked, leaning over his wife's form stretched out across the bed. "You're a million miles away."

"Something totally amazing happened to me today, Petey. I can't even put it into words. God's Spirit fell on Ted and me while we danced."

"What do you mean?" Petey massaged her back.

"I don't quite know. It is as though the Lord connected our spirits together. I feel so much love for Ted. I can't stop thinking about him. It sounds weird, but I know this love is from God!" Callie laughed into the down pillow like a schoolgirl in love.

A ping hit Petey's insides. "What do you mean?"

"Did you see us dancing?"

"No, why! Was it different?"

"It was. I was ushered into God's holy love through looking into Ted's eyes. How can I explain this? It's beyond description. All I know is that I felt like I was one with his spirit. I know it sounds weird..."

"Yeah, real weird. But things of God aren't always explainable, are they?" He tried not to let his insecurities surface. "Just don't forget me, okay?" His eyes became roasted coals and he licked her shoulder. "How about loving your own man for a minute?"

Callie stuffed her face back in the pillow and groaned. "Petey, the next session starts in ten minutes. I don't want to miss anything."

"As usual." He flew to his feet. "I'll see you over there!" He slammed the door on his way out.

She rushed into the bathroom and brushed her teeth, then pulled the curly wig back over her head. A double knock rapped against the door.

"One minute," she hollered. She hurriedly lined her mouth with lipstick, than opened the door.

"Mark?"

The pastor stood there sheepishly.

"Callie, do you have a minute?" He entered the cabin.

"Petey just left."

"I know; I saw him go. Are you okay?" Mark drew her hand to his chest.

Callie pulled it back.

A ping hit at Mark as well. He tried not to let it show. "Honey, what happened between you and Ted?"

"Oh, Mark, I don't even know. I've never tasted anything as powerful as this in the spiritual realm. I think Jesus has merged Ted's spirit with mine."

Mark stewed. "Callie, but God has put you with my spiwit and I am not sure God is calling you to minister to Ted now."

"No, Mark. It is not like that. I feel we are worshipping God as one."

"I have to ask you not to dance with him again. I cannot condone such actions between two mawwied people. We have to maintain a Godly standard in our assembly, do you understand, Callie?"

"I know, Mark, but God's all over me today. I need to allow His Spirit to move through me. In the long run you'll reap the benefits from my freedom in God."

"Yes, yes, of course, you're right, my child. Maybe God is moving you into a new place. Actually, I'm starting to feel my spiwit drawn to Laurina now. God has been restorwing our relationship. Maybe I should ask her to pway for me if you are too busy." Mark played to her insecurities.

Though Callie felt an overwhelming desire for Ted, she did not want to lose her position as Mark's top intercessor. She resigned herself and snuggled into his chest, caressing his aging neck. "Don't be silly, Pastor. I am not going away from you. Laurina can't replace me. You'll always be my first priority."

As the meeting progressed, Mark did not join in with the dancers. Worried that other couples might imitate Callie and Ted, he wanted to be alert to stop the session if need be. He sat on the couch and watched everyone *move into the spirit*.

Donna, in her shiny slippers, arched to the left and to the right like a ballerina as she abandoned herself to the music.

Kurt Hunter, Ted's younger brother, pirouetted in front of her and knocked her elbow. His eyes flew open with apology, but instead he found himself swallowed up by the force of her glare. Like a current of electricity, something began charging between them, back and forth, through the eyes. They slowed their movements and allowed the current to solder them together.

Donna tried to fight the strange happening, but she fell hostage to the grandiose feelings and welcomed the spiritual ardor with open arms.

Other dancers began *connecting*, including Penny Duncan and Cody Addison. As the music flowed, Penny opened her eyes and met Cody's penetrating response. The power zapped them, and they danced slowly and at arm's length. But the brazen look in their eyes made the onlookers blush.

Ted and Callie, who had been staring at each other from across the room with *lovesick* eyes, watched the magic take over, then flew onto the dance floor together.

Betty and Laurina were livid. Watching their husbands slink around another married woman, like cats in heat, was too much.

Mark caught it all and bolted out of his seat. He flipped the light switch on and off, hollering loudly, "Excuse me, eldership, intercessors, your pastor needs your attention."

Everyone stopped, dazed by the spirit moving them and unhappy that they had to *come back down to earth*.

"I must have your complete attention," Mark commanded. He positioned himself against the wall. "I'm aware of a stwange occuwwence going on between some of you in the dance. Dancing in such a way with someone else's mate is dangerwous and impwoper. It must stop now. I am your pastor and until I understand what is happening, I want eve*w*yone to stop dancing and p*w*ay."

Donna tiptoed up to Mark, still under the spell of love that had barraged her entire soul and spirit. She whispered in his ear. They spoke back and forth a few minutes before Mark turned back to the group.

"My wife insists this is from the Lord. I am not so sure. But, she ag*w*ees that we should spend the rest of this session in p*w*ayer to see God's heart on the matter."

The hesitation of the dancers irked Mark, but they relented to his request.

Mark pulled Donna into the small room near the fireplace and looked at her pleadingly.

"Donna, explain what you are feeling."

She giggled and said, "Mark, I don't know how to describe this. But I can assure you this kind of love is definitely from God! I believe the Lord is allowing us to experience His love through one another in a whole new way. This could be how He plans on bringing a unity within the church worldwide."

Mark had never seen his wife glow like this. It made him uncomfortable.

"I t*w*ust your judgments dear," Mark said. "But before I let this go, I want to p*w*ay and seek the Lord."

"Yes, dear, of course."

Penny returned home Friday morning feeling that she had been pierced by Cupid's biggest arrow. Her entire body reeled under the enchantment, and she found herself constantly ushered into a heavenly realm, quite unable to function on life's everyday mundane matters. The experience was beyond delightful. Yet she was confused because she was *in love* with her best friend's husband. The once sallow man now had become the most handsome and glorious man, and she could not stop thinking about him. Penny plumped down on the couch. What was she going to do? She felt as though she lost all her wifely feelings toward Rick. This worried her. And Laurina. She had to think of Laurina. But, at the same time, all she could think of was being with Cody and soaring into those heavenly places when they were together. It was phenomenal what took place in the spiritual realm. She hoped God would reveal what this all meant because she could not even eat. She had lost all desire for the things she normally liked to do. She just wanted to *connect*.

"Penny, what's up?" Rick asked, coming into the living room and catching her staring off into space. "You're a million miles away. Boy, that retreat must've been something."

"Oh Rick! I don't even know how to explain to you what happened. I think I'll just wait and let Pastor Mark do that tonight at service."

"Whatever." He longed to make love to his wife, but he could tell she was not there.

The phone rang and Rick answered. "Yeah, hi Cody, uh-huh, yeah…okay, just a minute." Rick covered the phone and said, "It's Cody, he wants to talk to you."

Penny's heart raced. She took the phone. "Hello?"

"Penny, how are you doing?" A nervous Cody asked.

"Fine, and you?" Penny started laughing.

Rick noticed and sat beside her.

"Penny," Cody urged, "I need to see you. I feel all this love for you. I really don't know what to do with it! How about meeting me before service tonight. Say, an hour before service in the front pew?"

"Cody, I need to see you too; I'll be there." Penny hung up the phone and swooned. She sank back into the sofa, starry-eyed and giggly.

"What's that all about?" Rick stuck his thumbs into his pant's pockets and waited for her answer. "Excuse me, Penny, am I missing something here?"

"Honey, something happened in the dance. Cody and I had this experience that seemed to merge our spirits together somehow."

"What?"

"I know Rick, I can't help what happened. This is the most holiest and glorious experience ever."

"So now I need to be jealous of Cody?"

The phone rang and again Rick answered. "It's Laurina." He balanced the receiver in his hand.

Penny took it. She took a breath than said, "Laurina, are you okay with all of this?"

"Cody told me he telephoned. To be honest, I'm feeling funny about the whole thing. I guess it's because I can't relate to what you guys are experiencing."

"I know. If you're uncomfortable with me meeting Cody, I won't. You know I love you Laurina and..."

"No, no, Penny, go ahead, meet with Cody. You both are experiencing something supernatural. See it through. I'm fine. Really. I trust you completely. I talked to Donna and she explained what happened to her. It really sounds amazing. I'll let you know if I get too jealous."

That night Penny waited anxiously in the pew for Cody. She took great care to look extra pretty. She had curled her long hair and clipped it back with a red bow to match her favorite red dress. She wrung her hands in her lap, waiting.

How odd she felt, responding like a young girl with a first time crush on a boy.

Whispers rose and Penny glanced over her shoulder. Donna and her new *connection,* Kurt, were seated a few rows back staring at each other like infatuated adolescents.

Cody caught her off guard. "Hey," he said, pinching her arm.

Startled, she blushed. He sat beside her reeking of cologne and breath mints.

"Hi Cody."

Their eyes met and *joined*. Awkward and self-conscious from the fierce sensations arousing them, they didn't quite know what to say.

"Maybe we should dance," Penny said softly.

"I don't think the Pastor wants us to yet." Cody reddened when he felt his body respond. He tore his eyes away and looked down.

"Something wrong?" Penny asked.

"I am…uh….not used to this kind of…I should go find my wife."

He kept his gaze averted, hoping his reaction would stop. It didn't.

"I'll talk to you later." He left the pew in a hurry.

Penny, stunned and confused, watched him go. She felt as though her heart was ripping in two.

"You all right, Hon?" Rick asked, coming up beside her. He saw her pain and wrapped his arms around her.

She began to cry. "He left me…I need him."

A disturbing pang of emotions grated at him. He hoped the pastor would shine some light on what was happening to his wife because he didn't like it. He was relieved when service started.

"Good morning, church," Pastor Mark said cheerily. He looked illustrious in a new suit and polished black shoes. His hair was swept up higher than usual.

The crowd cheered.

"God met us at the retreat this week! Pwaise God! Something very unique happened and I need to talk about this because some of you might be noticing some stwange new *unions* happening between certain members in this body. I want my *sweet* wife to come up here. She can explain this better than me. Donna?"

Donna hurried up beside him. Mark stayed put. "Good morning," she said, her husky voice full of excitement. "God is so good. The last three days were wonderful! God's holy, pure love has visited our assembly!" She began to laugh. "What He is doing is unique and life-changing. He is allowing us all to feel the depth of His love in a brand new way, by using the dance as a vehicle in which to experience the fullness of His love!"

The audience was captivated by the news.

"God's visitation might scare some of you, because to the natural eye it appears unusual, different, possibly even offensive. But I can assure you, what He's doing will benefit this body of believers and bring us together into one glorious union. We are becoming one with the Son of Man!"

She pulled in closer to the microphone. "Ted Hunter and Callie Graves were the first to experience this God-sent phenomenon. God's love united them through the eyes as they danced. At first I was shocked to see them look so intimate with one another, but as I watched these two people, people who never really noticed one another before, I knew that what was binding them together in the spirit was something supernatural."

Donna turned and swayed a little for full effect before exclaiming, "And than, it happened to me! Kurt Hunter and I have become so one in the spirit that I feel drenched with God's love for him!" She giggled. "We must all surrender to what God is doing!"

As Donna walked down to her seat, she locked gazes with Kurt. They both smiled widely.

Mark again took his place. "Seeing your mate dancing with someone of the same sex is not the pwoblem; seeing your mate dance with a person of the opposite sex will be difficult."

A stir charged through the congregation. Mark held out his hands, shooing them to be still. "After much pwayer, I feel I must allow God to move, and twust Him to bwing it all together for His glowy. I believe this is the way He plans on uniting His church. I need your submission here, people. Will you give God the go ahead to restore your lives? Can you twust you spouse so that Satan cannot destwoy God's plan? I will set guidelines to help us all move forward, of course."

In the elder's section Ted kept stealing glances at Callie across the aisle near Donna. When she smiled back at him, Betty cast her a dirty look.

The assembly, having not yet witnessed the new connection dancing, sat patiently waiting for further explanation of what they should expect to see or do.

Mark continued on the subject. "After service I'm going to allow God to have His way. I do not want to hinder what He wants to do. As your pastor who deeply loves you, I'm asking you to be patient with what might twanspire and twust me to oversee it all."

For the next hour the Pastor preached his sermon titled "God's Chosen Bride," emphasizing the importance of submission to God's Spirit and to the male authority.

Penny, impatient and fidgety, and dying to see Cody, kept looking back at him. He and Laurina were seated a few rows behind her.

"Penny, are you all right?" Rick whispered. He had never seen her so disturbed.

"I need to talk to Cody after service. Okay?"

"I'll come with you."

"No—alone." Penny pried her eyes away from her husband's astounded look.

Service ended with a triumphant shout from the musicians as the music ministers filed upto the platform and began to sing. Dancers flung across the vast red spaces in boisterous worship.

Penny rushed from her pew to where Cody and Laurina were sitting. She could not help herself. She felt driven like a madwoman. Laurina saw her troubled friend and patted the pew for her to sit down.

"Laurina, I don't know what is going on inside me, but I'm spiritually drawn to Cody so bad I can't function." She started crying.

Cody grimaced, leaned over his wife, and tapped Penny's hand. "I feel the same way, friend. I just want to be careful. The experience is so different. We need to make sure Laurina and Rick are okay with all this."

"I wish I could understand this," Laurina said. "But I trust you both, and know this is God's love. Go ahead and dance. I'll wait here and back you up in prayer."

Cody hesitated, not sure he should, then decided to. The love pulling at him made him feel woozy, and he wanted to taste more of it. He took Penny's hand and led her to the front of the sanctuary. Like whirling tops, they soon slowed down and allowed the energy to *join* them.

The Christians stopped, gaped at the couples connecting through the eyes—all married to someone else, now linked together like lovers. Ted and Callie boldly held hands and Donna and Kurt were spinning and spinning, their faces on one another. Others from the retreat were connecting as well.

"Hey, you okay?" Rick slipped into the pew beside Laurina.

"I don't know. I'm extremely jealous about now."

"Me too. I'm never going to dance like that. It's not me."

"Rick, never say *never*."

Donna and Kurt dodged the prying eyes in the sanctuary and moved to one of the private classrooms upstairs. Alone, without any spectators, they found themselves completely surrendering to the magical feelings flaring between them. Their arms and bodies moved, but their eyes remain fixed.

Kurt reached out and pulled the pastor's wife close. He could smell her perfume, her hair spray, and it intoxicated him. She responded and moved into his arms. Donna's age meant nothing to him. With this love, there was no boundaries.

As Donna moved her body full against him, massaging him with the beat of the music, he could not stop from reacting.

"Oh, oh, Donna..." he moaned, "I can't stop!"

"Don't."

Their lips locked and he soared with her into another place where neither one had ever been before.

oc *CULT*

CHAPTER ELEVEN

As the weeks flew by, more and more people were *connecting*. Now instead of solo dancing before the Lord all over the church, most of the members were locked in a slow dance with someone of the opposite sex. And because of this, the prayer benches were empty. Even Penny's favorite time praying with the Lord at home had all but stopped. Dancing replaced everything.

Different spiritual levels between *connections* depended on the depth of the experience during the dance. Mark and Donna had labeled the stronger unions, *mega connections*, and allowed them access to a private room upstairs above the sanctuary. To be considered a *mega connection*, the connected couple had to pass a series of written questions, describing in detail the spiritual experiences they had encountered during the dance. Those approved *megas* were issued yellow pass cards and allowed to enter the reserved room on Tuesday and Thursday nights through a security guard who kept watch at the door.

Cody and Penny had a pass card and looked forward to these nights. Entering the room was a delightful indulgence because it was there that the mega connections were allowed to respond to the spirit without any hindrances or worries of offending those members who were not on the same spiritual level. That meant dancing without restraint, allowing their bodies to connect as one as well as their spirits.

On Thursday night Cody and Penny arrived, both anxious to be together. The spacious room was not as full as usual, but they didn't mind. They moved to the music.

"Cody, it's so hard not to kiss you," Penny whispered into his face as they glided across the floor.

Cody laughed and said, "I know." Then, without warning, he bent over and smooched her smack on the mouth.

"Cody!" Penny chuckled.

"No one saw us. Besides, they are all kissing anyway. I already heard rumors."

"What rumors?" Penny asked quietly, slowing her gait in his arms.

"Let's go out to the car and talk."

They left the building and climbed into Cody's car.

"Penny, other people are kissing. I talked to Avery about it. He said God's love is so strong and sometimes the flesh gets in the way, but we shouldn't hinder what God is doing."

"What do you mean?"

"I guess we shouldn't feel guilty if we kiss."

"Okay," Penny said and bent over and kissed Cody full on the mouth.

He swooped her into his arms and kissed her long and hard. Their hands started flying everywhere and when they were touching skin, Penny broke away. Guilt pricked her hard.

"We had better stop, Cody."

The ringing phone brought Penny dashing out of the shower. She picked it up and pulled the towel around her dripping body.

"Hello?" she asked.

"Pen, hey, it's Marilyn. What's happening? Still want me to come over tonight?"

"You bet. Rick will be at a basketball game, so we have the house to ourselves."

"Good. See you soon."

Marilyn, dressed in baggy sweat pants and an oversized T-shirt, arrived about seven. She had just straightened her black hair and it rested stylishly against her chin. She set a bag on the kitchen counter. "I brought some banana bread and Sprite," she said.

"Thanks, Mar."

Penny set a bowl of dip and chips on the table, and then moved to the counter to slice the banana bread.

Marilyn poured the Sprite. "Penny," she said, "Did you know that on the church pulpit there is an indicator light that flashes different messages to people that testify."

"What? No way! Who told you that?"

"You mean Callie never told you? Ask her. She's always testifying."

"I can't believe that." Penny licked her fingers. "Really, are you serious, Mar?"

"I started cleaning the sanctuary and saw it himself. A digital apparatus is built into the top of the podium. Last week a friend of mine told me that when she was testifying, halfway through her speech a red message flashed across the podium saying, "close and sit down." She felt so embarrassed. I doubt she will ever get up there again."

"Really? How awful. You couldn't ever get me up there."

"I think it's strange, though. Don't you?"

"Not really. If Pastor Mark wants to keep our services in order, then I can understand the messages. I mean, if he has to publicly tell someone to sit down, that could be more embarrassing." Penny placed the banana bread on the table and sat down.

"Yeah, I guess so." Marilyn took a few bites of bread. She lowered her voice. "Pen, I'm worried about these connections. I can't find anything about it in the Bible."

"You have to experience it to understand what is happening. It's strange to the natural eye. But God is in this. Trust me, I am not the same anymore."

"I know. I can see that you enjoy being with Cody a lot more than with Rick. This is what bothers me. Jason and I are concerned about it all. Really concerned."

"I love Rick. But right now God is wanting me to love Cody and see Cody through His eyes."

"But scripture doesn't talk about this."

"Do you want me to pray for you, Marilyn? I think you might be feeling left out. You haven't had a connection."

"No. I have been praying. I don't feel right about it." Marilyn sighed. "Jason called his father. Since he is a pastor, we figured he could give us some guidance. His father told us this doctrine is dangerous. He told us to run from it."

"Marilyn, that's the devil talking. He wants to deceive you and lure you out of this church. You know God's called you here!" Penny leaned over the table and grabbed her friend's hands and held them. "Marilyn, I felt it! I am not deceived. I feel God is in this move! Look into my eyes. How can you say this love isn't from God. How can I be deceived after all the praying I do? God wouldn't let this happen to me. He knows how much I love Him. Besides, these connections are not just happening between males and females. Females are getting connected together and males, too. You know this." Penny tried to connect her eyes with Marilyn, but she looked away.

"It is wrong. Jason and I can't go along with this teaching."

"It is not a teaching, Mar, it is God's Spirit! We can't understand the things of God. The Bible says this!"

"The Bible says to avoid all appearances of evil. Now when visitors walk into our church, they see everyone practically kissing, dancing like something you'd see at a disco. People are walking out offended and shocked. I don't blame them!" Marilyn quieted down. "I hope you don't hate us when we switch churches."

"Stop it, Marilyn. Things will change. God's love is so powerful; we are all learning how to adjust to it."

"Penny, it has been over two months! It is getting worse. The *connections* are now being seen all over the city. Even you and Cody go out between services together. What do you do...together?"

Penny blushed. "What? Marilyn, stop saying all this! I won't let you leave. Please don't talk nonsense. Let me pray for you."

"God is the center of our lives. We have to follow Him."

"If you believe this, then you can't leave Grace Church. He is here, Mar, stay in the boat, okay? Don't listen to lies. Satan hates what God's doing and I don't want to lose your friendship."

"Why would you lose my friendship? I'll still be me if I leave. I still love God."

Penny didn't answer.

"Are you sure that maybe Satan isn't controlling the whole thing?" Marilyn added.

"Marilyn, I can't believe you said that." Penny got nervous. "I don't want you speaking that way about Grace Church. This is where God put me. I'm not running out on Pastor Mark. If we make mistakes, God will show us and correct them."

"Penny, the connections cannot be of God."

Penny plugged her ears with her palms. "Stop, Marilyn. I mean it. You're wrong."

"Penny, can't you see what..."

"I don't want to hear another word about it. God promised in the last days He would pour out His Spirit on man. He's doing it. If you refuse to be a part of it, that's your choice."

"That's right, it is my choice." Marilyn didn't want to push Penny away and ruin her chances of speaking with her again. "I don't want to argue, Pen. I'll keep praying and I know you will too."

"I don't have to, I know it's from God."

"Okay, Pen, let's drop it. I love you. We are friends and I am only sharing my heart with you. Like we always do."

"Yeah, well, you always have spoken what's on your mind." Penny flashed a weak smile.

"How about a hug?" Marilyn tilted her head to one side and held out her arms.

Penny lifted from her chair and wrapped her arms around Marilyn's neck.

They chatted another half hour on lighter matters, but their visit had become strained. Marilyn made an excuse and left for home.

Penny felt shaky, relieved she had gone. She quickly picked up the phone and dialed Laurina's house.

"Laurina? We need to pray for Marilyn and Jason. I think they're leaving Grace Church."

"I'll call Ted!"

Marilyn felt awful after leaving Penny's house. It had not gone well at all. She was glad that Jason was in agreement with her on all this. It would have been hard to go it alone. But

Jason, being an attorney, knew how to dissect the Word of God, and he was not one to allow feelings to override facts. Leaving the church and people they loved was not easy, but they refused to compromise scripture or sear their consciences. The strange spell moving through the couples had made them scared to even dance solo.

"Hey, Babe, how about a stroll in the park?" Jason asked his wife the next day. It was the kind of Saturday to be outside. He tweaked her nose, hoping to lighten her mood. "We can have a small picnic."

"Sure. I'll make some sandwiches."

He pulled her into his arms. "Mar, we have each other. God will see us through this. If He's moving us on...well, we have to accept it. We can't compromise what we believe in."

"I know, Jason." Marilyn kissed his cheek. "Let me get ready." She put together a basket of food and they headed for the fresh air.

The summer day was spectacular. The park, smelling like fresh-mowed grass, was laced with dense green trees, chirping birds, and thick, vibrant flower bushes. A warm breeze tickled their cheeks as Marilyn spread a cloth over the picnic table. Jason removed some Havarti cheese, a loaf of French bread, apple juice, and tangy lemon bars from the basket. They were preparing the food when they heard laughter rise from behind a large flower bush not too far from their table. Jason threw Marilyn a curious look. She shrugged.

"I don't think we're alone," he mouthed and grinned. He began humming and whistling to warn the hidden lovebirds.

A sudden rustling noise disturbed the bushes and Marilyn and Jason froze when out popped Ted Hunter and Callie Graves, all red faced.

"Ca..Callie?" a flabbergasted Marilyn asked.

Ted acted posh and Callie stammered, "Oh, h..h..hi guys. Fancy meeting you here. T..Ted and I were taking a break between worship."

Ted nodded at Jason and made small talk before making excuses to be back at the church. As they walked off, Jason slumped down on the bench and said to his wife, "What is going on?"

"It's my fifth call today, Pastor Mark," Petey urged over the phone. "Thought you might want to know. I've never had a Monday turn out so busy. Oh, and last night after service some of the worshippers didn't leave the sanctuary until early morning hours."

"Petey, thank you for keeping me informed," Pastor Mark stated without any emotion. "How are you and Callie doing?"

"I wish I could say good, but her connection with Ted has taken her right out of my life."

Mark felt the same way. Callie seldom made her appointments. "Give Callie time. I believe these connections will heal all the ma*ww*iages."

"Yes, of course, I know."

"Thanks Petey, you're a good worker. Keep me informed on any other pertinent news. God bless." Mark replaced the receiver and pressed the intercom button.

"Yes, Pastor?" his secretary asked.

"Sweetie, could you get Ted on the line and tell him I want to see him right away?"

Ted arrived ten minutes later.

"Afternoon, Mark," he said, dropping down into a chair, swinging one long leg on top of the other.

Mark gave a brusque nod. "Ted, Petey just telephoned me. Some of the ma*ww*iages are facing p*w*oblems. Some of the connections are disobeying the rules I've set and spending time together outside this church."

Guilt rushed Ted. He cleared his throat before speaking. "Yes, I know this." He hesitated. "Actually, Callie and I've met outside the church for lunch. Where do we draw the line, Pastor? I mean, we were friends before and never thought twice about sitting down for lunch. Now we see each other through God's eyes, and it's wrong?"

"Ted, I have to set boundawies. We can't have spouses forgetting their own mates." Mark picked up a stack of papers and shuffled them evenly together before placing them in his top drawer. "Another thing, you know Callie ministers to me on a regular basis each week. She has been canceling them lately. I don't want you meeting her duwing those appointed times. Can you make sure she is fwee to continue with her minstewial obligations?"

"Sure, Mark. And we'll obey the guidelines."

"Good, Ted. There is one other small matter that you need to take care of. Betty telephoned me today. She was cwying and angwy over your connection with Callie. She says you have lost intewest in her completely. I don't want anyone in this assembly being insensitive to their spouse. If it goes this way, I will have no choice but to stop the whole thing. Can you set the right example for this body?"

Ted eye's narrowed. "Yeah, sure, of course. I will spend the rest of the afternoon with my wife." He hastened to his feet and left the room.

Mark thought he would take a gamble. Since Callie wasn't coming today, he punched in Laurina's number and she picked up.

"Lauwina, this is your pastor. How are you today?"

A slight pause on the other end, then, "Fine, and you, Mark?"

"Gweat, I …I was wondering if you would be intewested in meeting me today for worship in the dance."

"Well, maybe that would be good. Cody is gone. This is a good time to work on our relationship. Where should I meet you?"

"How about the room for the mega connections? In one hour."

"Sounds good. See you then. Bye."

Mark quickly telephoned his wife at home and the recorder answered. He didn't leave a message.

Must be with that young boy again.

With time to kill before his meeting with Laurina, he left his office and strolled into the campus chapel. He sat down in a back pew and looked around. The lights were dimmed and soft music hummed from corner speakers. A few dancers, embracing intimately, spun about at the front altar area. Almost everyone had succumbed to the *new move of God*, and now it was common to see couples physically engaged, with bodies sandwiched together, lips practically touching, eyes locked. Still, Mark wondered if he was doing the right thing in letting it go this far. The reports of jealous spouses and sexual mishaps were starting to pour into the counseling office. It did look strange, and they were becoming the talk of the town. All the churches in town were boycotting them.

Mark's head spun round to the side aisle at the sight of two men, eyes foggy with love, moving together in a tight embrace in the dark shadows. They were almost kissing. He got up and moved to their side. It was then he noticed that one fellow was Owen Nason.

"Owen, I need to talk with you now." Mark ignored the other man.

Owen moved apart from his connection and followed Mark towards the back of the chapel.

"Owen, what are you doing? With your pwoblem, you shouldn't be dancing like this with another man. I want you to stick to gwoup dancing."

Owen looked annoyed. "Pastor, how come married couples can dance with someone else's spouse and I cannot?"

"In your case, you cannot. Marcy has put up with your stwuggles for years now. I think it is time to consider her for a change. Curb it now, Owen. This is an order."

Owen sighed and threw up his hands. "Whatever you say." He left the chapel. His connection, who had been waiting, trailed him out.

Mark knew that he was taking a beating by allowing these spiritual connections to continue. But, at the same time, he could not help but be drawn in by it all. It was an amazing sight to behold, and he wanted to understand and experience it fully for himself. He was yet to truly know what Donna and the *megas* were feeling.

Mark fumbled with the buttons on the cassette player and kept looking at his watch. She was late.

"Hi," Laurina said, startling him from the doorway.

"Oh, hello, Lauwina. Come on in."

The room was empty at that hour and Mark knew no one was allowed to enter until certain times. Laurina came near him and bent over, switching into her dancing slippers. When she finished, she faced him, smiling.

"I'm glad you could make it." He took her arm and drew her to the middle of the spacious room. "Thanks for coming."

"No problem."

The music played softly and Laurina let the pastor lead her around in slow circles. She kept her eyes pinned on his. He was enamored with her, but he kept his dignity and did not close in on her. He didn't want to scare her off.

Laurina had not yet experienced a connection either, so when she and Mark were jolted by a vigor that seemed to mesh their eyes, they were both surprised. Mark, overwhelmed at what was happening, moved in closer. Laurina responded and took his hand. She was so *drunk in the spirit* that she could barely stand. She leaned against Mark's chest, allowing his magnetic eyes to hold her up.

"Oh, Mark, God's given me so much love for you."

He put his arms around her, and like a dance instructor, guided her carefully around the floor. As the whirling dynamism drew them together as one, Laurina surrendered to the glory. Mark could not believe the experience. He embraced her, and she relaxed in his arms. He did not realize he was sexually aroused until her moving hips brushed against him. The sensation sent him spinning back to earth.

"Honey, I have to stop. My body can't take any more." He pulled away, not wanting to, but with her, knowing he had to.

"Oh, Pastor, yes, I understand, I'm sorry." She staggered backward. "I feel so one with you!"

They laughed, lifted their hands, and praised Jesus.

"Penny," Laurina exclaimed, as the two women took a seat near the window at *The Grill*. "It was amazing. Now I know what you and Cody are feeling! What an unbelievable experience! I cannot believe how much love I feel for the pastor. I feel like a jerk for doubting him. God loves him so much."

They rattled on about the wonders of the spiritual connection movement and then Laurina sobered. She asked, "Penny, have you heard from Marilyn?"

"Yeah, she called this morning. I feel this big wall between us now. I know the devil's deceiving her and Jason with lies."

"I called Ted. He is going to contact Jason."

"Good. Maybe he can persuade them to stay."

"I hope so. Marilyn and Jason are good people."

"I know. But no matter how much I love Marilyn, God comes first." Penny shook her head sadly.

"There are others leaving the church, Penny."

"Are you kidding? How many?"

"So far Ted said about one hundred have left."

"Oh, boy, the devil is really fighting mad. It is sad to see people being robbed of God's glory."

"The pastor doesn't want us talking to these *dissidents*. He says they are deceived and will not be part of God's Bride. We have to be careful to *stay in the boat* and not be persuaded to listen to their lies."

"Laurina, I am not going to talk to Marilyn anymore. I feel an evil spirit on her when we talk. Last time I was shaking. I don't want to be deceived. I'm going to talk to Rick about it."

"Yeah, Penny, I think we need to end our relationship with them now."

A gorgeous young woman, dressed quite stylishly, sashayed up to their table before the two friends could say another word. "Hi, Laurina," Janice Certs said. Her voice sounded like music.

"Hi, Janice!" Laurina said. "Do you know Penny?"

"No. Nice to meet you, Penny." Janice put out her hand.

"Hello. Nice meeting you as well." Penny gave her hand a welcoming shake. "Join us, please," she said, pulling out the chair next to her.

Janice sat. Her thick, almost white hair cascaded down her back. With her perfect face, high cheekbones and heavily made up almond eyes, she looked like one of the Revlon models in a magazine.

"Janice has been coming to one of the prayer meetings I attend," Laurina said.

The women made small talk, then Penny asked, "Have you had a connection yet, Janice?"

"No, not yet. I don't know how you handle it when your husbands dance with someone else. All I can say is I'm glad I'm single."

"I think when Rick gets a connection I'll be jealous. Right now he's too afraid to dance."

"He's the pro-golfer, right?"

"Yeah. How did you know?"

Janice shrugged. "Just knew."

"Cody and Penny are connected," Laurina said. "But I trust them both. I struggle a little with it, but I know God's in it. I lean on Him during the times I get insecure. Besides, Penny and I have a connection too."

Penny stroked Laurina's hand. "You're my best friend. You can trust me."

Laurina grabbed Penny's hand, and together they moved into the *connection* mode. The spell moved between them for a few minutes before Janice nervously tried to change the subject. The patrons eating nearby were noticing the two women looking at each other as if they were lovers.

"What do you want to order?" Janice asked, embarrassed, holding up the menu between the two women to purposely block the eye connection.

With the ogling interrupted, the threesome went back to their normal chatting. The waitress walked up and took their orders.

Marilyn phoned Penny early Tuesday morning. The summer's heat had not yet seared through the clouds.

"Penny, we're leaving the church," she said in a quiet voice. "Pastor Mark's in deception. The whole church is!"

"Marilyn, stop. I won't let you speak that way about our church. I can't believe you're listening to the devil's lies. Pastor Mark loves God."

"Listen to me. If you don't leave, you'll get hurt. Look at everyone, Penny. You say it's healing relationships, but it's not; it's tearing them apart. When was the last time you saw Marcy, or your husband? Everyone has 'new' friends now—their connections! The entire city is gossiping about it. God is not being glorified when everyone is mate swapping!"

Penny slammed the phone down. Her heart was pounding. She couldn't believe her dearest friend was rebelling against the church. Mark had warned them Satan would use certain people to divide the church and steer them away from God's holy love. She could not believe Marilyn would be one of them. She dialed the phone, trembling.

Laurina answered and Penny started crying.

"Penny, what's the matter?"

"I hung up on Marilyn! She was saying awful things about the pastor and the connections."

"Don't talk to her anymore. She's the one that's in deception. Stay away from them. We can't listen to their lies.

I almost listened to someone once...anyway, I thank God I didn't believe her lies."

"Boy, Satan is really out to destroy this church. He hates God's love."

"Yeah, and he'll do anything to take us to hell. We have to stand behind Pastor Mark. I will let the eldership know. They will probably disfellowship them."

"I know, Laurina. It is so sad! Will you call Callie for me and tell her? I want to pray."

"Sure. Bye, Pen."

The phone rang as Penny replaced the receiver.

"Hello?" Penny answered, thinking it was Laurina again.

Marilyn's voice cracked with emotion, "Pen, please don't hate..."

Penny slammed the phone down the same time Rick walked into the house.

"Penny, what's the matter?"

"Oh, Rick!" Penny ran into his arms. "Jason and Marilyn are leaving!"

"Are you serious?"

"Yes. I just hung up on her. I'm shaking all over. She was saying awful lies about Pastor Mark."

Rick raked his hair with his hand and sighed. "Jason called me too, Pen, a little bit ago on my cell. He tried to say the same things to me. We can't let their decision hurt us. Let's keep on going. Sad. I'll miss them."

Like ending a novel, Penny and Rick shut the book on their two dearest friends.

"Thank you for coming in this morning, Marilyn." Ted took a seat next to her on the office sofa instead of returning to his desk. "I received an alarming phone call from your friend,

Laurina Addison, yesterday. She says you're leaving the church. She's concerned about this, and asked if I would talk to you." He smiled and touched her forearm. "You have a good friend. She cares for you."

Marilyn planted her hands firmly in her lap as she looked up at him. She didn't know why she came today. Jason didn't want her to, but she wanted to be sure about their decision. Ted seemed sincere enough when he had called to arrange the meeting. She had spent an hour bent over her bed praying before coming, asking God for strength.

"Why didn't you want Jason with me?" she asked.

"I thought he and I might have lunch together another day and talk. I like Jason; he has been a great help for us here, and he has great potential for ministry. I hate to see him throw it all away, Marilyn." Ted picked at the tip of his nose with one finger and bent forward. "Marilyn, I'm afraid that you might be undermining your husband without realizing you're doing so."

"What do you mean?" She turned and faced him.

"The Lord called Jason to Grace Church and brought him under Pastor Mark. By leaving this church, he will be out of God's will. Do you want to be responsible for that?" He kept cool.

"This is both of our decision. We disagree with the connection…"

"Whoa!" He shot his hand up. "What demon is that talking? It sounds like a spirit of rebellion against this church government."

Marilyn squeezed her knees together. They were starting to quiver. "Jason and I are not rebelling…"

"Jason is not here. Let's talk for you. You aren't what?"

Marilyn was stunned at Ted's harsh tone. "My husband and I carry the same views. *We* are not satisfied with the teachings on the spiritual connections. There is no scriptural proof…"

"I can't have this church undermined," he interrupted. "If you want to be part of God's true church, you will have to submit to this counsel. You do want to be part of God's Bride, don't you?" He tried to sound sincere, but his eyes were impatient.

"Yes, of course."

"Then let me pray for you. Let's fight those deceiving spirits that want to destroy your soul. Stay joined with us, Marilyn. Fight. Be an up-lifter for Jason. Don't allow Satan to rob your husband of his future in Christ."

"I don't need prayer now. I need answers. Can you back up what's happening in scripture? Show me, so I can understand it through the Word of God."

"The Bible says our minds can't fathom the things of God." He got edgy and tapped his fingers across the back of the couch. "The Bible also says in the last days men and women would have dreams and see visions. God said He would pour out His Spirit on mankind. We are experiencing this now. Why do you want to run from what He is doing?"

"What about the scriptures that warn us against false doctrines and fables that corrupt the faith? The Apostle Paul tells us to test the spirits to see whether they be from God or not. Why would he say this if he didn't know angels of light would try and deceive God's people? In Bible College the teachers tell us to make sure everything lines up with scripture. Now you are telling me to do the complete opposite?"

"Christ said in the last days He would pour out His Spirit in new measures, like nothing we've ever seen before. This is one of those experiences. And it is holy. And to understand this, you must see with the spirit, not with your mind. I'm afraid you have chosen to look at this carnally instead of spiritually You're in danger of losing your salvation if you continue in this fashion."

Marilyn wished Jason were there. Ted's pitch was cutting and accusative.

"Marilyn," he continued, "I'm not going to allow you to corrupt the minds of those that want to have an intimate place with Jesus. You are choosing the way of darkness. And people in light cannot associate with those who chose darkness." He stood up. "You have a demon of rebellion, which is a form of witchcraft. Until you are willing to be delivered, I have to expel you from this church."

Marilyn was trembling as she stood, completely horrified at what Ted had just said to her. "I love Jesus," she countered quietly. "You have no right to make such a judgment on my life."

He walked behind his desk and stood there defiantly, not looking up.

"It is not my life you should be worrying about," she added. "Making out with another married woman in the park isn't exactly what I call spiritual." With that she walked out of the room and slammed the door.

Later that day Jason telephoned Ted's office.

Ted answered. "Ted here."

"This is Jason Elston." He was angry.

"Jason, I'm glad you called. I think we need to talk…"

"You had no right to harass my wife today and make implications against her character and her walk with God. If you slander our names or threaten my wife again, I'll sue you and this church! You are the one who is in rebellion to God. Not us!" Jason slammed the phone down.

Marilyn came up and clung to her husband, weeping.

"You all right, Mar?"

She shook her head yes and kept weeping.

"I feel so confused," Jason spouted. "I don't understand why this is happening. I thought God brought us here. Now our life is being ripped apart, we are losing all our friends. I feel lost, Babe."

"Jason, I am really proud of you. This is the hardest thing we have ever had to do. I guess now we know what it means to stand for Christ."

"Yeah, but I don't feel so righteous about now. I feel like a knife has ripped me apart. I feel let down by God too. I just don't know where to go from here. Grace Church was our life."

"We have to make Jesus our life now," Marilyn said. She soothed Jason with a tighter embrace.

"You are so right, Mar. We have put our trust in a church instead of God. That is why we feel so bruised now."

"We could be any one of those people right now, dancing with demons."

Jason looked into his wife's face. Tears fell freely. "I'm so glad I have you. Don't ever leave me."

They held each other and cried.

CHAPTER TWELVE

Sunday morning's pre-service was packed with dancers, mostly coupled up. Penny, seated in the middle section with Rick, watched Avery as he leaped like a deer across the front area and joined Ted's teenage daughter, Connie, in the dance.

"Penny," Rick said, interrupting her. "Did you see today's bulletin?"

"No, why?"

"Look," he handed her the newsletter. "Jason and Marilyn are disfellowshipped."

She read the front page. "I can't believe it. I guess its final now."

"Yeah, they were the last ones I thought would leave."

"Laurina said that they are really brainwashed."

"Well, we have to keep our eyes on Christ," Rick said. "It's over with them. We can't look back."

Someone brushed against Rick's back and he looked behind him. The stunning blonde he had seen at *The Grill* was smiling down at him.

Still looking at Rick, Janice sang, "Hello, Penny."

"Janice, hi, nice to see you again," Penny said. "This is my husband Rick."

"Hello." Janice grinned wider.

Rick's face turned the same shade as the red carpet. "Hello," he said.

"I heard you played golf," Janice said sweetly.

"I still do."

"I love golf. My father is an avid fan. I grew up watching all the tournaments on TV."

"Oh." Rick didn't know what to say. He was enchanted with her beauty.

She smiled again, then sat down behind him and put her Bible under the pew.

The choir took their place and the atmosphere was ablaze with anticipation of the *moving of the spirit*. Skirts flew up exposing moving thighs, arms reeled about like sails, and ballet shoes raced across the carpet. Penny quickly jumped up and joined Laurina in the dance. Within minutes Cody was at their side. Laurina patted her husband and left him alone with Penny to *connect*. She moved off to dance alone, but Pastor Mark bopped up beside her. As the music slowed, he took her in his arms and pulled her into *glory* with his eyes.

As Rick watched Penny and Cody dance, he tugged at his collar. He was still too uncomfortable at seeing them together, and he was still too chicken to try and *connect* with anyone.

Petey came over and scooted in next to him. "Hey Rick," he said, "Are you managing okay with Cody stealing your wife?"

Rick grunted. "Not too good with it. How about you? First the pastor, now Ted?"

"I guess I need to be glad I get to sleep with her nights," Petey joked.

Petey's bright tie looked out of place with his pale shirt. He crossed his long legs and moaned, "I only wish I knew what they were all feeling."

"Me too. I guess I just need to be pushed." Rick laughed.

"I'll talk to you later." Petey gave Rick a hefty pat on the shoulder, then left the pew.

Another light tap on his shoulder made Rick turn around. Janice leaned forward, with an apprehensive smile playing across her pretty mouth. "Want to worship with me?" she asked.

My God, she wanted to dance with him! How could he say no? He pitched her a floppy grin and said, "Sure. But I must warn you, I hardly dance."

"Me too. I have been too nervous to try it. So, now I am mustering up all the courage I have. Thank you for saying yes."

They went to the side aisle and began dancing without touching. But by the time the choir stopped to return to their seats, the two were completely entwined and looking as love struck as almost everyone else.

Pastor Mark, woozy from the deep spiritual encounter of the dance, jostled up the platform steps. "Pwaise God. Pwaise God," he shouted. "I'm in awe of what God is doing in our midst." He rolled up his shirt sleeves as he spoke. His casual appearance surprised, yet relaxed, the congregation, and they grinned, their fans now working quickly to cool down their perspiring faces.

"Church, I must admit, I was skeptical concerning these spiwitual connections, but this week God used Lauwina Addison to dwaw me into His glowious love. Dancing *solo* with God is wonderful, but being in a *spiwitual connection* is so much better!" He whooped and everyone whooped back at him.

"God merged my spiwit with Lauwina in such a way that I have found myself being ushered into places with God I never thought possible. Ohhhh...it is so divine! You people who have recently connected with someone, come on up here and tell us what God has done in you because of your spiwitual union and how God is changing your life!"

Mark gave over the platform and Laurina rushed up the steps.

"God's so faithful," she purred into the microphone, "I needed healing inside my heart with Pastor Mark. Over the year, hurts had built up between us, as they sometimes do in any relationship, but as I worshipped with him, God released my heart from those hurts and connected me to his spirit. Now I see him through Christ's eyes. God has replaced those hurts with His love and forgiveness. I urge everyone to jump on in to God's Holy love! At first I was jealous when my husband connected with a female friend. But now, since my connection with the Pastor, I am totally set free from all insecurities! I trust what God is doing!"

Laurina threw Mark a happy look and his heart fluttered. He felt warm all over.

She raised her voice. "We need to allow God to heal and restore our marriages and our relationships with one another. These connections will bring unity and freedom into our lives. If we release our mates, in time, God will give them back to us and we will all be one in Him!"

Ted Hunter was next to rush up to the platform. He loomed over the podium full of excitement. "I'm so full of joy I could burst. I didn't think it was possible to love or feel this kind of love. Some people are leaving this church, totally persuaded by Satan that this is not of God. But they are duped! This is of God and we must surrender our lives to His love or we will miss out on what God wants to do in us and through us! Let's love one another, church!"

Mark took back his position, this time soberly. "Now church," he said, "I have to bwing you all down to earth a bit here because I need to set some stwonger rules so that spouses are not being forsaken. I want all dancing to remain inside the church." Mark rubbed at his earlobe. "Because we're human, it's impossible for our bodies not to respond when we're feeling such stwong love. I want evewyone to be careful to respect one another and not move out of the spiwitual into the physical. No sexual intimacy of any kind is allowed between connections. Let's not taint God's love. Cover one another with pure love. Spouses, I know some of you are expewiencing feelings of jealousy and insecuwity. Use this time to seek delivewances against these evil spiwits. I want this church to be able to fully *release* their mates to God. Let's help God finish what He has begun. Let's connect with the Son of man!"

Mark ended the service and the music started. As tambourines began clanging, legs went flying. Mark sought out Laurina, Penny clambered after Cody, Ted and Callie scrambled together, and Rick turned behind him and boldly grabbed Janice's hand. All four couples spent the rest of the afternoon soaring in spiritual places.

Gayle inhaled, exhaled and then said it. "Dad, I'm worried about our church. This intimate dancing is turning away visitors and, frankly, me too."

Mark pressed the phone closer to his ear, not sure he had heard his daughter correctly. "What?"

"Why are you allowing everyone to swap mates and hang out everywhere?"

"Gayle, I set rules. I can't baby-sit evewyone. Stop wowwying. God will iwon it all out in His time." Mark, seated at home in his study, flipped through the pages of his concordance while impatiently letting Gayle drone on.

"Dad, I urge you to reconsider the whole thing. All the children are freaking out. They're confused at what they're seeing. It goes against their moral upbringing. I'm putting out a lot of fires at school. Kids just don't understand why their parents are with someone else now."

"I will hold a special session next week instwucting the teachers how to discuss this with the childwen. I want you to be the first to explain this so that your students understand and join in, not feel left out. God will touch them with His love too."

"Dad, my kids are only six years old."

"Not too young for God's love."

"And I suppose it's right for Avery to go goo-goo-eyed over Ted's seventeen-year-old daughter? She's underage to be running around with a man in his thirties."

"Gayle, get delivered from that suspicious demon or it'll ruin your mawwiage. Avewy knows he is not to be outside the church with his connection."

"Dad, please, this is not about me. Is mom home?"

"No."

"She's with Kurt, right?"

Mark kept silent.

"Dad, come on, it's Saturday. And he's twenty years younger than Mom. It looks terrible."

"Gayle, you need to relax and stop fighting God. I have evewything under contwol and I don't want you undermining my authowity. Do you hear me, young lady?"

"Lots of people are leaving, Dad."

"They are deceived. I hope you will twust your father and twust God." Mark cooed at her like talking to a baby. "My little girl, let's not argue. Come by the house tonight if you need to talk. You know I love you and that God is my life. I am not going to walk away from God, or you."

Gayle knew she was getting nowhere.

As she hung up the phone, Avery walked into the house with the two boys and placed three bags of groceries on the kitchen counter.

"Here, hope I didn't forget anything."

"Thanks Avery. Hey, want to take the boys to the zoo?"

"Um, no, I have other plans."

"Oh?"

"I'm meeting Connie at the college campus for worship."

"What, on Saturday? Come on, this is family time." She stopped unpacking the groceries and faced him.

"Gayle, God's moving and I just can't suppress His Spirit now."

"Avery, Connie is a child."

He picked the tip of his skinny nose and sniffled. "Gayle, stop looking at this through human eyes. This is a spiritual connection. I can't help the fact God put me with Connie." He selected an apple from the large bowl on the kitchen table, polished it with a clean towel, and chomped into it.

"Do her parents know she'll be with you?"

"Of course. Now stop worrying." Avery stepped behind his wife and kissed her cheek. "I have to get ready. I'm meeting her in half an hour."

Gayle did not know whether to scream or cry.

As months flew by and September brought the rain, the assembly became more lax with the rules pertaining to the *spiritual connection move*. They entered into the fantasy love full throttle, not caring that what they did might offend others. Most of the connections were sneaking outside the church, breaking the rules, and blaming their disobedience on the strong love. They were locking eyes at the parks, in grocery stores, libraries, theaters, and other public places, completely unashamed and uncaring of who was watching.

But the move went gloriously on. With each new problem, Mark would try to tame them with lengthy exhortations on proper behavior.

It was Thursday evening when a bubbly Donna arrived at the sanctuary with slippers under her arm, nodding at the other smiling churchites passing her. She climbed the stairs, two at a time, anxious to meet Kurt. Their *union* ushered her into glorious dimensions in the spirit that she never knew existed. The physical became the tool with which to obtain those deeper places. She found herself desiring only to be *in the spirit*. Cooking or going shopping or anything else that life's duties demanded became a drudge. The times with Kurt were what she lived for.

As usual, Donna bypassed the special room designated for the mega connections and entered the smaller classroom at the other end of the hall.

"Hello," Kurt said as she entered. He was lounging on a metal chair near the window, grinning.

Donna locked the door, then put on her dancing slippers and pitter-pattered over to him. She sat down on his lap and kissed him. The ghost-like, melancholy melody was already setting the tone for their anticipated spiritual journey.

"You look beautiful, my beloved," he said, pulling back to look at her. "Can you feel my love for you? God's love for you?" He took her hand and put it on his heart. They locked eyes, allowing the energy to connect them thru the dance. Slowly they rose and moved together.

"Kurt, can I trust you to cover me if I choose to do something totally different?" She stroked his baby face with her hands.

"Yes, of course," he said, rubbing her shoulders. Dancing with her was the most erotic experience he had ever tasted. Each time they met, they seemed to go higher in the spirit, and the bodily response he encountered transcended mere sex. To climax physically while moving into heavenly realms of glory was the ultimate experience, and his senses reeled under the expectation of doing it again.

"Kurt," Donna said softly, "last night I dreamed I was dancing naked in Christ's arms. You see I was completely open to Him. My nakedness represented that I no longer held anything back from Him. He had me completely. Than, suddenly, in the dream, Christ turned into you, and I was dancing naked in your arms."

Kurt listened, already feeling his body responding to her words.

"Will you let me experience you as Jesus, so I surrender myself completely to Him the same way I did in this dream? I feel God wants to use you to bring me into a new place with Him." She eyed him boldly. "The Lord wants to strip me of pride and selfishness, and clothe me with Himself—using you. Will you stand in Christ's stead for me?"

"Yes...oh...yes."

Donna undressed. Kurt stood there staring, speechless and fascinated.

With agile fingers she peeled away his clothing and they danced without restraint. As he merged into her flesh for the first time, their spirits soared, catapulting them out of reality far into the other side.

The tiny garden Callie had planted in her yard was the perfect spot to keep her busy while Ted was working. She had planted a garden of zucchini, cucumbers, radishes, and cabbage. She had the house to herself and wanted to do some canning before the vegetables rotted.

With her own brown hair tied up in a ponytail, she crouched over the garden with trowel in hand and plucked at the intrusive weeds which were hiding the overripe vegetables. The heat made her cheeks look like a spotty patchwork of reds and pinks.

Noticing a rather plump cucumber hidden under a patch of leaves, Callie plucked it, admiring its size. It felt unusually light, so she turned it over and discovered a hole in the bottom. An ugly green worm wiggled out. The entire cucumber was hollow. The outside of it appeared to be perfect, but the entire inside was rotten.

"This is the condition of your church. Follow My Word!"

Callie dropped the cucumber and jumped to her feet.

Who said that?

She waited, listening. A gentle but disturbing tug pricked at her heart.

"I rebuke you, Satan!" she retorted out loud, stomping on the cucumber. "I rebuke you in the name of Jesus. You will not get me to believe your lies!"

A staunch unrest settled over her for the rest of the day.

The following week the phone rang in Petey's office.

"Hello, Petey speaking."

Crying hit his ear.

"Hello? Who is this?"

"Petey, it's Betty Hunter. I...I hate to bother you now. I..."

"Are you okay?"

She cried some more. "Petey, to be honest, I'm not doing well with this. I...I feel jealous and...I mean I trust Ted...and Callie..."

"Betty, I understand. What you're feeling is normal." Petey swiveled his chair and reached for his notepad. Betty's outburst surprised him. She always seemed confident and calm.

"How do we release our mates, Petey? I feel like my heart's being ripped out. Seeing him with your wife isn't easy."

"Betty, your marriage will benefit from this, I promise you. And I trust my wife. Things will be fine." Petey repeated what he had said to all the upset callers of late, but he too, was not doing well with Callie and Ted's new relationship.

"Petey, I'm worried about Connie, too. She's spending a lot of time with Avery. She's only seventeen, and Ted doesn't seem to care."

"Have you told the pastor?"

"No one seems to listen. I feel like I am losing my family."

"Okay, let me get back with you. I will talk to Mark and contact Donna. Meanwhile, let me pray for you, Betty."

Petey said a quick prayer and no sooner had he hung up, the phone rang again. "Petey here."

"Petey, I need..." The caller choked on her words.

"Marcy? Marcy, what's the matter?" Petey scribbled Marcy's name underneath Betty's on the notepad. The two female leaders were crumbling. It was hard for him to believe.

"I need to talk to Donna. It's urgent." Her voice shattered into broken gasps. "No one is answering the phones in the counseling center."

"Is there something I can do?"

Marcy wanted to scream, but instead said, "No, Petey, just pray for me."

As soon as he hung up the receiver, the phone jangled a third time. Petey shook his head as he picked up and answered, "Hello? Petey here."

"Um...yes, hello. Uh...my name is Ellen Barker. You don't know me but I'm friends with Janice Certs."

"Yes, hello. I know you...uh...who you are."

He remembered she was the good-looking brunette he saw at the restaurant with Cody and Rick.

"I feel kind of dumb calling you...I mean...well...this might sound presumptuous, but I feel drawn to your spirit. I called to see if you would care to worship with me today."

Petey didn't know what to say. He hadn't moved into the connection thing at all, and was struggling trying to cope with all the problems from it.

"Oh," she continued, when he didn't respond. "I hope I don't sound too forward. I'm shy and don't dance much. It's easier for me to call than to approach you in person."

"No, I'm glad you called. I...I am shy too about it all. Would you like to meet me here at my office at one? We could worship in the college chapel." Petey felt the blood rush to his face.

"Yes. Great. I'll see you then."

He hung up the phone. A large smile crept across his face. He quickly relayed the urgent phone messages to the pastor's secretary. Relieved to hand the problems over to someone else, he bent over his desk to get some work done. As he began to tackle the stack of papers on his desk a knock hit his door. He groaned.

Ted peered in. "Got a minute?" he asked.

"Sure, come on in," Petey said.

"I wanted to get with you and make sure you're okay with the time I'm spending with Callie." He didn't sit. The memory of having sex with Petey's wife the day before was still too fresh. He was anxious to leave.

"Well, to be frank, it's not easy. First it was Mark, now you. I'm feeling sort of out in left field right now. But I do know God's doing something wonderful. And I trust my wife completely. Don't worry. I won't stop what God is doing between you both."

Ted shuffled his feet and kept his eyes to the floor. "Good, good, I'm glad you understand. Let me know if you have any problems with this. I'm willing to work out any disagreements that might arise."

"Ted, before you go, I should tell you, Betty called me crying. She is very distraught over these connections. And she is worried about Connie and Avery. I passed her call onto the Pastor's secretary."

Ted fidgeted. "She's a very insecure person; clings to me like a wet napkin."

Petey did not say anything.

"I'll get her some prayer," Ted affirmed.

"I've had some pretty strange calls from others as well today, Ted. I had one woman ask if nude dancing was acceptable between connections. Can you believe that?"

"Yeah, I've had some weird calls along that line as well. That's why we need guidelines. Too many people wanting to do their own thing." Ted stooped over, gripped Petey's hand, then whisked out the door.

At eleven o'clock Laurina Addison entered Mark's office wearing a mauve knit sweater and straight black skirt. He escorted her to a conference room, locked the door, and turned on the music. As they released themselves to the supernatural prism, Mark's hands roamed up Laurina's shoulders and down to the top of her chest. Under the beguiling hex, she allowed his touches, until he slid his hand over her left breast.

She jerked out of his arms, ending the journey.

"Honey, oh honey, I'm so*ww*y. I got ca*ww*ied away in the spi*w*it. I didn't realize I touched you there."

"Mark, I want to stop now."

He trailed her to the door. "Please, Lau*w*ina, I won't do it again. Don't misunderstand my heart."

"Mark, let's not defile this relationship."

"Don't go mad. Let's talk." Mark caught her arm.

"I'm not mad. I understand the love is strong. It's just that our past…"

"I know. I know. I don't want you to think that I was t*w*ying to touch your b*w*easts ever before. Forgive me. Let's p*w*ay now."

Laurina gave in and smiled. "Don't worry about it. I know lots of people are making mistakes."

They ended the session and Mark returned to his office. He was turned on and frustrated that Laurina was such a challenge. He had to get a release today.

He dialed Callie's home phone and perked in his seat when she answered.

"Callie, it's your pastor. How are you?"

"Mark, hello. I'm fine, thanks."

"Callie, I know you have been busy with Ted, but, he has p*w*omised me that he would not hinder your minist*w*y to me. You canceled our last appointment, and well, I need your spi*w*it today, Honey. I don't want to have to talk to Ted about it again…or put rest*w*ictions on…"

"Oh, no, no. Don't talk to Ted. I can come over now if you want me to. I am free for a few hours."

"Gweat. I'll see you soon." Mark clapped his hands.

At one, Petey and Ellen, both self-conscious with each other, walked into the darkened chapel. As they did, Ted passed by with his arm around another woman. Petey watched him lead the woman out of the chapel looking glazy-eyed and giddy. Three or four other dancing couples remained. Petey, not sure he was feeling anything spiritual, did enjoy being close to such a lovely lady. He let her eyes catch his, though he knew it was lust that made him gaze back, nothing else.

As they danced and cuddled closer, the pastor's wife flew into the chapel with her connection, Kurt, and Frank Serris, whose wife and step-daughter moved to California, and a pretty wife of one of the Bible College teachers. The noisy foursome interrupted the silent dancers with buoyant laughter, charging the room with energy. Immediately they began spinning around each other, allowing their glassy orbs to dart back and forth between their parties. Hooked by the power tying their eyes, they skulked across the floor, coming together, hands touching, pulling away, and spinning some more, then slowing until they were swaying together in one close circle.

The onlookers slowed, their own dancing interrupted by the hypnotic and noisy activities of the new group. But they completely stopped, open mouthed and staring when a sudden frenzy, like a tornado, pushed the foursome to the ground, their bodies thrust together like dominoes under the power of the *spirit*, climaxing, and jerking pleasurably into the one next to them. They yelped, groaned, and moaned as their spirits spiraled them into the cosmos.

The orgasms went on, and Petey didn't want to watch anymore. If this was what he had to do to go deeper in God, he didn't want it. He took Ellen's hand and led her out of the chapel. Still, not willing to let her go just yet, he took her back to his office.

After leaving Mark's office, Callie didn't feel much like dancing with Ted. Still, she missed him. She went to his office.

"Is Ted in?" she asked the receptionist.

"No. He left the office early."

"Did he go home?"

"Actually, I think he's dancing with Suzie Hatley."

"Suzie?" Callie's face fell. "What do you mean?"

"Oh, they connected this afternoon in the chapel. I think he tried to find you."

"I was with the pastor. Where do you think they are?"

"Probably at the sanctuary."

Callie glanced at her watch. It was almost four. Petey hadn't called either. Her husband always telephoned during his lunch hour. She walked across the hallway to Petey's office. He was gone too. She felt panicky.

She decided to go to the sanctuary. She knew she shouldn't spy on Ted, but she couldn't help herself. She was lovesick for him, and had to be with him! She sped into the grand parking lot, parked, and rushed into the sanctuary. She climbed the stairs, two at a time, and found them alone, cuddling in the corner of the *mega's* room.

Callie stormed at them, screaming, "Ted, Ted...I need you now!"

Ted put up his hands in defense as Callie started pounding on him. Suzie reached for Callie's arms to restrain her.

"Callie, what's the matter?" Suzie hollered.

"Stop touching her!" Callie shouted.

"Callie," Ted snarled. "Get it together. Stop this! I'm with Suzie now. I can meet with you tonight, but not now."

She burst into hysterical sobs. "What's happening to me?"

Ted motioned for Suzie to wait. He put his arms around Callie and led her back downstairs. "Callie, I don't understand your outburst in there."

"I can't release you very well, Ted. I'm sorry…it's too hard." She wiped at her eyes. Mascara ran down her face.

"Callie, its God's love that drew us together. Now God's doing the same between me and Suzie." He leaned her against the wall in the foyer and lifted her chin with one finger. "Are you okay?"

"Ted, we had sex. Doesn't that matter?"

Ted pulled her into his arms. "Of course, but Callie, the love pushing us together is from God. We slipped. But we've got to move on, keep connecting. We have to deal with this through spiritual eyes. Are you with me, Cal? We are not through; we have many more spiritual journeys together." He wiped her cheeks.

She clung to him. "Come on Ted, let's go somewhere. I need you."

Ted distanced her with both arms. "No, Callie, I'm with Suzie now. Go home. I'll call you later."

"I feel like I'm dying, Ted."

"Callie, maybe God's allowing you to feel this pain. Maybe he wants us not only to experience His love, but He wants us to identify with His pain as well. Maybe these connections are part of experiencing God's agony for us."

"But seeing you with Suzie makes me crazy."

"Don't think about…"

"Ted, are you going to sleep with her?"

"Callie...no!"

"We did it so much, I thought...we were close..."

"Suzie's waiting, I have to go." He chucked her chin and kissed her mouth. "I'll see you later, okay? Please, don't worry."

He left her there.

Callie drove home in a weepy daze. Petey was not home and she called his office. His number was forwarded to the front receptionist's desk.

"Is Petey there?" she asked.

"Oh, Callie, last time I saw him he was with Ellen Barker."

"Who?"

"Tall brunette. I think they had been dancing. I don't think he is coming back here."

Ted never called and Callie spent the rest of the evening sobbing.

CHAPTER THIRTEEN

Service that weekend was in full swing as Janice Certs swung through the busy aisle and sat down beside Rick, rubbing up against his shoulder. Her blonde hair was piled high on her head and the tiny loose strands teased the base of her elegant neck.

"Hello, how are you?" she asked flirtatiously, before leaning forward and smiling innocently at Penny who was seated on Rick's other side. "Hello," Rick said, his mouth almost reaching his ears. She was a knockout. He could barely think of anything else since they had connected.

"Hi Janice," Penny responded politely. She was experiencing a lot of skittish emotions since Rick connected with Janice. She didn't like the feeling.

Rick took Janice by the hand and led her out onto the *dance* floor. Penny wondered where Cody was? She skimmed the crowded aisles and front altar, and when she spied Cody dancing with another woman, a worse feeling hit her. She slipped off her shoes and yanked on her dance slippers, then sped down and flew in between Cody and the woman. Cody, though surprised, did not mind. He gestured a sorry motion to the other woman and took Penny's hand. He focused his glossy blues on hers and she smiled and released her glazed-over eyes to his. She felt better.

When the lights flashed on and off, the dancers returned to their seats. Mark waited at the pulpit, flipping through the pages of his notes. He had left his suit coat behind, along with his tie. His shirt was open at the neck and he was sweaty from dancing. The audience gave him complete attention.

"I realize how difficult this new move of God is on mawwiages, but the outcome will be for good. I urge you to *let go* and *let God. Release* your spouses to their connection. We must release them in order to let God unite us. I know that thwough these connections God will restore all the mawwiages." He rolled up his shirt sleeves. "We are getting calls about jealous spouses. This has to stop. I am ordewing evewyone who is feeling insecure to get delivered from those demons. You are hindewing your spouse and it must stop!"

Donna came up behind Mark and put her hand on his forearm. He stepped aside. Her demure form seemed out of place with her dominating gestures.

"My connection and I have a newfound freedom in God that surpasses the physical," she began. "We have learned to go beyond it into glory. God is using these connections so His love will unite us. Do not let the outward appearances confuse you or stop you." Her arms moved this way and that. "The connecting of our spirits does not end with the dance. It's an on-going bond. If your mate is willing to release you and allow you time with your connection outside church, this is now acceptable. But your mate must agree to these terms. We must consider our spouses. Let's move ahead with caution and careful considerations."

The service ended an hour later with jubilant shouts of *Hallelujah* and *Praise God.* But Mark's financial advisor and elder, Joe Fellows, did not share in the excitement. He and his wife Christina had already noticed the connections parading outside church, at parks, grocery stores, and movie theaters. They picked up their Bibles and left the sanctuary.

Penny and Cody danced until midnight.

"I'll drive you home," Cody said. He stuffed his loose shirt back into his pants and eyed her eagerly.

"Let me tell Rick. Wait here, I'll see if he's upstairs." Penny hurried up the stairs and ran into Petey coming down. He was with a tall brunette.

"Hi Petey. Hey, is Rick up here?"

"Yeah, he's in the far corner." Petey squeezed Ellen around the waist and kept walking.

Penny was glad to see Petey finally connecting.

"Where's Callie?" Penny called after him.

"Who knows?" he yelled back.

Penny spotted Rick in the corner embracing Janice. Their lips were almost touching. She didn't want to break into his spiritual encounter, so she swallowed the nabbing sensations she felt in the pit of her stomach, and returned to Cody's side.

"Let's go," she said to Cody. "By the way, Cody, where's Laurina?"

"She went home two hours ago. She wasn't feeling well."

As they walked outside and entered the back parking lot, Avery drove past with Connie Hunter snuggled close beside him. It was than that Penny remembered her first week at Grace Church and the words the pastor said to the congregation, *"No fwontal hugs allowed. Let's maintain a standard of holiness..."* She shooed away the memory and squeezed Cody.

He turned off the car's engine in front of her apartment and leaned close. "Penny, I can barely contain the love I feel for you." The potency of the moment drew their faces together, and they locked mouths. "Oh, Penny, you are so beautiful, so beautiful... Jesus in you..." He murmured as he kissed and pawed her.

Beaming headlights broke into their darkness and they flew apart.

"It's Rick. I better go." Penny pushed her sweater down and scrambled out of the car.

Rick came up to the car as she shut the door. "Why didn't you wait for me?" he demanded.

"I didn't want to break up your worship time with Janice." She bent down and waved Cody on. He looked worried, but drove away.

"I don't like you sitting alone in the dark with him," Rick fumed, not letting on he saw them kissing.

Penny did not answer. She moved to the house and unlocked the door. Rick stormed in after her, kicking shoes and the garbage container. Confusion rattled his brain. He hated Penny kissing Cody; yet, he was doing the same with Janice. He felt guilty and angry.

That night they slept apart on opposite sides of the bed.

The next morning after Rick left for work, Penny dropped to her knees. It was the first time in a long while that she had spent time with Jesus. It was long overdue. She had to turn to Him because she was feeling ashamed for kissing Cody, and ashamed for feeling jealous of Rick. She had to release Rick and do what the pastor said, but when she wasn't with Cody, those feelings tore at her. As she began to pray, instead of the presence of God meeting her, a strong conviction settled over her. She suddenly knew that God did not want her kissing Cody.

She wept. "Father, forgive me!"

"Thanks for meeting with me, Rick," Cody said the next day at *The Grill*. I know we should have been getting together more often since this new move of God started. I know you were upset last night, and I want to apologize."

"Cody, hey, I understand."

Cody tossed Rick a relieved look. "You do?"

"Yes, I wasn't angry at you. I do feel jealous, but at the same time, I can't stop thinking of Janice." Rick scanned the menu. "I'm not even hungry. I am so torn by all these feelings. You are my friend, and I don't want to compete with you."

"I understand. Laurina is going through the same feelings. What's hard for her is that the pastor wants to be with her more then she does with him. She just doesn't have the same powerful connection as Penny and I do."

"I think that is what is happening with me and Janice. I don't know that I have had a great spiritual experience so far with her, but I do know that I am lusting after her big time. I feel guilty about this."

Cody laughed. "Well, we are human." His rough face creased into a frown. "Just do what you feel God's leading you to do. Be careful. Just keep connecting. Each connection is on a different level."

"I don't like you kissing my wife, but at the same time, how can I stop you when Janice and I have been making out."

Cody looked down. "Let's trust God with each other over this. I promise, Rick, I won't kiss her again. You are my friend and I will honor your marriage."

Rick nodded. "You know, Cody, God has set me free through my connection with Janice. I don't even think of golf anymore."

"Praise God!"

Elder Joe Fellows telephoned Mark's office Tuesday morning. "Pastor, how are you?"

"Fine, Joe, fine. What can I do for you?" Mark asked, looking at his watch, anxious for his meeting with Laurina within the hour.

"Mark, I'm concerned about this connection doctrine. My wife and I disagree with the entire thing. We can't find supporting evidence in scripture to back up such a theory. We're also concerned about the negative effect it's having on the children, visitors, and the marriages."

"Joe, I appweciate your concern, but until you expewience it yourself, you will have these doubts. Be patient."

"Pastor, my wife and I cannot be part of this any longer. You won't discuss it during our board meetings, and I am shocked that adultery is being considered something sent by God."

"Joe, what do you mean *adultewy*? I don't condone such a thing!" Mark sputtered.

"I am sure you know of the numerous couples who are falling into sin."

"They are being pwayed for and counseled. God's love is stwong and it is new to us, therefore we need to be patient and merciful with those that make mistakes."

Joe raised his voice. "Mark, you are in a delusion if you think this move is condoned by God! I will not be part of it! I resign as of now."

"Joe, you always were too independent. This is your downfall. I will not let you twample on my authowity. I will have no other choice but to put you out of this body."

"Do what you have to do. But I will not be part of this evil doctrine."

Penny and Cody parked near the water's edge. The sun beat down through the windshield. There was no one in sight.

"Cody, we can't kiss anymore," Penny said as she leaned her head on his shoulder.

"I know. I told Rick I wouldn't kiss you anymore."

"You did?" Her head flew up.

"Yeah. Sort of feel it's the right thing to do."

"Well, God told me in prayer not to."

"I don't believe that was God, Penny. If God is giving us this love, He understands our flesh will get in the way."

"Than why did you promise Rick not to kiss me? If it's not wrong, we shouldn't be stopping. Right?"

Cody touched her cheek. "I don't really think Rick expects we will stop. He's kissing Janice."

Penny pulled away from his touch. "What? He is?"

Cody didn't answer.

"He is something. Tells you to not kiss me, but he is having his make-out sessions with her!"

"Penny, it's not like that with him. He is feeling the same way we are. He didn't ask me to stop kissing you. I volunteered to on my own."

"You did?"

"Yeah. And about God talking to you, why would Donna be kissing her connection if it was wrong?"

"Really? She does?"

"Yep. She told me herself. She said they have bypassed the flesh. Don't pass it around. Not everyone is ready to go to those spiritual places."

Penny laughed. "Brave one, aren't you." She started kissing his ears. "Still want to keep that promise?"

Cody groaned and pulled her close. Passion flared and this time he could not stop at the kissing.

"I want you, Honey," he drawled huskily. "Oh Penny, God's love is too strong..."

"No, we shouldn't, Cody. What about…"

His mouth stopped her from saying any more.

Penny arrived home at eight that evening. Rick's car was parked out front, but the house was dark. She wondered where he was as she unlocked the door and flipped on the light switch. Janice and Rick popped up from the bottom of the couch with tousled heads and crimson faces, looking as if they had been caught stealing hubcaps.

"What's going on here?" Penny screamed.

"Penny, I didn't expect you so soon," Rick sputtered, jumping to his feet.

"Obviously not!"

"We were praying."

"Yes, and I'm the president!"

"I'll take her home now."

"I thought you didn't want me alone with Cody. What's this?"

"I thought you'd be here hours ago."

"Yeah, sure," Penny replied with sarcasm. She did not look at Janice. Instead she stormed into the bedroom and slammed the door. Why was she yelling at Rick when she just had sex with Cody? She felt shamed—and sick to her stomach that Rick might be doing the same thing with Janice if he had not already. What was happening to their lives?

Penny heard the front door open and close. She waited for hours for Rick to return, but he never did.

"Hello church, how was your week?" Pastor Mark asked his flock Friday night after the singers took their seats. More security officers stood guard at each entry door and a dozen more ushers lined the back wall. Hundreds of *connection couples*, no longer concerned about being with their spouses, were seated together all over the auditorium, smiling happily. Others, having trouble releasing their mates, sat stone-faced.

"Tonight, along with my sermon, I would like to speak on some important issues. As your pastor, I'm concerned for your health and well being, especially with all the dancing going on. I want to make sure you're eating well and getting enough sleep. I'm aware that some of you are here dancing until four in the morning. Starting today, the sanctuawy closes at one."

The majority of the congregation responded with disappointed groans.

"Now for bad news. I hate to tell you all this, but Joe and Chwistina Fellows have been disfellowshiped and I am asking all of you to avoid them."

The crowd mulled over the news for a few seconds, and than a small buzzing went up.

"He refused to submit to this church government, and he is in rebellion to God's Word. He is not to be associated with. I know some of you are confused as to why so many are leaving the church. But, this is the way God is sepawating the sheep from the goats, the tares from the wheat. We must stay in the boat!"

When service ended, Callie watched from the pew, torn at the sight of Ted and Suzie dancing. All of it was too much. She stood to leave. As she did, Petey and Ellen strolled onto the floor, laughing and connecting. Her husband's arm clenched the lovely woman's thin waist, and he looked too happy. Their mouths were inches apart as they pranced together.

"Excuse me!" Callie shouted over the music, pounding on Petey's back. "I need you now!" She ignored Ellen.

"Wha...? Callie, what's wrong?" Petey faced his tormented wife.

She grabbed his arm and pulled at him. "I need you. Period."

Ellen threw Petey an exasperated look as others close by stopped and watched Callie's tantrum.

"Callie, demons of jealousy are attacking you now," Petey said, looking from Ellen's impatient expression back to his wife's ragged one. "Let's pray and get you delivered. Ellen can join us." He hid his irritation with a wan smile.

"What?" Callie said in a loud tone. "*No*, take me home. Now! I need you now!"

"I have to go now, Ellen. I'm sorry." Not wanting to cause a scene, Petey grabbed Callie's arm and ushered her out the sanctuary without waiting for Ellen's reply.

Meanwhile, the pastor's daughter was feeling just as miserable as Callie. She sat in the pew watching her husband float by in Connie's arms. Her husband's distant behavior grew worse each day, and Gayle found no comfort from him or her parents. She looked around, jealous that others were enjoying themselves so well. She wanted to understand, to step into the boat and discover why everyone flounced around, willing to look so foolish.

She decided to go to the foyer and dance solo. Sitting alone and watching Avery make love eyes at another woman was not helping. As she started to dance, she couldn't help but smile at the man tumbling about in front of her, looking ridiculous with his long arms flipping around his head and his feet bashing the floor like a clumsy elephant. Without thinking twice, Gayle flew into the man's path. He didn't see her, and sent her reeling to the floor on her bottom.

"Oh my, excuse me," the man exclaimed, bending over and pulling her back up with his hand as fast as she went down.

"Oh, my!" she said.

"Did I hurt you?" he asked. He was slightly overweight, but had a nice face. He grinned wide at her.

"No, I'm fine, I think." She laughed. "Would you mind if I joined you in worship?" she asked.

"Oh, sure. God is good; come on."

In one swift movement the big guy whisked Gayle high into the air, and from there she spiraled into glory. She forgot everyone and everything.

Penny and Marcy met for a late lunch on Monday at *The Grill*. Other church members poured into the busy café, most of them with their spiritual connections.

"Penny, I feel left out. Do you think God's forgotten me?" Marcy sipped at her coffee.

"Marcy, your time will come. God hasn't forgotten you. Cheer up." She noticed Marcy looked pale.

"Caring for a child doesn't give me much time to dance."

"Why don't you ask Owen to take Willy more? Or I can babysit." Penny spread jam over her croissant.

"Owen works so much and I hate to make him miss out on worship. And I wouldn't keep you from Cody." Marcy smiled. "I'll find someone to watch him."

"Marcy, please, I can watch Willy. How about tomorrow?"

"No, really, I'm fine."

"Marcy, are you feeling okay? You look tired."

"Just didn't sleep well last night."

Penny patted her friend's hand.

The cafe door opened and Avery walked in with Connie. Connie, who wore a bright purple ribbon in her hair looked very seventeen.

"There's Avery with his connection," Penny leaned forward, resting her chin in a hand. "Connie's so young; seems weird to see them connecting."

Marcy nodded. "I know her. She's pretty mature for her age."

"Hey guys!" Laurina came flying up to their table waving. "I thought I might find you here." Her auburn hair was swept up in a ponytail.

"Hey back," Penny said, her voice strained. She had a hard time looking at her friend.

"How come you didn't return my call, Pen?"

"I forgot."

"Oh." Laurina tried not to look hurt. She had been sensing Penny's estrangement toward her of late.

Marcy broke the ice. "We're people watching," she said.

Laurina followed Marcy's eyes to the elder and teenager. "I see."

"Laurina, you've lost weight," Marcy added, still trying to make everyone comfortable.

"Almost ten pounds. All this dancing's been great for weight loss." She sat down.

"There's Ted," Penny said.

Ted slid into a side booth with Suzie Hatley. He was dressed to kill in a flamboyant flowery Hawaiian shirt and khaki-type pants.

"He never dressed like that before," Laurina laughed.

"I wonder where Callie is?" Penny asked. "Is Suzie a new connection?"

"Yes," Laurina said. "They danced for hours last night."

"Boy, I hope Cody doesn't get another connection…" The words flew out before Penny could stop them.

Laurina flushed and pulled the menu close to her face.

"Oh, Laurina…Are you okay? I mean…"

"No problem. I trust you and Cody." She peeked around the menu and forced a smile. "All of a sudden I'm starving!"

Penny decided not to tell Laurina that she was meeting her husband after lunch.

Penny arrived home still flushed from the memory of making love with Cody in a small room on the college campus. They hadn't even danced. As soon as Cody bolted the door, they were at it—like inmates who hadn't had sex for years. Afterward when they were done, Cody insisted God would forgive them for their weakness.

She threw the keys on the counter. Rick was gone as usual. She grabbed a box of donuts from the refrigerator and poured some cold milk into a tall glass. As she bit into the donut, she couldn't help but smile. She had never experienced sex like that before. It was beyond description. She felt fire with Cody, absolute fire.

The phone rang. Penny picked up. It was Laurina.

"Pen, have you seen Cody?"

Guilt rattled her spine.

"I can't find him anywhere," Laurina said.

"I am sure he will call. I have to go, Laurina. You caught me in the shower." Penny hung up without waiting for a reply. The guilt stalking her was not just from the sex—she was in love with her best friend's husband.

Rick couldn't get enough of Janice. He knew meeting with her in a cheap motel was not proper, but he didn't want to dance anymore. He was completely taken in by Janice and did not want to share her with anyone else.

"I love you, fine lady!" He kissed her hard.

"Rick," she moaned pleasurably. "Don't hate me, but I hate your wife. I am so jealous of her. Just the thought of you with her makes me crazy. I know these connections are supposed to help marriages, but I don't want your marriage restored."

Rick swung to his side and propped himself up with an elbow. He looked into her almond eyes. "What are you saying?"

"I want to marry you!" She pulled his head back down to her lips.

Rick knew they were stepping outside the realm of God's will, but he could not resist a love that moved him like dynamite moved a mountain.

Mid-December brought an unusual blanket of snow. The evening wind howled and slammed against windows as the swirling snow bounced everywhere. Three inches already covered the ground.

Marcy sat at the kitchen table in the parsonage watching Donna cook. "Thanks for seeing me on such short notice," she said.

Donna looked over and smiled. She wiped her hands on her ruffled apron. "Marcy, I know this is tough on you. But, let me tell you, there is no perfect marriage out there."

"I know. But I seem to be losing my will power. My mind has been jumbling and I am so tired all the time. I have no energy for little Willy. I am worried that I might not get out of bed tomorrow."

Donna walked over to Marcy and sat beside her and took her hands in hers. "You are stronger than you think. Have you been seeking deliverances?"

"Yes. But nothing seems to help me."

"There must be a stronghold demon somehow holding on to you. We need to really seek God to show you what is allowing this demon to stay and torment you."

"But, even if I do get deliverances, how do I handle Owen's gay lifestyle?"

"Marcy, he is a Christian. You must give him continual grace. All I can tell you to do is keep trusting the Lord. If Owen is trying, you must be patient."

Marcy lowered her voice. "Do you think William will get his demons?"

"That is why we have the deliverance teams. Now is a good time to have those prayer warriors praying for your son. Let me pray for you."

Donna placed her hands on Marcy's head and prayed loudly, demanding demons to leave Marcy and William alone.

At the end of the prayer, Donna stood. "Marcy," she said, "Mark will be here soon, so I will see you next week at our regular scheduled time. Okay?"

Marcy nodded and put on her coat. "Thanks, Donna." She gave her a hug and left through the front door.

Mark, inching his Cadillac up the snowy driveway, waved at Marcy who was slowly backing out.

He came through the garage into the warm kitchen. The house smelled of apples, cinnamon, and chicken soup.

"Marcy doing better?" he asked his wife.

Donna, standing at the stove adding cloves to a pot of apple cider, said, "She needs a connection."

Mark removed his coat and straddled the stool, watching his wife. It was one of the rare occasions when they were home together. Usually one or both were dancing or in prayer meetings.

"Mark," she set down the wooden spoon and faced him. "I think Frank Serris might have slept with one of the teenage girls."

"What?" Mark shouted. "Fwank is causing this church too many pwoblems!"

"We can't prove anything yet, but one of the school teachers told me the girl's mother suspects her daughter and Frank might have had sex. Another member had called her after seeing the two going into a motel last week."

"What is she doing with him at that age? Why aren't the pawents supervising her wheweabouts?"

"Apparently both parents have been busy with their connections. They didn't think Frank would be a threat. They allowed him to take her to a show and to the amusement park, but only because he said other church members would be joining them. Obviously one of those times they decided to hit the motel instead."

Donna filled two bowls with chicken soup. She pushed one over to Mark.

"We'll have to put restwictions on him. He disgusts me! What bothers me about this move, too many people are abusing it. I'll talk to Fwank tomowwow. He will not be allowed near any young ladies." He moaned, "I am not sure if letting the spiwitual connections have fweedom outside the church is a wise thing."

He walked to the sink, washed his hands, and returned to his soup. "Have any cwackers?"

Donna opened the cupboard and handed him a small basket.

"Mark, we can't let a few mistakes plug up what God wants to do. You need to keep insisting the congregation release their mates and seek deliverances." She joined Mark on the stool beside him.

"How are things going with your connection?" Mark snapped. He crumbled a few saltine crackers into the soup.

Donna shook her head. "Don't start with me, Mark. I am not your problem."

"This is the first time you have made me dinner in over a month."

She didn't reply.

"So, how far have you and Kurt gone in the physical?" He kept sipping his soup.

"The physical isn't important Mark. It's only a vehicle used to go deeper in God." Donna patted her artificial tresses away from her face as she raised the spoon to her lips.

"Not evewyone is mature enough to understand what you are saying, Donna."

"I don't think kissing will hurt anyone."

Mark raised his eyebrows.

"Mark, there are those of us who want Jesus so bad we're willing to overlook our bodily responses for a deeper spiritual experience. Yes, I have done this. Are you shocked?"

He winced.

"Of course," she quickly added, "The entire church isn't ready for this."

"I don't want to know how far you've gone," he said with irritation. "But I do have to keep this church in line and not allow evewyone to be committing adulterwy. There are already too many people falling."

"Why don't you hold a special meeting for the mega connections and allow them more freedom for physical expression, instead of the whole church? Then we can enforce stricter guidelines for the less spiritual members. We need to give God room to mature these spiritual unions."

Mark slid the crackers to Donna.

She pushed them back.

"Today's Wednesday. Let's see, I'll a*ww*ange a meeting for next Tuesday night," he said.

By the following afternoon the snow had melted and a steady rain fell instead. Betty Hunter could hear the raindrops spattering against the bathroom window as she hung her head over the toilet bowl. She felt another wave of nausea and threw up some more. She wiped her mouth on her sleeve and struggled back into the living room. Though everyone else was losing weight from dancing, the twenty pounds she lost was from depression. She was unable to accept Ted with another woman. No matter how hard she tried, she couldn't. She swallowed, waited for her stomach to settle, then reached for the phone on the coffee table. She called the counseling center.

The receptionist answered.

"This is Betty. I need to talk to Donna. I'm not doing well." Her voice was shaky.

"Hold on, Betty. I'll put you through."

The minute passed slowly.

Donna's voice came over the phone. "Betty? Are you okay?"

"Donna? No. I'm…" her voice faltered, then she shrieked, "Come over, Donna. I'm losing control…I'm throwing up, I feel insane…!"

"I'll be right over, Betty. Hang on."

Donna hung up and telephoned her husband's office across the hall.

"Mark, we need to get to Ted's house. Betty needs help. She's really distraught. Sounds like she's having a nervous breakdown."

"Where's Ted?"

"I think with Suzie. He's not taking his cell phone either. I left a message for him."

"I'll meet you in the corridor. Donna, don't tell anyone else about this."

Mark grabbed his coat and hurried out of his office.

He and Donna pulled up at the Hunter household fifteen minutes later and parked the car. They scrambled to the front door and knocked. There was no answer.

"Betty?" Mark yelled. He knocked again.

"I think the key is under the pot there," Donna said.

Mark found it and unlocked the door. All the lights were off. Whimpers came from the living room.

"Betty!" Donna rushed over to the limp form slumped on the floor and gathered the despairing woman into her arms. "Mark, open the curtains. Get some light in here."

Betty looked drunk. It made Mark uneasy. "Has she been dwinking?" he asked.

Betty's breath smelled sour. "Yes. I think so," Donna said, rocking Betty. "Shhhh, Betty," she crooned, "You'll be fine."

"I'll go see if they have any coffee in the kitchen," Mark said.

"Good idea."

Betty opened her eyes and slurred, "Donna, Ted's having an affair again."

"Now Betty. That's ridiculous. You are allowing the past to hinder you from God's love now. You need to relax and release Ted to the Lord. I promise He will restore your marriage."

Betty closed her eyes at the rushing memories.

"Don't allow Ted's mistake to turn you away from God." Donna's rigid voice was reprimanding. *"Ted repented of his affair. It's your duty before God to forgive him and cover him. And Laurina. She is young, vulnerable...give her a chance to grow too."*

"But Donna, I don't trust him. He's done this before..."

"Before you were saved. He's been faithful up to now. Betty, submission is not easy during times like these, but if you can submit to your husband, God will reward you. I believe your lack of submission to him could be why he had the affair."

"What? I teach classes on submission. How can you say this?"

"Maybe God is showing you areas you have not yet surrendered to..."

Betty bawled. Donna continued to rock her. Mark came back into the room.

"Call Ted again. See if he's back in the office yet," Donna said.

Betty's cries turned to choppy moans.

"You're boring, Betty. Boring...boring...boring..."

"Let's lay her down," Mark said. He and Donna scooped her up onto the couch.

Donna sat down beside her and massaged her feet.

"I'm so sorry," Betty whispered. "I wish I were stronger."

Donna's cell phone went off.

"Hello?" Donna answered.

"This is Ted."

"Ted. Mark and I are at your house. We need you here. Now!"

"I'll be there right away." He voice was edgy.

Connie burst through the front door and stopped in mid-flight. "Mom, what's the matter?" she asked, walking slowly toward the trio.

Donna got up and led Connie into the kitchen. "Your Mom is having some hard times, now. She needs some rest."

"She is freaking out again over Dad's connection, right?" Connie swung out her hip, impatiently balancing her fist on it.

"Connie, your mother needs prayer and support. We must all be patient..."

"She's jealous of me and Dad with our connections," Connie retorted.

Donna's voice rose. "Aren't you being a might selfish, young lady?"

Connie pouted and sank into the kitchen chair, embarrassed by Donna's scolding.

Ted walked in disgusted at the sight of his wife acting like a nut case. Mark threw him a cool "do something" look. Ted resigned to the silent order and sat down with Betty and pulled her into his arms.

"I've got you," he said. "Calm down, Betty." She whimpered into his shoulder. Her raw emotions made him tense.

Donna returned. "Let's pray for her now."

Connie came back into the room and rolled her eyes. "I'm going over to Sally's house to spend the night," she said, and walked out the front door without waiting for an answer.

The group prayed for Betty until she stopped crying.

The next day Callie walked into the college bookstore deep in thought. She had peeked into the chapel and had seen Mark dancing with another pretty woman. He seemed to have a new connection every week. He never called her anymore to meet him, and when she called, he made excuses. Boy, how the tables had turned. She was sure his many female *dancing* partners were keeping him quite virile. The rejection of Mark and Ted had been difficult, but she refused to let them see her grovel anymore. Getting used to Petey's connection helped strengthen her against those insecure demons, and she was determined to *release* Petey and not hinder his spiritual journey. She had a reputation to maintain, and she would not allow demons to ruin her. Crying herself to sleep every night or stomping her feet would not bring Ted back or keep her husband away from that gangly brunette. She had decided not to think about it, but to focus on other things. Just put it out of her mind. It seemed to be getting easier because she didn't hurt as much.

She purchased two books, than decided to go back into the college chapel and dance solo. It had been a long time since she worshipped alone with God. The pastor was gone and only a few couples were there worshipping at the front. Callie decided to go to the back of the chapel where no one could see her. She began twirling softly and let the music soothe her.

She didn't see Avery come in. The pastor's son-in-law watched her for a few minutes, and then joined her. She opened her eyes to find the lanky elder looking at her with a buoyant expression. That familiar energy flew between them with a wonderful jolt. Avery reached for her hand and drew her right against him.

Together they soared higher than either one had gone before.

Cody had an hour between college classes and was tempted to take a walk and enjoy the sunshine; but instead he opted to pray. It had been a long time since he spent quality time alone with the Lord. He knew he couldn't keep running from the guilt he was feeling, all too often now, from sleeping with Penny. He had to face it and take it to God. He went into the small prayer room near the college chapel and knelt at the bench. As he started praying, he heard the door open and close. Looking around, Cody saw an attractive woman kneeling on the other side. He went back to his prayers, and soon felt a hand on his back. He felt a sizzling in his spirit and began laughing under the *power*. He looked up into a lovely freckled face. Her sapphire eyes locked with his turquoise ones and together they *danced*, without even standing up. After an hour of being drenched in the supernatural ardor, they came back down to earth. By this time their bodies were wrapped together, like two drunks falling over one another.

"Hi, I'm Lorie Welch," the pretty redhead said, still looking into his eyes.

"Hi back. I'm Cody Addison." His eyes twinkled.

"Yes, I know." She kept smiling, still reeling from the experience. "Do you feel what I feel?"

"Absolutely. Want to dance?"

"Absolutely."

He took her by the hand out into the chapel and they danced nonstop for two more hours.

"What do you mean you have other plans?" Penny asked Cody that evening over the phone.

"Penny, don't be jealous, but I got a new connection today. She wants to meet with me tonight at the sanctuary."

Penny's heart plummeted. "Do you want to meet her?"

"Yeah."

"But we always meet on Thursday nights."

"Just this once."

"Who is she?"

"Lorie Welch."

"Lorie? That pretty redhead?"

"She's okay."

"Yeah, sure. So, does this mean we're through?"

"No, Penny. You are my *mega*, not Lorie." He didn't have the heart to tell her that he felt more captivated spiritually than he had ever been before. "We can meet tomorrow morning. I'll take the day off and we can go downtown."

"Really, Cody? Oh, that sounds wonderful." She let him go, despite the topsy-turvy emotions plowing through her. Dealing with Laurina was hard enough, but now sharing him with another pretty woman made her crazy. It was too much. Releasing her husband had been torturous, but releasing Cody was like facing death. The spiritual unions didn't seem to be restoring anyone like they were supposed to do. Months were flying by, yet it seemed everyone was either losing their minds, or completely suppressing them so as not to feel any pain. Everyone involved in the *move of God* was riding on a giant roller coaster. No one knew when to expect a dip, a curve—or a drop.

She decided to go to the sanctuary and worship alone, convincing herself she was not checking up on Cody. But she knew better.

Marcy had packed a light suitcase and put a coat on Willy. *Should I leave a note?*

Little Willy stared at her from the doorway. "Momma, Momma!" he said cheerily, holding his hands out for her. Marcy decided against the note and picked William up. He looked up at her with wide happy eyes.

"Time to go, sweetheart." Marcy grabbed the one suitcase and left the house.

She belted her son into the back seat of her Honda, then backed out of the driveway and sped to the entrance of the freeway. She turned south. Soft rain beat against the car roof, lulling the boy to sleep. Marcy's eyes twitched and her head spun. There was no other way to save her child.

A few hours later she took the Eugene Exit and drove a few more miles until she saw *vacancy* flashing on a motel sign to her right. She pulled into the parking lot and cut the engine. Willy was still asleep in the back seat. She clutched the steering wheel for a long time, listening to the rain beat against the windshield. Taking a deep breath, she wiped at the tears that were running down her face and climbed out of the car. Quickly reaching into the back seat, she retrieved Willy and ran inside the warm office.

They gave her room 7. How ironic. In the scriptures, seven symbolized perfection and completion. She smiled slightly. Inside an old television set was perched on a desk near the double bed. One dresser and a few cheap paintings furnished the small room. Marcy laid Willy down on the bed, then locked the door. She didn't go back outside to get her suitcase.

She opened her Bible to the book of Psalms. She bent over it crying. There was no other way. She had to make sure Willy would not get Owen's demons. She carried the open Bible to the bathroom and set it face up on the floor. Next, she reached over and turned on the tub's faucet. As the warm water filled the basin, she sat back on the cold floor in a stupor. Once the tub was full, she turned off the knob and returned to the bed. Willy was still sleeping. She was glad; it made it much easier.

She lifted him into her arms, and stared at him.

Goodbye, my sweet.

She moved back to the bathroom and lowered her son into the bath water. He woke as she pushed his little head under.

"Take him God, in Jesus name!"

She held him down until his small body thrashed no more.

CHAPTER FOURTEEN

News of little William Nason's death charged through the church office like a hurling boomerang.

"Ted," Mark said, rushing into Ted's office. "I'm holding an emergency meeting in thirty minutes. Get the elders together. This is a sad, sad day."

Ted rose from the chair. "Yes, it is. I'll get right on it."

Mark moved to leave, but hesitated. "Ted," he asked nervously, rubbing the creases on his forehead, "what could have possessed Marcy to do something so cwazy?"

"I don't know. She was getting counsel, prayer…"

"The church will suffer from this. It was on the news this morning. They also mentioned the spiwitual connections. They made our church look pwetty bad."

"God will be our defense."

Mark returned to his office, deeply troubled. The intercom buzzed. He hit the button. "What is it?" he asked.

"Pastor, Channel Five News is on the line. They want to question you regarding William's death."

"Tell them I'm in a meeting and will be unavailable for the rest of the day."

"Yes, Pastor."

Perspiration forced him to remove his suit coat. What on earth possessed Marcy to kill her own child? He felt angry with her. Her monstrous actions would bring the police around. What would he do? He had to talk to the assembly and make sure they kept quiet. Further investigations might lead them to look into other matters, which made him jittery about Frank

Serris. He would have to contact the key people who knew about Frank's weakness and make sure they wouldn't talk to the media either.

Thirty minutes later Mark entered the conference room, looking remorseful and confused. Everyone was there, including Gayle and Donna.

Gayle went to her dad and consoled him with a big hug. He returned the squeeze and wiped a tear from his eye.

"I am sure you all know that last night Marcy Nason dwowned her three-year-old son in a hotel bathtub in Eugene." He faced the group.

Gayle took a seat between her mother and Avery. Everyone was grieving.

"Dad, who found Marcy?" Gayle asked.

"Marcy called the police herself. She told them she did it to fwee William fwom demons. It was on the news this morning and I am getting calls from other stations asking to interview me. But, I just can't talk to them now." He put his head down.

"Where's Owen?" Avery asked.

"He was questioned by the police, and now he's with his parents. He's taking it hard."

Gayle was crying. "What will we do?" she asked.

Donna spoke up. "Mark, I think you need to talk to the press. If you don't, it'll look like we're the reason why Marcy did this. The news is already starting to portray our church this way."

"She's right," Ted said.

The others in the room agreed.

Mark sat down. "I don't know," he said, "It might not be wise for me to have my face plastered on all the television stations. We need to keep a low pwofile. Right now I have to think of how to appwoach the church with this news."

"Remember," Donna said, patting at her big hair, "the church handled Becky's suicide. They'll do the same in this situation. Have faith in your sheep and in what God is doing here. We can't let the news media distract us from the truth or from what God is doing in our lives. Marcy was driven by demons. She made a choice to step outside our covering, and disobeyed God in the process. Now her child is dead. This is the result of rebellion. We must strive harder to walk with God and not allow this ordeal to hinder this church from moving deeper into God's holy love. Let's deal with it, and move on."

The elders piped up in agreement.

"Mark," Ted added, "If you like, I'll take care of the press interviews."

"Yes, yes," Mark replied, "That's a gweat idea! Ted, you're a whiz at business. You can handle their tough questions. Hopefully this will all die down soon. Meanwhile, I will pwepare for tonight's service. I am deeply concerned about my...um...our church's reputation, and so let's evewyone pway today that God will defuse this bomb."

Gayle felt morose. She knew that the spiritual connection dogma had already ruined Grace Church's reputation. This murder would only add fuel to the fire.

No music played at that night's service. Everyone sensed something was amiss when the pastor moved up to the podium with his head hung low and his mood grim.

"I have some bad news," he said. "Last night a tewwible thing happened."

No one moved. Even the babies seemed to sense the solemn spirit by refusing to cry.

"I want you to know that what I am about to say is difficult. Please, keep in a spi*w*it of p*w*ayer as I speak. I ask that all of you remain quiet."

Mark placed both hands flat down on the podium and looked around at the sea of curious faces. "Some of you might have seen this morning's news. Last night Marcy Nason killed her son, Willy."

Gasps rose. Mark put up his hand to silence them. "Please, I know this is a shock. Please, do not speak now." He continued to tell them what happened, and for the next half-hour the assembly let him speak. Many wept at the news, while others just sat there stunned.

At the end Mark said, "One final thing. I am asking each one of you to remain loyal to this church du*w*ing this time. The police will want to talk to some of you who know Marcy. Let's be careful not to gossip and put her th*w*ough any more anguish. As it is, the media is t*w*ying to portw*ay this church as the cause of her p*w*oblems. Satan is mad and is turning up the heat on us for what God is doing here. Let's fight for each other, and for God's Word. Let's not allow the devil to destw*oy us any further."

Mark sighed long, than added, "Marcy, that poor girl, walked out f*w*om the covew*ing of this church and left herself wide open to demonic attack. I warned you all, if you leave G*w*ace Church, you are placing yourself in a dangew*ous place. Do not give into the devil! Stay joined with me, church! Let's p*w*ay."

Mark led the mournful congregation in prayer.

When the praying subsided, Donna reached for the microphone beside her pew and began speaking in tongues. She stopped suddenly, then began to interpret in English. The prophesy encouraged the hearers to follow their pastor and brought a renewed hope into the room.

Mark took advantage of the uplifted mood. "Church," he cried loudly, "Let's worship God and shout the devil right out of this place! Choir, get on up here!"

Most of the assembly acted on his faith and rushed to the floor in response to the upbeat melody.

Penny, Laurina, and Callie did not dance. They were heartbroken. How could their friend do such a horrible thing? Marcy had never spoken to any of them about any problems she might have had, and she seemed so together. She was a pillar in the church. How could she have fallen in such a way? How could she have murdered the son she had longed for and loved so dearly? It was a hard thing to cope with. They sought each other out for comfort and sat together in a back pew, talking into the wee hours of the morning.

A week went by and church services returned to their normal high-paced mode. Penny sat on the edge of the pew watching everyone dance. Rick and Janice, as usual, were nowhere to be seen. They seldom ever showed up at church anymore. When would things turn better? She felt so blue. She lost Marcy, Marilyn, Rick, and now Cody. Marriages were supposed to be restored by the spiritual connections, but hers was in complete disarray. And how could she go back to Rick when she loved Cody so much? Would God take that love back? She scanned the group of dancers. Where was Cody? She hated that he had a new connection. Sharing him was like asking her to give up her life. It was unbearable. All she wanted to do was cry all the time.

She decided to go upstairs and see if he was there. As she hit the top of the stairs, the music switched to a vigorous, joyful tune. The area was packed.

Penny's heart raced when she spied Cody near the wall bopping and spinning with his new connection. The blatant desire on his face enraged her. Panicky, she ran down the stairs, and pushed her way through the crowded foyer, away from her torment, out to the safety of her car.

Ellen Barker had promised to dance with another gentleman that evening after service, so Petey sat in the front pew watching them. He didn't like the man touching her shoulders. Ellen sensed Petey's discomfort and whispered into the man's ear. He took her hand and led her out of the sanctuary to dance in the foyer.

Before jealousy had time to smother him, someone tapped on Petey's shoulder and said timidly, "Would you like to worship with me?"

Petey looked up. Betty Hunter stood there in a chic flowery dress wearing a worried look that he might say no. The elder's wife had lost lots of weight, and though her face looked unsure, Petey found her invitation and new look appealing.

"Sure, I guess so," he said with an impish grin.

Betty lit up.

Petey rose and took her hand. "You're the first elder's wife I've danced with." He removed his glasses and put them on his Bible, than moved into the aisle with her, careful how he touched her.

"I haven't danced since this *move* started, so thank you for obliging me."

"No, how come?"

"I had to learn how to release my husband first. And all that good stuff…" She smiled and leaned into his body.

He did not expect her to be so bold so fast. As the beat of the music slowed, Petey pulled her to himself tightly. Within seconds he was consumed with the gold flecks of her eyes. The swell of the spell hit them both powerfully and unexpectedly, and Betty, for the first time in over a year, found herself laughing with glee.

Meanwhile, Gayle asked a friend to watch her two boys, and she left the church with her connection. It was the first time she had agreed to go with him outside church property. She tried to maintain a right spirit about it all. She didn't want to do anything that would disappoint her students or her own children.

The *spiritual lovers* parked in an old Chevrolet on a dead end street near the old beer factory. The beguiling hex moved them to such passion that Gayle did not stop his hands from moving up under her clothes. She had never allowed him to go beyond kissing, but tonight she could not stop. Together they slid backward across the old patched up leather seats. But it was the throbbing mass of guilt, not her partner's sex, which penetrated Gayle and brought her tumbling back down to earth.

"Penny, you look terrible. What's up?" Callie asked, tightening the belt on her flannel robe. Her large Doberman sniffed excitedly at Penny's legs. "Come on in, sit down."

"I am sorry to barge in like this. Last night was hell for me. I just need to talk to someone."

"Spill the beans. There is nothing you can't say to me." Callie sat down beside her, tugging at her wig. "I'm suppose to meet Avery in an hour, but this headpiece won't sit right."

Penny gave a small chuckle. "It looks fine."

Callie commanded her dog to go, and it scampered out of the room.

"You have a connection with Avery?" Penny asked

"Yeah. Wow! It's a mega for sure. I'm totally gone!"

"Is he still connected to Connie?"

"No. She had a hard time with us, but I think she is moving on now." She didn't mention that a crying Connie followed them for days before Avery had to report the problem to Ted.

"Oh, Callie, that's what's happening to me. Cody has another connection. I'm so jealous, I'm sick!"

"I know exactly what you are feeling. When Ted connected with Suzie, I went bonkers. I was so possessed I ran up to them while they were dancing and started beating on Ted."

"You did?"

"Yeah. And I did the same to Petey. It scared me."

"And now?"

"And now I'm *soaring*!"

"But…but, do you *love* Avery?"

"Totally. I can't think of anything else. It doesn't even bother me anymore that Petey is with Ellen. I am glad, because it frees me up to see Avery." Callie squeezed herself. "He makes me feel alive! And God's love is pouring on us every time we are together."

"I'm worried. I'm so in love with Cody, and Rick doesn't come home anymore. He's with Janice constantly. They don't even go to church."

"You need to report that. He should be at church."

"Well, since the pastor allows connections to go everywhere together, how can I tattle on Rick? They will just tell me to release him."

"Yeah, probably so. Do you and Rick still...you know...sleep together?"

"Have sex? No."

"Neither do Petey and I."

"Callie, this is why I am worried. I have...slipped with Cody. More than once."

Callie stood and looked at her watch. "Oh, Penny, I have to get ready. Listen, don't be too hard on yourself. Mark and Donna already told us mega connections that it was okay to use the physical to get into the spiritual. We are only human."

"But, not sex...when we did it, we weren't dancing."

"God forgives you. Don't feel guilty. You're not alone." Callie let a sly smile slip out and she patted her friend on the cheek. "Jesus' love is uniting everyone. Let's let Him iron out the mistakes. Pastor Mark says God's allowing jealousies and mishaps to manifest so we can seek deliverances and come into that perfect unity."

"Thanks, Callie, for being a good friend." Penny rose to go. "I guess I'm still down after what happened to Marcy. I heard she is in a mental ward."

"Yeah. She is. I miss her too."

"By the way, the pastor has wanted to dance with me. He's called my house a couple times. But, I made excuses. I'm too down with Cody."

Callie's countenance sobered. "Oh? Let me warn you, Mark can get pretty intense and....just don't let him pressure you into something you aren't comfortable with."

"What do you mean?"

Callie put on a quick smile. "Maybe you should meet him," she said matter-of-factly. "It will get your mind off of your troubles. That's how I got over Ted. I decided to just jump in and dance!"

The phone buzzed.

"I have to get that, Pen." Callie walked into the kitchen and picked up.

A muffled sound pursued and Penny heard Callie retort angrily, "I'm fine. Tell Mom to stop worrying about us. It's gossip, that's all."

More muffles and Callie returned to Penny.

"Problems with the family, Cal?" Penny asked.

"My family is harassing me to leave our church. Ever since the news reports about Marcy, they think our church is unsafe."

"Those news reporters will say anything to get a story!"

"My family believed it."

"My aunt is worried too. I ran into her at the store last week with Cody. Boy, was she confused. It's hard to explain this stuff to people who are not in tune with the spirit of God."

"Yeah. Now listen, Pen, I have to get going or I will be late for my *beloved*!"

The shades were drawn in the parsonage and five lone candles lit up the darkness. Pastor Mark admired his new connection. She wasn't pretty, but he liked her full figure and uninhibited touches. Each time with her was like opening a bottle of bubbly champagne.

"Pastor, you make my head spin with love, I feel Jesus soooo much," she said, her thick arms roaming his back.

The single woman had pursued him for weeks before he agreed to dance with her. Afterwards he was glad he did. He found her company refreshing. She was a frisky gal who was willing to try everything and anything to reach the *heavenly* places. She didn't have a self-conscious bone in her body.

"Honey, I'm feeling your spirit, let's go deeper in God now."

The young woman smiled, and bounced toward the bedroom, her frizzy brown hair bobbing onto her shoulders and her large hips swinging as she went.

As weeks flew by, Cody was spending less time with Penny and more time with Lorie. Penny knew it was because she was too jealous. Every time Cody did get with her, they fought. Penny knew her insecurities turned him off, but she felt powerless to the rage welling up inside of her. Guilt, shame, jealousy, envy, obsession, hatred, anger, and confusion consumed her emotions, and they didn't let up. She swung from one awful *demon* to another.

Thursday night Penny called Cody. He was out. She couldn't handle the rejection. She jumped into her car and sped to Lorie's home, crying. Cody's old Ford was there. She hit the steering wheel and zoomed away toward home. She called Callie, but she was out. And of course she couldn't talk to Laurina. They had been at odds with each other for a long time now. She just couldn't face her when she was in love with her husband. Laurina never said anything to her, but she could see the hurt in her eyes. They simply drifted apart. The pastor said once they released their mates, God would bring them back. She knew Laurina was agonizing, patiently waiting for this. But how could she give up Cody now? How would she start loving Rick again? She felt nothing for him anymore. Sure, jealous pangs hit her at times when she saw him with Janice, but her love for Cody couldn't be beat.

Three hours later Penny got back in the car and drove to Cody's house. She was relieved when she saw him getting out of his car. She quickly pulled over and jumped out.

"Cody," she said, running up to him. "I can't handle you kissing her!" She sobbed hysterically.

Cody shut his car door. "Penny," he said, "you have got to stop this."

"Are you sleeping with her?"

He didn't answer.

"You are! Oh, God, I can't take this!" She bent over, dry-heaving, shaky. "I love you! How can this be of God when I am so tormented?"

"Penny, you need to get delivered. You have demons pushing you to this extreme. God put me with Lorie. Why are you fighting what God is doing?"

Cody put his arm around her and she clung to him.

"I'm s..s…sorry. I know I need prayer."

He let her cry.

"Can we go parking for a little while, Cody? I need your spirit."

"I can't tonight, Penny. Laurina is home. I'll call you tomorrow." He pulled away. "Go home and get some sleep. I still love you. God loves you."

"You never want to be with me anymore."

"That's not true. I'll call you tomorrow. I promise."

When she arrived home to her apartment she had never felt so alone.

And as usual, Rick didn't come home. This time it bothered her.

The next morning Penny telephoned Cody. "Cody, Rick never came home last night! He doesn't come home at all anymore."

"For how long?"

"This whole week. I only saw him twice. He came and got some clothes and left again."

"That's not good. No wonder you're so insecure."

Penny was weeping. "I f..f..feel like I'm dying, Cody."

"I'll contact Ted and call you back."

Penny hung up and flung herself across the bed sobbing. The sound of someone unlocking the front door startled her. She dashed out of bed and wiped her eyes. Rick walked into the bedroom sporting an icy look.

"You aren't supposed to live with your connection!" Penny screamed.

"Like you really care." He opened a drawer and took out some clean underwear.

"Rick, we're married; did you forget?" She stomped after him.

"Are we married?" he jeered.

"At least I keep my connections within church guidelines. You don't even dance with yours. I'm calling the counseling center!"

"Don't worry, I'll be home tonight," he growled. He shoved past her into the bathroom and locked the door.

"What, you won't even dress in front of me now?" She screeched, pounding on the door.

Rick opened the door and said, "You're crazy."

She swung at him and he pushed her onto the bed and slapped her face. "Leave me alone!" he yelled.

He ran out the door and didn't come home that night either.

The next afternoon Ted ushered Penny into his office and motioned her to sit. He moved behind his desk and sat down, swiveling his chair while he stared at her.

"So," he said without any sentiment. "Cody says you're having marriage problems."

"Yes, I…Rick doesn't come home at nights anymore. He's with Janice."

"How do you know he's with her?"

"I know. And Cody saw them together."

"I talked to Rick this morning, Penny. He says you haven't been treating him fair."

"What? Well, we did get into a fight last night. But it's because…"

"Penny, if you'd be a better wife and submit to Rick, and *release* him, maybe he would want to stay home." His tone was cool.

"What do you mean?" She sat up, uncrossed her legs, and sank her face into her hands, sobbing. "How do you know what kind of wife I am? You don't even know me."

Ted pushed the Kleenex box toward her. "Submission is the key here, Penny. If you don't get delivered from these man-hating demons that are causing you to react so crazily, you will miss out on what God wants to do in your life. You must allow God to finish the work He's doing in Rick and Janice. Just as God's doing between you and Cody."

"Aren't you going to put restrictions on them?" Penny blubbered.

"Why? And make matters worse? It's you who needs to change. Even Cody told me you've been manifesting demons of insecurity towards him as well. If you don't get delivered, you can find yourself removed from this church, and I don't think you or God wants this."

"I'm feeling attacked by you…"

"Penny," Ted said gruffly, "submit to my counsel or face the consequences. Rick has agreed to come home nights. Let's take it from there. Release him to God."

"I need Jesus now…" she sobbed, running from the room before Ted could utter another threatening word.

ОС *CULT*

CHAPTER FIFTEEN

Laurina Addison had not had a mega connection like most everyone else. It seemed the men were drawn to her more out of a spirit of lust than of a love. She just didn't trust their motives and refused to be pawed at. She felt left out. And no matter how hard she tried to release Cody, she was having a hard time doing so. On top of that, Penny's crying jags over her husband and Lorie's complete disregard for her position as Cody's wife, weighed her down. Leaving the church was not an option; she would never do that. The last thing she wanted to do was end up like Marcy in a mental ward, or be in delusion like Marilyn and lose her salvation. It was hard, but she would endure the trials for the sake of the Lord, trusting Him to give her strength. So far she had dealt with her troubled heart by staying away from Penny and Lorie. It had been easier to handle that way.

But lately Cody seemed to lose interest in her. They seldom made love, and her polite pleas for attention only made things worse. This was the real test of faith. She thought she had it together and could push the pain out of the way, but she found out how wrong she was when she came home unexpectedly that evening, catching her husband making out with Lorie. Furious, she ordered the woman to go. Lorie responded with a rolling of the eyes and a defiant stance. Laurina wanted to smack her, but instead she picked up the phone and said with a bite, "I am calling Mark. Do you want to stay, Lorie, or do I tell him you are demon possessed? You know, he will believe me. We are very close."

"You had better go, Lorie. Take my car." Cody handed her the keys to his car. The redhead threw Laurina a raw look and left.

"Are you sleeping with her?" Laurina exploded. All the months of holding things in flew out.

"No."

"You liar! Tomorrow I'm calling Mark. You touch her, you touch Penny, but you never touch me!" Anguished sobs wracked her body.

"Give it up, Laurina!" he yelled, pacing the floor. "You don't want to connect because you are paranoid every man wants to have sex with you! "

Laurina swung at him, clubbing his chest with her fists and leaving a trail of bloody nail marks down his neck.

"Get off me! I'm contacting Mark myself about you. He is used to your tall tales!" He threw her against the wall and ran out the door.

She fell to the floor whimpering.

"Laurina," Avery admonished the next afternoon in his office, "I can't control your husband. But, God can. I suggest you pray for him instead of attack him."

Laurina squirmed. Cody, seated next to her, raised his nose and squared his shoulders.

Avery pivoted his chair away from his spotless desk and examined his fingernails. "We are all adjusting to seeing our mates with someone else. Learning to look through spiritual eyes instead of physical eyes will keep everything in perspective. Cody is in God's will. Let him be, Laurina."

Laurina's jaw dropped. She looked from Avery to Cody, astonished.

"Laurina," Cody said, his southern accent sounding too forced, "I need you to let me experience God's love through Lorie. Yes, we have not been perfect, but I promise you, I love you. I am looking forward to the day God brings us back together."

"Making out with Lorie is not spiritual! I am supposed to let you do that?"

"Again," Avery almost hissed, "we all make mistakes; forgive Cody, Laurina. I'm here for you, so are any of the counselors. But if you butt heads with our advice, then you may very well end up outside looking in. Do you want to face an excommunication because you're unwilling to cooperate?"

"No." She slouched forward.

"Now, Laurina, you've given us problems in the past, and I feel it is imperative that you get prayer if you want to remain in this church."

"She will," Cody insisted, not too pleased at Avery's harsh words, but still not willing to go Laurina's route to give up Lorie.

"Good, God bless you both."

I cannot open my eyes.

I try. I pry and pry at them with my fingers. They will not open. I am desperate and afraid. What is happening? I am crawling around the floor, clawing at my face.

"I'm blind! In Jesus name, In Jesus name, let me go!"

Penny shot up in bed, terrified. It was the third time she had had the same dream. She reached for the alarm clock. It was 8:00. As usual, Rick hadn't come home. Sunlight filtered through the white blinds, casting long fingerlike shadows on the wall beside her. She climbed out of bed, pulled on the cotton robe, and headed towards the bathroom. She had no energy. Each step felt like she was balancing bricks with her feet. Her reflection in the mirror revealed sleepless eyes and pale skin. She pinched her cheeks to find color.

Where are you God? You seem so far away.

She turned on the shower to let it get warm, then brushed her teeth. At once, as though panic just woke up itself, she felt her insides being pummeled as fast as the water whipping against the tub.

"Ugh!" She bent forward, dizzy. The toothbrush clattered to the floor. She felt lightheaded, depressed. Did she have the flu? She didn't think so. But her head was swirling badly and she wanted to go back to sleep. She forced herself to shower. She was so numb, so out of it, that she didn't realize the water had been beating down on her for ten minutes while she just stood staring at the wall. Slowly, she turned off the water, climbed out, and dried off. She moved to the kitchen in slow motion. She felt strange. What was wrong? She picked up the phone and punched in Cody's cell number.

The recording answered.

She called the ministry's office. "Is Cody Addison around, by any chance?" she asked.

"I don't see him," the receptionist said.

"It's urgent. This is Penny Duncan. I need to talk to him."

"Actually, I believe he's worshipping in the chapel with his connection. Do you want me to see if I can find him?"

"No, forget it!"

She slammed the phone down and sank to the floor, drawing her knees up to her chest, rocking with the rhythm of her jagged and pitiful cries.

God, help me, I'm drowning, help me... I hate this... Jesus, Jesus...I don't want to be in love with Cody. I want Rick...

The phone rang, forcing Penny back from her stupor. She grabbed at the kitchen counter and pulled herself up.

"Hello?" she answered.

"Penny?" It was Cody. "I heard you called."

She moaned.

"Penny, talk to me. What's wrong?"

"I don't know. I feel funny. I think something's wrong with me. I can't think. I'm so tired."

"Where's Rick?"

"Work."

"I'll be there in ten minutes."

Penny answered the door still wearing her robe. Cody was wearing a new blue suit.

"Penny, you look awful."

"I'm so depressed, Cody. I really think I need to go to the hospital. I haven't been able to eat for days. I have no energy...I just can't cope with..."

He rushed forward and held her, apologizing for neglecting their union. "Shhhh, Penny, don't be down. I am here. We'll work this out. Just rest now, relax. Let me love you. You need to be filled up with God."

He pulled her head up to meet his gaze.

She responded, letting her eyes merge with his.

His hands skimmed down her hips and around her backside, but she pushed aside the nabbing voices screaming at her to *stop, stop, stop,* and gave in to the desire that would make her forget her troubles; at least for the moment.

Rick came home late in the evening and avoided Penny's disapproving looks. He plopped down on the couch with a bag of potato chips and picked up the remote control.

"Rick, can we talk?"

"About what?" he said without emotion. He kept his attention focused on the television.

"Rick, do you love me?"

No answer.

"Are you in love with Janice?"

"I love you both."

"Something's wrong, Rick, this <u>connection doctrine</u> has <u>destroyed our marriage</u>. The pastor says it's supposed to make our marriages better, but after a year things are worse. In fact, Cody told me about twenty people are getting divorces. Will we be next?"

He didn't answer.

"Look at us. We can't stand each other anymore. You used to love me; now you love another woman." She hesitated. "And I love another man."

"Go to bed, Penny. I'm too tired to talk."

"That's it? I love someone else and you don't want to talk?"

"I trust you," he muttered.

"Rick, I need to get away. I'm confused and I feel so far from God."

"Where?" Rick asked, irritated that she kept talking.

"To San Diego for a week...to stay at Aunt Joann's condo out there by the beach. I'm leaving tomorrow. I'm going alone."

"Since when did you plan this?"

"Since today." She had called her aunt after Cody left her feeling ashamed. "I am facing a nervous breakdown if I don't get away and pray. I am confused and feel like I'm losing my mind."

He didn't answer.

What a nightmare their life had become. They simply existed together under one roof, nothing more. Anything they once had together had gone with the wind.

The airplane flew high away from her home and Grace Church, but Penny did not feel any less depressed or relieved. Her heart was still enslaved to her chaotic world back in Portland.

She was glad Aunt Joann had agreed to let her use her beach getaway. She had wanted to join her, but Penny insisted she needed to be alone. She needed the time to hear from God. Something was very wrong. The guilt, fears, and anxieties haunting her should not be.

She arrived at the condo late afternoon, exhausted. The two and a half hour flight seemed like a lifetime. Should she have left? Time would tell.

Too mentally fatigued to check out the place, Penny crawled into the double bed and fell into a deep sleep. She woke up four hours later, greeted by darkness and stale air. She edged out of bed and cracked a window. The breeze grabbed her, and so did the fantastic view of the ocean. Picking up her jacket, she walked outside and strode along the beach, praying silently as she did. The fresh air seemed to calm her jitters and alert her senses. She started noticing her surroundings. A long wooden pier, dog walkers, joggers, and laughing people seated at a bonfire. Everyone's life looked so normal, so content. What had happened to hers?

There was no food in the apartment, so she walked over to the beachside hamburger joint, all lit up with bamboo torches. As she sat there eating, she realized it was the first time in a week that she actually *tasted* what she ate. Maybe the trip was right. She took in a deep breath of the ocean air.

Although the next day was nippy, Penny stayed on the beach all day, stretched out on a blanket, reading, watching seagulls doing nosedives and toddlers chasing Frisbees. Spring wanted to burst through the air, but winter's chill still didn't quite want to let go.

The first two days passed by slowly. Penny still hadn't gone to her knees. Her overwhelming shame for being in love with another married man seemed to convince her not to pray. But on the third day, Penny knew she had to face all her sins and weaknesses and let God have them. Would God understand her? Would He even listen to her? She had thought a long time ago that He had told her not to kiss Cody, but Cody had convinced her it was not God. Deep down, she believed it had been the Lord's warning.

She always had a special relationship with Jesus, setting aside time every day to pray. She had come to know His gentle presence and His still small voice. But she had pushed Him aside to justify what she wanted, not what He wanted. Everyone was convincing everyone else it was right, yet, they could not see that they were becoming just like Joe Fellow's dream—when everyone was dancing and Jesus was standing in their midst alone and ignored. They didn't want to give up their fun to hear what He had to say; otherwise they would realize kissing led to sexual improprieties. How awful that she had become one of those people in Joe's dream.

Penny stood at the window, watching the waves beat the sand. Wow, where was all this insight coming from? Her mind seemed to be clearer than it had been in ages. Was God talking to her now? Things seemed to make sense. Why couldn't she have seen this before? Of course God wouldn't want them kissing! It was tainting His *move*. God had tried to warn her.

She felt freer than she had in a long time. Dropping to her knees, she repented and asked the Lord to forgive her for committing adultery. Then she asked God to help her love her husband again. That was it. She got up.

For the first time in weeks she felt lighter, hopeful. She found herself beaming happily.

Thank you, Jesus.

Looking back over the years, she realized it was those quiet times with God that seemed to be the only thing that gave her stability and made any sense to her. Everything else was a blur of confusion. It was humbling and a relief to have found Him this way again. And tonight, she wouldn't trade all that drenching love she felt in the dance for what she had with the Lord right at that moment.

She went to bed and slept soundly. The next day she kneeled and prayed for over an hour. Afterward she opened her Bible and read. She gave the entire morning to finding Him again. The rest of the afternoon she took long walks down at the beach. She felt alive. The anguish she felt for Cody seemed to be on hold, and her concerns for her marriage remained at Christ's feet where she had laid them that morning. When she went back to bed that night, she expected another peaceful sleep. But she was wrong.

I am dancing in church, spinning and twirling; arms raised in adoration to Jesus. I feel holy before God. The skirt on my dress swirls high in the air with each spin, flashing slender thighs and silky underwear. I am oblivious to the male eyes watching me. I dance all over the sanctuary, up and around the pastor, weaving in and out of the elders. The congregation begins to dance too. My attention is on God, on God, on God...

One by one the men in the church dance up and form a tight circle around me. The pastor sashays forward and pulls me against his body, resting his hand upon my breasts. The male members gyrate, possessed, faster to the music, their lusting eyes open wide while shouting praises to God. The other females in the church are dancing and shouting to God in unison with the men, but their eyes are closed, not seeing anything...

Penny woke with a start. Like a tiny light poking its way into a black chasm and illuminating its once bleak surroundings into something tangible, Penny suddenly saw what she had not quite got before. Waves of shame hit her. Any physical display during the dance was not of God.

"Oh God, oh God! Satan is out to destroy our marriages! I need my husband. I need you, Rick. Oh Rick, what have I done?" She leaned over, holding her stomach, crying out to God until she could weep no more.

The spiritual connection movement infested the satellite churches as well, and their troubles were climaxing as fast as those in Grace Church. Married couples faced tremendous emotional upheaval trying to release their mates to their connections. Complaints crammed the phone lines to Grace Church's main counselor's office. To maintain control, counselors used fear tactics and harsh directives to subdue the irrational flare-ups. Afraid of being *put out*, the church members surrendered to the biased counsel and, like dutiful robots, obeyed the church government without question. To keep from manifesting jealous rages, they learned to shut off their hearts, searing their consciences in the process so as to subdue their torment. Others dealing with the chaos and distress found solace in booze and sexual promiscuity. Spouses that once testified of good things happening because of their connections were filing for divorce. One hundred cases were filed at the courthouse and Mark, anxious not to lose his entire congregation, still promised God was in control and that the marriages would reunite. He compromised his rules and stopped excommunicating the divorcing members. This gave the go ahead for others to follow suit and end their marriage.

News reporters were snooping around the sanctuary more and more, showing interest in the bizarre spiritual connection doctrine. The same night Penny arrived back in Portland, Channel Five news took the first plunge and aired a special report about the strange "spiritual" mate swapping practices being promoted as God's love, and all the resulting divorces caused by it.

Callie answered the door looking fantastic. She wore a green silk dress, and her wig was coifed in myriads of tiny curls. "Penny! You're back!" she hooted, but corked her excitement at seeing Penny's sour response.

"Are you alone?" Penny peered nervously over Callie's shoulders. Rick was nowhere to be found when she arrived home from the airport, and so she drove straightaway to Callie's house.

"No, Avery is here. Come on in."

"No. Can I talk to you alone? We can sit in my car."

"Pen, what's going on? You're scaring me?"

"I'm fine. But I need to talk to you." She brushed at her long hair as it was whipped into her face by the wind.

"Come on in, I'll tell Avery."

Penny plunged her hands into her coat's pockets and stepped back. "No, I'll be in the car."

"Okay." Callie looked perplexed. "I'll be right out."

Penny got into her car and turned on the heat. The night air was brisk and the full moon cast an ominous glare across the hood of the car.

Callie opened the passenger door a few minutes later and climbed in beside Penny. "What's up, Pen? You're acting strange."

"Did you see the news?"

Callie laughed. "Sure! Now everyone can see what God is doing in our church!"

"Callie, those people think we're nuts!"

"How could they not when they don't see with spiritual eyes?"

Penny jacked up the heat to clear the foggy windows. "Callie, God showed me something while I was in San Diego. I think our church is in deception!"

"What? Penny, why would you say such a thing? Did you talk to Marilyn?"

"No. I talked to God."

"Penny, stop listening to the devil. God's spirit is weeding out the grunge in our lives, so of course some people will make mistakes. It is the cleansing process. But in time God will bring us all into a perfect unity."

"Callie, I had a dream that I believe was from God. In my dream I was dancing in church, not realizing my underwear was showing every time I twirled. All the men encircled me with leering eyes. The women were dancing behind them with their eyes closed and could not see their lust."

Callie flinched and looked away. "That doesn't mean anything."

"Callie, there's more. In the dream Pastor Mark approached me in the dance and he touched my...my breasts."

Callie jerked around. "E...E...Everyone's made mistakes," she sputtered guiltily.

At that moment Penny understood her own encounter in the pastor's bathroom years ago when Pastor Mark touched her in such a strange way. And Laurina's secrets about him...her charge that he was too "affectionate." Her dream was from God!

She turned and pressed Callie's shoulders. "Did Pastor ever touch you, Callie? Did he? Tell me?"

"Whew, it's getting hot in here!" Callie fumbled for the car door.

Penny leaned over and barred Callie's exit with her arm. "He did, didn't he? That is why you got the boob job. For him! Callie, what are you doing? Why are you protecting him?"

"Penny, it's a lie. You are wrong. I am not going to listen to you accuse me..."

"Callie, don't you understand? Satan is destroying our marriages. And our pastor is allowing it. We should not be kissing and..."

"I'm going. You're deceived, Penny!" She jerked up the handle.

Penny sobbed, pleading. "God set me free! I feel love for my husband, Callie! It's not Cody I love, it's Rick!"

Callie halted, with one foot hanging out the door. "So, you think the connections are wrong?"

"I don't know. Maybe it's from God, I mean, the love is powerful, and that is hard to imitate, but God never intended us to be mate swapping! I mean, look at everyone. Cody told me there were at least fifty cases of adultery reported to the church office last week." Penny dipped her head. "I already told you I committed adultery too."

"Don't be so pious. Most everyone has by now. Mark said to repent and go on…"

"See! See! Hear what you are saying? It's like no big deal to you. Since when does God's Word condone adultery?"

Tears slugged down Penny's cheeks. "I don't even know if I will get Rick back now. Oh, Callie, you must fight for Petey! Don't do this with Avery!"

"Where is Rick?"

"I don't know. He wasn't home." Penny slid her shaky hands around the steering wheel. "I haven't been able to find him. I am sure he is with Janice. He loves her now, not me."

"Maybe your connection with Cody opened you back up to Rick, Pen. Have you considered that? Remember, Mark told us God would reunite the marriages. Don't let the devil lie to your mind. Do you want to end up like Marilyn and Jason?"

Penny felt confused.

"Be careful, your dream could have been a ploy from Satan. It simply seems to me that you are moving back toward Rick, proving that these connections are from God." Callie refused to talk anymore. "I have to go; Avery's waiting."

Penny gave a defeated, "Okay."

She drove home with troubling thoughts stinging her mind like pesky mosquitoes. Maybe Callie was right. Could God's love be moving her back to Rick? Was she mistaken about the dream being from God? She had to find Rick and talk to him.

When she reached her apartment, Rick's car was still gone. Inside, taped to the refrigerator door was a note: *Gone to California with Janice. Since you took a vacation with who knows who, I figured I deserved some rest too. Ted knows about it. Rick.*

She crumpled the note and threw it at the wall. She was too late. Slumping to the floor, she sobbed bitterly.

Callie scurried back into the house and flew over to Avery, who was lounging on the sofa eating popcorn and watching a baseball game on television. "Avery, I think Penny Duncan is deceived! She was talking nonsense about the connections being of the devil. I have never seen her act so strange. I'm worried."

The bases were loaded. He didn't want to disrupt the game. "I'll call her later."

She plopped down in his lap. He stretched his head around to see the screen.

"She told me she had a dream from God showing her that our church was in deception."

"I'll take care of it," he said, as the pitcher hurled the ball.

"I hope we don't lose her. I love Penny. She's been a good friend."

"There it goes! There it goes! A home run! Great play." Avery pushed her off his lap and sat forward, bouncing and cheering at the TV. "Callie, make me some more popcorn; this game is going to be a doozer."

"Avery? Are you listening? You should get some people to pray for Penny right away."

"Right, right. I will. Come on. Stop worrying." He pinched her bottom as she got up. "Now, make some popcorn and join me. Let's enjoy this time together."

Penny didn't go to Friday night service. She wanted to sort out her feelings and think about what she needed to do. She had no idea how to contact Rick. He wasn't answering his cell phone. The wait was pure hell.

Early Saturday morning a rap-rapping hit her door. Penny peeked out the curtain and saw Cody standing there with his hands in his jean's pockets, looking worried. Low dark clouds hovered over Portland and the radio had reported possible snow. The unusual March cold wind played tag with Cody and he pulled his suede coat up around his neck. Despite her resolve to end her relationship with him, she felt weak-kneed when she saw him standing there.

Penny cracked opened the door, still in her robe.

Cody pushed his way in. "Penny, why didn't you call when you got back? I've been worried. And Avery…"

"Avery probably told you I was leaving the church." She stayed aloof.

"Are you?" He took her by the shoulders and put his face close to hers. "What is going on?"

His touch made her reel. Oh, God, give her strength. She wanted to fall into his arms and cry. Instead she stiffened and pulled away. "I need my husband. But Rick is in California. Ted let him go with Janice. How is that supposed to be good for my marriage? How is this supposed to be of God? I heard about all the divorces."

Cody rubbed her arms and played on her frail mood. "Penny, Penny, come on. Don't do this! It's me. Don't be far from me. God put us together. Let's talk. Come on. I need you now."

She wouldn't look at him. A tear slid down and tickled her mouth.

"Rick will return. God is restoring marriages. Trust me." He pulled her into his arms. Penny resigned to his comforting shoulder and rested on him.

A loud jerky rat-tat-tat on the front room window startled the pair. They flew apart at the sight of Laurina's torn reflection.

"W..wha?" Cody stumbled toward the front door.

"Laurina?" Penny wanted to shrink.

She came through the door shrieking. "Leave him alone, Penny! He's *my* husband! Cody, don't do this! I need you!"

Cody restrained his wife. "Laurina, stop this! Right now. Stop this. You're giving in to demons!" Laurina slumped to the floor, weeping and shaking.

"No, no, she's right, Cody!" Penny rushed over to Laurina and shouted, "This is wrong! Laurina, forgive me. You are right. This is not of God. Cody and I have sinned. Please, please forgive me." She clutched at her friend, crying too. "I need Rick just as much as you need Cody. But he's gone. He's gone with Janice. He loves Janice!"

Laurina pulled Penny close and they clutched one another.

"You are my best friend," Penny wailed, rocking her friend, "and I have wronged you. I have sinned against you and God. Oh, Laurina, forgive me. Forgive me!"

"You're my best friend!" Laurina choked out.

Cody stood there, irritated.

"Cody," Penny yelled at his stoic response, "She needs you, not me!"

"No," he said almost in a whisper. "This is not my problem. If you can't stop giving into demons I can't do anything for you."

He walked out the door.

oc *CULT*

CHAPTER SIXTEEN

The next day at mid-morning Penny entered the counseling center in dirty jeans. She hadn't brushed her hair and she wore no make-up. Worry lined her eyes. Trying to be brave, she sucked in mini breaths as she spoke to the receptionist.

"Is Avery available?"

The smiling receptionist and the normal hubbub of student activity at the college gave her sudden doubts. Her life was such a shambles, yet here at the church things seemed fine. Doubts began to plague her. Maybe she had stayed away from Grace Church too long. Maybe the devil did get at her. She felt sick.

"Yes. Go right on in. He's expecting you."

Avery smiled as she entered, careful not to let her see his surprise at the way she looked. "Hello, Penny. I'm glad you came by. Callie has been so worried about you." He led her to the leather chair near his desk. "Have a seat."

She didn't sit. "I...this is not easy to say...so I'm just going to say it. I want to do the right thing before God." The little bit of strength she had mustered up for the meeting wanted to scamper away. She fought it.

"Yes?" He sat back on the edge of his desk and crossed his arms.

"I committed adultery with Cody Addison." She turned beet red. "More than once."

Avery didn't flinch. "I see. Well, let's pray and ask God's forgiveness."

"That's it?" she charged angrily.

"Let's not make a scene, Penny. Repent and go on. This move of God has been a difficult temptation to the flesh. It's understandable that this would happen. God's love is intense. Repent and keep connecting."

"Don't you think you should talk to Cody?"

"Why?"

"You want us to keep seeing each other?"

"Let God finish what He's started."

"The news is right. We are all crazy."

"Penny, Cody told me already that you guys had slipped. He also said you have gotten your heart back for Rick. This is what the pastor has been trying to tell us. You need to stay in the boat and allow God to complete His work in your marriage. Rick will respond in time." Avery saw her shoulders slump and he moved beside her. "The news reporters don't understand any of this. How can they? You belong here. This is where God has called you."

"I'm so confused." She tried not to cry.

"Penny, will you give God another chance? Will you give Grace Church another chance? Callie is willing to meet with you twice a week and pray for you. I will join her too. We love you. We want you to hang on! You're part of us. We are one in the Son." He stretched his arm around her and gave her a jolly shake.

His soothing speech coerced her.

"Okay," she relented, "I guess so." She left his office trying hard to tame her screaming thoughts.

The next week became a blur. Penny met with Callie and Avery for prayer, but nothing changed. Her desire to see Rick tossed her head around like it was caught in a spinning agitator inside a washing machine. She attended church services, but did not join in the dancing activities. Her heart was not into any of it. Any love or joy she had was gone.

Rick came back on a Saturday. Her heart beat hard as he came into the house, hauling two suitcases behind him.

"Hi, Rick," she said softly. She wanted to run into his arms and hold him. But his steely glare stopped her. Her heart sank and hope shattered into fear. Trembles, like small aftershocks, gripped her body. She had never seen him look at her with such contempt or loathing before. He ignored her and went into the bedroom.

She followed him. "Rick, I love you."

He unpacked his suitcase and tossed his dirty clothes into the hamper.

"Rick, do you love me?"

"At this moment, no."

She didn't know how long she could hold onto her composure. His reactions were killing her. "Rick, I just want you to know that I will not be seeing Cody anymore. It is you I want."

He picked up the hamper and headed for the laundry room.

She knew if she fell apart it would make things worse and he would leave. She swallowed, prayed a silent prayer to God for strength, and let him be. She moved to the kitchen and made him a nice dinner, hoping it might knock down the barrier between them.

He finally came into the kitchen. "I'm not hungry," he said, putting on his jacket.

"Please don't leave me now," Penny pleaded.

He wouldn't look at her as he opened the door and walked out.

Penny had tried to persuade Rick in a kindly fashion, but he would not listen. For the next week he only came home to change clothes and, when he did, he barely spoke to her.

She had enough! She was going to go find her husband, no matter what counsel said. She threw on her sweater and ran out the door.

God, I'm losing it. I'm losing it!

She drove to Janice's apartment. Rick's car was there. She scrambled up the sidewalk to the door, pounded on it, and rattled the doorknob. No answer. Like a crazed person she pounded and kicked at the door.

She hollered, "Open up, Rick. I know you're in there. Open up!"

No answer.

Penny kept kicking.

"What are you doing?" Rick's angry face appeared in the upstairs window.

"Rick," she begged, calling up at him. "Please don't do this to me. I can't take this anymore. I love you."

"You're crazy. Go home."

Penny's heart mangled when Janice poked her head out the window and crooned, "I love your husband. And he loves me."

"You husband stealer!"

The noise alerted the neighbor, and a big burly man opened his front door. "Everything all right?" he asked.

"No!" Penny screamed. "My husband is having an affair!" She ran off like a wounded animal.

Oh God...Oh God...What do I do?

It was two o'clock. Penny jerked her car into drive and squealed out of the lot. She had to report this! She headed for the college campus.

She ignored the receptionist and stomped into Ted's office, standing there like an angry Cheetah ready to pounce. "Ted, Rick won't even speak to me. He won't come home anymore. He's living with Janice!"

"Penny, slow down," Ted demanded, moving up out of his seat at her dramatic entry. "What's this all about?"

"He's not even going to church. You know this. I don't understand why you aren't putting restrictions on them. Especially with all these divorces…"

"It is not your call, Penny. You need to start submitting to this church authority and let us make those decisions."

Penny got angry. "He's *my* husband!"

"He's God's child."

"He is living with her. You don't care! How can this be God's will?"

"Maybe you are the reason he's staying away." A sardonic grit replaced his features.

"What? What?"

"Penny, you had better get some deliverances from these man-hating demons." He tapped his toe and crossed his arms with insolence. "I've warned you before. I won't have rebellion in our camp. One more outburst like this and you're out!"

Hot explosions erupted inside her. "I didn't do anything wrong!" she screamed. "Why is Rick right and I'm wrong? All I want is my husband back." Her legs were shaking so bad she didn't know how long she would be able to stand.

"You can't even see the deception clouding your eyes, Penny. I mean it, one more time…"

"Okay!" Although she was rumbling with rage, Penny backed down. His threat was real, and she didn't want to be put out.

She didn't know how she made it home and through the front door. The tremors that started in Ted's office got worse. They seemed to have control of her inside and out. She needed help. She took the phone and called Laurina's number, praying she would be home.

Laurina answered.

Penny gasped into the mouthpiece, "Please, come help me, Laurina!" She could say no more. The heaves overpowered her. She dropped the phone and fell onto the couch, shuddering uncontrollably.

The slimy serpents flicked their tongues at her, calling to her to come closer, just a little closer.

Stay in the boat...stay in the boat...

Nausea swept over her.

I can't do it.

What demon is that talking?

The incessant banging on the door did not stir Penny, nor did the shattering of the living room window. She lay rigid, frozen, unable to stop the quicksand now pulling her down, down, down into its hell.

"Penny? Oh my God? Penny?" Laurina shouted as she broke away the jagged pieces of glass with her purse to get her hand inside the window to unlock it. Penny was lying unconscious on the couch. Hurriedly Laurina slid the window open and climbed in, rushing to Penny's side.

"Penny, Oh God, help her," Laurina cried. She pulled her into her arms and shook her. "Penny? Penny? Oh, God, You're alive!"

"Take me to the hospital...I'm dying..." She was gasping. The darkened circles around her eyes gave her the resemblance of a frightened raccoon.

"Penny, I'm here. I'm here! Jesus, dear Jesus, help her!" Laurina was scared. She lay down on top of her friend and ran her hands over Penny's distraught face, cooing her and consoling her the best way she knew how. "It's going to be okay. You're okay. I'm here. Jesus is here." Laurina looked around and spotted the tape player. Hurriedly she got up and turned it on. Grace Church choir music wafted into the stillness and Laurina lay back down on her friend and stroked her until Penny slowed to a whimper.

Laurina wanted to cry. "Jesus, Jesus, we love you. We only want to serve you. What's happening? Help us!"

A week later a numb Penny waited at the kitchen table for Rick to arrive. He had called earlier and told her he needed to talk. Since her breakdown she felt sluggish and disinterested with life, almost afraid to breath for fear she might rebound and lose it again. She couldn't function at work and quit her job. Everyone there knew she went to Grace Church and they whispered behind her back.

Tires scrunching up the driveway made her jump. Would Rick be willing to work things out? She felt dread rise up like bile as she recognized his familiar stomp, stomp at the front door. Sucking in air, she got up and stood there, waiting for him to walk in.

He pushed open the door and faced her. This time his eyes looked tired and resigned, not angry. Penny had set her hair and dressed nice, hoping he might open up to her. Hope poked at her heart. Would he?

"Hello, Pen." He had a hard time looking at her. The pain in her eyes made it hard for him to say what he had to say.

"Hello, Rick."

"I know I haven't been doing things right. Truth is, I have gotten in way over my head with Janice. I couldn't stop."

"I did the same with Cody. But it's not Cody who I want. It's you." She inched toward him, but he backed up.

"Don't, Penny. I need to tell you...I love Janice. I can't live without her."

The last of whatever reserve Penny had gave way. "Rick, I love you. I love you! Please, don't leave me. I need you. I don't want anyone else. God has shown me that these connections were not supposed to go physical! I have repented. I am praying for us, Rick!"

Her open pleas did not anger him this time. He felt exhausted. He was tired of carrying the guilt on his shoulders. It had to end. He couldn't keep pretending he was in God's will. He knew better. This was it. It was time to leave the church and make a decision that would put an end to all the suffering he was causing Penny. He went to her and drew her into his arms.

"I am so sorry, Pen. I never intended this to happen. I am confused too. But, I love Janice now. My life is with her. I can't undo what has happened. It's done. I'm sorry."

Penny was wracked with sobs.

"You were a great wife," he said softly. "It is not you. I know I hurt you by avoiding you all these months. I was running from the truth. Don't blame the church. I made my own choices. It's time I live my own life now. I gave up everything for you, and ended up losing you. And now my heart does not want to go back. I want to be with Janice. Start over. Maybe try some golf again, if it isn't too late."

"Where are you going?" Penny cried into his shoulder.

"We're moving to the Midwest. Back to Illinois."

"Of course."

Rick pulled back and tipped her chin. "Penny, I will always remember you. You are a wonderful lady and I will miss you."

Penny had no more tears to cry. She nodded. He kissed her cheek and left their home. He was gone, forever. The dream in San Diego had been from the Lord. The spiritual unions were not right. And more than that, she could see that the entire love potion, poured out onto the assembly, was a delusion, a pseudo love to trick them, a gift from Satan. She stood there anesthetized from feeling anything. God had warned her a long time ago, but she had refused to hear Him. Her own disrespect for God's Word had caused her to lose her husband. What a price she had paid for playing with fire. And Marcy, what had caused her to crack? What gave the devil so much reason to destroy their lives? She felt that panic swell up again.

You can do this, Penny. Get a grip...you have a sound mind in Christ Jesus.

She tried to remember when connections began dating outside church and when rules ceased to matter. The last year was hazy. What month did kissing become accepted as a vehicle to get into the spirit? What service did Mark condone French kissing under *certain spiritual conditions*? When were divorces allowed?

Would God give something that would cause them all to tumble so far into sin? That was the key right there. He wouldn't. No. God wouldn't ever compromise His Holy Word. Marilyn and Jason saw it all clearly. They tried to warn her. But she refused to hear the truth. She chose to follow silly fables, crazy feelings, and esoteric experiences. She deserved now what she got.

She moved to the kitchen table and fell down in the chair. How tired, how old she felt. Without thinking, she leaned forward and lowered her head, smashing her cheek against the table's cool glass surface. Wide, lifeless eyes stared at nothing, and her slender arms dangled haphazardly at her side. She missed Marcy. Poor Marcy. And Marilyn. How mean she had been to her friend.

Call her.

No. She's a dissident.

The whirring noise from the refrigerators icemaker seemed to move with the rhythm of her clanging heart. It buzzed, stopped, buzzed, stopped, buzzed. She remembered Joe Fellows letter! He had sent a letter to all the members warning them about the devilish doctrine of mate swapping months ago. What did she do with that? Oh, yes, she tore it up and never read it. Mark had warned everyone not to or else *the enemy would corrupt their minds.* Didn't she always do what the pastor said? She laughed. Did she even know how to make decisions on her own anymore? Joe did. Marilyn did. Jason did, and so did hundreds of others who had left the church, refusing to participate in the spiritual connections. But she didn't. Why?

Her cheek warmed against the table's top and her trapped ear began to tingle. Would she end up in hell? She had participated in such an evil deception. The week before, Gary Evans, the Kentucky satellite pastor had run off with his connection, and one of the Bible college teachers was arrested for abusing his wife. Over one hundred divorces too. Pastor Mark tried to blame the "heydays" on rebellious members who disobeyed his rules. The satellite pastor from France, who bravely warned against the spiritual connection doctrine, was disfellowshipped and his urgent admonition erased from the service tape. Mark's explanations of the unusual problems were blamed on Satan because *God was moving.*

All the hours they allowed demons to take control and thrash them around. She couldn't even get angry or disagree with someone without the "what demon is that talking" retort. With all the people now spinning out of control, it was obvious who was actually *in control* of those "demonic deliverances." What a joke. Everyone spent hours and hours to get delivered, and then they all committed adultery!

The memory of Cody's kisses burned more than her trapped ear.

It's no good. No good.

Focus…focus…don't lose it. Stay strong.

Call Marilyn!

She raised her head. Lord? Her cheek and ear were a numb red. How long had she lain there? Is that you? She stood and wobbled.

I can do this.

With nervous hands she grasped the phone and hit Marilyn's number.

CHAPTER SEVENTEEN

The following evening Marilyn answered the door. Her brown eyes twinkled. Jason came up behind her, grinning excitedly. Penny flopped into their arms, unable to hold back the tears.

"I can't believe I'm here," she cried. "God helped me!" She wept with her friends for a while, hugging, before they finally moved into the house. A delicious aroma of roast beef caught Penny's nose. She had always loved Marilyn's cooking.

The two women sat down on the oversized couch opposite the fireplace, and Jason took the rocker nearby. Marilyn had placed a vase of carnations, Penny's favorite flower, on the coffee table.

"Penny, let me tell you something right now. Jason and I love the Lord. We have not lost our salvation." She chuckled. "Everyone in Grace Church thinks we are roasting in hell right now."

"Mar, it's been a long time. It is so good to see you. I want to apologize for hurting you. For not listening to you…"

Marilyn's hand flew up. "Whoa, don't say any more, Penny. You were victim of a tragic spiritual holocaust. You obeyed because you trusted Mark. He led you astray."

"Yes, but I let him do it. You and Jason didn't. I have to take responsibility for my horrific choices. No wonder the Apostle Paul admonished us in scripture to guard our salvation with fear and trembling. I had a lot of repenting to do. My choices have ruined my life. I am broken and bruised and I don't quite know how I will come out of this." Penny twisted her hands and looked down. "I am so ashamed of what I got involved in. Right now, I am glad you are both here for me."

"Penny," Jason said, "We know how you feel. We went through quite a grieving process this last year. We still haven't fully healed. It will take time for all of us."

Marilyn knew it was hard for Penny to be there. She grasped Penny's hand and said firmly, "Penny, you're safe here with us."

Penny snuffled on her shoulders. "I treated you like poison! Oh, Mar, I shut my heart off. I betrayed you!"

"Shhh, don't worry about that. We're together now."

"Hey," Jason said, "Marilyn made a wonderful dinner. What say we go eat?"

The trio moved into the dining room. The cherry wood table was set with pink flowered china. Sprays of pink and yellow daisies in crystal sat in the middle, queen over the surrounding bowls of salads, vegetables, and assorted breads.

"It looks lovely, Mar," Penny said. She sat down and took her napkin.

Marilyn went for the dinner and Jason took his seat. "Penny," he said, "You don't need to face your struggles alone. We are here for you. God will see you through."

Marilyn returned with a platter of sliced beef and buttery baby potatoes.

"Let's pray, gang," Jason said. They bowed their heads and Jason said a short prayer, than said, "Dig in, Pen."

Penny obliged and helped herself to the meal. "I have a hard time sorting this all out," she said, "I feel lost now; Grace Church was my life." She passed the steamy platter of beef to Marilyn.

Jason poured drinks and said, "After Mar and I left, we flew back East to spend time with my folks. My father spent hours going through the Bible with us, showing us just how awful the spiritual connections were. It was a smack in the face for Mar and I to admit that we had put our trust in feelings and experiences over God's truths."

He sat down and put some corn on his plate. "At Grace Church everyone is always striving for a "feeling" or an "encounter" of some sort, instead of walking by faith and being content with finding solace, joy, or comfort in the Word of God. Why do you think everyone is now mate swapping? Everyone presumed it was from God because they were habitually taught that the more spiritual manifestations they received, the more "in tune" with God they were. This is a complete contradiction to scripture. God used dreams and spiritual experiences when He needed the Apostles to implant life-changing revelation to the church, such as Peter's vision on the roof when God wanted to graft in the Gentiles to His promises."

Jason took a few bites and kept talking. "What Grace Church is doing is implementing their own doctrine, and going outside of scripture to do so. Scripture has already revealed God's heart and plan—through Jesus and the Apostolic writings. There is nothing more to be revealed to the church. In fact, Jesus revealed everything that He wanted us to know right up to the end, through the Book of Revelation. This is where Grace Church did error; they went beyond the Bible and opened themselves up to deceiving spirits. It is walking by faith, not by sight, that keeps our Christian walk stable, not fairytale excursions to la la land. "

"But His Spirit was so real…some of the connections were not…"

"Penny," Marilyn added, passing the bread to Jason, "Satan is the biggest counterfeiter. Scripture tells us that he will disguise himself as an "angel of light" to try to fool God's people. Sure, God created feelings, but they are to be in submission to God's Word, to work together with the truth, not to be a replacement for scripture. How many of us at Grace Church really walked by faith? We were all too busy soaring in the spirit and seeking spiritual experiences simply to satisfy our own selves. It feeds the flesh, but does little to build faith. Sure, we were told it made us more spiritual and closer to God, but how so? That's the delusion we all fell for. We became dependant on a "feelings" drug, so to speak. We were like alcoholics, and had to have more and more "wine"— because we loved the feeling of being intoxicated more than obedience to His Holy Word."

Penny ate and listened attentively. Their words were undoing so much of the confusion inside her head.

"We need to look at Jesus' life as the example on how we should carry ourselves as believers," Jason said, buttering his bread. "Did His prayer times with His Father focus on how high He could *fly in the spirit*? No. Even when Satan tried to tempt Him in the wilderness to exploit His supernatural authority, Jesus refused. Christ's every word and action were to bring salvation to the lost. He accomplished His mission by speaking truth and caring for the people. Even when He showed great compassion and healed the people, He asked them to keep it quiet. He didn't want people to cling to Him to see miracles; He wanted them to follow Him for who He was in the Father. He died, sacrificing His entire life for us, all by faith…and what are the churchites doing now to further Christ's command to preach the Gospel? They are committing fornication among themselves and expecting everyone to accept it as being from God. How can such immorality further the gospel of Jesus Christ and save souls?"

Penny put her fork down. "How could I have been so duped?"

"Penny," Marilyn reassured her, "You are here now. That is what's important."

Jason continued. "Look at Marcy Nason..."

"Marcy?" Penny asked, "Have you seen her?"

"No." Sadness crept over his features. "But she is a prime example of what happens when a church ignores scripture. She was forced to hide a lie, and was told it was okay. She lost her mind in the process."

"What lie?"

Jason and his wife glanced at each other.

"You didn't know?" Marilyn asked.

"Know what?"

"That Owen was gay?"

"What?"

"This is why Marcy drowned Willy. She was afraid he would get Owen's homosexual demons."

"Oh, no! She never told me. Why didn't she tell me?" Penny's hands flew to her face. "I never knew..."

"No one did, Pen," Jason said. "The pastor and Donna coerced her not to tell. They told her she had to submit to Owen's lifestyle and forgive him if he fell. He took advantage of this and didn't do much to change his life. He continued to see other men throughout their entire marriage. Marcy was living a double life and forced to hide his sin. She was greatly distressed."

"Oh, my, poor Marcy. To hold all that in, never say a word."

Marilyn soothed Penny with a hand pat. "Marcy was told that if she left Grace Church, she would go to hell. Same thing we all believed. Willy's murder is the result of Mark's treachery to manipulate all of us. Marcy did not want to endure any more mental anguish, and she worried about Willy's future, so in her mind she found the only solution that she thought would take care of the problem and end the 'curse' on her family. The demonic deliverances combined with the spiritual connection movement is what pushed her over the edge."

"So, we shouldn't have been rebuking demons? But in scripture Jesus did."

"Yes, but He is the Son of God. No demon can stand still in His presence. Jesus allowed those demons to manifest to prove how real and cunning demons are, to teach us that we should never put down our guard against their shrewd and destructive ways. So, from looking at the examples in scripture, the connection doctrine should be no surprise at how easily demons can cause havoc, even with Christians, if we let them."

"Yet," Marilyn continued, "Ephesians 6 clearly shows that we are to resist the devil by using the sword, which is His Word, and not give the devil rights to 'pierce us with his arrow.' The only thing God wants inside of us is His Holy Spirit. Remember, Jesus' death gave us victory over the enemy. When we walk by faith and stay true to God's Word, God's Holy Spirit will keep us demon free."

"But, why were those demons able to take control of some of those people in church? Remember that skinny guy?"

Jason and Marilyn threw each other a questioning look, unsure whether to say more.

"What?" Penny asked.

"Well, could be a lot of reasons," Jason said slowly. "We are trying to sort it all out ourselves. The supernatural manifestations and Mark's sin all played a part."

"Mark's sin?"

"Mark's sexual sin," Marilyn stated.

"With who?" Penny sat back, extending her legs out in front of her, and crossed her arms.

"With Jolene Dexter," Jason added.

Penny remembered! Her first service...the Dexters and Laurina's strange testimony...the first dissidents.

"Jolene's husband told us that Mark exposed himself to Jolene after a prayer meeting. To cover his sin, Mark dragged those two couples through the dirt. They were going to sue, but it was too hard on Jolene, so they let it go. They have been treated like lepers, and they did nothing to warrant it."

"I remember that ordeal so vividly because of Laurina's testimony. She always had a chip on her shoulder with Mark. But she never told me why. I figured it out a few weeks ago."

"You did?" Marilyn leaned forward curiously with wide eyes.

"Yes. After I got back from San Diego I went to visit Callie to warn her about the connections. It all came to me than. Along with my suspicions that Callie had sex with Mark."

Marilyn and Jason were open mouthed.

"The boob job, guys. Come on, Callie was changing her whole appearance for him. After that her marriage wasn't the same. Poor Petey, he was always trying to compete with the pastor."

"It makes sense," Marilyn agreed.

"Marilyn, remember the day we met? At the parsonage?"

"Yeah."

"That day when I was in the bathroom cleaning and the pastor came in? I never told you what he did."

"What?"

"He leered at me, then stood very close to me and ran his hand up and down around my waist and hips, really slow like, and the whole time looking at me weirdly. It was like he was testing me, or checking my reaction."

"Why didn't you tell me?"

"Would you have believed me?"

"No, probably not."

"Besides, I didn't want to believe it myself. I kicked it out of my head and refused to let it bother me. I convinced myself for years that he was just being nice. I am just glad I was not his type. I'm too flat chested."

They all laughed.

"What a creep!" Marilyn charged.

Jason got up and poured everyone more drinks.

"There is something else you should know," Jason said cautiously, eyeing his wife to see whether he should proceed or not.

She nodded her approval.

"Mar and I stopped speaking in tongues."

"I don't understand. Why would you do that?"

"My father has been a pastor for a long time. He never heard anything like what happened at our church. He went over scripture with us again about speaking in tongues and wondered if our misguided teaching on tongues might have opened the door to demonic intrusion. He didn't think one man's sin could allow demonic interference to such an enormous extent on an entire church body."

Jason got up from the table and returned with his Bible. He flipped the pages to the book of Acts. "If you read in Acts 2, you can clearly see that tongues translated means languages. It wasn't a babbling unearthly sound that made all the men of other nations amazed on the day of Pentecost, it was the fact that they all heard the Jews speaking in their own languages, languages the Jews did not previously know how to speak."

"But...the power...the feelings...the..."

"Listen to yourself, Penny. It all goes back to relying on feelings and experiences. Those languages back in Acts were given by God to convince the unbelievers of Christ's death and resurrection. When the men heard all the Jews speaking in their own native language the beautiful works of God, they marveled. It opened them to the Gospel message, and this is when Peter stood and preached Christ to the crowd. Satan has, as usual, played on the senses of many believers and convinced them to embrace his counterfeit. Mar and I believe the tongues we opened up to were not of God. We thought long and hard on all this, and we have come to the conclusion that all the strange demonic possessions and intense occult spells binding people's spirits came right on the heels of the unified *singing in the spirit* move. We believe we were worshipping Satan during that time. The demonic activity that is destroying people's lives right now as we speak is phenomenal. What gave it access? One man's sin? No, the entire congregation forsook the Word of God and found themselves knee-deep in the occult."

Penny remembered her Aunt Joann's argument about tongues, that witches did the same.

Jason paused as Penny's face fell. He flipped the pages and skimmed his finger down the text and read. "'For the time will come when they will not endure sound doctrine, but according to their own desires, because they have itching ears, they will heap up for themselves teachers; and they will turn their ears away from the truth, and be turned aside to fables.' This is in Second Timothy."

He read another verse. "'Nevertheless, because of sexual immorality, let each man have his own wife, and let each woman have her own husband.'"

Penny let him read more scriptures about evil appearances and how to walk a holy life.

"Now you can understand why that love spell was able to come into the church," Marilyn added.

Penny sighed and clamped her hands down in her lap. It was a lot to take in.

"God warns us all through scripture to beware of false prophets and ungodly doctrines for this very reason," Jason said at last.

"Penny," Marilyn reached over and lovingly squeezed her husband's hand, "Mark could never come up with scripture to prove the connection doctrine. The scriptures he used were general, and taken out of context. Elder Joe Fellows tried to talk to him over and over on the matter, but Mark would not listen."

"God tried to warn me not to kiss. But I was too loyal to Mark."

Marilyn nodded. "We all idolized Mark and the spiritual experiences more than God. We let Mark be our Bible. We gave him our life instead of Christ."

After coffee, they returned to the living room, and talked until eleven.

"Penny, I'm glad you're staying the night." Marilyn put Jason's Bible in her hand. "Take this to bed with you. Never be without it."

In her room, Penny snuggled up under the thick quilt, and closed her eyes. She was worn out. As she began to drift off to sleep, voices came rushing at her, harassing and pushy.

Get out... run now... escape!

They're in deception. Don't listen.

Don't talk to dissidents. They are liars. They are going to hell!

You will go to hell...you will go to hell...you will go to hell...

Reeling from the attack, Penny prayed out to God. Could she fight this? She was so weak. Then she remembered what Marilyn said about using the Word of God to fight the devil's lies.

The sword. Use the sword!

The same scriptures she heard earlier at dinner bounded into her head, displaying in her mind like the large green directional signs posted along freeways. Swiftly, the antagonistic voices disappeared and Penny fell asleep.

"Oh, dear God!" she screamed the next morning as she rushed into the kitchen.

Marilyn glanced up from the stove with spatula in hand, and Jason, seated at the table with a newspaper, set down his glass of orange juice.

"Grace Church is a cult! We were in a cult!"

Laurina rocked slightly as she waited for Mark to get off the phone. He kept peering up at her over his reading glasses. She didn't want to be there in his office, but Avery had told Mark about her troubles with Cody. Things were worse. Cody spent all his free time with Lorie, and she felt shut out and closed in, both at the same time. Her wacky emotions would not subside, and only seemed to intensify. She got prayer, went to church, danced, tried to connect, but nothing helped.

The entire assembly had changed. No one was the same. Everyone had swapped spouses for someone else. Members were dodging news reporters all the time now, but some still managed to sneak into services and take notes. Every news channel had already reported on their "odd" behavior, and it did not look like the gossip in the town was letting up either. The heat was on Mark big time.

He hung up and sat back into his chair. "Sorry for the inte*ww*uption," he said.

She crossed her legs and swung her ankle up and down. "So, what do you want to see me for?"

"I heard you were having t*w*oubles moving into the connections…and releasing Cody."

"Why do you say that? I danced with you and it was wonderful. I mean… I really felt God's love. And, sure, it is hard to see Cody with Lorie so much. I admit that. I'm human."

"Cody will be fine. He loves you." Mark chuckled and leaned forward, folding his hands over the desk. "Maybe we should t*w*y that dance again? I wasn't the one who stopped the connection. You were. Remember? Maybe that is why you haven't had any success in getting another connection. You're running f*w*om what God wants to do between us."

She shrugged.

"Why don't we take care of this p*w*oblem right now. Let's go worship, and afterwards you can tell Ave*w*y he's w*w*ong about you."

Laurina couldn't help but snicker. Avery was a cad and a spoiled one at that. She never did like him. Anyway, maybe Mark was right. Maybe she was allowing a spirit of unforgiveness toward him to hinder what God wanted to do in her. "Well, okay."

He led her to the college chapel, hoping by dancing around others first she would relax. It worked, and in time she responded to the *spirit*.

After some time had passed, and the floor became too crowded with students and office personnel, Mark whispered, "Let's go to the confe*w*ence room."

She had been hit a few times by some of the more buoyant dancers, so she agreed.

Mark shut and locked the door once they got there, and flipped on the cassette player. They continued dancing, and soon Laurina was *gone*.

Mark became woozy and *drunk*, and his body's urgent reaction spun him back from the surreal flight to seek and fulfill the physical pleasures he was experiencing. Boldly he slid his hand up Laurina's ribcage, and pulled her tightly against him. He grabbed her breast with one hand and clasped her bottom with the other. His attack broke her spiritual rendezvous, and she tried to break free from his grasp, but he wouldn't let go.

"Stop," she cried, fighting him.

But he persisted, tightening his grip and pushing his hand up under her skirt. "I can't," he panted. "Let me go, Honey. Let me go!" His mouth came down hard on hers.

She wanted to gag. He was pawing her everywhere now. Why did she agree to this? Oh Lord, help me! This is not right! She started crying the same time Mark reached his peak.

He let her go abruptly.

Laurina ran to the door, flipped the lock, and ran out.

"Cody, please listen to me! Mark tried to rape me!" Laurina followed him around the kitchen as he put together a sandwich, but he seemed disinterested.

"Laurina, stop exaggerating."

"Cody, he shoved his hands in my underpants!"

Cody screwed the lid back on the mustard jar and looked at her. "Okay, so, forgive him. You know this love is hard on a man's flesh."

Laurina fell down beside him at the table, thunderstruck. "You are sticking up for Mark? You don't care what he tried to do to me?"

"It's just that I don't want to go through another scene like we did before. And this time, everyone is making mistakes, so how can we blame Mark?"

"Everyone? I'm not, Cody."

Cody took a bite.

"Are you still making mistakes?"

"No."

"I am releasing you to Lorie every day, trusting you, trusting God...you had better not be sleeping with her!"

Cody got up and poured himself some more soda.

"Cody, are you?"

He ignored her.

"Are you!?" she screamed.

"Let it go, Laurina. I'm here; I love you. Stop badgering me to give you details of my connection. It's not important. What's important is that we are submitting to God and working out the kinks."

"I hate you." Laurina glared at him. "You want me to pretend these spiritual connections are making our marriage stronger when all I feel is contempt and anger at you. Look at what it did to Penny and Rick. He's gone! Penny's life is shattered. Doesn't that bother you? Look at all the divorces. Doesn't that bother you? What about our marriage? Don't you worry about us?"

"I suggest you talk to the church counsel with your accusations."

"I will!" She got up, and stormed from the room.

Later that afternoon, Penny rapped on Callie and Petey's door. Meeting with Marilyn and Jason had set her free; she couldn't leave Grace Church without trying to warn her friends.

Petey answered, shirtless, wearing a pair of jeans. "Hey, Penny. I'm watching a football game in the bedroom. Come on back."

Penny followed the pat pat of his bare feet down the hallway into the bedroom. All the lights were off and the curtains closed. The small television blared with the excitement of the game.

"Is Callie home?"

"No," he said, turning down the volume, "but she should be home in about thirty minutes. Why don't you wait?" He plunked down on the bed and leaned his back against the pillows. He patted the mattress for her to sit.

"When did you get a TV?"

"Oh, a few months ago."

She sat down and puckered her brows at the open can of beer on the nightstand. What had happened to Petey? He had been a tower for the Lord. "Petey," she said, trying to muster up the courage to say it correctly, "I'm leaving the church."

"What?" He removed his glasses and set them aside. "You're joking, right?" He threw her a funny look.

"That's why I'm here. I wanted to come by and tell you I'm leaving. Grace Church is a cult, Petey. The spiritual connection doctrine is not of God."

"Pen, you are hurting because Rick chose to walk against God's will and leave the church. Don't follow his footsteps.

Stay with us. Don't let his mistakes make you view the connections as bad."

"Petey, how can you say that? Look at all the divorces."

Petey pulled her down beside him and rolled over, pinning her down with his body.

"Wha?"

"Relax, Penny, you just need to be loved." Moving his face close to hers, he began stroking her hair and cheek.

She gasped, "Petey! W...what are you doing?" She had never seen Petey act this way, almost lewd. She tried to get up.

"Let's connect and let God's love heal you."

"NO!" she pushed at him. "Let me up! The connections are wrong, Petey, don't be deceived!"

She recoiled at the evil spirit showering through his eyes and she shoved harder, hollering, "I don't want this kind of sick love!"

She bolted up off the bed and out of the house, not looking back.

The next day Mark telephoned Laurina early.

"Please, come to my office. I need to talk to you about yesterday."

Laurina wanted to hang up, tell him off, but knew she couldn't. "When?" she asked snottily.

"Now if you can."

She thought it over. "Okay. I'll be there soon."

"Lauwina, I'm glad you came by," Pastor Mark said, greeting her at the door when she arrived thirty minutes later. He shut the door behind her.

"Don't lock it," Laurina snapped.

Mark ignored her remark and walked back to his desk.

She wouldn't take the chair close to him, but instead sat on the far sofa.

"Lauwina, I want to apologize for going overboard yesterday..."

"And maybe fifty other women in this church..." she retorted.

"Honey, you're out of line. I'm here to patch things up, but you don't seem to want to do this."

"You practically raped me."

"That's not twue!" He lifted his hands in a "I don't know what to do" gesture. "I've twied to be a father to you, watch over you, guard your heart..."

"Fathers don't stick their hands down their daughter's pants."

He pronounced his best lisp. "I need your support, Lauwina. The ministwy is difficult enough. Wunning this church is not easy. And you don't make it any easier for me. Why don't we come to some form of happy medium and..."

"Mark, you want me to forget what happened?"

"How can you blame me for something God's doing between us?" He baby-talked.

"God didn't tell you to have sex with me." She felt herself trembling, but stood her ground.

"I am sowwy. What more do you want me to do, beg?"

She looked away and crossed her arms, rubbing them briskly.

"I hope you will not let this go any further than this room. This eldership is aware of your past...and know you like to make up stowies."

Laurina threw her finger at him as she talked, "You know you did wrong!"

"You have a histo*w*y of wanting attention, and saying whatever you can to get it, young lady. You are in a no win situation here. I am asking you to forgive me, and let's move on."

He lowered his voice. "I love Jesus and I want to expe*w*ience His love fully. You will never be able to release Cody or yourself to God's spi*w*it if you don't open up to what God is doing. If you get stiff eve*w*ytime a man touches you, how will you be able to unite with this body?"

He kept going. "To you I was touching your b*w*easts, but to me, I was touching the body of Ch*w*ist, joining myself to His Spi*w*it. This is a place you have not yet obtained in the dance, because you're bound to your fears. Some of us do want Jesus, not sex, as you are accusing me of. I care about you. I love you with God's love." He rose. "Do you believe this, Honey?"

Laurina looked down and twiddled her fingers.

"My pet, I need you to love me back too. I'm hurting now because you think I'm out to have sex with you. If you can just relax and let God inside you, you'll see my t*w*ue heart. You don't want to leave this church and be alone, do you?"

"No. I just want you to stop touching me."

"I apologized."

Nothing.

"You do know what will happen if you undermine me, don't you?"

Nothing.

He walked to her side and sat down.

"Mark, why are you doing this?" she sobbed. "I've been a good church member. Don't you know I want to trust you? I've tried. You make it impossible!"

"Lauwina, stop giving in to these demons. Think of what your actions will do to Cody. He's the youth pastor."

"Cody?" she spat. "Cody's too busy with other women!"

"Then release him, Lauwina, and quit fighting God's Spiwit. If you don't, I will have to expel you out of this body."

"Than I'll expose you to the media! I'll tell them…"

"Thweats, Lauwina?"

His arctic look gave her goose bumps.

"Will you tell them I raped you? No, Lauwina, You have nothing to say to anyone."

"I'll tell them you're into women's breasts!" She jumped up and charged out of the room.

Mark had never seen Laurina act so defiantly. He hunched forward, worried. Why did she have to fight him all the time? Look at Callie; she blossomed into a beautiful rose because of him. But Callie was not Laurina. God, how he loved Laurina, how he wanted her. Had for years. He stood up and went to his desk.

He buzzed his secretary. "Get Ted in here right away," he said.

Ted arrived looking tired.

"Didn't sleep last night?" Mark asked. "You look tewwible."

"Too many problems to deal with. More divorces too. And the media is turning up the heat."

"I know. I know." Mark paced.

"I don't quite know how to handle all the cases coming into the counseling center."

"Why don't you put some more mature Chwistians on staff to help?"

"That might be best."

"Listen, Ted, Lau*w*ina's causing me, ah, us, some more p*w*oblems. She's th*w*eatened to go to the media with…uh…some lies. I have no choice but to put her out. I am concerned that she will undermine this move of God. Maybe she's been talking to dissidents."

Ted's brows shot up. "Are you sure, Mark? Laurina has her outbursts, but Cody is a pillar in the church…"

"Ted, keep your personal feelings out of this. I am hoping by doing this she might bounce back around. She is not submitting to this church government, and I have to do something to get her to change. Call Cody, and let him know of our plan. I don't want to lose her either, but I'm plain worn out in fighting with her. A little psychology might be good in this case. Whether Lau*w*ina knows it or not, she is part of us."

Ted stretched, his long back rising up toward the ceiling, and sighed. "All right, it's a plan."

CHAPTER EIGHTEEN

Laurina seethed. "You can't do this!" she shouted, and stood to her feet.

Ted hissed at her, "Shut up and sit down. You're creating a scene." He hunched over his cluttered desk, his eyes biting.

"My husband is the one having an affair, and I'm being put out? I have done nothing!"

Ted loved her fire. He wished he could tell her so. "Mark's orders yesterday. Coming from the highest authority. I have no choice but to disfellowship you."

"You allowed Penny's husband to run around with Janice and look what happened to her. She lost her husband. You think you can coerce me into letting Mark feel me up any time he wants? No way!"

Ted's left eye twitched. What was she talking about?

"You've never taken care of your problems, Laurina. You have rebellious spirits and this church can't put up with them anymore."

Her eyes were molten lava. "I'll expose you, Ted. And Mark!"

"You're outnumbered here, Laurina."

She blew. Ted's clutter went toppling to the floor as Laurina whisked her arm across his desk. She left him there trying to catch the mess, as she charged through the reception area yelling, "You have no right to disfellowship me. I'll fight it. And you know it, Ted. You know I can."

The roomful of co-workers did not bat an eye. These types of outbursts had become a common occurrence.

Laurina turned off the car motor and slowly walked into her empty house. Evening had shrouded the sky, and not even the stars were out that night. She had driven around for two hours crying before heading back home. She didn't know how long she stood in the dark. She was now disfellowshipped from Grace Church—her whole life was over.

What was she supposed to do? Surrender to Mark's advances? She didn't understand why she was booted out. Things were so twisted; nothing made sense anymore. Everyone was crazy...everyone. And where was Cody when she needed him? With his connection of course.

Where was God in all this? Didn't He love her? Why would He allow her to be so scorned? She thought she had been faithful. She tried hard to move into His love. She couldn't help that she was weak.

She had no one to turn to. She was a dissident now. Oh, God! She was a dissident! Maybe she should have forgiven Mark! At least she'd still be inside Grace Church. Now she was out...it was too much to bear! How could she live?

Paranoia crept up her spine as the wall clock's tick-ticking behind her got louder.

A movement.

What's that? Who's there?

She tried to hit the light switch but they came at her fast and furious, from every direction—black, eerie, creatures with no eyes and ghoulish grins.

Stop, stop, stop...

Fists flying, she batted at the empty air.

But they covered her. The last thing she remembered was feeling a pinch on her cheek from the zipper on her sweater.

"I have to call Laurina," Penny told Marilyn over the phone. "I have to try and get her out of there. Besides, I owe her...for sleeping with her husband. I'm so ashamed. She's my dearest friend. I have to tell her."

"I don't know if that is wise, Pen. Look what happened with Petey. Maybe you should stay away now."

"No. I wouldn't feel right if I just walked away. You tried to warn me and Rick, remember? I have to do this now, too."

"I guess you're right. I'll be praying while you phone her."

Penny hung up and called Laurina's cell phone. No answer. She redialed her home number. She was about to hang up when someone picked up.

"Hello?" Penny asked. "Laurina, is that you?"

A funny muffled noise answered.

"Laurina, is that you?" Penny shouted. "Laurina? It's Penny, are you there?"

Laurina's voice shuddered, "Penny, Ted kicked me out of the church. I didn't do anything wrong. I'm not rebellious; I love Jesus!"

"Laurina, listen to me, Grace Church is in terrible deception."

"My whole life is ripped apart. Seven years...my marriage... friendships. Penny, I passed out...I feel sick."

"Laurina, I'm coming right over and I'm bringing Joe Fellows. You have to know the truth. Jesus loves you and would never reject you for standing up for what is right."

Laurina choked over her sobs. "Please hurry." The phone slipped from her ear and she fell back to the floor.

An interview with Pastor Mark's daughter a week later was the breakthrough for Portland's Channel Five News. The connection doctrine scandal was the hottest story in local news, especially since reporters had secretly filmed footage of dancing members. All the stations were following the bizarre *soap opera* as it went.

The live interview was held in Gayle's home.

"What made you leave your parents' church?" the woman reporter asked as the cameraman stood nearby zooming in on Gayle's distraught face.

Gayle, dressed in a blue wool suit, wore a forlorn expression. Her hair was pinned back tight, and she faced the camera looking as if she wanted to run. "At the beginning I questioned the strange doctrine," she said, "and argued with my parents about it. But they insisted I was wrong and put a lot of pressure on me to stop interfering with what they said God was doing." She paused, looked down and said, "My father has a way of twisting people around his fingers, including me. I tried to be the good daughter and obey...so, I fell into the web of deception along with everyone else."

"And the reason you finally left?"

Gayle fidgeted with her fingers. "A few reasons. My husband stopped being my husband; I started doing things I shouldn't have with my connection, and...the clincher, when my children asked me one night if my husband's connection would be their new momma. My eyes opened right at that moment."

"Did you have sex with your connection?" the reporter asked boldly.

The question flustered Gayle. She stuttered, "I...I'm ashamed at what I s..s...succumbed to."

"I understand your husband Avery is a Bible college teacher. Where is he now and what does he think of your decision to leave?"

"Avery thinks I'm deceived. He's in love with his connection and is still in the church."

"What do you think can happen to the people remaining?"

"They'll go crazy, like I almost did."

"What would you like to say to your parents now?" the reporter asked.

"Turn back to God."

That Sunday morning a swell of news reporters congregated outside Grace Church, hoping for a word with the infamous Pastor Mark. Security guards kept the reporters at bay, refusing to let them enter the sanctuary. Pastor Mark was shuffled in through the back door, and members, entering through the main doors, ignored the belligerent reporters and snoopy cameras.

Inside the oblong structure, the sanctuary was no longer packed. Four hundred members had already left the church either because of the false doctrine or to marry their connections.

Everywhere people were slow dancing in the aisles, stuck together like glue, moving under the power of Satan, their eyes syrupy-sweet and locked in beguiling bondage.

The lights flashed, the choir stopped, and the dancers reluctantly broke apart.

Pastor Mark took the platform and shouted into the microphone. "My flock, my dedicated members, your pastor loves you!"

The members did not shout back this time. Tension had been mounting over the last few services.

"I know the media is casting a dim light on our church, but we'll stand victorious!" He waved his diamond-cuffed arms over his head. "As most of you saw on the news a few days ago, my daughter's been swayed into deception by the evil one. I have not allowed tears to destwoy my faith. I twust God she will return. I have no doubt in my mind…because she is one of us! She is part of the Bwide of Chwist! But, until she is restored, I am asking each one of you to stay far fwom her. The power of Satan is nabbing the saints of God like flies. We must be careful." He puffed out his chest.

"My sheep, those of you that are still here are headed for *glowy*. Pwaise God! You have remained faithful!"

He charged the podium with his hands. Leaning forward he bellowed to the audience, "Others are leaving, deceived by the enemy and I must report who they are. Lauwina Addison and Penny Duncan are both disfellowshipped and not to be associated with. They are undermining this move of God and in rebellion to this church government."

No one blinked. They were no longer surprised at the large exodus of people leaving Grace Church.

Donna climbed the stairs in her dance slippers and stood beside Mark. He stood back as she exhorted into the mic. "Some will leave and never return, but many will return because God is in them! I know Gayle will come back. I love my daughter! I am confident that she will be here again testifying of the great work God has done in her. I am not defeated, but I am strong in the Lord, standing my ground, unwilling to bend to the lies and works of the devil. This is the time of testing! Don't follow the footprints of those who refuse to open up to God's glory. If you do, you will end up falling off the cliff, out of God's will for your life." She steered her shapely body from right to left as she spoke to the audience. "No other church has been blessed with such a Holy visitation! You can't find God moving like this anywhere else! Someday other churches will be coming to us hungrily wanting the same. Don't let the devil win; fight to victory! Married couples, hang on! God is separating the wheat from the chaff. Pray, church, let's get back to prayer!"

Laurina had moved out of her house and in with Penny. Cody would not talk with her or see her. She tried to pinpoint him for days to talk, but he had moved out of their house as well, and she could not find him. It took a few weeks for her to get up off the couch and move again. Marilyn, Jason, and the ex-elders, Joe and Christina Fellows, had spent a lot of time at Penny's house, talking, praying, and counseling the women out of God's Word.

Both women started to feel stronger, although they knew their recovery process would take years. They had been in a cult, and learning to reason and make decisions on their own would be a challenge. Together they attended group sessions specifically designed to help ex-cult members. It wasn't long before the zombie-look in their eyes began to disappear.

"Penny," Laurina asked one afternoon, while they were eating ice cream and talking. "Let's call Callie. If she has slept with Mark, we need to get her out of there and expose what he's doing."

"I don't think she will listen. She'll hang up on you. She wouldn't listen to me."

"Let's try. I feel like I have to try."

"I know."

Laurina called. She was surprised when Callie picked up.

"Cal?" Laurina quickly added, "Don't hang up. Please!"

"Why are you calling here? I don't want to talk to you or Penny!"

"Cal, you know me! Please, listen for a minute."

Laurina didn't hear the dial tone, so she kept talking.

"Mark tried many times to seduce me. He grabbed at my breasts…that is why I left! He would have raped me if I hadn't stopped him."

"Laurina, those are lies."

"Callie, I don't know what you and Mark have done together, but don't let him con you anymore. You need to leave. You can come stay with me and Penny."

"Mark never touched me."

"Okay, but the connections are wrong…"

"No. They are beautiful and from God. You are in delusion, Laurina."

Penny motioned to Laurina and she grabbed the phone. "Cal, this is Penny. Did Petey tell you I came to your house three weeks ago to see you?"

"Yes."

"Callie, Petey tried to come on to me…"

"Why are you lying, Penny!?"

The phone went dead.

"She'll never come out," Penny stated.

Laurina moved to the couch and sat down, pulling her legs up under her. "Penny, I have been thinking, maybe I need to tell the authorities about what Mark did to me. And," she looked down, "Tell them about Frank Serris molesting his step-daughter."

"You're kidding?" Penny asked, moving down beside her.

"No, I am not kidding. Cody knew about it. Avery told him. And he told me. Mark shipped his wife and daughter to the California fellowship to quiet it all. It happened around the same time you arrived, Penny, when Mark tried to seduce Jolene Dexter."

"Isn't it the law to report something like that?"

"Yes. It is. So, I am going to do this now."

"Do you feel strong enough to do this?"

"No. But I have to."

The news regarding Frank Serris and Laurina's civil suit brought against Mark for sexual misconduct drew others out of the woodwork. Five more lawsuits against Mark put further pressure on the church and caused greater scandal in the community. Like ants wading through wet cement, the elders trudged forward to deal with the mess, hanging onto their pastor's promising words, "*Its not twue, its not twue*"—but things got worse.

"Ellen, I need to know exactly what happened," Ted asked Ellen Barker Tuesday morning in his office. His eyes followed her long legs, one dangling over the other, moving rapidly in nervous motions.

"Pastor Mark invited me to join him at the parsonage to worship. He...he attacked me—until I screamed." She fussed with the buttons on her blouse.

"Why did you wait so long to come in? You said this happened a few weeks ago?" He raked his hands through his weedy-thin hair.

"I was scared. I didn't want to go against Pastor Mark. He threatened to disfellowship me if I came here."

"I understand. Tell me what happened."

"We were dancing in his living room. I figured it was okay. Donna had been there when I arrived."

"She left?"

"Yes. It was wonderful at the beginning. God's spirit was really moving and I felt connected with him. Then he moved in close to me and started touching me here." She patted the top her chest.

"Did you let him do that?"

"Yes…but then he moved his hands down." She blushed. "At first I sort of let him, I mean, the love was so strong and I was caught up…"

"Then what did he do?"

"He turned. One minute we were dancing, the next minute he had me pinned to the couch like a crazed man. He wouldn't get off."

"And?"

"His hands and mouth were everywhere. He got his pants open…I got scared and screamed."

"Did he expose himself?"

"Yes." She looked away. "He apologized afterwards, even telephoned me couple times…"

"To keep you from reporting it?"

"Yes. He threatened me if I did."

Ted's mind was racing. He drummed his fingers across the other stack of reports issued against Mark. Grace Church was going under fast. He had to do something. As his eyes traveled over Ellen's figure, a brainstorm hit him.

"Ellen, thank you for sharing this. I will get back with you. Meanwhile, don't talk to anyone else about this."

"Will I get in trouble with the church?" she asked meekly.

"No, Ellen. You did nothing wrong here. Don't worry. Keep plugged in to what God is doing. Move on, and don't let this mistake by Mark hinder your walk with God." He tried hard not to let his excitement show. "This church government will do everything to correct the problem. I don't want this incident to weaken your faith in this move of God or steer you away from His plan for your life. It is vital that you stay where God has put you. Will you trust me?"

"Yes, I love Jesus…I want to please God."

"Good. You're a brave woman. I'll call you next week and give you an update on this."

"I did the right thing talking to you, didn't I?" She asked again, worried.

"Stop worrying. You are not going to be disfellowshipped." He rose with a big smile and put his arms around her. "I'll call you soon."

Ted clapped his hands and chuckled out loud after she left his office. He picked up the pile of reports from his desk and kissed them.

Wasn't he the one running the show most of the time? Always getting Mark out of tight spots? Pay back time!

He buzzed Petey.

"Petey, Ted here. Contact the elders, everyone except Avery, and set up an emergency meeting in my office in twenty minutes."

"Is the pastor going to be there?"

"No. He's not in today. I don't want him aware of the meeting. Understand, Petey?"

Petey was pokey in his answer, but Ted knew he would do what he asked, especially since Petey was connected with his wife.

"Petey, do you understand?"

"Yes, I'll get right on it."

"Oh, and Petey, I want you here as well."

CHAPTER NINETEEN

The nine men filed into Ted's room with curious expressions. Some of them sat on the couch, some stood. Petey, by Ted's directive, took the chair by Ted's desk. He felt self-conscious and out of place.

Ted closed the door. He walked to the front of his desk and leaned back, balancing on its ledge, his arms folded. "What I have to say is confidential," he said. "Pastor Mark is not aware of this meeting. Neither is Avery. I want to do the right thing for Grace Church. There are reports that are coming into my office that need to be addressed...about Mark." He eyed each man briefly. "So, if any of you are uncomfortable with what I am about to say, feel free to leave now. But, I must tell you we are swimming in scandal now, especially since our church is involved in lawsuits and legal issues with the police. We have to discuss this or we will lose our church!"

The elders eyed one another apprehensively, but none of them moved from their places.

"As you know, Laurina Addison has filed a suit against Mark, charging he got frisky with her against her will. New suits have also surfaced this week by other women who have left the church." He held up the stack of reports. "Yes, Laurina could be telling tall tales, but these other charges against Mark are too similar and cannot be ignored. Especially after today."

The elders listened up.

"Ellen Barker has made a formal complaint to me too." Ted put his arms down and stepped forward. "Mark exposed himself to her in a forceful manner and, of course, practically raped her. I know you're thinking that we've all made mistakes in this move of God, many have slipped, but Mark's taking this too far."

Petey's jaw dropped. "Ellen told you this?" His throat felt parched. After connecting with Betty, he had stopped dancing with Ellen. She did not handle the rejection well. Especially since they had been intimate together on numerous occasions. Would she mention their tryst together?

"Yes, Petey. You know her. She isn't the kind of woman to make up such stories."

Petey shook his head in agreement and said, "You're right. She isn't."

"Ellen's willing to remain quiet about it, for now, but if she talks and the press gets wind of this, our church will cease to exist. We're talking about a ten million dollar church and Bible College, and our jobs. Everything God's doing here will be destroyed."

"What do you propose we do?" one elder asked.

"It's important that we save this church. Mark is not carrying out his pastoral position in an appropriate manner. I am now starting to think that Jolene Dexter was not making up a story. Mark has a problem. As elders, we can change this—by voting him out."

Nervous eyes darted to one another around the room.

"We can keep going. Keep this church afloat. If we don't do something now, we are all history, and we might all individually face legal troubles once Mark goes down. I assure you, he will go down. We will too if we don't clean house now."

"Let's do it," another elder said. "Ted's right. Things are out of hand now. We have to stop this balloon from bursting."

Ted shook the papers in his hand. "Let's gain control of the church so we can deal with these properly."

"I'm in favor," one elder said.

"Me too," said another.

"Count me in," a third rattled.

The vote was unanimous.

Petey looked around feeling funny. He was witness to a coup he wasn't sure he wanted to be seeing.

Ted sucked in air. "I have an idea. Mark has been talking about taking a vacation this month. If I can persuade him to leave this week, we can approach the congregation while he's gone and save this church."

"Who will take over the responsibilities once Mark is gone?" Petey blurted out, sorry he had.

Ted's brows shot up tenaciously. He didn't have to say a thing. He was senior elder. He had kept the church in order for years. They all knew that. He was the trunk holding the tree. He bent forward over his desk and placed both hands down, meeting their gaze head on. "I choose to nominate myself for pastoral position. Gentlemen?"

That evening Ted telephoned the parsonage. Mark answered the phone in his study.

"Mark here." He closed his Bible and leaned over his desk. The hour was late.

"Mark, it's Ted. How are you?"

"Fine, Ted. What's up?" He scratched his brow and took off his reading glasses.

"Mark, listen, I know you've been talking about heading for Hawaii. Why don't you and Donna take the trip this week? I...I think maybe if you disappear for a week or so, it might calm the media a bit…and give me time to put out the fires. What do you think?" Ted held his breath.

"You might be right. This morning reporters were camped outside my fwont door."

"I hope I didn't overstep my boundaries—I went ahead and made reservations for four, at the Sheraton in Maui. I figured my brother and your connection would be going."

"Gweat! Good job, Ted. I need this bweak."

Ted could feel his palms sweat. If anyone needed a break, it was he. Mark had managed to dodge all the harassing reporters, lawyers, social workers, and police, putting the full responsibility of it all on his shoulders. He wanted to spit, he was so angry.

"You leave Saturday morning on Hawaiian Airlines. Don't forget to tell your wife."

"Oh, yes, yes, of course. Oh, and, Ted, you will watch over my flock?"

"Oh, absolutely, Mark, absolutely. You can count on me."

While Ted was on the phone with Mark, Laurina was standing over Penny's stove dipping fish in tangy lemon batter. She wiped her messy fingers on a towel. "You guys, I have decided to move to California."

"You have?" Marilyn asked, standing beside her at the counter mashing potatoes.

"Yes. Cody is filing for divorce. The church is giving him the go ahead because I'm a *demonized* dissident. I can't get him back. It's over. I need to move on, get away. Give myself time to heal." She dropped three fish filets into the pan of simmering oil.

"I'm going to miss you." Marilyn said with sorrow in her voice. "But, I understand. Jason wants to move back East."

"Come on you two, don't leave me," Penny implored as she sat at the table dicing vegetables. "It will be terrible with you both gone."

"What about you, Pen?" Laurina asked, turning around. "Are you going to go back home?"

Penny's eyes got misty. "I can't go back to Illinois. Rick's there and my family won't know how to console me. I wish I could turn to my parents and sisters for strength. But I can't. There is too much distance between us. For now, I will stay put."

Laurina grabbed Marilyn's hand and moved towards Penny, crying. "I'll never forget either of you. I wouldn't have made it without your support and friendship."

They all came together and hugged.

"It's going to take me a long time to walk into another church," Penny said, returning to her task cutting the vegetables. "I don't even know if I can. Right now I can't even look anyone in the eyes."

"I hear you," Laurina said. "It's like I don't trust myself yet, or I don't trust what might come out of my eyes. I'm still scared of that power. I worry it might still be there."

Marilyn took Laurina's hands. "Girl, you have prayed and asked the Lord to forgive you. Trust Him now to protect you. You have closed the door to that evil, and you are moving forward in truth. Remember, it is the Word of God that will heal you and keep you protected against such evil atrocities. Satan has no more rights to you."

"Thanks, Mar. I know this, but I have to get it in here." She pounded her heart. "I still feel so broken."

"Yeah, and I notice that little things now stress me out," Penny added. "I cry at the drop of a pin now."

Marilyn set the potatoes on the table. "Well, you both have come out of a cult, escaped from a demonic spell, and all the while going through a divorce at the same time. Even the strongest person would have a hard time dealing with all that at once."

Penny put out the plates and Laurina removed the fish from the pan and placed the hot dish on the table. "I still can't believe Rick is gone. I miss him so much. I wonder if my heart will ever feel normal again."

They sat down, prayed, and passed out the food.

"Even though Jason and I never got into the connections," Marilyn said, "we feel so far from the body of Christ. We've been hopping from church to church for a year. We have come to the conclusion that our relationship with Jesus is all that matters. We had put our trust in a man, in a church, and now we are resting and putting our trust in Him. Church begins here." She pointed to her heart. "Going to church doesn't make you a Christian any more than going into a garage makes you a car. It is a great feeling to look up to Him for guidance for a change, instead of trying to find it everywhere else."

Penny said, "I don't know how I feel about God anymore. I gave my life to Grace Church, for prayer, for ministries; and now my life's in shambles. I feel so let down. I know God didn't do this to me, but I feel dead inside. How can I ever trust another church?"

"That was our problem," Marilyn expounded, "We gave our life to Mark's empire, instead of to God. We idolized a man and let him make our decisions for us. We lost ourselves. We thought we had freedom, but we didn't. We gave our minds over to someone else to control, and we stopped thinking."

Marilyn shook her head sideways. "Look at all those Bible College graduates who sat in the pew doing nothing. Jason was one of them. Mark was too insecure to let them use their degrees. He didn't want anyone to usurp his position. And when one of them did want to do something with the degree, like Suzie Hatley's husband, who wanted to minister with the youth in New York, he ousted them from the church and told everyone they were in rebellion to God. Can you believe that?"

Laurina coughed out a laugh. "Hey, remember that rare time when that other minister took the pulpit and Mark got jealous?"

"Oh, yeah, I forgot about that!" Penny hooted. "That poor man! The look on his face."

"I get so mad at myself for allowing Mark to manipulate me." Laurina got serious again. "I'm just not a strong person."

"Baloney!" Marilyn argued. "You are here. That means you are stronger than you think. Look how many are still dancing with demons?"

"Like Cody."

"He is the weak one, not you."

"I knew from the beginning Mark had problems." Laurina clenched her jaw. "Why didn't I listen to Jolene Dexter when she told me to leave? I would have spared myself a lot of grief. And maybe I'd still have Cody."

"Do you think Cody would have let you go?" Penny asked. "I sort of doubt it."

"You're probably right. Look at our lives. We've gone backwards. I'm in a worse state now than before I became a Christian. This is what confuses me. Besides Mark's sexual sin, we all prayed and trusted God."

"We put experiences before the Word of God, Laurina," Marilyn said dogmatically. "No matter how many women Mark felt up, we were just as guilty for not obeying scripture. Our sin was no greater."

"Yeah," Penny agreed. "No one's going to control my Christian walk, my mind, or my decisions ever again. I don't ever want to feel another spiritual experience again. My goal is to find the Christian balance…His way. I walked by feelings for so long…I have a lot to learn about faith."

"What a delusion to think God was only moving at Grace Church." Laurina shook her head in disgust. "Like God is so small."

"I wish I could be happy again." The dark circles under Penny's eyes had become permanent stains. "I spend most of my time trying to keep my thoughts from jumbling."

"Hey," Marilyn exclaimed jumping from her seat, "How about celebrating our freedom?" She bounced from her chair and grabbed a bottle of champagne out of the refrigerator. "A toast with the forbidden fruit?"

Penny chuckled and went for the glasses. "I forget what the stuff tastes like. But if I'm correct, I believe the Bible says a little wine is good for the stomach. My stomach can use it."

"Amen," Laurina agreed.

Ted took the platform Sunday morning after song service wearing his best blue suit. With the constant news of the numerous divorces and lawsuits happening in the church, edginess hung over the place. Ted sensed the distressed mood and leaned over the pulpit confidently, echoing into the mic, "Good morning everyone."

Coughs, rustling Bible pages, and fanning noises were the only response.

Ted didn't back down. "I'm glad you made it, despite the August heat and the searing hot trials now facing our church."

Suzie, Ted's connection, and Connie, his daughter, were holding hands in the pastoral pew, supporting Ted with proud smiles. His wife, Betty, was gleefully sitting in the elder's section leaning up against Petey. Avery and Petey's wife, Callie, were nestled together in a pew two seats back. Cody Addison was nearby, his fingers wrapped around Lorie Welch's forearm.

Ted put on a sympathy look. "Today I will not be preaching a sermon. I have unpleasant news to bring you. But first, I want to pray for God's wisdom and discernment."

He prayed slowly, carefully, and then took a deep breath before scoring his point. "Some of you watch the news; not all of it is rumor."

Skeptical looks shot back at him.

"I know I should be saying this when Mark is present, but under the circumstances, I don't think I would be able to give out the information honestly if he were here. This is extremely difficult for me to bring, and I am asking all of you to hear me out." He moved from side to side, challenging the listeners straight on.

"As you know I am the senior elder, and I have been with Mark all these years, as a dedicated and loyal servant for him, as well as the Lord. So it is with a grieving spirit and a broken heart that I stand here today."

The audience got restless. Ted hurried along, "Our pastor is guilty of the sexual charges filed against him."

Silence, then grumbling rose. How could they cast stones at Mark when they themselves were intimate with their connections?

Ted put up his hand. "Hear me out, now. This is a serious charge I am bringing, and I wouldn't dare do it if it were not backed by facts. Our church is under fire, and if I don't step in and discuss this with you, this body, Grace Church will no longer exist. I had to make a decision to expose Mark's weakness so that we can start to move this church back toward healing. God is doing something here that must be preserved. Mark has allowed sin to pervert God's love. And these sexual charges are damaging us and our witness!"

"The elders and I are in agreement, church. We have voted him out of the pastoral position. He is no longer our pastor."

Heated murmurings traveled across the vast room.

"What do you mean?" one member stood and shouted. "He's our pastor. He's a man of God. How can you do this?"

"Yeah," another female member shouted, "He's the reason this church exists."

"I will not undermine him!" Callie screamed as she pounced to her feet. "Ted, you have a dissident spirit!" She shook her finger at him, all red faced, and angry. Others stood with her, shouting agreements.

The elders felt the heat and were worried, but they stood up and walked to the platform and stood behind Ted to show their support. Half the assemblage quieted.

Ted urged the people to let him finish. "We must stand against the sin and uphold God's truth. All of us on the church board have done what we know is God's will. We can only pray for Mark, and hope he repents."

Callie rushed from her pew, her big hair making her small frame look top heavy. She grabbed the mic on the pastor's pew, ignoring Suzie and Connie's angry comments. "All of you that are behind our wonderful pastor, raise your hands," she shouted. Her bounteous chest moved up and down as she shook her fist in the air.

Half of the church was in an uproar, and they waved and shouted, "We love him!"

Ted was speaking in the microphone to calm the mass, but Callie kept shouting, "Lets take a stand. Pastor Mark's not here to defend himself against this vicious attack. I've prayed for him for years; these are all lies. Let's honor him. If you are with Mark, get up and walk out!"

Avery, still rigid in his pew, glared at Ted with rage. How dare they not consult with him? He jumped to his feet and yelled, "Let's go!"

The crowd roared when he stood. Callie came back to his side, and together they stormed out of the pew, down the aisle, and toward the foyer. Their flight ignited a small stampede as hundreds of Mark's loyal *churchites* shuffled into the aisles after them.

Petey watched his wife in astonished disbelief. His throat was dry. What should he do? Betty squeezed his hand, but her eyes told him she was not staying. Petey was mortified. "Are you coming with me?" she asked.

Petey felt numb all the way to his toes. "I can't," he said. "Won't you reconsider?"

Betty stood up. "I can't either." Tears soaked her eyes when she left his side to follow the fleeing crowd. She didn't look back.

Cody nudged Lorie. "You staying?" he asked, fearfully. She nodded and grabbed Cody's hand possessively. He sighed with relief, his heart beating fast.

Frank Serris was bustling, almost running, out of the sanctuary, so was Owen Nason, with his male connection.

When Mark's people were gone and the commotion died down, Ted nodded to the elders, and they returned to their pews.

The church had split up and Pastor Mark had no idea.

The pastor and his wife returned from Hawaii nine days later with a mob of reporters and cameras greeting their flight. Their connections kept a good distance behind them as they trudged through the airport trying to dodge the media pests. Mark would not answer the barrage of questions; instead he walked ahead, smiling at the cameras, enjoying the attention.

At baggage claim, one reporter stuck his mic under Mark's nose and asked, "What will you do now that your church has split?"

Donna heard the question and felt her heart skip a beat. Mark turned from the camera to hide his surprise. The foursome retrieved their baggage and settled into a taxi. Donna didn't say anything. Her mind raced. She knew something was up. Mark did too. He sat quiet and distant, looking out the window.

After the cabdriver dropped their connections off, he delivered Mark and Donna to their house. It was early evening and the air was clear and warm. As the pastor and his wife exited the cab, they spied the large manila envelope pinned to the front door. Mark hurriedly paid the driver and retrieved their luggage. He looked at Donna. She walked over and grabbed the yellow document.

"What's that? Another lawsuit?" he asked. His gut told him it was more serious.

"It looks like a court order." After what the reporter said, she felt skittish. She let her thoughts drift back to sandy white beaches, to Kurt, his touches, his laughter. She tore open the envelope. Her heart pounded like a jackhammer. The letter read: "Official Order: Mark Garrett has been removed from his Pastoral Position by the unanimous vote of all board members at Grace Church. Enclosed is a court order denying him access to the Bible college campus and church premises."

"What is it?" Mark insisted, at the sight of her face dropping.

She looked at him blankly and handed him the notice.

He read it, then shouted, "How can they do this to me?" He dropped the document and wept.

Donna unlocked the door with trembling fingers. Quickly she ran into Mark's study and dialed Ted's cell number.

I am free.

"Ted here."

"Ted? I'm with you. What do you want me to do?"

Mark wiped his face, his blue eyes blazing.

What am I doing? I am Pastor Mark. My sheep will follow me!

Penny pulled her car off the road and parked, dropping her hands and forehead on the steering wheel, sobbing as the traffic whizzed by. She could barely get up in the morning lately, let alone function at her new receptionist job. She thought enrolling in a few night courses would pull her out of her depression, but it didn't.

Laurina had moved to California to live with a distant relative and Marilyn and Jason moved back East. Losing their support was hard; she missed them, but they too, had to find themselves. Some days she thought she might be doing better, but then, out of the blue, she would be pulled back into that black hole. She had barely talked to her aunt since she left the church two months earlier. She had been too embarrassed to face her—especially after all the news reports—and had not returned her calls.

Penny peered up over the wheel. "Dear Lord," she said softly, "I'm so confused. I believed in You. If you're not real, I have no reason to live. I loved You…what went wrong? How can I trust you?"

A flicker of movement caught her attention in the rear view mirror, and she looked up. The reflection of an old silver-haired man in dark glasses, balancing on a cane startled her. Where had she seen him before? She spun around in her seat.

Where did he go?

She rolled down the window and stretched out her head, but no one was there. Then that familiar Bible verse came flying at her: *The Lord openeth the eyes of the blind and the Lord raiseth them that are bowed down. The Lord loveth the righteous.*

An unusual calm filled her and, like warm honey, inched up her toes, through her belly, and into her heart. She grinned and took a deep breath as a sudden newfound sense of hope permeated inside her.

She looked back up at the mirror, startled at her own smiling face. She was going to make it.

She zoomed back onto the road and headed towards Aunt Joann's house.

Time to know my family…

THE SIGNS OF A CULT

Destructive cults can be political or religious. Some push a new age philosophy, or practice aberrant forms of therapy. But they all engage in some form of control and exploit their members financially, physically, and psychologically. Cults are close-knit groups, usually with a self-appointed leader who claims to have special knowledge or a special calling, and who dictates control over its members' lives.

Signs of a cult:

- The group is centered round one authoritarian leader or small group of individuals.
- Beliefs, values, or practices contrast with the normal culture or tradition.
- The smallest details of daily life are governed in tight control by the leader/leaders. Decisions are governed by the rules or ideologies of the structure/leader.
- The group is led to believe that only they have "the truth," usually based on new insights or revelation.
- Emphasis is on experience and emotions instead of scriptural truths.
- Members usually believe that their group is singled out for persecution.
- Complete obedience is expected within the group.
- Leaders control members by getting them to believe they will face death, expulsion, rejection, or God's wrath if they walk outside the governing structure.

• The group puts great emphasis on secret, hidden or inner truth.

What members might experience inside a cult or cult-like environment:

- **Mental Abuse**
- **Inability to Form Friendships**
- **Loss of Free Will/Cannot Make Decisions**
- **Child-like Behavior**
- **Separation From Family Members**
- **Loss of a Healthy Conscience**

If you, a family member, or a friend, suspect cult involvement, please contact a therapist or cult expert for support; or email the author at:
is@globalstrategicresources.com.

ABOUT THE AUTHOR

June Summers is a full time writer for Global Strategic Resources, Inc., a company that also promotes defensive means to counter physical and spiritual threats against Americans. She is co-author of *Inside the Red Zone*, Physical and Spiritual Preparedness Against Weapons of Mass Destruction. Escaping from a religious cult 20 years ago, June now advocates the importance of maintaining a sound  Biblical balance against the present evils deceiving our world today. Currently she resides in Las Vegas, Nevada with her family.

Quick Order Form

Please send me _____ copies
   of *ocCULT*. $13.95 each.
Please send me _____ copies
   of *Inside the Red Zone*. $19.95 each.

Name:_____

Address:_____

City:_____State:_____Zip:_____

Telephone:_____

Email:_____

Sales Tax: Please add $1.50 for books shipped to Nevada address.
Shipping and Handling: $4.00. Add $2.00 for each book.
International: $9.00. Add $5.00 for each book.
Payment:

☐ Check (pay: *Global Strategic Resources*)   ☐ Credit Card

☐ Visa   ☐ MasterCard   ☐ Discover

Card number:_____Exp. Date_____

Name on card:_____

TO ORDER:
Website: http://www.globalstrategicresources.com
Fax: Send this form to: 702-259-9579
Email: is@globalstrategicresources.com

Global Strategic Resources
1725 S. Rainbow Blvd., Ste. 2, Box 171
Las Vegas, NV 89146
Tel: 702-259-9579